# Voices from a Far Field

Calvin Bowden

Llumina
Press

Requests for permission to make copies of any part of this work should be mailed to Permissions Department, Llumina Press, 7101 W. Commercial Blvd., Ste. 4E, Tamarac, FL 33319

ISBN: 978-1-62550-443-2

# Voices from a Far Field

# Prologue

Even at his best, a man is a mess. He's strong-willed and impatient, gets dirty at work and play, and often doesn't smell good. However, if you're one of those who suspects that life has some purpose other than filling one's belly and stirring up the bed lint, you might have seen, on occasion, something else under all that male bluff and bluster. You might have discovered a warm, humane creature that has, at times, given serious thought to the more meaningful things of life. Such a man is the one I'm going to tell you about. His name is Heck Tennel. Heck was my best friend back when the Great Depression bore down on East Texas farms. Both of us were as poor as winter weeds and dumb as mud about some things, but that didn't stop Heck from wanting to improve his life.

What is the meaning of life anyway? Does it have a purpose? Perhaps not, but if it doesn't, why do so many folks keep asking that question?

Heck's main purpose back then was taking care of his sick little brother and his sisters, saving money to pay down on a piece of good land and finding a proper girl to marry. Fate didn't give him enough time to make the money he needed, but he came real close to hitching himself to a proper girl. It was his love for that pretty girl that almost got him killed.

Heck is old now, like me; but when he was young, his hopes and plans made lights pop on and whistles blow. He believed, as did all other men inclined to be sentimental about such things, there is no love like the first one early in life. (It might be that way with women too, but since I'm not a woman, I don't know.)

Heck's first real love was special because it fulfilled all his expectations about beauty, tenderness and grace, and all those other things that make life better than it has to be. It also gave him his first real chance to escape the unpleasantness that had troubled him up to that point in his life.

When I mention love, I hope you don't think I'm talking about the physical part of it that men are often accused of thinking about too much. That part can happen with any woman, is over in minutes, and is often forgotten. The other part, the part that puzzles us the most, won't let a man forget, not even after he's old enough to know better.

Some say it's foolish to dwell on things that appear to have slipped away forever. You'll have to decide if that applies in this story about Heck Tennel which begins in May, 1934.

# Chapter 1

Stepping into the shade along the front wall of the City Café in Two Rivers, Texas, Heck Tennel fixed his eyes on the second story window of Walter Norton's law office across the street and hoped he hadn't allowed sentimentality to overcome good judgment. If so, he'd walk into serious trouble when he went up there to meet with Norton. Whatever possessed him to take such a chance?

The August sun, up less than three hours, was already hot. Being away so long had caused him to forget how uncomfortable the Texas heat and humidity could be in the summertime. It was made even more intense by the coat and tie he'd worn for the occasion. In spite of his discomfort, however, the heat was not his primary concern. He was more worried about whether Walter Norton could be trusted. If the lawyer had lied in his letter, the sheriff would be waiting to arrest him.

Only two people in the world could have persuaded him to come back to Two Rivers after so long, and up until the previous week, he had neither seen nor heard from either of them in more than sixty years. Sixty years. It seemed only yesterday when his world suddenly fell in on him. He had never been able to figure out how so many bad things came out of serious effort and good intentions.

Heck's gray hair and neatly-trimmed white mustache, accented by his white coat and wide-brimmed white Panama, gave him a distinguished, festive look that contrasted sharply with the strained expression on his face. In spite of the uncertainties of the moment, however, his flashing brown eyes, set beneath bushy eyebrows, suggested a fierceness that had never acknowledged defeat. This hint of defiance also showed in the set of his jaw, and the way he held his shoulders erect.

Standing there quietly studying the second story window, oblivious to traffic and an occasional passerby, it occurred to him how puzzling it was that a man could love a girl from his youth to old age. A powerful thing, that special feeling a man has for a woman once in his life, if he's lucky. Like a pretty tune, it won't go away no matter how many songs he's danced to since. And now, it had lured him back home where it all began.

Heck glanced at his watch. Ten to nine. Since Norton's office wouldn't open for another ten minutes, he decided to wait inside the air-conditioned café. Approaching its side door around the corner, he saw in a newspaper rack the headline of the August 12, 1995, *Town*

*Gazette:* NO SIGN OF LOCAL OUTLAW-TURNED-HERO YET. A fresh wave of doubt rushed over him about the wisdom of coming back. It also caused him to look around for a deputy wearing a large hat and cowboy boots.

How could the news media know he was coming back? He glanced at the lawyer's office window, more distrustful then ever of the man who had sent for him.

Inside, he sat down in a booth under a window affording a good view of the buildings on the other side of Main Street. He ignored the stares of two young men in the next booth and ordered coffee from a cautious young waitress whose expression said she was afraid of him. He recalled that strangers had always been eyed suspiciously in small Texas towns.

He took a sip of hot coffee and adjusted the blind to improve his view as one of the men in the next booth said to his friend, "You reckon he'll show?"

"Who?"

"The man that was just eighteen years old back in thirty-four when he helped Bonnie Parker and Clyde Barrow rob our local bank. It's all in the paper. Right after that, he messed up by getting crossways with the richest family in Two Rivers. Besides bank robbery, his run-in with the rich folks got him indicted for felony assault and rape. After that he took off, changed his name, and went on to become this town's only hero in the big war. Fought in Europe and the Pacific. Got shot up real bad. Received lots of medals. But nobody here knew that for a long time because he wasn't using his real name. Says in the article he later sent back all his medals and told 'em to shove 'em."

"Why'd he do that?"

"Nobody knows. The TV people are in town to get in on the returned-war-hero-love stuff. Maybe they'll find out. Don't you ever read the paper? It's been front page news for a week."

"There ain't nothin' goin' on I can do anything about. Besides, I always figured that if something important happened, you'd tell me about it since you're so danged smart."

"Look at this picture. Even back then, that Tennel kid was already taller than most men. Shoulders as wide as a barn. But with them dark, close-set eyes and that George Washington nose, he wasn't much on looks." He laughed. "Check out them baggy overalls, and that ol' cap. What a hayseed."

"Don't resemble nobody I ever saw."

"Of course not, dummy. It's been over sixty years. Nobody knows what he looks like now. Why, he could walk through the door and we wouldn't recognize him from this ol' picture. Guess that's why the news hounds haven't spotted him yet. If he had enough gall to come back, that is."

"What's the big deal, him comin' back after so long? The rich folks in this town don't like poor boys any better now than they did in thirty-four. So why would he do it?"

"Love, it says here. And some rich ol' lady. She left orders to have him brought back."

"Why?"

"It don't say. But it does mention it would be mighty risky because of them felony warrants outstanding against him."

"After thirty years? Warrants that old ain't no good now."

"Proves how much you know, buddy. Says here, there ain't no statute of limitations on a felony indictment. That only applies to charges prior to indictment."

"Reckon that Tennel fella had a thing goin' way back then with the rich woman who had him brought back?"

"This don't say. But my grandpa don't think so. He said young people back then weren't like they are now. He also told me the rich woman was a nice lady."

"Then who did he rape?"

"It doesn't say."

Heck finished his coffee, glanced at his watch and slid out of the booth, giving the two young men a cold stare as he passed them. They stared back, apparently more suspicious of him than before. As he approached the cash register, he heard one say to the other, "Did you get a look at that ol' geezer's eyes? Dark and flashy and as cold as ice. Gave me the creeps."

Outside, Heck paused at the corner again to survey the area across the street. So far, no sign of TV reporters or anything else out of the ordinary, but he had lived too long and been through too much to become careless now.

He was still puzzled by the fact that Miss Cilla's letter, forwarded to him by Norton, had been written three years ago. In it, she said how happy she was to find out he hadn't died, as she'd been told by her sister and others for so long. She implored him to return to Two Rivers immediately so she could give him a "most urgent message" in person. She said it was "critical to the happiness of both of us for whatever number of years we have remaining." The letter also stated she would make amends for some of the wrongs done him in Two Rivers. Norton's accompanying letter was vague, saying merely that he'd been retained by Miss Priscilla Vandergriff to assist in her legal affairs.

Heck didn't trust lawyers. Outside of Miss Cilla, he had never trusted any of the rich and powerful people in Two Rivers, least of all her father, B.M. "Blood Money" Vandergriff, and her horse-faced sister Josephine. They had never tolerated challenges to their authority in "their" town, and never forgot those who dared to do it. If Norton had him arrested, it would be because of them. Heck suspected Blood Money had long since died, but wouldn't believe it until informed of that fact by the lawyer. *Bad people seem to live longer than most,* he thought, sadly. *Like the song lyrics go, only the good die young.*

He moved out into the street, telling himself that if anybody deserved to live a long life, it was Priscilla Vandergriff. He remembered her as a kind, pretty woman, and smart. She was so browbeaten by her older sister Josephine and her dad that she became withdrawn, a trait which some took as a sign of mental retardation. Those who liked her called her Miss Cilla. The ones who didn't called her Miss Silly.

It was hard to understand how a man like Blood Money sired a child as kind as Miss Cilla, even more puzzling that such a refined lady, ten years Heck's senior, took such a liking to a poor country boy like him. He could only imagine living the elegant life of the Vandergriffs.

Pulling himself more erect, Heck stepped up on the opposite sidewalk, thinking, *too late now to worry about trumped-up charges filed against me when I was eighteen. This is the last chance to see Miss Cilla and find out about her important message. According to my calculations, she's eighty-nine now.*

Heck noted the visible changes in the immediate area. Blood Money's bank, Two Rivers State, had expanded into the adjoining building, and some of the other businesses had new fronts. All had been air conditioned, judging by their closed doors. Driving in earlier, he'd noted other improvements, a shopping center on a new loop around the north side of town, and a large Wal-Mart Super Store. All the streets he'd seen were paved now, and lots of new houses stood inside the loop and beyond. The thing that had not changed was right underfoot - - still surfaced with the same shiny, red brick from his boyhood.

Heck studied the faces of people walking by, feeling even more ill at ease as he moved toward the lawyer's office. Glancing at his reflection in the glass wall of the bank's expanded facilities, a twinkle came to his eyes. *You don't look half-bad for an old hayseed, Heck Tennel, alias Roger Wills.*

He'd read somewhere that a poor boy, once grown, should never return to his hometown for any reason, because he can never change the image of what he used to be in the eyes of those who knew him early on, no matter how much he had changed. In an effort to escape that depressing prospect, he had reached into his meager savings to buy himself the white trousers and coat, and a yellow tie. Combined with a discount store's imitation Panama and white Chinese-made shoes, he figured he looked good enough to convince any Two Rivers snob that he had never touched a hoe nor dragged a cotton sack down a sandy middle.

The owners of the building he now entered hadn't seen fit to install an elevator to the second floor, but had dressed up the stairs with plush red carpet secured by gold-colored tacks. Wallpaper and florescent lighting had been added to the stairwell, but the steps still squeaked like they did when he went up them a long time ago to talk to Doc Samuels about his sick little brother Billy. Poor Billy.

Upstairs, he moved down a carpeted hall, past the office Doc Samuels had occupied, to a glass door where large gold letters read WALTER NORTON III, Attorney-at-Law.

*A third generation apple not falling far from the tree,* Heck thought. As a boy, he had known the first Walter Norton as one of Two Rivers' high moguls: chairman of the Democratic Party, president of the Rotary Club, and head of the Chamber of Commerce. At the time of Heck's hasty departure, Norton had already been Hispaniola County's district attorney for three terms, an advantageous position for handling all of Blood Money's legal work.

Nervously checking his reflection again, Heck adjusted his clip-on tie and moved the Panama to a more rakish angle. If a policeman or an FBI agent awaited him, he didn't want to look like a common criminal when marched down Main Street to the county jail. If they could catch him, that is.

Pushing through the door, Heck found himself facing a well-endowed blonde behind a long mahogany desk. The entire setting, large oil paintings on paneled walls, thick carpet, spoke of money. He held no grudges against any honorable man for achieving success, but in this case it turned his stomach.

"May I help you?" she purred.

*Amazing how much better the upper crust treats a poor man when he dresses up.* "I'm Roger . . . I mean Heck Tennel. Norton's expecting me."

"He surely is." Her face lit up. "We've been wondering if you'd come." She stood up, allowing him to observe that the rest of her body looked as good as her upper half. "Please have a seat. I'll tell him you're here."

Heck nodded toward the door marked PRIVATE. "Anybody in there with your boss?"

"Oh, no." She produced another saccharine smile. "He'll just need a moment to go over his list of what he's supposed to do now that you're here."

*Or to call one of his flunkies down at the sheriff's office,* he thought.

He remained standing near the door, poised for a jackrabbit start in case the blonde lied. He'd show them what a seventy-nine-year-old could do when he's got crocodiles snapping at his heels.

The blonde returned and sat down behind her desk. "Mr. Norton will be with you presently. Care for a cup of coffee?"

"No thanks." He shook his head. His eyes moved down to the bosom she apparently was very proud of, judging by the way it was pushed up. Nice to know such a beautiful sight could still produce a stirring in a certain area of his body.

Presently a buzzer cued the secretary to say, "You may go in now."

Her words reminded Heck of a game they had played at the Panther Holler one-room schoolhouse in the first grade. He said, "May I?"

She gave him a puzzled look as he turned to enter the private office.

A short, fat man with a big belly and bald head stood up behind his desk as Heck closed the door behind him.

"Mr. Tennel, I presume." He smiled.

Heck nodded, but didn't take the lawyer's outstretched hand. "You presume right." He looked around to make sure a deputy wasn't lurking about.

"Have a seat." The fat man pointed to a chair. His eyes swept over Heck. "You're much taller than I expected. As I recall, your father was – ah – short."

"I'm not like my dad in lots of ways," he snapped.

Norton's expression reflected a sudden spark of appreciation, causing him almost to look trustworthy. But then the fixed politician's smile returned to his face.

Sitting down, Heck continued to study the lawyer, noting a decided resemblance to the ancestor who had filed criminal charges against him in 1934. That feature alone was enough to prevent him from ever developing a liking for this man.

"How did you come to be called Heck?" he asked in another apparent attempt to break the ice.

"It wasn't considered good manners to say 'hell' in public when I was a pup in Two Rivers."

Norton started to laugh, but smothered it in the glare of Heck's cold eyes. "I see."

"Miss Cilla's letter said she had an urgent message which she would deliver to me herself." Heck leaned forward. "When can I see her?"

"Miss Priscilla is dead."

"Dead? But her letter . . ."

"Written just after her health took a sudden turn for the worse."

"But you sent a letter too. You didn't say anything about her dying."

"Would you have come if I had?"

"Probably not." He settled back in his chair with a sigh and looked through the window at the clear sky. "Miss Cilla was a nice lady. I wish I could've seen her again before she died."

"She tried hard to locate you as soon as she found out for sure you were still alive. So did I. You weren't easy to find."

"How *did* you find me?"

"We pulled lots of strings with the government, the V.A., our congressman, but got nowhere 'til I went back to see your daughter Sissy that last time. It was just before Miss Priscilla died. Sissy gave me your assumed name and the address of somebody who might know where you could be reached. We immediately followed up to see if her information was valid."

"Sissy was told a long time ago never to do that. I wonder why she finally did."

Norton held up his hand, rubbing his thumb and forefinger together. "Miss Josephine paid Sissy's mother five thousand dollars way back there for a written statement saying you had died and promised her that same amount every year for as long as she lived. She did that so Miss Priscilla, convinced of your death, would stop looking for you. When Sissy's mother died in seventy-three, Sissy threatened to tell Miss Priscilla how her mother had lied in that statement if Miss Josephine didn't agree to continue the five thousand dollar annual payments to her. Miss Josephine agreed, but when she died in nineteen seventy-six and the payments stopped, your daughter was – how should I put it – very unhappy."

"My daughter would have fit in well with B.M. Vandergriff Enterprises," Heck said. "Like him and her mother, she never allowed principle to get in the way of going after what she wanted."

Norton gave him a cautious look. "When I visited Sissy that last time, she thought I'd come by to resume the payments. When she found out I represented Miss Priscilla and was there to question her mother's old statement, she grew mean as hell. Grabbed her shotgun and threatened to shoot me. That's when I offered her a certain – ah – consideration for the truth of the matter, plus a lead on your whereabouts. She proved to be a shrewd businesswoman. Wouldn't take my first offer, or my second. And right after she did accept and gave me the information I needed, she left this part of the country. Haven't seen or heard from her since."

"Neither have I." Heck looked at the documents on Norton's desk. "But I didn't come back to chit-chat about Sissy and her mother's crooked deals. I came because I loved Miss Cilla and she asked me to. She was my best friend, even after Miss Josephine had me filed on. Always treated me like I was somebody. Okay, tell me her message so I can blow this town before the sheriff grabs me."

"I represent Miss Priscilla, not the state, or the sheriff." The lawyer's eyes were steady. "I explained that in my letter."

"So you did, but all you lawyers pee through the same blanket. Otherwise, why would you tell the news media I was coming back and put me on the run again?"

Norton threw up his hands. "I didn't tell 'em. Maybe some of those people we contacted trying to find you leaked it."

"Or your top-heavy secretary. Regardless, I'll listen to Miss Cilla's message and get out of here while I can."

"It's not that simple. Miss Priscilla's instructions to me were very clear. If she died before you came, I was to give you nothing here. You'll have to pick up all the things she left you at that special place which she said only the real Heck Tennel would know about."

"The real Heck Tennel? You think I'm an imposter?"

"I don't know who you are for sure. Even if I did, it wouldn't matter, because I have to follow orders. You realize, I'm sure, that Miss Priscilla was the only one in Two Rivers able to identify you. Everybody else has left, or died."

"Cracker Carver is dead?"

"Your Negro friend isn't dead, but you two were too close. Even if you are an imposter, he'd back you up if he thought Heck Tennel sent you."

"Cracker wouldn't lie."

"Who knows for sure? There's too much at stake for me to take a chance. Same goes for your daughter, if I could've located her and brought her in for this meeting. But neither one of them have seen you in so long, even they might not recognize you. The stakes were too high to take chances."

"I see. But what I don't see is what Miss Cilla could have to say to me that would cause her to insist on you being so careful."

"You'll find that out tomorrow morning, if you know where that special place is. Miss Cilla said it was where Heck Tennel picked up some letters and notes from somebody special in thirty-four."

"*That* place." He felt a flush of excitement as old memories came rushing back.

Norton went on, "Go there in the morning at ten and pick up Miss Priscilla's message. I'll meet you at the old Vandergriff house. If you're Heck Tennel, you'll know where that is too."

"You think you're real foxy, don't you, Mr. Lawyer? You've fulfilled your promises to Miss Cilla and can revert to being just one of the local good ol' boys. You'll tell your D.A. buddy I'm back, and he'll have the sheriff and some TV reporters waiting for me in the bushes."

Norton's gaze suddenly hardened. "You'll have to wait 'til in the morning to find out, won't you?'

"I will if I don't decide to hightail it out of town first." He stood up.

Norton gave him a sober look. "If you don't show up out there, you'll be making the biggest mistake of your life."

"I doubt that, Mr. Lawyer. I've made some real humdingers in my day."

"Heck Tennel – Roger Wills – whoever the hell you are, I'll see you in the morning, if you decide to stay in town, and you really are the man we've been looking for." He stood up and held out his hand.

"No offense intended, Mr. Norton. But shaking your hand would be like saying I forgive ol' Blood Money and his heartless daughter Josephine for all the misery they caused me – and you know who." He stopped, swallowing a sudden lump in his throat. "I can't do that."

Heck merely glanced at the big-bosomed secretary as he walked briskly out of the office and, still absorbed in what he'd just been told, failed to notice people coming up the stairs. Too late, he saw the bold letters CNN on the camera in the hands of a large man trailing along behind three women. Heck stopped, remembered there was no other exit and attempted to brush by them without speaking. One of the women caught his arm.

"Are you Heck Tennel?" she asked.

The large man raised his camera, and the others stopped to hear his answer.

"No." He pulled his arm free. "But if you'll hurry, you can catch him in Mr. Norton's office. They're about to sneak out through the back door."

As they rushed upward, Heck descended the stairs as fast as he could, returned to his 1984 Ford two blocks away, and drove back out to the new motel on the north loop. He went to his room with his pulse still pounding, took off the coat and tie and lay down on the bed to digest what Norton had told him. The lawyer's statements about Miss Cilla mixed with other freshly renewed memories to put his mind in a whirl. *Should I run or stay? There's a lot at stake either way.*

The lawyer mentioning that "special place" had been so disturbing that he found it impossible to relax. He, in fact, had gotten no rest or a good night's sleep since receiving the two letters from Norton. The long drive back to Two Rivers had pushed him to the point of collapse. Stiffness in his legs and lower back caused by sitting so long behind the wheel doubled his discomfort.

Getting up, he pulled a pint of Crown Royal out of his battered old suitcase, took a big swallow and lay back down with a sigh. After closing his eyes and lying very still for a few minutes, he finally unwound enough to fall asleep.

Hunger pangs and cramps in his hips and legs woke him. He sat up to look at his watch: 3:50 p.m. Refreshed by the long nap, he stiffly rose to his feet and ran in place for several moments, slowly at first, then more briskly as he loosened up. He dropped to the floor and did twenty push-ups.

Feeling better after a shower and a shave, he redressed, leaving off the tie, and called room service, figuring ordering in would lessen the odds of being recognized by the wrong people. He hadn't told Norton where he was staying, or the name he registered under, but he didn't want to take any unnecessary chances.

Thirty minutes later, he left the motel and drove west on the loop. Turning onto Panther Holler Road, another surprise greeted him. The formerly sand and red clay surface had been blacktopped and renamed "Josephine Vandergriff Road." The sign made him feel a little sick to the stomach.

He told himself all the way down from northern Idaho not to visit the old sharecropper house on Panther Holler Road where he and his family lived so long, because that would stir up too many bad memories. His meeting with Norton had rekindled enough stored-up anger for one day. But now so close, he realized staying away wouldn't be easy. He felt drawn to the cropper house.

Two miles out Panther Holler Road, he slowed down in anticipation of seeing the one-room schoolhouse he had once attended and the Baptist Church he joined at age twelve. Disappointment swept over him when he saw neither. The school was gone, and one made of brick replaced the little frame church.

He pressed the gas pedal and stopped again where a dirt road turned off into The Settlement, a small community of Negroes. The road looked the same except for its sandy banks. They were higher, the pines and hardwoods shading it, much taller. *At least there's still something around that hasn't been covered by asphalt or named after a Vandergriff.*

Hesitating, he looked north along the blacktop, then down the dirt one, undecided on whether to visit the old cropper house before dark, or go into The Settlement in search of his friend Cracker. His real name was Abraham Lincoln Washington Carver, but he'd always been called Cracker. As a boy, he loved RC sodas and crackers.

Glancing at his watch – 4:45 – and believing there was enough daylight left to visit both his friend and the old home place, he turned toward The Settlement.

The deep sandy ruts and ungraded ditches looked much like when he used to visit Cracker. The sight brought back more memories, especially how white people looked down on him because his best friend was a Negro. He had been called some vile names because of it. He and Cracker had worked and played together so long, he never thought of him as a black boy. He was just a boy like him, a fellow human being, his trusted friend. When Heck was twelve, Cracker saving him from drowning in Morales Creek forever strengthened their bond.

Heck approached a half dozen small frame houses set back in the woods on the left side of the road, all built since he left. Moments later, he spied the familiar lane leading to that part of The Settlement which he remembered. He drove in among older frame houses and stopped in the approximate spot where Cracker's family used to live, now nothing but a mass of rotted boards and rusty tin among a thick growth of weeds and pine saplings.

Getting out, he looked around for signs of life, saw no one, and was beginning to believe his arrival had gone unnoticed when a screen door creaked open. Then another. He turned to find several adults and some children watching him from small front porches. An older couple at the first house stared from unfriendly eyes. The children's expressions were a mix of curiosity and fear. The less-than-hospitable reception puzzled him.

A boy, who looked about ten years old, slowly approached him, speaking loud enough for the others to hear. "You a sheriff, mistuh?"

Heck shook his head. "Nope."

"Bill collector?"

"Wrong guess again."

Two older boys joined them. One said, "Then you're an insurance man." He pointed at the old Carver house. "Nobody lives there no mo'."

"So I see." Scrutinized by the older strangers, he sensed a mounting tension in the air that he had never experienced here as a boy.

He turned back to the boys. "I'm looking for Cracker Carver, and I've got a dollar for the first one who tells me where I can find him."

"What did he do?"

"Nothing," Heck said, suddenly irritated. "He was a friend of mine a long time ago. Now, quit trying to build me up as some kind of monster and tell me where I can find him, or direct me to whoever's lived around here the longest."

The boy pointed at the old couple. "Maybe they know him. Do I still get a dollar?"

Heck took out his wallet, gave him a one and walked over to the porch where the old man and woman were sitting. "I'm looking for Cracker Carver."

"I heard," the man said gruffly. "Nobody 'round here got no white friends no mo'."

The statement left Heck at a loss for words for a moment. Moving closer, he said, "Cracker and I used to work in the fields together. All the people in The Settlement were friends of mine back then."

"You don't look to me like you ever worked in no fields. Least of all with no colored man."

"It's a common mistake, judging a man by his clothes," he said sharply. "Some might say it's kind of like judging a man by the color of his skin." The old man dropped his eyes as if he might have spoken too harshly. "Did you ever know any Carvers?"

"They're mostly dead, or moved off somewheres," the old man said, looking at the remains of the house where Heck first stopped. "Which one of the boys you say you're lookin' for?"

"Abraham Lincoln Washington Carver, better known as Cracker. Big fella, about my height and age."

The old woman's face lit up. "You mean Reverend Carver?"

"Reverend?" Heck gave her a surprised look.

"He don't preach no mo'. But he lives on down the road a piece." She pointed. "Last house befo' you get to th' branch."

Nodding politely, Heck thanked them and returned to his car. He remembered the branch well where he and Cracker caught sun perch.

He drove by several more small houses on the main road before a wood bridge came into view. He pulled into the driveway of the house next to it and cut the motor. Looking around, he saw no one in the "reverend's" yard, or on the porch. Typical of Settlement houses, this one was small and simple in design, but unlike most of the others, it had been painted recently. Its premises had a neat, uncluttered appearance. A late model Ford was parked under a lean-to carport.

Going up on the front porch, Heck knocked, softly at first, then louder when he didn't get a response. Hearing nothing, he knocked a third time and detected a stirring in one of the back rooms.

"I warned you kids about pesterin' me," a man called out. "Get away from that door."

"That you, Cracker?"

No answer. Presently a tall, stooped-shouldered Negro with white hair and a gray mustache came into view. After studying the figure outlined against the bright sunlight, he moved slowly to the middle of the living room and stopped again. Still not recognizing the visitor, he moved closer, stopping abruptly to stare open-mouthed for a moment.

"Good God-A' mighty," he muttered. "It can't be."

"Hello, Cracker." Heck smiled. "Are you gonna stand there all day like a young bull lookin' at a new gate, or open the door and let me in?"

Cracker moved a hand up to his chest, swaying slightly before he took a deep breath. "But you're dead."

"Do I look dead, pea picker? Old, like you, but a helluva long way from bein' dead, by God. Now, unhook the screen so I can get in out of the heat."

"Come in ol' Cracker's house and fill me in. My Lord!"

Heck stepped into the room and embraced his old friend who met him with open arms. When they finally stepped back to observe each other more closely, Heck saw tears in Cracker's eyes and for a moment thought he felt moisture of some mysterious origin in his own.

"You nearly gave me a heart attack, Heck, you devil. Showing up in my door against the light, all dressed in white, I thought for a minute you'd come back as some kind of angel. Of course, my good sense told me right away that wasn't possible in your case."

"Glad to see you too." Heck slapped him on the shoulder. "What's this I hear about you being a preacher now?"

Cracker's expression became sober as he pointed at the sofa. "Sit down and I'll tell you." After they settled in, Cracker turned to face him again. "About the preacher business. Well, it was like this. One day soon after you left, I decided I just couldn't make it any more without some outside help. Lord knows, I needed it, what with all that trouble the white folks put on me before you lit a shuck. If you remember, I nearly got myself killed. And afterwards, nobody would hire me to work their crops any more. So I got down on my knees and went to The Man. And He came to me and lifted me up. After that, I did a lot of reading about such things. I studied the Bible. Our old preacher helped me."

Taken aback by a totally new Cracker Carver, Heck searched for the right words. Finally, he said, "I . . . I don't know what to say. You've changed so. All for the better, mind you. I'm impressed." He laughed. "I'm sure you found preaching to be a helluva . . . I mean a lot better than choppin' cotton for fifty cents a day."

"You always were the craziest white boy I ever did know. And I can see you still got lots of the devil in you. I can see him dancin' around in them fiery, brown eyes. That's what caused me to recognize you standin' in the door with your jaw stuck out and big fists on your hips like you was rarin' for a fight."

Heck smiled. "Or lookin' for a good lookin' woman to rassle? So what have you been up to, besides puttin' the fear of the Lord in retired cotton pickers and young whore chasers?"

Shaking his head, Cracker replied, "That would take lots of tellin', because lots of water has gone through the swimmin' hole since you left. I'll get us some coffee, or some iced tea, and then we'll talk more. Which one do you want?"

"Nothing stronger? We might as well do something befitting the occasion. Hell, we might not be around in another sixty years."

"Ain't that the truth? Well, I got a little something special in the kitchen for colds and such. Be right back."

Heck watched his friend limp out of the room, more impressed than ever by his new image and the fact that he had worked so long trying to help others as a preacher. He was indeed a man re-made.

Looking around, Heck was also impressed by his old friend's housekeeping habits. The clean room and good furniture were a far cry from what either of them was accustomed to in their youth.

Cracker returned with half a bottle of Seagram's and two glasses, giving one to Heck before he sat down and poured each of them two fingers.

"I was sitting here thinking how well you've done," Heck said. "You don't even look like a clodhopper anymore."

Cracker smiled. "You talk funny too. So, tell me. Where have you been hiding all these years?"

"Different places. Midwest, Alaska, up north and out west."

Cracker waited expectantly for more details, but instead of supplying them, Heck raised his glass to propose a toast. "Here's to all reformed, re-treaded and retired clodhoppers. May the rest of their days be lit up by clear skies and the bright smiles of pretty girls."

"I'll say amen to the clear skies," Cracker said, taking a sip of the whiskey. He gave Heck a serious look. "You can at least tell me if you've got a family, can't you?"

"Just my daughter, Sissy." He winked. "The only one I know about, anyway."

Cracker, apparently not seeing the humor in his statement, said, "You mean you never found a woman to settle down with that you thought was as good as the one who got away in thirty-four?"

Heck's expression suddenly became sober and he turned to look out the window, not answering him. Undeterred, Cracker said, "I know it's not because you didn't have lots of chances. A tall hunk of a man like you. You were always better looking than you thought you were in the old days, and I'm sure you got over being afraid of pretty city girls. I just hope you didn't let bitterness from what happened here cheat you out of a full life."

Heck turned and gave his friend a thoughtful look, as if he might pursue the subject, but didn't. He smiled instead, slapped Cracker's knee, and told him, "This ain't no funeral. Stop talkin' like a preacher and tell me about your family."

"I had a good wife, Heck." Cracker set his glass down on the coffee table with a sigh. "I guess that's hard for you to believe, knowing me so well during my wild-seed time. Jeanette gave me four healthy children who are scattered all around the country now. She died five years ago."

"I'm sorry. But sounds like you were a lucky man."

Cracker's eyes met his. "Luck didn't have nothin' to do with it, Heck. I straightened myself out and lived right. Now, I'm not necessarily saying I believe you didn't, because the Good Book tells me I'm not to judge."

"I understand," Heck said. "I'm just surprised I'm being given a lecture on morals by a man who used to chase heifers and wild women like Tiny Lucy."

Cracker cringed. "Did you have to mention her? I do believe you'd spit in the eye of the devil himself if he showed up and tried to give you some pointers."

"He's mad at me because I did spit in his evil eye so many times. So what are you doing now to keep your mind from going back to those tough times and loose women?"

"I fill in as relief preacher at a couple of little churches. I write an article for the *Baptist Journal* from time to time. Even tried to write a book, but figured nobody would want to read about what happened to me and my family. Guess I need to write about somebody more interesting, like Miss Priscilla. Or you. Might too, some day, now that you're back. I suppose you went on to do great things with your music and singing."

Heck's expression became grave. "Didn't have much music left in me when the running and the shooting died down." Holding out his left arm, he tried to make a fist, but could get his fingers only half-closed. "Couldn't make a decent 'C' chord if my life depended on it."

Cracker shook his head. "What a shame. Always figured you'd go far in the music field."

"If things had gone like they were supposed to . . ." He stopped and stared at his glass, as old memories came rushing back. Then he went on, "Maybe Dad was right. Maybe I aimed too high. When a man does that, things happen to put him in his place."

"How many times do you reckon that's been said to me?" Cracker gave him a skeptical look. "It always sounded bad, and hearing it from you doesn't make it sound any better."

"You might have a point, so I'll change the subject. What's happened to the people in The Settlement? I felt a lot of anger in the air. Got the feeling they didn't want me in here because I'm white."

The silence in the room grew heavy as they held each other's gaze for a moment, causing Heck to feel like he was in the presence of a stranger. Then Cracker's gaze softened and he said, "Negroes have grown out of the old ways, Heck. In the process, seems nobody cares about anybody any more. Colored against colored, white and colored against each other. Negroes don't have to constantly worry about empty bellies or getting lynched now, so they found other things to be mad about. Looks like some of us might never be happy any more unless we can learn to accept the good things from our past. It takes a lot besides equal rights legislation to make a person happy."

A mischievous gleam suddenly appeared in Heck's eyes. "Maybe they should have to chop cotton a couple of summers, and saw a wagonload of firewood with a crosscut two-hander for four bits a day." Leaning, he looked past Cracker at the woods timber beyond the window. "Didn't there used to be a trail out there leading back to the Sproggs' place?"

"And to that old bachelor's place."

"I guess they're all dead now, along with the others we used to know in the thirties."

"That's the truth," Cracker said, nodding. He gave Heck a curious look. "So what brings you back after all these years? I know it wasn't to find out who died."

"Miss Cilla sent for me," he said with a sigh.

"But she's . . . "

"Dead. I know that now. But I didn't find out until this morning. Her attorney Walter Norton *the third* told me.*"*

Cracker was thoughtful for a moment. "Miss Cilla was an awfully nice lady. Many's the time she brought groceries to the poor and sick in The Settlement. She was always afraid her daddy or Miss Josephine would find out about it, but my people loved her so nobody ever spoke of it in town. She's the one who talked my parents into letting me go back to school. She even helped Daddy with money out of her own allowance so I could do it."

"Looks like you spit in the eye of the devil too, getting an education with Vandergriff money."

"After you left, Miss Cilla kept coming by to see if I'd heard from you. Always real disappointed when I told her I hadn't. When Miss Josephine put it out that you'd died, she kept coming. Then, toward the end, after she got real sick, she came out again. Told me she was very sorry things turned out the way they did with you, and that she wanted to do something to make things as right as possible under the circumstances. She looked real poorly, bless her heart. Didn't weigh more'n a sack of flour by then." He gave Heck a questioning look. "But she died over three years ago."

Heck nodded. "Her lawyer had a hard time finding me. When he did, he sent her old letter that she never mailed."

"He didn't include a letter from anyone else?"

Heck's eyes flashed. "You mean, from *her*?"

Cracker nodded.

Heck shook his head. "She'd long forgotten me, I'm sure."

"Could be she's what Miss Cilla's urgent message is all about."

"You think so?" He shook his head. "Naah. Can't be." He stood up and began walking back and forth across the room. "Finding out for sure would be very risky."

"In what way?"

Heck stopped pacing and turned. "I'd have to go to the old Vandergriff place in the morning to find out what Miss Cilla's message is about. I think I'll be arrested if I do."

"Arrested? After all these years?"

"Got a feeling ol' Blood Money and Miss Josephine still run this town through six feet of dirt. But their cronies won't make a move before Norton finds out for sure I'm who I say I am."

"Heck, aren't you ever going to forgive and forget?"

"Did you?"

"I made my peace. You should too."

"Don't you think I've tried?"

"I expect you found out that just up and sailing away from your roots and your troubles won't do the trick. A ship can pull anchor, but it's still got to carry the freight in the hold. Look at all the troubles I had laid on me. If I could stay around and tough it out, anybody could."

Heck had become so absorbed with their conversation he forgot to watch the time and, when he glanced at his watch, the sun had already set beyond the trees. Looking out at the shadows in the woods, he finished his whiskey and placed the glass on the table. "Gotta go if I'm to see anything out on Vandergriff Road before dark."

"It's already too late, Heck. Spend the night. Go out early in the morning."

"I've enjoyed our visit, but don't want to spoil a good thing." He thought a moment. "I'll just bed down in my car on a country road someplace. Can't afford to go back to town with those news hounds prowling around."

A hurt look came over Cracker's face. "You weren't too good to stay overnight with me back when I was just a nigger and you were nothin' but an ignorant redneck clod roller."

"You've got yourself a boarder for the night, preacher. But I should warn you. I snore."

"You can kick on the wall and bay at the moon for all I care. When my head hits the pillow, I'm out for the night."

They talked until it became dark in the house. Cracker turned on a light and prepared sandwiches for supper. After eating, they again talked about the old days, recalling the good times and the dangers they faced as boys. Cracker stood up finally and stretched. "All this reminiscing reminds me of a little ditty my sweet Jeanette and the kids recited every night. It went,

"To bed, to bed," said the Sleepy Head.

"Wait a while," said Slow.

"Let's have a snack," said Greedy Gut,

"Before we go."

He looked at Heck. "I wish you'd known my wife. She was really something. I sure miss her."

He escorted Heck into a spare bedroom where he turned down the sheet and switched on an oscillating fan, apologizing for his lack of air conditioning. He showed him where to find clean towels and wash cloths in the bathroom, then turned in.

Heck got his battered suitcase from the car and took out his shaving gear and some other items he would need in the morning. He brushed his teeth and had returned to the bedroom, dressed only in his shorts, when Cracker reappeared.

"Heck, I . . ." He stopped short, staring open-mouthed at the scars on Heck's chest, stomach and left arm. "Good God Almighty. What on earth happened to you?"

"Well, it was this way. I was living in a very hot place and couldn't afford air conditioning, so I ventilated myself."

"Be serious. What happened?"

Reaching for his suitcase, Heck pulled out a fresh shirt, but in his haste jerked out some other items that fell to the floor. Several pages of handwritten yellowing notebook paper spilled out of a frayed brown envelope. Ignoring the spill, Heck slipped his arms into the sleeves of the shirt and began buttoning it. "I got a little careless in the Sahara one day when me and the boys had to save some British snobs from Rommel's troops. Or did it happen later, on that scenic Iwo Jima beach? You know how hard it is for a world traveler to keep all of the fine vacation spots straight after visiting so many." He glanced down at the spilled pages.

Cracker continued to stare at him with a shocked expression. "I didn't know about you being in the big war until the other day when I read it in the local paper. I had no idea your wounds were so serious."

"You shouldn't have been surprised --- dumb country boys make the best cannon fodder." He again glanced at the brown envelope. "You?"

"No. I was twenty-eight at the time we got in it, and I already had four kids."

"You're better off. My good intentions earned me a couple of extended visits to the V.A. hospital. Free room and board. Silly gowns that showed my ass every time I stood up."

Cracker's eyes bored into him, unimpressed by his attempt at humor. "But you must have got something. Some medals. A pension, maybe."

"Oh, I got some medals pinned to the front of my backless gowns. And a couple of congressmen up for re-election came by to have their pictures taken with me. A few other war profiteers thought they had to do something too, so for a year or so after my discharge from the hospital, they had the government give me almost enough to buy beer and rent a cheap room. That went on until they found out who I really was and what I was charged with. Then one of those Republican doctors called me in for a physical, to see if I was still disabled. Figuring I'd be arrested on those old charges, I didn't go. Surprise, surprise . . . the pension stopped."

"But that wasn't fair," Cracker said, frowning.

"Fair? You, a black raised in Hispaniola County talk about fair?" He sat down on the side of the bed. "By that time, the government had already paid for a few courses in night school for George Wills. Enough for me to get my G.E.D. But there was no demand for half-educated cotton pickers."

Cracker looked at the spilled sheets of paper. "What's that, some of your old government papers?"

"Oh, nothing." He began gathering up the pages. "Just a lot of stuff I wrote down to pass time on long winter nights."

"If it's about your life after Two Rivers, I'd like to read it, if it's not too personal. Maybe I can match it up with some of the things I jotted down and write a piece about it."

Heck hesitated, glancing at the envelope in his hands. He handed it to Cracker. "I don't guess there's any harm. I'm tired of looking at it anyway. But you'll be bored to tears."

Cracker took the envelope and turned it slowly in his hands as if he'd been given a priceless collector's item. "I'm sorry you got shot up in the war, Heck. I'm sorry you had to take on all that suffering on top of what you left here with. And I'm sorry it's been so long since I laid eyes on you. Good night, my friend." He disappeared down the hall.

Heck turned off the light and lay down with his mind in turmoil over the day's events and the old memories rekindled by talking to Cracker. Nights had always been bad for him. He'd found a man could put on an act for those around him during the day to cover up his true feelings. Big talk and big smiles always help. But lying down at night brings him face to face with his true self.

Heck often dwelled on his experiences through the years, and reviewed them many times during the long drive back to Two Rivers. So the events of his early life in the area were very clear in his memory. Reminiscing with Cracker further sharpened his recall -- as though it had all happened yesterday. *Funny,* he thought, *how the mind hangs on to the things that bother the most.*

He sat up on the side of the bed in the darkness and asked himself, *Should I try to sleep at all? Maybe a drive some place - - anywhere - - just to keep the night from pressing in on me.*

Driving had helped before when the aches of his old wounds, both physical and mental, kept him awake. During some of the most troublesome, he found himself almost overwhelmed by the fact that Josephine and Blood Money Vandergriff had cheated him out of what he'd wanted and needed most in this life. At times, he settled the inner storm by telling himself that even though the completeness he had known with his one true love was brief, many men were never that lucky. But attempts at the better-to-have-loved-and-lost consolation prize, plus brief liaisons to satisfy physical urges, had always left him with an emptiness he could not reason away.

Somewhere out in the nearby woods a whippoorwill issuing its "Chip-fell-out-of-the-white-oak" call, over and over, reminded him of another evening long ago, sitting on the front porch of another house with the girl he loved, listening to the same sound.

Grimacing from the tightness of old wounds and an aching left hip, he lay down again and let his mind rewind. This time to Hank Slater's cotton field that warm day in May, 1934, when Cracker stopped chopping cotton to sit down beside him in the shade for a short rest and a drink of water.

After downing about half the water in his Mason jar, Heck turned his eyes out to Willa Sproggs hoeing cotton in the late-morning sun. Beyond her, doing more talking than hoeing, were two of Cracker's friends, Kite and Sam.

Willa paused to glance at him and Cracker, eager to join them at the end of the row. Heck looked away not to give her the satisfaction of knowing he was watching her.

"Cracker, I never should've allowed Willa to bring me a drink of water that time over in Seth Ryan's hay loft."

At nineteen, Cracker was one year older than Heck, one inch shorter at six feet, but heavier. He gave Heck a puzzled look. "You white folks got it on us coloreds in some ways, I know. But when it comes to women, man, you is as dumb as I am po'. Take all she's got and enjoy it. There comes a day when a stud horse can't jus' jump up and bust out'n th' pen like he done as a colt. You'll cry a bucket o' tears fo' every race you coulda run but didn't."

"Can't you see? She's tryin' to catch me in her baby trap."

"So? It's her trap too. If she wants a baby, give it to her. Mamas been takin' care of their babies ever since men been helpin' make 'em. That's what they do best."

"I know about all them babies that don't have daddies. But that wouldn't be right for me and Willa knows it. She knows I'd marry her if I got her pregnant. I can't get married now."

"I can hear them wheels a' grindin' in your hard head. Don't wear out what little brains The Man blessed you with befo' you hafta use 'em for somethin' that ain't so easy to figure out."

"I got bills I can't pay now, what with Papa bein' a cripple and unable to work and a step-mama who won't. Billy is real sick and needs a doctor bad. I've been tryin' to talk Mama into getting' a job, but so far no luck. Even if she was willin', she don't know how to do nothin'. Marna's old enough to work and she's willin', but there ain't much farm work she can do. There ain't enough of that for us men."

As Willa came nearer, Heck, noting how Cracker was staring at her, said, "Don't even think about it."

Cracker turned quickly, giving Heck a sheepish look. "Think about what?"

"Don't what me. You know what."

"Thinkin' ain't doin'. I ain't that dumb. I want to live to a ripe old age, not get hung in my prime."

"Then don't let Ubis Sproggs catch you oglin' his daughter like you just did."

"Wasn't oglin'."

"Was too."

"Oglin' or not, that don't keep me from wonderin' about things, like how come a white man can – you know – do it with a colored woman, but a colored man can't do the same thing with a white lady."

"Because his juice makes black babies, dummy."

"And a white man shoots white baby juice. You get the same thing either way, a half-and-half youngun."

"Of course you do." Heck gave his friend a look of disbelief. "That's why white men folks won't allow their women to cross over. Don't make no difference if it's their sister or wife, or no kin at all. And as long as they're in charge of things, it ain't gonna happen."

"That's the only reason?"

"You ain't never heard of any man, black or white, who wanted to support another man's good times, have you? And if the woman's white, and that good time shows up half-black, Katy bar the door. It marks a white woman, pulls her down into the gutter. She can't claim it's her husband's or that it belongs to her boyfriend that she's about to marry."

"Somethin' tells me that still don't answer the real why of it all."

Heck squirmed a little, glancing at his friend. "That's most of it. If you know the rest, don't make me say it."

"It's 'cause whites don't quite see us as real human bein's, ain't it?"

"I think you're a might fine human being."

Cracker looked out across the field again with a sigh. "Life's a shitter, ain't it? On top of bein' black, I had to be po' as a cow paddy that's laid in th' sun all summer long."

Heck's voice was suddenly defiant. "You ain't no poorer'n I am. And you've had almost as much schoolin'. There ain't no jobs for whites either. You think the rich businessmen care whether poor whites like me live or die? That's the way things are, and there ain't nothin' neither one of us can do about it. It means we gotta work harder, if we want to make things better."

Cracker seemed not to have heard him. Then he said, "Life sho' ain't no Saturday night musical for me or you. And that's a fact."

"So what is it?

"I don't know 'xactly what it *is*. I'm still trying to figure that part out. So far, I just know what it *ain't*."

Heck looked out at the big-busted Willa, knowing that if he waited until she got to the end of the row, she'd come over, sit down next to him and put her hands where they had no business being when he was supposed to have his mind on work. She'd done it many times before and got her way.

"Cracker," he said, "are there any colored women like her? You know, wantin' it all the time."

"Sho'. They's the best kind. What's the matter? Ain't you ever hit the pine needles with a colored woman?"

"Nope. Had a chance to once right after Ross died. I'd quit goin' to church. Back-slidin', I was, runnin' around with that worthless Slick Haskel and drinkin' Ubis Sproggs' moonshine. I almost climbed on, but it just didn't seem right."

Cracker shook his head in disbelief and Heck went on, "Most country boys our age are already married. Girls younger'n us, like Willa there, are getting' hitched. But after about nine months of good romps, the babies start poppin' out and the fun's over. A man stuck like that will be dirt poor the rest of his life. He can't never break out of the mold and make his life better." He sat up straight. "Well, by gollies, that ain't for me. Not with a girl like Willa, anyway. The girl that I get hitched to has to lift me up, not pull me down."

"Hmmph," grunted Cracker.

"It's like Grandpa Tennel told me once. A man oughta breed up, not down." He let out a long sigh. "But before I can marry up, I've got to get me some land of my own and make lots of money. No high-caliber girl will take a likin' to any boy that's in the shape I'm in now."

"Don't know why not," Cracker said. "You're big and strong, and in spite of a nose like an eagle and eyes like a hawk on the prowl, you ain't bad lookin' for a po' country boy."

"You ain't no girl, so how would you know? I'm no John Barrymore, and that's a fact. Jus' thinkin' about talkin' to a pretty, high-class girl I see in town, my legs turn to jelly and my tongue gets all twisted. Around country girls like Willa, I don't have that problem. So why do you reckon it happens around city girls?"

"Don't think I want to even guess, seein' as how you've already told me I ain't qualified. But if I was to guess, I'd say it's 'cause you've got yo' brain loaded down too much with high-thinkin'. You know, like how you're gonna be a big-shot land owner some day, pee in tall cotton and raise lots o' spotted cows."

"And I will." Heck's eyes flashed. "All I gotta do is buy me a big piece of rich bottom land next to a creek somewhere. This ol' sand ain't no good for cotton. Look at them puny stalks."

"That's 'cause it was planted too early. Cotton's got to have hot weather to come up in and grow. And he didn't use no store-bought fertilizer. That old cow lot stuff ain't rich enough."

"Maybe, but whether the soil's sandy, red or black, a man can't amount to much unless he owns lots of it. Have you ever noticed how big landowners are always rich? They've got nearly 'bout all the money."

Cracker grunted. "So how you gonna get all that land, Mr. Know-It-All High-Stepper?"

"I'm gonna play and write songs. Put me together a band and sing and entertain folks all around the country like Jimmy Rodgers does. I'll get a record contract too." He picked up a clod and tossed it at a big ant. "Right now, of course, I've got to concentrate on just makin' enough money to buy groceries for my family and take Billy to ol' Doc Samuels. I've got to get Billy well." He picked up another clod and tossed it at the retreating ant. "But I'm not gonna let anything keep me from breakin' out of the rut I'm in now."

"Dreamin' an' schemin' don't cost you nothin' 'cept another kick in the slats," Cracker said. "But don't bank on God helpin' you out when it happens. I done tested that route."

"I'm not that dumb, dummy. A man's got to help hisself. I've already decided God don't have nothin' to do with what happens to poor folks." He kicked at another red ant. "I come to that way o' thinkin' right after Daddy got his legs cut off and Ross died."

"Maybe your God is different from colored folks' God," Cracker said. "Preacher told us our God's got a hand in everything that happens to us. He didn't say why. Appears He stays mad at us all the time. Always figured that's because He's white."

"Can't be. Our scrawny little preacher Homer Percy told us the same thing. Which is why I quit goin' to church. I figured somethin' was wrong with God if He could've kept all the bad things from happenin' to my family and didn't." He took another drink of water from his jar. "That's when I started believin' that bein' rich is better'n bein' religious."

Cracker gave him a questioning look. "You sho' do a heap o' speakin' out for a man who don't know beans 'bout women and ain't never had no money. I guess you gonna tell me next how the rich think about folks like you and me."

"Ain't hard to figure out. Like I already told you, they don't give a poot about what happens to us. But they need us. That's because they can't be rich unless there's lots of people like us willin' to have nothin', just barely getting' by. I figure it takes at least five thousand po' folks to make one rich one. O' course, the richer one is, the more poor folks there's gotta be."

"One thing's fo' sho'," Cracker sighed. "Ain't no colored man ever gonna be rich."

"Says who?"

"Nobody said." He held out his hand in front of Heck's face. "That's what says it, loud as a freight train's whistle."

"Looks okay to me." Heck inspected it. "It can chop and pick cotton as good as mine can."

Cracker's eyes flashed. "It's black, you bushy-headed pea picker."

"Ain't either. It's kinda brown, like maybe a white man might've laid down in the shade of your family tree way back there." He laughed, slapping his leg. "Maybe you're kin to Blood Money hisself. Both his daddy and grandpa owned slaves, you know."

Cracker threw up his hands. "You can be the aggravatin'est white boy I ever done seen. That ain't funny." He grunted. "You don't know nothin' 'bout nothin'."

"I know we gotta get off our cotton choppin' butts before Mr. Slater catches us lyin' down on the job like two fat hogs." Shielding his eyes with his hands, he glanced at the sun.

Cracker mumbled something, but Heck couldn't make out anything except "white trash" and one "nigger."

"Who said I was white trash?" Heck asked.

"There you go agin, playin' who said. Nobody said. Them looks you get in town does the tellin'. And don't say you ain't never noticed. It's the same look us coloreds get from folks who think they're better'n us."

"Oh, shit!" Willa cried out as she started chopping furiously at something with her hoe, causing them to turn and look at her. Cracker's friends, further out in the field, also stopped to watch.

"Lizard, most likely," Cracker said.

"Or a field mouse," Heck said. "Mice always scare women for some reason. You reckon it's because they're afraid they'll run up inside 'em?"

"Maybe."

Willa started chasing whatever it was, chopping and cursing, screaming so loud they could make out every word she said.

"See there?" Heck said. "She ain't got no class a'tall. A woman ain't supposed to cuss like that."

Cracker got to his feet and picked up his hoe. "Mr. Slater's gonna cuss worse'n her if we don't finish this patch o' cotton by twelve."

Heck picked up his hoe. "You'd better enjoy it, because after today there's no more farm work in these parts."

"Who said, Mr. Smarty Pants?"

"I said. I've already checked with all the farmers hereabouts. They're done workin' what they ain't plannin' to plow under. There ain't no jobs in town either. I looked."

Out in the field, Willa finally caught up with the intruder and chopped wildly. She stooped down and picked up a large field mouse. Turning to Heck, she yelled, "You coulda at least headed off the damn thang to save me chasin' his ass all over the goddam field. Lord knows, you ain't done nothin' else to give me any relief for over four months."

Cracker nudged Heck with his elbow. "That's a call to th' bushes if I ever heard one. Me and the boys won't tell nobody."

"Too hot," Heck said. "Besides, I'm supposed to be home by eleven. To load the butter and eggs in the wagon and finish my run in time for our musical tonight. It's Saturday, you know."

Cracker gave him a frightened look. "You can't leave now, not with Miss Willa still here and on the prowl. If you got to go, at least take her wid' you. If'n you don't, she's gonna pester me fo' sho'."

"Can't do that. She'd hold me up. If I don't make all my stops, I'll lose some of my customers. You and your friends can quit too if you're that scared of stayin'. Black folks don't like to work on Saturday nohow."

"That's a fact. They mostly like to go to town, but Kite and Sam need crap shootin' money for tonight. And I needs a little extra too, 'cause this is my night to see a good-time gal."

Heck shrugged. "A man's got to do what he's got to do." He moved out toward the end of the cotton rows.

Cracker grabbed his arm. "Lookahere, Heck," he said, frightened now. "You know us colored men don't like bein' left with no white lady by herself no day of the week."

"Hell, Cracker, Willa can take care of herself."

Cracker tightened his grip on Heck's arm. "It ain't Miss Willa I'm worried about. She'll touch me. And if I don't do nothin' but say hello, she'll scream rape so loud the High Sheriff'll hear her all the way to town and I'll be a hung nigger by sundown. My friends too, most likely."

Heck stopped and looked at Willa who had begun chopping toward them again. He told Cracker, "I could try to get her to go up to Mr. Slater's house and work around there the rest of the day. But I doubt he's got anything for her to do 'cept weed this puny cotton. And you know her daddy. Ubis Sproggs is the meanest man in the county. He'll beat the tar outta her if she comes home early for any reason. Just work away from her. Tell Kite and Sam to do the same."

Pulling his arm out of Cracker's grasp, Heck began clearing the grass at the end of the next row of small cotton. Stopping suddenly, he looked at his frightened friend. "What do you mean, she'll pester you?"

Cracker shifted his large feet in the sand and gave Heck a nervous look. "She'll, uh, touch me, Heck. She's done it befo'."

"You mean, like when you worked past her or something? It was probably an accident."

"Weren't no accident, no suh." He vigorously shook his head. "White ladies don't touch colored men like that."

"Just where did she touch you?"

Cracker passed his hand over his thigh and crotch.

"Cracker, I never knew you to lie to me before."

"And I ain't lyin' now. It's more like I'm dyin'. That white lady'll get ol' Cracker in bad trouble if you leave her out here. I ain't got the will power you got. My nature's got a hair trigger."

"All right, I'll do what I can. But if she won't leave, you and your friends may have to skedaddle."

"Can't. That would put me twix a rock and a hard place. The white man would want to know why. If I tell him, I'd be askin' for trouble fo' sho', and if I didn't, we'd all get fired, and no whites would ever hire us agin. We'd be branded as troublemakers and loafers."

"I'll talk to Willa. Now, let's go to work."

Because she was so large in her thighs, buttocks and bosom, Willa appeared older than sixteen. Besides being filled out better than most grown women, she was as strong as a young buck because her bootlegging father had always made her do manual labor. At 5'7", she was six inches shorter than Heck, but he guessed they weighed about the same, 165. Her hands were as tough as a man's and long hours in the sun had coarsened her freckled face. She seldom combed her long, reddish-brown hair.

He had known Willa all her life, and walked to school with her every day her dad had allowed her to go. She quit altogether when Heck dropped out in the middle of the eighth grade.

When he drew near Willa, she stopped, fixed teasing brown eyes on him from beneath her floppy felt hat. Brushing her hair from one eye, she smiled and blocked his row so he couldn't get past without touching her. Her meaning was clear. She wanted a tumble.

"Hi," she said, continuing to smile. "Thought you'd never come out here so we could talk without them niggers hearin' us."

Heck kept cutting away the grass and small weeds around the cotton and chopping down the most stunted cotton plants. Out of the corner of his eye, he saw an anxious Cracker hanging back, waiting to find out if he could persuade Willa to leave the field with him.

When he found Willa blocking his way, Heck stopped and met her gaze. "As soon as I finish this row, it'll be time for me to go," he said. "Why don't you walk up to Mr. Slater's house with me and see if he's got some chores you can do there to make out the day? It's awfully hot for May."

"The Slaters wouldn't pay me nothin' for doin' what they can do," she said, placing her hand on his arm. "But I could walk part of the way with you if you want to stop for a while over there in them trees and cool off."

Heck glanced back at Cracker. "Didn't your daddy know you'd be alone with Cracker and his friends when I left today?"

She jerked her hand away. "He don't care who I work with as long as I bring home thirty-five cents. Besides, why should it matter? I ain't scared of them niggers."

"Cracker's scared o you. You know blacks are afraid to be left alone with a white woman out like this. I think you should leave when I do."

She stamped her foot, sending a shower of dirt over Heck's old brogans. "I ain't gonna do somethin' that'll cause me a beatin' just to get away from them damn nigger friends of yours."

"Cracker said you touched him."

A smile curled her lips. "Whatsamatter, big fella, jealous?"

"Willa!"

"He's a lyin' nigger." She pursed her lips. "But he is a friend of yours, and any friend of yours is a friend of mine. Besides, I feel sorry for him at times. Ain't you never felt sorry for nobody?"

Heck had always found it hard to decide if Willa was teasing or lying when her talk turned sentimental. It caused him to recall his granddad's warning: "Connivin' women use all sorts of tricks to get a man to do what they want him to do."

"Stop that kind of talk, Willa. You'll get Cracker killed."

She opened another button on her faded blue shirt and moved the garment in and out to stir up the air. "It's powerful hot this mornin'."

She fanned some more, revealing the tops of her large breasts. She never wore a brassiere, always bragged she didn't have to. He stared at her bosom, just like she knew he would, and right away, he felt his resolve begin to weaken and something else harden. He started hoeing again, faster now, but she moved up alongside him.

"Whatsamatter?" she asked. "You ain't started listenin' to that wimpy preacher Homer Percy agin, have you? I thought you quit goin' to church."

When he didn't respond, she stepped closer, reaching her hand around to grab his privates. He kept hoeing, hoping he could pull away before he felt himself begin to swell. When she moved in again he knocked her hand away, determined to leave for town on schedule.

"I guess you forgot," he said, "about me tellin' you I ain't takin' no more chances on makin' a baby with any girl right now. There are too many other things I have to do."

"You ain't got no more sense than your nigger buddy." She kicked another shower of dirt his way as her face became redder than usual. "You're just a field hand, Heck Tennel, like me. You and your high-fallutin' ideas. You ain't never getting' out of workin' at some other kind of hard labor as long as you live. And don't think for a minute you can convince one of them dainty little town pretties to hit the pine needles with you, 'cause you ain't got enough good looks or brass to ask 'em. And even if you did, them kind ain't gonna hitch their buggy to no plow horse. So wake up. Try to be more like Slick. Be pleased with what you can get, or already have."

He kept chopping and thought, *she's right about Slick. He don't refuse any girl, or a drink of whiskey, or a crap game.* He told her, "I'm not makin' no crap shoot outta my life. There has to be a better way of livin' than what I've seen so far."

"There is, if you'd climb down off your high horse and dive into the clover. Take what little good that does come your way and enjoy it."

"I'm okay," he said, not looking at her as he kept working.

Drawing up alongside again, Willa lowered her voice, sounding almost like a real lady for a change when she said, "I want some of the good things too, Heck. You think I want to work in these fields 'til I get as hard and wrinkled as an ol' saddle, live in a pig sty and get beat up every time I don't please my daddy? And maybe end up with some man who treats me like a cow? I ain't never been treated with no tenderness or kindness by nobody 'cept you, before you started considerin' yourself too good for me. Can't you see I need you to help me out of this mess?"

"I've got my own mess to worry about, Willa. And, by damn, nobody, or nothin' is keepin' me from doin' whatever it takes to climb out of it!"

Shocked by his angry outburst, Willa fell silent and watched him work away from her. Recovering quickly, she reverted to her usual habit of yelling at him, "You'll be sorry, Heck Tennel. Sorry, sorry, sorry. For bein' so uppity, for turnin' your back on your own kind, and me. Somethin' bad will happen to you. You'll see."

Heck hurried to finish the row, not bothering to look back lest Willa see it as an indication he'd changed his mind about stopping in the woods. But he kept thinking about what she'd said. Maybe Slick Haskel's way was best, and maybe he'd enjoy life more if he let his passions run wild like Cracker did. *But without giving my plans a try, for sure I'll end up being what Willa said, sentenced to life at hard labor. Heck, you have to measure up. That's what I promised my brother Ross, on his deathbed worrying about what would become of our family.*

Heck walked along a branch until he got to a field of young corn. He went down a long row, crawled through a barbed wire fence and crossed an open meadow on his way to the Slater house. Mr. Slater sat in the porch swing smoking his corncob pipe, intently watching him. He was an old man, seldom working the crops any more, other than plowing with the riding cultivator or weeding his garden.

Mr. Slater pulled his watch from the bib pocket of his overalls, opening it. "Thought maybe Willa had changed your mind about goin' into town today," he teased.

Heck pretended he hadn't heard the remark as he moved up in the shade of the porch to sit down. Taking off his straw hat, he began to fan himself. "Sure hot for May."

"It ain't too hot to reach up here and take your money is it?" Mr. Slater pulled some change out of his pocket.

"No, sir. It ain't never that hot."

"Got your week's wages figured up and counted out. Three dollars and thirty cents."

Heck took his money: six silver half-dollars, one quarter and a nickel. He studied the coins a moment as a sense of pride swept over him. Then he closed his hand, shook it, and listened to them rattle. "That's a might pretty sound." He pulled a folded magazine ad out of his chest pocket of his overalls, unfolded it and carefully wrapped the coins. "If I could keep Daddy from takin' it all, I'd have enough to pay Doc Samuels' to visit our house to see Billy."

"Billy ain't no better?" Mr. Slater gave him a concerned look.

"No, sir. I'm awful afraid he'll die if I don't find a way to get him some doctorin' real soon."

"What's that, a picture of some kind?" Mr. Slater fixed his eye on the ad.

Always quick to show it to anybody with the slightest interest, Heck handed it to Mr. Slater. "A Martin guitar advertisement I found in an old magazine that somebody throwed away over on the main road. Just somethin' to look at. I can't afford to buy one."

"Real purty." Mr. Slater studied the picture. "You and your paw still holdin' them musicals, are you?"

"Every Saturday night. Why don't you and Miz Slater come over tonight?"

"Been wantin' to. I like fiddle music." The old farmer handed the paper back to Heck. "Sorry about work playin' out, boy, but with cotton so cheap, I can make more plowin' it under, just like the rest of the farmers around here. I'll plow under the peas too, 'cept what we got in the garden."

"Thank you for your concern, Mr. Slater, but we'll make out some way. I've still got my butter and egg route." He would've told him about selling a new product beginning today, but a good Baptist hated whiskey almost as much as he did dancing. It appeared they thought anything fun was a sin. "I'm tryin' to get my stepmother to go to work, but she claims not to know how to do nothin'. Won't even look for a job."

"I hear tell Brother Percy is lookin' for somebody to clean up his church every Monday. If she could get on there, maybe the big church in town would hire her part-time too."

"Thanks. I'll talk to her about it when I get home, if I can do it without Daddy hearin' me. He won't allow her to work anywhere but home, but since she makes me and the girls do everything there, she really don't have nothin' to do but sleep, primp and complain about how she's wastin' her life."

"How come your paw won't let her go to work?"

"Daddy told me one time she's got a weakness."

"You've had a heavy cross put on your shoulders, boy, what with your older brother dyin', and your daddy bein' crippled. If you can't get your step-mama to go to work, how in thunder will you support your family? There ain't that much to be made sellin' butter and eggs."

"Find chickens that'll lay twice a day, and a cow that gives ice cream."

Mr. Slater laughed. "If gall will take you anywhere, boy, you'll prosper. Power to ya, by Gadfry."

Leaving his hoe propped against the porch, Heck headed for his mule out by the barn. Riding the mule allowed him to work a full four hours on Saturdays, because it took him less time to travel to and from the field. He could make the four-mile trip in about thirty minutes if he kept Maude in a slow lope or trot.

Riding down the lane to Slater Road, he soon approached the eastern border of Panther Holler Woods, a thousand acre tract of virgin timber bordered by a four-wire fence. He would ride along it about two miles to where the road intersected Panther Holler Road, then turn south to his family's house about one mile from the big wood's southern border. From home, it was five miles to Two Rivers.

To keep his mind off the big woods and its spooky history, he hummed a couple of tunes and tried to remember the words to "When the Work's All Done This Fall." But he couldn't keep his eyes or his thoughts free of what might be lurking just beyond the fence adorned with red and black metal signs about every hundred yards warning:

STAY OUT
TRESPASSERS WILL BE SHOT
SURVIVORS WILL BE PROSECUTED

As far as Heck was concerned, the signs were a complete waste because no man in his right mind would dare enter the forest. Ever since age five, when he found out it was where the crazy old miller Fritz

Kesselmeir murdered his wife and her lover, he had been afraid to ride or walk past by himself. His fear was given an added urgency one time when a panther screamed as he walked by alone at sundown. Almost messing in his overalls, he ran all the way home.

He'd witnessed only that one blood-curdling panther scream, but had been told by others hearing them several times each year. The old bachelor Loony Toons, who lived down the road from their place, claimed to hear them often, but few people believed him. Loony had a vivid imagination.

Riding on the right side of the road next to the ditch, he finally arrived at Panther Holler Crossing where he turned his mule's head toward the bridge over Morales Creek. Casting another nervous glance at the big timber on his left, he kicked Maude in the ribs and began whistling, "Oh, Susannah" as he tried to make himself think of the new items he'd have for sale that day. Selling bootleg whiskey in a dry county was very risky, but not nearly as scary as riding by Panther Holler Woods alone.

He passed the dim outline of an abandoned lane leading off the main road to where the old miller's gristmill once stood deep in the woods on the banks of Morales Creek. Before the murders, and preceding the building of the fence, county farmers took corn down that lane to have it ground into meal.

Even though Maude walked on the far side of the road, they were still no more than twenty feet from the big woods, causing him to keep a wary eye out for a panther along the fence. He kicked Maude in the ribs, but she maintained a fast walk.

Heck always hoped to meet someone on the road to accompany him by the place, but had never been so lucky. No more than a dozen families lived within two miles of the bridge, close enough to hear him yell for help. A car seldom came through because only a couple of dairymen in the area could afford an automobile.

With his fears mounting, Heck pulled a well-used Hohner harmonica from his back pocket and began playing "Buffalo Gal" loudly. Feeling dizzy from the effort, he dropped the instrument back into his pocket and again listened for sounds beyond the fenced area. The clop-clop of Maude's hoofs on the hard, dry roadbed gave him some comfort. They were almost to the creek.

On the other side of the bridge, the road curved sharply to the right, then went up a hill where it leveled off on its way to the Vandergriff Road intersection. There were four old sharecropper houses at that intersection.

Heck and his family lived in the one facing Panther Holler Road. His dad and sisters would be waiting there to ride into town with him.

When he turned sixteen, his dad let him keep his earnings until the end of the week, at which time he had to give them up. He appreciated the temporary possession that gave him the privilege of rattling and counting it, plus the pride in knowing he'd earned it himself and that it would go for a good cause.

At eighteen, his dad had agreed to return half his week's wages on occasion, subject to the amount required for household expenses, his mood, and whether he needed a fresh supply of Ubis Sproggs' home brew.

Heck worried about no more work to be found, not even as a laborer at the big Vandergriff Lumber Mill in Two Rivers. The mill paid the highest wages in town, ten dollars for a six-day, sixty-hour week. However, if you got hurt, like his dad did, they'd let you go without benefits of any kind.

The road narrowed at the bridge, and as Heck urged Maude toward the wide, rough planks, he began singing "You Are My Sunshine." He was feeling much braver now. But just as her hoofs struck the boards, a car suddenly appeared in the curve ahead, roaring toward them. He jerked wildly at the reins to stop the mule or make her jump off the bridge, but she refused to cooperate.

It was so quick: the blur of the speeding car, the sound of locked wheels in dirt ruts, a cloud of dust. It was get out of the way or be run over, so he jumped off the mule, barely clearing the ends of the big boards as he fell on his back in the water below.

A sharp pain stabbed him at the base of his neck when he hit the bottom of the shallow stream. Had he broken something? *Wonderful. Another medical bill we certainly can't afford.*

# Chapter III

S pitting and gasping for air, Heck scrambled to his feet in the waist-deep water looking for the mule. If she was hurt or killed he'd really be up the creek. No transportation and no way to run his milk and butter route, a guaranteed financial disaster.

"Maude!" he yelled.

She wasn't in the water, on the bank, or the bridge. Wiping his eyes, he looked in the distance and saw her running up the hill toward the house, apparently not seriously hurt. *Thank God.*

Checking himself, he was further relieved to find nothing broken, a happy conclusion quickly replaced by panic when he reached into his open bib pocket and found his week's wages gone.

"Dammit to hell and back," he yelled. He sank to his knees and began feeling around for the coins on the soft, sandy bottom.

Not finding them by touch, he plunged beneath the surface in an effort to spot them. But the water was too muddy. All he brought up was burning eyes.

He took another deep breath and resumed running his fingers through the mud. He still didn't find them, and after several more attempts realized he never would.

He crawled up on the bank beneath the bridge near a piling and began frantically combing the grass. Then out along the water's edge. Nothing.

"Damnation," he said out loud, in disgust. "I can't take Billy to the doctor now, and Daddy'll beat the tar outta me."

"Are you all right?" asked a calm voice from above.

Heck jumped. He peeked upward along the edge of the bridge toward the unexpected sound. An angel? *Naah. This could only be the devil's handiwork.*

He moved cautiously from under the bridge to find a tall stranger watching him from the side of the road. Dressed in a white shirt and tie, khaki pants and a snap-brimmed Sunday hat, he looked more like a politician than a farmer.

"I ain't dead," Heck told him. "But right now I don't know if that's good or bad. Damnation."

The stranger moved closer. "From the way you were yelling, I was afraid I'd hit you."

Heck wiped more water from his face. "I would've been better off if you'd killed me. I lost a whole week's wages!"

"Sorry I surprised you like that. I was moving too fast for that curve."

Heck noticed an object showing above the man's belt on his left side, the butt of a pistol. "Are you a security guard?" he said, thinking Blood Money might have sent him out to ride the boundaries of his Panther Holler Woods.

The stranger's smile vanished. "No." He looked up the road where the mule disappeared. "Can I help you with the animal?"

"She'll stop at the house." Heck climbed up the bank.

"I'd offer you a lift, but I've got passengers in my car."

Just beyond the bridge Heck saw a parked grey Ford sedan with a man and a woman in the back seat. He could barely see the shorter of the two, but he could tell by the hair that it was a woman.

"I can walk to the house."

"What's your name?"

"Heck Tennel. Who are you?"

The stranger held out his hand. "Jake Vest. Maybe your money fell on the bridge and rolled through the cracks as you took that dive. Let's have a look see."

They went down the slope and searched the area, but found no coins. When they returned to the road, Jake asked, "How much did you lose?"

"Three dollars and thirty cents."

"For the whole week?" Jake gave him a puzzled look.

"And I was lucky to get that. After today, there's no more work."

Heck watched Jake walk to the male passenger's side of the Ford, lean down and say something. Heck couldn't understand what they were saying, but did hear Jake call the passenger "Clyde." The man passed something to Jake who promptly rejoined Heck and told him, "Maybe this will help your feelings a little."

Heck looked in awe at the twenty-dollar bill in his hand, fighting an urge to grab it. He'd seen very few bills that large during his lifetime.

"I didn't lose that much," he said. "Besides it was as much my fault as it was yours."

Jake pushed the bill into Heck's chest pocket. "That'll replace yours with a little something left over for damages. You're a mess."

Heck suddenly found himself liking the stranger. "Thanks. I'll put it to good use." The first thing that came to mind was paying for Doc Samuels' house call with enough left over to buy Billy and the girls new tennis shoes.

"Not many people live along this road, I've noticed," Jake said. "You're the first person we've seen since leaving Two Rivers."

"Everybody that's goin' to town is already there by now, I guess."

"Of course." Jake smiled. "Going to town on Saturday. The highlight of the week, right?"

"For some. For others it's the musical we give every Saturday night at our place. If you're still around about the time it gets dark, why don't you come by for a while? Turn right at the next road. You'll hear the music. Daddy might even let you put something in his hat."

"I may do that. Got to go now." He offered his hand.

Heck shook his hand, then watched Jake walk back to the Ford and drive away. He slowed down at the intersection, as if undecided which way to go, then turned right toward the Slater place.

Heck pulled the greenback from his pocket, stretched it, and twisted it to hear it rattle as only new paper money does. It was the most money he'd ever received at one time, and he liked the way it made him feel. He wondered about Jake's passenger. *Must be very rich to afford that shiny new Ford and give away twenty-dollar bills to total strangers.*

Heck headed for the house at a brisk pace, each step producing a squashing sound in his wet brogans. In all the excitement, he had forgotten about the dangers lurking in the woods beyond the fence, but now that it had come back to mind, he quickened his gait and cast a cautious look over his left shoulder.

Topping the hill, he slowed down some and soon approached the Vandergriff Road intersection. A quick look at the front porch told him his dad was waiting for him. Early Tennel sat in his homemade wheelchair - - nothing but a straight chair, a few boards, and four wheels Heck made from cuttings off a gum log.

Before Early's accident at the mill ten years ago, they'd lived in Milltown. That's where Heck's mother died when he was almost two. Thelma Pascal, one of Early's girl friends prior to his marriage, moved in right away to help his dad take care of him and Ross, but they didn't get married until Thelma got pregnant with Marna later that year. Elsie, born two years after Marna, was four when Early had the accident, and Heck was eight when they were ordered out of Milltown for failure to pay rent and buy commissary groceries. With no income, Miss Cilla and Brother Percy persuaded Blood Money to let them live rent-free in the old dogtrot sharecropper house where they were given enough groceries by Brother Percy's Baptist church for a few weeks to keep them from starving. After that, Heck and Ross cleaned stables for local farmers and sold bottles they found along public roads for barely enough to buy food they couldn't raise in their garden. Their plight was improved a little when a nearby dairyman gave them a Jersey milk cow.

Located on the edge of the farm that also provided the site for the first Vandergriff family home, the shabby old house was where Amy and Billy were born. Curt Truesdale, Blood Money's farm foreman, lived in it up to the time they moved in. Curt took his family to the main house vacated when Blood Money transferred his family to their new mansion in Two Rivers.

The old tin-roofed structure was the first in a row of four unpainted bats-and-boards houses at the intersection, and the only one facing the main road. Three shacks facing Vandergriff Road stood just beyond a wire fence running from the corner of the cow pen to the dilapidated barn where Heck kept his mules and milk cow. That first one was where they held their Saturday night musicals, rain or shine. The others, more run-down, no longer had windows or doors.

All three of the smaller houses looked out over the road from atop a high clay bank with only one cut in it from which they could be reached by wagon or car. That cut also served as a driveway into the back yard of the house Heck and his family lived in. Towering oaks and sycamores shaded all four structures.

The hot air had almost dried Heck's clothes by the time he got home, and the remaining dampness gave him some relief from the heat. Comfort, and anticipation of starting the butter and egg run into town, quickened his entry into the backyard. He spotted Maude grazing out near the barn, apparently undisturbed by her narrow escape.

At the top of the cut, their mixed-breed terrier Spot charged out to meet him, barking excitedly, and in the process sending several frightened guineas and some Rhode Island Red laying hens scurrying to safety. Heck reached down to pet Spot, who licked his hand and jumped up in his arms.

Early had pulled himself along the walls of the dogtrot to the back porch, and the expression on his face indicated he was upset. Of late, he seemed always mad about something. Quickly turning away, Heck looked around the yard for Billy and his sisters, but didn't see them. They often disappeared when Dad was in one of his bad moods, and didn't dare reappear until after he'd vented his anger, usually on Heck.

Early's left leg had been severed just above the knee, the right one at the ankle. Heck had constructed a leather pouch for each stump, crude devices that allowed his dad to pivot himself out of his wheelchair on his longest leg when he went to bed or to the privy. Even those simple maneuvers had become difficult for his obese frame, the result of prolonged inactivity. He had also taken to ignoring personal hygiene, seldom bathing or shaving. At age 44, he had no special interests to occupy his time, and was convinced those things which made his life meaningful before – work, fishing, dancing and sex – had been take away forever by Blood Money's mill saw.

"You're late, boy." Early's brown eyes flashed. "Where you been, mixin' it up with that trashy Willa Sproggs agin?"

Heck walked up the porch steps and over to the wash pan on a shelf between two rotting posts. "No, Daddy. I quit at ten, just like I always do on Saturdays. I had an accident is all."

"Don't tell me you lost the money."

"I fell in the creek."

His dad leaned forward. "Then you did lose the money."

Heck suddenly found hope in his dad's words. *If he believes there's no money, I can keep the entire twenty and spend it as I please.* But as quickly as that exciting possibility came to mind, it vanished. *Dad will know when the doctor comes out, or when he sees the kids' new tennis shoes.* That would earn him another beating with the razor strap.

Heck poured clean water in the pan from the bucket on the shelf and reluctantly pulled the twenty from his pocket. Early became so excited he didn't bother completely turning his head toward the edge of the porch before spitting a long stream of tobacco juice. Some of it spattered on the floor near Heck's feet. His dad jerked the money out of his hand, inspected it, and gave Heck a suspicious look.

"How'd you come by this much money, boy? Did Ubis Sproggs give you an advance on what you're gonna sell for him today?"

"No, Daddy," Heck replied, quickly telling him what had happened. "I told the man I didn't want to take it all because it was partly my fault, but he gave it to me anyway."

"Hmmph. You and your grand ideas. You're just like Ross was, in some ways. I'll tell you what I told him lots of times. You ought not to be so damned particular when it comes to money. Poor folks like us deserve it more'n them that's got more'n their share. Who was the man anyway?"

"Said his name is Jake Vest. He was dressed up real nice."

"Well, boy, you done the right thang by brangin' in lots of cash this week." His dad looked at the bill. "Otherwise, I don't know how this fam'ly woulda made out the month."

Every reference to how bad off they were made Heck feel guilty about how little he earned. He finished washing his hands and face and told his dad, "That's why I let you talk me into sellin' Ubis Sproggs' shine, remember? With the extra money that'll bring in, I was in hopes you'd let me keep enough of this twenty to buy Billy and the girls some new shoes." He didn't dare mention his Doc Samuels plan. Early didn't believe in doctors or preachers.

"Nope. I need it all. Even that might not be enough after what happened this mornin'."

"Is Billy worse?" A sinking feeling swept over Heck.

"Will you quit worryin' over Billy and start thinkin' about the rest of the family for a change? Billy'll be all right. It's the cash that's important. Blood Money sent his bitchy daughter Josephine out here this mornin' right after you left for work. She didn't even get out of her big Cadillac to tell me we've got to start payin' rent on this ol' ramshackle house. No more free rides, she said."

"But we've been livin' here over ten years." Heck frowned. "The preacher and Miss Cilla got her daddy to promise you we could use this house as long as he didn't need it for anything else. Blood Money owes you a helluva lot more than that, him and his damned sawmill."

"Well, he changed his mind, the money-grubbin' ol' bastard. Miss Josephine comes drivin' up real slow-like with her dumb sister Cilla in tow. Said times was hard on everybody, even them. Can you imagine the brass it took to tell that lie to a poor man like me?"

"How much is the rent?"

"Ten dollars a month, with the first month's tab due now. We can keep usin' the barn, the garden spot and the pasture."

Heck sat down, sickened at having his plans ruined.

His dad went on, "I told Miss Josephine I wouldn't have no money 'til you got home from the field, so she said she'd be back in the mornin' for it. We can pay by the week."

Heck did some quick figuring and decided he might still have enough money for Doc Samuels if sales were good on the route, a highly doubtful prospect. He looked around for his stepmother, telling himself it was time to talk to her about the part-time job at the church. Even though she wasn't his birth mother, Heck had always called her "Mama" out of respect for what she'd done for the family early on and the fact that she was the only mother he'd ever known. Grandpa Tennel told him she was nothing like his real mother.

"Where's Mama?"

"Asleep, I reckon. She don't do much else around here no more."

"I need to talk to her." Heck started down the hall.

"There ain't no time for that," his dad said hotly, shaking his head. "Besides, for a change I'm glad she's asleep, 'cause it gives me a chance to mention something else I been meanin' to brang up. 'Specially since you brought in a little extra."

"What is it this time? You out of booze?"

"No, more important than that." Averting his eyes to look out at the mule, he went on, "It's about this, uh, problem I've been havin' lately. Started when I had my accident, but during the last year or so it's got out of hand."

When Heck said nothing, his dad glanced at him without turning his head and continued. "In plain man talk, I can't do it no more with your stepmama. Don't expect you to understand the pity of that, you bein' so young. But it's the worst thang that can happen to any man."

Early shifted in his chair and spat again, still not looking at Heck. "So I been thinkin' that what I need to get me goin' again is a little visit with Frieda Haskel."

"You'd spend that money on a whore?"

"Not so loud." He glanced around to see if one of the girls might have been listening and leaned closer. "Hers ain't no different from any other woman's. A man just pays for it in a different way, is all. I figure if she does her special on me the way Cotton Murphy described, it'll bring back my nature." He looked out in the yard. "Like thangs are now, I'd as soon be dead."

The painful way he said it convinced Heck his dad might have tender feelings about some things after all. He felt obliged to make some allowances for his problem. Anything his dad said, or the blunt manner in which he said it, never surprised him. For a long time Heck suspected something was amiss in his parent's love life; of late he'd not heard any attempted tumbles followed by an exchange of angry words. Their bedroom was across the hall from his and Billy's and the doors were always left open.

"Dad, can't you put off the visit a while longer? Wait 'til after I buy some things for Billy and the girls."

"I ain't gettin' no younger, boy. So, I'll be keepin' all the twenty. It won't hurt Billy and his sisters to go barefooted the rest of the summer. We can buy some groceries and pay this week's rent out of the butter and egg money."

"But the whole twenty?"

"Cotton said it won't be over five dollars, unless I get her special. That'll cost more."

Heck didn't like it, but he knew better than to try changing his dad's mind. "I'll find Marna. She can put our stuff in the wagon while I hitch up and load the shine."

Feeling his dad's eyes on him as he went into the kitchen, he didn't dare go in and talk to his stepmother. He'd have to do that another time.

Stopping at the pie safe, he pulled out three cold biscuits, punched his finger in each one and filled them with ribbon cane syrup. Not seeing Marna by then, he headed for the wagon, eating on the way.

His half-sisters were nowhere in sight, so he brought the tub from the barn that he had set twelve quarts of moonshine in the night before. After sliding the merchandise into the bed of the wagon, he made sure the jars were separated and covered with hay, and went back for the mule harness.

Worried about selling whiskey in a dry county, Heck knew what would happen if caught by Sheriff Emmet Sloan or a city policeman. And more frightening, what would happen to his family if he had to go to jail. *I can never let that happen, no matter what.*

By the time he hitched up the mules, Marna and Elsie had come from the woods out back and brought the box of butter and eggs from the kitchen. They very carefully placed it in the bed of the wagon and slid it forward enough to be reached from the seat.

Even though she'd just turned sixteen, Marna looked older because of her large bosom and hips and the way she fixed her brown hair when she went to town. The fourteen-year-old Elsie was short like her sister at about 5'1". Her eyes were blue, her hair red, the same as Thelma's. Because of her fair complexion and constant exposure to the sun, her face had freckled like Willa's. Marna's skin, on the other hand, was a clear medium olive. Both girls already had a keen interest in boys, but wouldn't socialize in circles outside the family because they were ashamed of their flour sack dresses and frayed tennis shoes.

"Elsie," he said, "where's Billy and Amy?"

"Billy ain't feelin' good today. Amy's with him under the big oak."

Heck turned and called out, "Billy, come here a minute, buddy."

His eight-year old half-brother appeared presently at the corner of the house, walking slowly toward him. Pale and thin, he had dark shadows under his big brown eyes.

When he came within reach, Heck placed his hands on his frail little shoulders and gave him a smile. "What's this I hear about you not feelin' good this mornin', podner?"

Billy fixed his sad eyes on Heck. "I've been talkin' to Ross."

His statement rendered Heck speechless for a moment. Recovering, he made himself smile again as he patted Billy on the shoulder. "Yeah, well, I think about Ross a lot too. How do you feel?"

"Not very good, Heck. Amy said I ought to lay down and rest some more."

"That ain't a bad idea, little brother, but don't you want to come to town with us and get an ice cream cone?"

Billy shook his head. "I want to stay home." With that, he turned and shuffled out of sight around the corner of the house.

Fighting back tears, Heck gripped his hands so tightly his fingernails bit into his palms. He wanted to hit somebody, to kick, or scream, but all he did was watch and remember the indifference his parents showed regarding Billy's health. Thelma had always shrugged off his condition as nothing more than the natural result of her crippled husband's weak seed, made less potent when he had the mumps the year before.

At times like these, Heck even fumed at God for allowing his little brother to be born sick. Amy was sickly too, but not as bad as Billy. Thelma blamed Early for that too, because he was drunk at conception. Neither had been allowed to go to school after Billy's condition worsened, and their dad made Elsie stay home to help Amy look out after him so Heck could work full-time in the fields. Marna was ordered to quit school and go to work after the fifth grade.

"No use gettin' all worked up over Billy again, Heck," Marna said. "You've done all you can. Even if you could afford to send him to a hospital, Daddy wouldn't let you, seein' as how he believes all doctors are quacks."

Elsie told him, "Daddy said Billy's gonna be all right. He is, ain't he?"

He started around to the driver's side of the wagon. "If I have anything to do with it, he will."

"Heck," Elsie said, "Marna said Brother Homer told her that whatever happens, it's God's will."

"Could be Marna's been listenin' to the preacher too much lately," he said.

"He come by again last Wednesday," Marna said, giggling. "I think Mama's gettin' the hots for him. She told me she's glad he comes by, because she needs somebody to talk to. She also said she's got other needs that ain't bein' attended to since papa got to where he can't . . ."

"Marna!" Heck said, frowning at her. "Not in front of Elsie."

Elsie smiled. "Oh, I know all about sex. Marna and Willa told me. Yuck."

Heck set the brake, gave the reins to Marna and went back to the porch to get his dad. Pushing the wheelchair down the ramp at the end of the steps, he rolled him out to the left side of the wagon where he helped him climb into the seat. Still holding onto the reins, Marna climbed over the seat to sit on a box beside Elsie.

Going to the driver's side, Heck climbed up and took the reins from Marna. He told his half-sisters, "Hold onto the back of the seat so you won't fall over backwards like you did last Saturday. And don't make me have to look for you when it's time to come home."

He glanced at the house. Still no sign of Thelma. He regretted not finding the chance to tell her about the job at the church, because his daddy's being away would give her an opportunity to go check it out.

Releasing the brake, Heck tapped the mules with the reins and swung them around toward the cut in the bank and looked at Billy and Amy under the big oak until they'd passed from his view. Billy had lain back down and Amy was near him playing with a homemade rag doll.

"What's in the tub, Heck?" Elsie asked.

"Lemonade," he responded shortly.

Marna cleared her throat, causing Heck to look at her. Turning her eyes away with a smile told him she knew about the shine.

Once they were out in Panther Holler Road, Heck glanced toward the bridge in the hopes he'd see Cracker and his friends coming home early. No sign of them, but looking back did give him an idea for talking to Thelma about that job.

"What you stopping for?" Early demanded, spitting over the front end of the wagon on Maude's tail.

Heck didn't look at him. Turning to Marna instead, he told her, "I forgot something. Come up and drive."

"Marna can't drive in town," Early complained. "And I won't be able to get out of the wagon."

Jumping to the ground, Heck told his dad, "Wait for me at Mr. Meade's"

Marna clucked the team forward. Heck climbed the red bank and cut back through the woods toward the house.

Now that it looked like he would lose the entire twenty dollars and not knowing how much he'd sell on his route or if anybody would throw anything in the hat that night, the family's future seemed shakier than ever. He had to convince Thelma to take that job at the church.

# Chapter IV

U pon approaching the side yard, Heck peered through the trees to determine what Billy and Amy were doing. If Billy was asleep, he didn't want to wake him up. He was surprised to find both of them had disappeared.

*They probably went inside,* he told himself, continuing toward the back porch. That's when he heard children's voices out on Vandergriff Road. Changing directions, he walked around the barn to a spot near the high bank and overheard Billy ask his sister, "How come you think Mama wanted us to go see Miz Sproggs all of a sudden?"

"I think Mama's gonna have company again, that's why," Amy answered. "Remember how she done the same thing last week when the preacher showed up all of a sudden?"

*Company? Preacher? What's going on?* Heck wondered.

"Now don't you worry, Billy," Amy said. "We'll stop to rest on the way so you won't get too tired."

*What to do?* Heck puzzled over the unexpected developments. *Stop the kids, or go talk to Thelma? Billy's in no condition to be walking to the Sproggs place. On the other hand, they shouldn't overhear a discussion of the family's desperate situation. Billy's a born worry wart. But heaven only knows when I'll ever again catch Thelma home alone.*

A car turned off the main road and swung up into their backyard through the cut. Racing to the corner of the barn, Heck watched the Reverend Homer Percy stop his Model A Ford near the back steps and get out. Without calling out a greeting, he walked up the steps and disappeared into the dogtrot on his way to the front of the house.

*That's strange. What's happening? Did Mama already find out about the job and send for the preacher? Maybe Daddy and me sold her short.*

Curious, Heck circled the house, approaching it from the corner room where he and Billy slept. Stopping there to listen, he heard Thelma laugh in what they called the living room, which was actually his parents' bedroom with a fireplace and an old sofa in it.

He crawled through the screenless window, tiptoed to the door and peeked across the hall into the front room. Thelma and the preacher were sitting next to each other on the sofa. He jumped back as if he'd done something he wasn't supposed to do and seen something he wasn't supposed to see. Embarrassed and confused, he tried to decide what best to do. He diminished his sudden feeling of guilt by telling himself, *I came back to the house for a good reason.* That made him feel a little better.

But then an important question popped into his mind. *Do I have any right to eavesdrop on a preacher and my stepmother for any reason?* He suddenly saw a certain resemblance to his own way of thinking about preachers that he had always seen in his dad. He also suspected he might be about to learn what Early meant by Thelma's "weakness."

Burdened with guilt, he turned toward the window and, making his first step to exit, the old floor went *squeeeak!* Heck froze.

"What was that?" the preacher asked.

Thelma said, "Oh, just this rotten ol' house leanin' and settlin'. Don't pay it no mind."

Heck drew his foot back and once more leaned against the door frame to listen.

"I'm sure glad you come by to counsel me, Homer . . . I mean, Brother Homer. Hope you didn't get tired of waitin' for Early and the kids to leave. I'm about to go crazy here with nothin' to do and a husband that can't comfort me."

"What's a preacher for, if he can't do God's work, Sister Tennel? I'm just sorry I had to leave so soon the last time because of another appointment. We'll now continue talkin' about your problem today. But Brother Tennel really needs to be here too."

"No way," Thelma said. "What I have to say can't be said in front of him."

"But I should at least talk to him about those Saturday night musicals he's having. He's running a regular den of iniquity, with all that dancin' and drinkin'. I fear you and him and all your children are goin' to hell if it's not stopped."

Heck peeked around the door facing again and saw Thelma move closer to the little preacher, who had taken off his coat.

"Well, Brother Homer, Early ain't here, so let's forget all that Hereafter stuff and concentrate on the *now* stuff. You remember, I was tellin' you how God looked the other way and let my crippled husband give me two kids in this ol' house. Don't know what's worst, to get bred by a cripple that just got over the mumps, or one that's drunk as a skunk. I've been afraid he might give me another'n, the way he's been strainin' and makin' me do thangs. But I reckon God finally looked my way, 'cause he fixed Early so he can't do his husbandly duty no more."

"Sister Tennel, that's a personal matter. I'm here to counsel you about . . ."

"Don't stop me now, preacher, 'cause I'm on a roll. As I was sayin', every time my man's tried to get in the saddle lately, he can't even get the horse up on its feet, let alone out of the stable. To tell the truth, he ain't been no whole man since he got his legs whacked off. For a while back there I saw a little hope, but his manhood just got weaker and weaker 'til it finally petered out altogether. It's because of that I'm hurtin' so. Not wantin' babies don't keep me from havin' the cravings."

The preacher swallowed and pulled at his collar. "Have you got down on your knees and gone to the Lord with this problem, Sister Tennel?"

"I sure did. But my own nature kept gettin' in the way. I tell you, Brother Homer, my nature's about to bust. I ain't but thirty-nine years old. I'm in my prime. Why, I lay in there every night thinkin' about how I'm bein' cheated out of life's greatest reward." She laid her hand on his leg, squeezing it. "You got to give me some relief. It's God's will."

Brother Homer looked down at her hand. "But our souls would suffer, Sister Tennel," he muttered.

"Preacher, I don't see no reason for me to make a fuss about my soul when it was God that give me my nature. Besides, I'm already in hell, sufferin' the way I am. I want relief now, and after that another kind of help. I want somebody to help me get away from this sorry ol' house, my sick kids and a snuff-dippin', booze-swiggin' husband with a love pole that's as limber as a wet noodle. I want somebody to find me a place to live in town. I want to go dancin', see bright lights for a change, and happy faces."

Heck felt sick. He hadn't thought she was that low. *Besides her not going to work, she won't even be here to help out around the house.*

Across the hall, he heard the preacher tell Thelma, "But dancing is a sin, Sister Tennel."

"It ain't no more of a sin than the life I'm forced to live. I've got to get away from here, I tell you."

"But what about your family?" the preacher said, pulling at his tie. "Heck's already got a heavy burden to bear."

She placed her leg against the preacher's and pushed her breast against his arm in a way that reminded Heck of Willa. *How dare Thelma do such a thing in Daddy's home? Looks like Grandpa Tennel had good reason to dislike her.* His fists automatically closed, opened and closed, opened and closed. *These two need a lesson in morals, best started by me throwing that hypocrite out of the house with a bloody nose.* But he hesitated, considering the evils of jumping a man of the cloth. And worse, two killings added to his problems when Early got wind of this.

"Heck's done all right so far," his stepmother said. "And Marna and Elsie do most of the cookin' and housekeepin'. Plus we'll soon have Willa Sproggs in the family. She told me that herself. Strong as a man, she can help Heck support the family, and she can push Early around in that confounded chair of his'n."

Heck drew back to digest what Thelma said. *So Willa already considers me hooked, does she? Well, strike me down dead as a mackerel if ever I so much as touch her again.*

He glimpsed Brother Homer scooting away from Thelma until he found himself against the arm of the old sofa. Looking like a trapped puppy, he turned to her and whimpered, "I've come to counsel you, Sister Tennel, that's all. I'll start with a prayer. Get down on your knees."

"Whatever you say, preacher. But hurry, 'cause I'm about to bust."

Heck uncurled his fists and exhaled slowly, relieved to hear Homer Percy getting on with what a preacher is supposed to do. As he turned to leave, he heard his stepmother say, "I need to hold on to you while we pray."

Brother Homer's voice was shaking. "Of course, Sister."

Heck peeked to see which part of the preacher Thelma was holding onto and found her squeezing his hand. Amen no sooner escaped his lips than she pulled him back on the sofa, moved up against him and placed her arm around his neck.

"Sister Tennel," he said, pushing her away. "Perhaps I'd better go now."

Thelma quickly placed her leg over his as if she thought he was about to get away. "You pray real nice, preacher. It done me a world of good. But like I said, I got other needs that God saddled me with, and he sent you here to help me. I'm sure in your high callin' you've helped other women like me."

Brother Percy strained ineffectively against her grasp. "Restrain yourself, Sister Tennel."

"Don't fight it, preacher. You said yourself in the pulpit one time that woman was made for man. Well, I ain't got no whole man, and I ain't had for a long, long time. Don't make a liar out o' God, preacher."

"But Brother Tennel will - -"

Thelma said, "Early brothered out a long time ago. You're my man now. I know you want somethin' fresh, 'cause I've been watchin' you cuttin' your eye at them fleshy women in church, even when that skinny wife of yours was by your side. You want 'em, and you want me."

Disgusted, Heck started toward the side window as the sound of a car was heard turning off Vandergriff Road onto the main road. He got to the window in time to see Ubis Sproggs' Ford hoopy pass on the way to town.

*Lordy mercy. Daddy'll find out about the preacher bein' here for sure. Ubis loves spreadin' bad news and seeing people hurt each other. Considering Daddy's dislike for preachers, maybe I should warn him.*

By the time he reached the hall door, it was too late to stop his stepmother and the preacher from beginning what Heck considered a killing offense. She'd already pulled out his tallywhacker which, from the looks of things, was not responding to the preacher's better judgment. Her free hand placed one of Brother Homer's on her bare breast.

"Oh, my God," the preacher moaned.

"My sentiments exactly," Thelma moaned. "There ain't no turnin' back. You're gonna give up the ghost here and now."

She lay back on the sofa and pulled the little preacher down on top of her as Heck whirled and headed for the window. He was crawling outside when Thelma shouted, "I feel the spirit movin' in me, Preacher. Make it move faster. Faster."

Heck was so angry and disgusted he ran all the way to Nathan Meade's place where he jumped into the wagon just as Marna turned into the front lane.

Early and the girls turned to give him a curious look, and Marna said, "What you been up to? You're as red as Frieda Haskel's petticoat."

Out of breath, he couldn't answer her. Not now. Not ever would he be able to tell anybody in the family about what he'd just witnessed.

"You didn't bring nothin' back with you," his dad observed. "I thought you said you forgot somethin'."

Heck didn't dare look at his dad for fear of revealing the truth in his eyes. Finally catching his breath, he asked him, "Did a car pass you?" He hoped Ubis Sproggs had turned off before overtaking them.

"Ubis come by."

Heck avoided eye contact. "Did he, uh, stop and talk?"

"Waved is all. Why""

Heck sighed. "Just wondered." *The bootlegger didn't spot the preacher's car after all. So, for a while, my troubles will continue to be just the usual ones. Somebody, or some power, surely looked out for that backsliding preacher and Thelma. Wish somebody would do the same for more deserving members of my family.*

# Chapter V

Nathan Meade had been a close friend of the Tennels for as long as Heck could remember. He was 89 years old now and, like Grandpa Tennel, had fought in the Civil War as a teenager, only he had fought for The Cause as a member of Quantrill's Raiders of Kansas. He claimed he knew Jessie and Frank James and their cousins, the Dalton brothers. One time in the school library, Heck read about the Jameses and the Daltons, and was surprised to discover that if Jessie James had lived, he'd be the same age as Mr. Meade.

As a boy, Heck heard the whispers of those who believed that Nathan Meade was the famous outlaw, but everybody knew Jessie was murdered by the coward Bob Ford. There was a song about the event entitled, "The Dirty Little Coward That Shot Mr. Howard" which Heck's granddaddy asked him to sing from time to time at their musicals.

The library book also said Jessie's brother Frank survived the war and their outlaw exploits and died in 1922, six years after Heck was born. That meant Mr. Meade couldn't be Frank James, as some suspected. At an early age, Heck learned Mr. Meade held the outlaw brothers in high regard, and ever since Heck could remember, a faded sign bearing one of Frank's quotes hung on the wall in Mr. Meade's cabin. It read,

If there is another war in this country,
it will be between capital and labor.
I mean between greed and manhood.
And I'm ready to march in defense of American manhood
as I was when a boy in the defense of the South.

The words hadn't meant much to young Heck, but he'd thought about them a lot since, mostly when he heard the old folks speak of such things. They talked about the South and the James brothers in soft, reverent voices, the same hushed tones used when discussing deceased relatives.

During frequent childhood visits, Heck learned a lot about manly honor and duty from Mr. Meade. His old friend also taught him how to play the guitar and told him about his pistol, an old Smith & Wesson Scofield, the kind that broke open at the top. The kind Jessie James used, he said.

Mr. Meade was waiting for them on the front porch. In spite of advanced age, his small frame was still erect and his eyesight so good that he used spectacles only for reading. His cabin consisted of one room and a lean-to shed on one side for cooking and canning. He supplemented his home-raised pork and chicken with game killed in the big woods behind his place, and he always had vegetables, canned or fresh, from his garden. He kept a cow for milking too, but she was dry now and the hawks and wolves had carried off or eaten his laying hens, otherwise he wouldn't be buying eggs and butter from Heck. His only cash income was a five-dollar per month confederate pension and what he could get for the furs he trapped on Morales Creek.

As usual, Mr. Meade had his holstered pistol attached to his belt. He strapped it on every day when he got up, wearing it wherever he went. No one had ever tried to make him take it off, not even Sheriff Sloan, a widely feared man. Miss Josephine Vandergriff told Heck that Mr. Meade and his Grandpa Tennel were just useless relics who refused to accept the present but wouldn't die. Heck didn't believe her, but he knew better than to argue the point with the woman whose word was law in Hispaniola County.

Taking one pound of butter and one dozen eggs from the box and one jar of moonshine from the tub, Heck joined Mr. Meade on his little front porch. They exchanged "Howdys," and Mr. Meade's eyes lit up when he saw the jar.

"That got here just in time to prime me for your musical tonight. Much obliged."

"I told the girls it was lemonade," Heck said softly, glancing at the wagon to make sure they hadn't heard him.

Early called out, "Don't tarry, boy. We got lots of deliveries to make today."

"Okay, Daddy." Heck went inside and placed the butter and eggs on a sturdy wooden table in the center of the room. When he turned, he saw Mr. Meade taking a drink of the home brew.

"Man!" His old friend smacked his lips and stamped the floor. "It's got a kick like a Missouri mule, but it's mighty good stuff. I'll take a quart a month. How much I owe you?"

Heck smiled, always happy to please a customer. "One dollar for the lemonade, seventy-five cents for the butter and eggs."

Mr. Meade pulled two dollars out of a worn leather change purse. "Keep the change."

"Thanks," Heck said, placing the bills in his pocket. "See you tonight at the musical."

When Heck started toward the door, the old man said, "You makin' it all right, Heck? I hear work is scarce, gettin' slim to none."

"I'm makin' it fine, Mr. Meade. Thanks for askin'."

"Well, anytime you need a friend, you know where I live. Now, be careful in town with that, uh, lemonade. Keep a sharp lookout for Emmet Sloan and his policemen friends."

"As careful as a loose dollar bill around ol' Blood Money hisself." He smiled and headed for the wagon.

Mr. Meade always came to their Saturday night musical, dressed in grey pants and floppy felt hat of the same color. He could still give the rebel yell when some of the old Southern songs were sung. But they stopped playing "Dixie" for him. The last time they did, he jumped up and started shooting his pistol. The scared women and girls ran from the house screaming.

Heck climbed into the driver's side of the wagon seat and took the reins from Marna. He sensed his dad's eyes on him, but still didn't look at him for fear the truth about what he'd seen at home would show. As they entered the main road, his dad finally broke the silence.

"I still ain't figured out why you was so concerned about whether Ubis Sproggs talked to me or not."

Knowing for sure now that his father suspected him of hiding something, Heck became even more nervous. He kept looking straight ahead, pretending not to hear.

"I guess you know your step mama's got the hots for that scrawny little preacher. All her talk about goin' to church again to seek the Lord's help didn't fool me."

Surprised by his statement in front of the girls, Heck glanced back at Marna and Elsie to see if they'd heard. When their eyes met his, he knew they had.

His dad added, "Them girls know all about man-woman stuff. What do you think they go to town fer?"

The girls giggled, and Heck found himself hoping they didn't turn out to be like their mother.

Early went on, "Thelma don't know that I know about her havin' the hots for that little shrimp. But a man would have to be blind not to see the way she looks him over when he comes by to talk to us about savin' our souls. Ever since you joined the church that time, he's been after us to join up too. He's tried even harder since you quit goin'. Got to keep my eye out for him, make sure he don't come by when I ain't home."

Heck recalled walking up the aisle to shake the preacher's hand at age fourteen. Looking for relief and compassion from a power stronger than those influencing his life to that point seemed the right thing to do at the time. A moving experience, but diminished by his parents not even as much as mentioning the event on the way home. They never offered him support or recognition for anything he did or tried to do. It caused an empty feeling deep inside that he hoped would go away some day.

By the time Ross died, Heck already leaned toward believing he needed something more solid than faith in the hereafter to make life better for himself and his family in the present. Ross's passing convinced him that no compassionate, all-powerful being with the ability to prevent death would have allowed it to happen. Oh, he still believed there was something out there bigger than him and all other human beings, but he hadn't decided just what it was or what it had to do with him. What he couldn't believe was the myth that there was someone sitting around on a throne in the sky who had directed that Ross should die, or that his dad should have his legs cut off, or that his little brother should be born sick, and working folks should have no jobs. No indeed. If a man wants things to be better in his life, he has to stop looking for help from a power that exists only in the minds of desperate poor folks and start doing things that pay real dividends.

Heck made two more deliveries on Panther Holler Road, leaving eggs and butter at one place, a jar of moonshine at the other. After each, his dad promptly asked for the money received.

Approaching the entrance to Milltown, they passed a white cottage on the side of the road where the prostitute Frieda Haskel lived. Her little house looked respectable enough, freshly painted and bordered by flowers and a white picket fence. Once when Heck asked his Uncle Tim how Frieda could practice her profession without being arrested, he was told that she paid the sheriff a monthly fee to leave her alone, and gave the police chief Herman Heyduck a free tumble whenever he wanted one.

Heck saw his dad staring at her house and heard the girls whispering to each other and giggling. His dad pretended not to notice.

Heck turned into the narrow dirt street leading into Milltown, passing two barefoot children playing with an old automobile tire. Located on the northern fringes of Two Rivers, Milltown was where most of the Vandergriff sawmill workers lived. Except for the foreman's house, occupied by his uncle and his grandpa, all the others were built alike — three rooms in a row, "shotgun" style. That allowed one to see all the way through from the street if the back and front doors were open. All had corrugated tin roofs, unpainted exteriors. None had running water or inside toilets.

Butter and eggs were available at the mill's commissary, but cost three times as much as Heck's, and were seldom fresh. Heck undercutting the commissary prices angered Blood Money and Miss Josephine when he started the route, and they had ordered the mill guards to throw them out. But when the guards moved to do it, some of the workers surrounded them, making it clear by their presence that harm would befall those who carried out the owner's orders. The guards did something they'd never done before, or since; they backed down.

By the time Heck made two deliveries on a side street, word had spread about their being in the addition, so at the next turn some of his shine customers waited for him in a huddled group. After glancing up and down the street to make sure there were no guards or policemen in sight, he handed each man a jar, taking a dollar in return. Telling them to spread the news about his new product and that he would be back the following Saturday, he moved on to the back street to deliver more butter and eggs.

Heck saw more children now, who stopped to stare at them and watch silently as they drove by, obviously wanting the fresh goods they were selling but knowing their parents had no money. Their sad faces were devoid of emotion, frozen in forlorn silence.

"What's everybody starin' at us for?" Elsie asked. "We don't look no worse-off than they do."

"They know we have food in the wagon," Heck told her. "I expect some of them are hungry. Their dads probably got laid off."

"They wouldn't be hungry if they grew their own stuff like we do," Marna said.

"They've got no place for a garden," Heck replied. "And Blood Money and Miss Josephine wouldn't allow it if they did. What little they can afford, they have to buy at the commissary. Them that's got jobs are paid in script that's only good at the commissary."

Heck delivered eggs and whiskey to the Alvin Jones family, collected the money and returned to the wagon to find two little girls quietly staring at the cloth-covered apple box. As he drove away, other children joined them, walking alongside and behind the wagon with their sad eyes fixed on box. They said nothing.

"Make 'em go away, Heck," Elsie said. "They give me the creeps, watchin' us like a bunch of scarecrows."

"Just don't speak to 'em," Early said. "You do, and they'll think we're gonna give 'em somethin' for sure."

Heck made deliveries until he had only one dozen eggs left, and the children were still silently following the wagon. He felt sorry for them, but told himself his own family needed the money from the sales more than the children of Milltown needed his last dozen eggs. Try as he might, however, his logic didn't overpower that little voice within telling him he should help them. He pulled the mules to a stop.

"Heh, now," his dad said. "What you stoppin' fer?"

"Because I'm stupid, I guess," Heck looked down at a girl about ten years old who had pressed in close to the front wheel. "What's your name, child?"

"Mary Eileen McDuffy," she said shyly.

Heck nodded toward the other children who had run up behind her. "Where are all your daddies?"

"Mine's somewhere out yonder," Mary Eileen said, pointing west. "He's walkin' to Californy. My mamma said he'll be sendin' for us as soon as he gets there and finds work. My friends' daddies went with him."

"But don't some of your daddies work at the mill?" Heck asked.

Mary Eileen shook her head. "They got laid off. And Mama said our credit ain't no good at the company store no more. Our mothers can't find enough washin' and ironin' no more to pay what we owe, so the sher'f is comin' real soon to move us out."

Heck jumped down, walked to the side of the wagon and uncovered the apple box.

"Stop that," his dad said. "I need the money them eggs'll brang."

An excited murmur ran through the group of children pressing in around Heck. He pulled out the last dozen eggs and told his dad, "Take it out of my share of the money."

"You're as dumb an' starry-eyed as Ross was," his dad said.

Heck told the children to line up, and they quickly complied. He gave each of them one egg until they were gone, and as the lucky ones ran off to announce the good news to their mothers, Heck met the disappointed gaze of two little girls left empty-handed.

"You two meet me here next Saturday," he said. "I'll give you two eggs each for not complainin'. How does that strike you?"

Their expressions brightened and they waved as he climbed up and drove off.

White people lived along the main thoroughfare and the side streets where they'd made deliveries up to that point. Turning down an alley now, Heck headed to the rear of Milltown, and on the way passed several Negro children with adults. His uncle told him how Negro muleskinners were the best he'd ever seen. He said they had a special way with the big mules used to pull the huge logs from the woods to the log wagons and around the mill. Heck knew most of the children and their parents, and while all knew what he was selling, they seldom bought anything.

Swinging the mules around, Heck drove into another side street on his way back to the main thoroughfare which he would follow to Grandpa Tennel's house, and on the way Negro men and women watched him as he passed. Some nodded greetings. Others waved shyly. He returned their greetings with a wave and a smile, but his dad kept his eyes fixed straight ahead, ignoring them.

Arriving at the house where his grandfather and uncle lived, Heck turned the mules into the side yard and drove all the way to the back before stopping. His grandfather's black mare Belle whinnied softly from a nearby pen.

Granddad Ibsen Tennel came out on the back stoop, waving at the girls who jumped out of the wagon. In spite of his 90 years, Ibsen remained alert and active, fully capable of walking downtown and back without a cane.

"Help me down," Early ordered, more impatient than usual to get out of the wagon. Seeing surprise in Heck's eyes, he added, "I decided to stay and visit with Papa while you run into town."

Dad's furtive expression and abrupt change of their Saturday routine set Heck to wondering. *What's the real reason he's not going to town as usual? Don't see how staying here could have anything to do with his intentions to visit Frieda Haskel. Until I brought home $20 this morning, he could only dream of a romp under her sheets. Anyway, stay alert. He's holding all our money.*

"Daddy," Heck said while supporting him as he hopped along on his longest leg toward the back door, "I need my share of the money from the shine. Ubis gives us twenty-five cents on each jar, so my share is one dollar and fifty cents. Just add that to my half of the twenty."

"Can't do that," his dad said gruffly.

Heck stopped. "But I need the money. And don't forget, seventy-five cents on every jar of that shine goes to Ubis. You know how mean he gets when he thinks he's been cheated."

Early gave him a look that suggested he was about to box his ears like he'd done so many times before when Heck challenged him. Sensing himself on shaky ground, Heck remained quiet.

"You ain't gettin' half o' nothing this week, boy," Early said. "Marna said this mornin', the only thing she needs for the kitchen is coffee and a sack o' meal. I'll give you a dollar for that." He pulled two half-dollars from his side pocket. "Now, take me in out of the sun."

Heck didn't move. "All right, I'll forget new shoes for the girls. But what about Billy? You want him to die? At least give me five dollars so I can have Doc Samuels go out and take a look at him." *There. It's said. And I don't give a shit what Dad thinks or what he'll do to me for saying it.*

"Dammit, I told you there ain't nothin' wrong with Billy but the spring punies. I'll get Marna to give him a strong dose of Black-Draught and he'll be fine. I'm still head o' the house, and I'll decide what's best for Billy. I'll also decide how the money's to be spent. Now, quit whinin' like a titty baby in church and take me inside."

Struggling against his rising temper and his dad's weight, Heck took him up the steps and through the house to the sofa in the front room.

"You're runnin' a little late," Grandpa Tennel said. "Everything all right at home?"

"As good as it can be with a crippled rooster and a healthy hen in the same coop," Early said.

Marna and Elsie sat down on the sofa, but Heck continued to stand, eager to get to town and find somebody willing to pay an inflated price for the last jar of shine. Ordinarily, he would have taken the time to go through the house and admire how neat and clean it was. This one, bigger than the others because Uncle Tim was a mill foreman, they kept spotless.

Grandpa Tennel had a high regard for cleanliness, in more ways than one. He only went to the third grade in school, but was a self-educated man, having read many of the classics in addition to the Bible. He also knew his figures better than the math teacher at the one-room school Heck attended.

The familiar front room was sparsely furnished, as were all the others, but it had an organized look about it. The only decorations were a large framed picture of Heck's grandmother and a smaller one of a mounted Robert E. Lee.

Ibsen talked to Early with the patience and kindness of a concerned, loving parent. He'd always been that way in spite of his son's shortcomings, the main one being his taking up with and marrying Thelma Jones so soon after Heck's mother died. Heck found out later, that prior to becoming his stepmother Thelma was known as a loose woman who associated with local white trash such as Cotton Murphy, his dad's closest friend during his younger days.

Early threw Heck an angry look, obviously upset because he hadn't left for town with the dollar. Heck decided to stay put - - the only way he could think of to protect his full share of the money. Convinced his dad had an ulterior motive for not going to town, he feared all the money being spent, even Ubis Sproggs' cut. Heck, troubled enough already surely didn't want to be explaining anything while looking up the barrel of a swindled moon shiner's twelve gauge Winchester.

# Chapter VI

Grandpa lay down to take a nap after Elsie and Marna drank some iced tea and left to visit a girl they knew in Milltown. Early ordered Heck to help him out to the front porch.

Placing his dad in an old car seat, Heck sat down in a hide-bottomed straight chair nearby. Increasingly curious about his dad's motives, he said, "You usually don't want strangers gawkin' at you. Lots of people will be passin' by here goin' or comin' to town."

"Well, I sure as hell can't spit in the house." He opened his snuff box and deposited a pinch of the powdered tobacco inside his lower lip. "Ain't it past time you was getting' into town? We'll need that meal and coffee next week."

"I ain't in no hurry." Heck leaned back against the wall.

As they sat with nothing more to say to each other, Heck noticed how Early kept looking up the dirt street at the entrance to Milltown. *Who's he expecting? As far as I know, Frieda Haskel don't make house calls.*

A couple of minutes later a sputtering, flat-bed Model T Ford hoopy swung off the main road in a cloud of steam and dust. As it came closer, Heck recognized the driver with the long flaxen hair flowing out from under an old cloth cap turned backwards. It was Cotton Murphy, his dad's best friend from his youth and Thelma's old flame, ex-convict and known thief. Through the years, Heck had heard tales about the Cotton/Early duo's record-setting whiskey-drinking and wild-oat-sewing.

Cotton cut the motor, crawled over the door of the topless jalopy and headed for the porch, smiling broadly. Unlike Early, he had all his body parts which still worked according to what Heck heard through the grapevine.

Early shot his son a nervous glance, and said to Cotton, "Didn't know you have a car. Surprises me you can find money for gas even."

Cotton smiled, never self-conscious about the wide gap between his front teeth. "Didn't have no car 'til I won it in a crap game last Saturday night. You bein' cripple and all, I brought her over for that little trip you said you wanted to make. Ready?"

"Trip? What trip?"

"Hellfire, Early," Cotton said, stamping up on the porch. "I knowed you lost your feet, but I didn't think you'd lost your memory too. The trip over to Frieda's, o' course. The mail carrier give me your message."

Heck remained silent, curious as to whether his dad was still willing to blow their whole wad on the whore after Cotton let the cat out of the bag.

"Well, uh," his dad stammered, "not right this minute, I reckon."

"Get real, Early. Heck's a grown man, in case you haven't noticed. We'll take him with us. Frieda'll fix him up too."

Unbeknownst to Cotton, Heck had already decided there was nothing in this world that could prevent him from going with them. And as soon as Frieda made his dad take off his dirty overalls, he would grab his share of the money and head for town.

"Well," Early said, his face flushed with anticipation of his renewal. "I did tell Heck what I had in mind doin' sometime to get me started again."

"Then come on," Cotton beckoned. "If you keep settin' there like a fat toad on a log, you'll soon be so old Frieda can't do you no good no matter how hard she tries to get you fired up."

"Don't tell Papa where I went," Early told Heck. "We'll be right back."

"No danger in me tellin' Grandpa." Heck dropped the front legs of the chair down hard. "I'm goin' with you."

"You'll have to wait outside if you do. This ain't gonna work for me with you in the house."

"I'll stay out of sight. Just make sure you don't pay Frieda more than her usual fee." Heck moved over to help his dad out to the car.

Early looked at the Ford, then at Cotton. "Will that hoopy get us to Frieda's and back without fallin' apart?"

"She won't go nowheres without no gas," Cotton said. "Got any gas money?"

"You've already got gas, smart aleck. Otherwise you couldn't've drove over here."

"She's about out though. Didn't put but a quarter's worth in her yesterday."

"Dad-gum it, Cotton." Early took hold of Heck's neck so he could be pulled up. "I thought you was a friend of mine."

"I am, for a fact. Didn't I tell you just last month about all them thangs Frieda said she'd do to get you started agin? But friendship won't burn worth a hay fart in a T-Model Ford."

*Cotton will always be a moocher,* Heck thought as his dad reached into his pocket for some money.

"How much you need?"

"A gallon'll push her over there and back, I reckon. Fifteen cents. It'll be twenty-five cents more if'n I have a flat."

Cotton took the three nickels and said, "The real question is, are you primed and ready?"

"Well, now that you mention it, I sure could use a shot of Irish whiskey, if you've got any."

"You ain't gettin' cold feet are you, Early?" He laughed, slapping his leg as he glanced at his friend's stubs. A sober expression swept over his face and he added, "Dammit, I'm sorry. Just a figure of speech, as a good politician would say."

"Yeah, sure," Early replied, obviously not impressed by the humor or the apology.

"Hell, Early, no need to be scared." Cotton's face brightened. "You've made it with Frieda before."

"That was a long time ago," he said, struggling to keep up with Heck on his longest leg. "It was before . . ." He looked down at his stubs.

Heck found himself feeling sorry for his dad, and hoping he was able to do everything with Frieda that would make him feel like a whole man again. But not with his share of the money.

"Frieda ain't never seen me in this condition. She might not do her best work with a cripple."

"Frieda ain't interested in them missin' parts, Early. What you gotta do is concentrate on your best qualities. Frieda told me not long ago, that you was the best qualified man she ever remembered doin' business with."

"She said that?" Heck saw his dad's face light up.

"If I'm lyin', I'm dyin'."

Heck pushed his dad up into the ragged front seat as Cotton climbed behind the wheel and called out, "Turn her over, boy."

Heck turned the crank six times before it started, then had to scramble out of the way to keep from being run over. He jumped up on the back of the flatbed contraption as it passed by.

They bounced off the main road into a graveled driveway leading to Frieda's backyard and stopped behind a rose-covered trellis that blocked their view of the road. The parking area was especially designed to provide privacy to Frieda's customers. She apparently didn't want any of them worrying about their vehicles being spotted by wives or friends.

When no one made a move to get out, Heck wondered if his dad still wanted to go through with his plan. He watched him turn a cautious eye toward the screened back porch and the open hall door beyond.

"She must be tied up with another customer," Early said. "Otherwise, she woulda come to the back door."

"The door'd be closed if she was busy, scaredy cat," Cotton said, climbing down. "You're worse'n a boy fixin' to lose his cherry, for cryin' out loud. Give him a hand, Heck."

Heck helped his dad to the ground, then over to the screen door that Cotton had already had rapped with his bare knuckles.

A plump woman with long black hair and skin that looked as soft as a baby's bare rump appeared in the hall door. Upon seeing who her callers were, she smiled and moved out on the porch. "Come on in, boys," she said. Her big smile showed even white teeth that didn't impress Heck nearly as much as her large breasts, half of which were in full view above her silk kimono. They weren't freckled like Willa's.

When they entered the screened-in area, Frieda turned all her charms on Early. Gently patting his shoulder, she said, "Hi, big boy. How come you stayed away so long?"

Early blushed as he threw a glance at her pretty face.

"Have fun, lover boy." Cotton slapped him on the back. "I'll pick you up in about an hour. Don't be too tough on Frieda." He laughed.

Ignoring his friend's remark, Early returned Frieda's greeting and smiled nervously. His face and eyes lit up in a way Heck hadn't seen since the accident.

Upon passing through the carpeted hall into the richly furnished living room, Heck realized how out of place his dad was in his soiled, frayed overalls and his needing a bath and a shave. He too felt out of place and made himself look even worse by his sudden clumsiness when Frieda brushed against him to give a close-up view of her bosom and a strong whiff of her perfume. He almost lost his grip on his dad's arm as they moved toward the sofa.

Heck guessed Frieda was in her late thirties, but age hadn't affected her the way it had the wives of the farmers he knew. Her breasts and hips still looked round and soft, but not too heavy, and inside work had kept her skin so clear and supple he wanted to touch it. He also marveled at her small waist, and the smooth, flowing way she carried herself. If a man didn't know better, he'd swear she was a lady of the highest order.

Making himself concentrate on the business at hand, Heck eased his dad down on the clean, soft sofa and stepped back.

"You shoulda gone with Cotton, boy," his dad said. "Take a long walk somewhere. I won't be needin' you 'til he comes back to pick us up."

"My, Early," Frieda said, looking at Heck. "You've got a mighty fine-lookin' son. Tall as a virgin pine and wide as a Studebaker across the shoulders." She winked and reached out to pinch Heck's cheek. "Honey, you can come back to see me any time you're ready and willin'."

A sudden stirring in the groin caused Heck to momentarily forget his dad's presence. Recovering from the Frieda's spell, he said, "See y'all later."

Heck went down the hall, crossed the back porch and opened the screen door, but didn't step outside. Releasing the door to allow it to slam loud enough to be heard up front, he turned and tip-toed to the rear wall of the porch, stopping near the hall entrance. *I'll wait right here until it's safe to go back and get my money.*

At first, all he heard was the rustle of Frieda's kimono as she moved about in the living room. Then came the sound of her patting part of his dad's body.

"How have you been makin' out, Early?"

"My life's a pisser, honey. Can't work. Can't dance. Can't hunt or fish. But I'd put up with that if I could be a man in bed. I ain't been able to do it for a long time now."

Heck heard Frieda pat his body again and kiss him. "Well, honey, I'm gonna fix the part that needs fixin' the most. And after a good time today, you'll be your old self again."

"You really think you can fix me up?" he said with childish exuberance, more like a plea than a question.

"Sure, honey. But first you've got to relax. How about a shot of good Irish whiskey for openers? It's the brand you always drank."

"I'd sure like that, Frieda. Damn, you look good. I've missed touchin' some as soft and purty as yours. Can I touch 'em?"

"You sure can, big fella. Ouch! Don't squeeze so hard." Her silk kimono made a swishing sound again, and she said, "I'll find us some good music on the radio."

A Jimmy Rodgers song, "Waiting for a Train" came drifting down the hall, and it so absorbed Heck that he didn't hear Frieda's footsteps until she got to the kitchen door. He jumped back when she called out to his dad, "You and Heck still having your musicals?"

"Yeah. It's the only time we're halfway happy out at our place these days. Heck's got a callin' for music, you know. I've always wished you'd show up."

"A girl in my business doesn't go to public gatherings, unless she wants her eyes clawed out. Women have a very low tolerance for competition."

Frieda returned to the living room and Heck began worrying about his share of the money and getting to Doc Samuel's office before it closed. He heard his dad give out with a loud grunt, after which Frieda laughed, suggesting that she had touched him in a sensitive spot.

"That's good whiskey. Lots better than the rotgut Heck's selling for Ubis Sproggs."

Heck grimaced, wishing he hadn't mentioned the new line, considering Frieda's relationship with the chief of police and the sheriff.

"Mercy, that feels good," Early moaned. "But you used to always want to see the color of my money before getting' down to business. How much do you charge for your special these days?"

Heck held his breath, visualizing her taking all the money and putting it somewhere he couldn't find it.

"For old time's sake, I'm just charging you my regular fee, five dollars. If my treatment works, and you want another before you leave, it'll be ten."

Heck rolled his eyes. *Wish they'd get on with it. Please, Frieda, pull off Dad's overalls before y'all go into the bedroom.*

Frieda must have started rubbing his dad's longest leg and what lay between it and his shortest one, because Heck heard him moaning.

"How about a nice, warm bath in my high tub?" she asked.

"Do I smell that bad?"

Heck nodded, smothering a laugh.

"I'll draw you a full tub of water and put you in it. Then I'll rub you down real good. After that, I'll do something that'll shake loose the clapper in any bell, no matter how rusty it is. First, let's take off all your clothes."

Heck smiled. *Frieda, you boilin' sex pot, you're a jewel among women. But how strong are you?*

His question was answered by the thump of his dad's longest leg on the floor as they headed down the hall.

Giving her crippled customer words of encouragement on the way, Frieda got his dad into the bathroom near the end of the hall. Early grunted, Frieda giggled and Heck heard the sound of running water.

"Let it run until it's nearly full," she said. "I'll get some towels and my special soap."

Heck moved cautiously across the rear entrance to the bathroom window, but found his view blocked by a drawn shade. That meant he wouldn't be able to tell when Frieda closed the bathroom door. He couldn't be seen going back up the hall. Not hearing Frieda in the hall, he returned to opposite side of the door.

Frieda returned moments later to turn off the water and Heck heard grunts of ecstasy from his dad as Frieda began stirring about in the water. She said, "I'll suds you up real good down there. How does that feel?"

"Lordy mighty," Early exclaimed. "If it felt any better, I'd keel over graveyard dead."

The sound of splashing water and Early's blissful moans continued as Heck tried to decide how long he should wait before going up the hall for his money. He hadn't heard the bathroom door close yet.

Frieda must have removed all her clothes too, judging by what his dad was saying. "You're still as fine lookin' as you was back when I come by the last time, Frieda. You wuzn't much more'n a little girl. Since then, you've growed some more in all the right places. My God, them's purty."

"Then take one." She cooed. "I'll lean down closer. Oh, Early, honey," she moaned. More splashing, followed by, "It's my turn now, honey. Raise up your hips so I can put this stool under you."

Heck had never heard his dad groan so. If he didn't know better, he'd believe he was dying. Figuring now or never, he moved into the hall and peeked around the bathroom door facing to make sure neither was looking his way.

He recoiled quickly, shocked and ashamed after looking squarely at Frieda's bare bottom as she stood over his dad in the tub of soapy water. Bracing himself for another look, he inched his head forward until he could see inside real good, then jumped back again, shaken and embarrassed.

His dad was lying back against the end of the tub, eyes closed and holding onto Frieda's breasts with both hands. Heck couldn't see what Frieda was doing to his middle parts, but whatever it was, it made him feel so good his entire body started trembling.

Taking a deep breath, he peeked again and, when Frieda lowered her head some more, darted past the door and tiptoed down to the living room. With his pulse pounding like a drum, he picked up his dad's overalls and began going through the pockets.

"Oh, Lordy, Frieda, honey!" Early cried. "Pull the plug quick. It's time."

With shaking hands, Heck counted out his share of the whiskey and produce sales: $7.15. He left the twenty-dollar bill because there wasn't enough change to half it, and as he turned to flee, he heard Frieda's surprised cry, "Oh, my! How did you get out of that tub so quick? Now, don't be so rough, honey. This floor's hard on a lady's back."

Heck wondered how his dad had managed to get out of the tub at all, but didn't tarry to dwell on the puzzle. Moving through the front door and across the porch, he headed for grandpa's place in a fast walk.

*I hope Daddy'll be so pleased with his renewed nature that he can control his temper when he finds some of the money missing.*

# Chapter VII

A city block from where Panther Holler Road intersected West Main, those who came to town in wagons turned off the main road to cross Iglesias Creek on their way to the hitch lot. The fording allowed a driver to stop and soak his wheels. That caused the wood in them to swell and press tightly against steel rims. While doing that, his animals could drink their fill from cool water.

The unpaved hitch lot was the place where farmers left their mules and wagons when they came to town to shop and visit or sell their produce and poultry to city residents. Sometimes, items were merely bartered for things the farmers needed but couldn't buy.

Following the ruts leading into the creek, Heck became edgy about transporting that last jar of moonshine in a dry town. So far, he hadn't seen a police car as he searched the area beyond the far bank. He did see several wagons on the hitch lot. Teams of mules, unhitched and haltered to the rear wheels, munched on hay put down for them. He also saw a group of men wearing overalls, floppy felt hats or drooping, cloth caps, standing quietly where the lot cornered on Main. Men collected there early every Saturday morning, remaining there all day to watch each passing car in hopes of being picked up as a day laborer. Heck didn't approach them about buying the shine, because he knew they had no money.

After soaking his wheels for about five minutes, he pulled up on the opposite bank into the hitching lot and began offering the whiskey for five dollars to those he trusted. No takers.

He found a vacant spot and unhitched the mules, tethering them to the back wheels. Tightly wrapping the jar in a paper sack, he headed toward the main business district.

He walked less than a block before spotting Marna and Elsie. They had come downtown to do what their dad had predicted, look at boys. They would probably go home disappointed again, as no city boy with a car and nice clothes flirted with girls dressed in worn-out tennis shoes and flour sack dresses except for all the wrong reasons. Heck knew that reality had never disturbed Marna. He once heard her say, "If I ever meet a good looking city boy with a job and a car, I'll do anything to get him to marry me. I'll do it to get out of living in this old cropper house, dressing like a hobo and eating turnip greens, dry peas and gravy all the time."

Heck slowed down, allowing his sisters to get far enough ahead not to interfere with a sale in case he ran into the sort of guy who had a hankering to take a nip now and then and five dollars to spare. Seeing no one that looked promising, he stopped in front of the Liberty Theater to wait for a prospect. The marquee announced the Saturday western movie inside starring Buck Jones, his favorite. Oh, for the luxury of taking his mind off eking out a living, if only for a short while. But he had neither the money nor the time.

Spotting no potential buyers, he pushed his long hair up under his hat as best he could and headed for Doc Samuels's office, not bothering to make eye contact with the well-dressed people he met on the way. *To hell with their haughty looks and superior attitudes.* But appearance didn't bother him as much as not being able to stop and strike up a conversation with a pretty girl he saw.

Two blocks later he went up a stairwell near the bank, mounting the squeaking wood steps two at a time on his way to the doctor's office at the end of the hall. The other offices on the floor, occupied by insurance agents, lawyers and a dentist, were already closed for the weekend.

He smelled the medicines in Doc Samuels's office, a sickening odor reminiscent of the time his Uncle Tim brought him there to have his tonsils cut out. A horrible experience. Returned home, he almost bled to death.

Coming to Doc Samuels's office, Heck passed through a screened door and allowed it to slam shut behind him. The noise brought a nurse out of the back room in her white, starched uniform.

"Howdy, Miz Finley. Is Doc Samuels in?"

"And what kind of problem are you having today, Heck?" she asked curtly. The woman seldom smiled. "Those tonsils didn't grow back, did they?"

"No ma'am." Surprised that she remembered him, he relaxed a little. "I come to ask Doc Samuels to go see my little brother Billy."

"Is he too sick to be brought in?"

"No, ma'am. Daddy wouldn't let me."

She went into the back room, reappearing shortly. "He's waiting for you in the examining room. Good luck," she said with a mischievous gleam in her eyes.

Heck found Dr. Samuels sitting in front of his old roll top desk writing on a pad of paper. He made no effort to turn or speak.

The doctor, almost 70 years old, still had a full head of thick, black seldom-combed hair. He was dressed in a white shirt and black suit as usual, and had a black, smelly pipe in his mouth. He finally dropped his pen, swung his chair around and fixed dark fierce eyes on Heck. "Why, you're Tim Tennel's nephew." He said gruffly, leaning forward. "Whatsamatter? Did them tonsils grow back?"

In spite of his fear of the man, Heck made himself look into his eyes. "I want you to go see my little brother Billy today. He's real sick."

"Then why didn't you bring him in?" Doc Samuels raised his eyebrows.

"Because my dad's with me. He don't believe in doctors."

"I see," he said, rubbing his chin. "Well, we are a pretty unsavory lot. But even the worst of us have to be careful about going out to houses where the head man doesn't believe in doctors."

"Like I said, Daddy's not home now. He's, uh, tied up. That's why you have to go out right now."

The nurse appeared in the doorway, caught the doctor's eye and beckoned him to join her in the outer office. They moved out of his view and talked in hushed tones for a moment before the doctor returned to his chair.

"Heck, did you ever find a way to get your daddy those artificial legs you talked to my nurse about a few years back?"

"No, sir. I'd have to hold up ol' Blood Money Vandergriff's bank for that. A thousand dollars is just a little more than I can afford right now."

"I see. Well, about your brother Billy. What seems to be wrong with him?"

"He don't feel good, and he don't, doesn't look good either. He's pale as a sheet, and weak. Thelma – that's my stepmother – said it's because Daddy's seed was bad at the time."

Heck thought he saw a sudden sparkle in the doctor's eye, but it quickly disappeared and he finished his plea with, "What's the goin' rate for a house call?"

"The goin' rate? At last accounts, it was five dollars. That includes the goin' and the doctorin'. Payable in advance when I go into hostile territory. Do you have that much?"

"Yes, sir." Heck pulled the money out of his pocket. "There's five for you, and two dollars fifteen cents for Perkin's Pharmacy for Billy's medicine."

Obviously impressed, Dr. Samuels gave Heck a serious look as he watched him count out the money on his desk. "I'll take a look at Billy, boy. But from the symptoms you've described, I think I may have to bring him to the hospital for some tests."

"I ain't, don't have that kind of money. You've got to get Billy well now, without doin' all that. I don't want him to die like Ross did."

"Ross, yes. Too bad your daddy wouldn't bring him to see me before his appendix burst. Well, regarding Billy. If he does have to come in later, hospital tests cost lots of money. At least a hundred dollars, I suspect. They require payment up front too."

"Oh, no. For me to put together that much money legal, I'd have to beg a loan from Blood Money Vandergriff hisself. That'd be harder than pullin' a hickory stump out of a red clay hill." He shook his head. "But I'd be willin' do anything it takes to get Billy well." He turned to leave, but stopped. "Please tell Mama what's wrong with Billy, so I'll know as soon as I get home."

The doctor gave Heck a mock salute. "Will do."

Heck went back down the stairs and approached the bank, stopping at the glass front door to peer inside. He dreaded facing the richest, unfriendliest man in town, but since a sense of desperation about Billy had pushed him this far, he couldn't stop now.

Several sad-faced farmers standing near the door caused him to wonder if they had just been given some bad news by Blood Money. As he hesitated, he heard them mention something about tight money and what a mess the country was in. One of them said, "Franklin D. Roosevelt is our only hope."

Looking through the door again, Heck recalled that he had only been in the place twice in his life, both times with Uncle Tim. He had been allowed to accompany his uncle into Blood Money's glassed-in office on one of those occasions, but his presence went unacknowledged. The experience had, however, proved something he'd heard but never witnessed: Blood Money was the only Texan who could break wind and belch at the same time. In most cases, a loan applicant could predict the outcome of his plea by which way the gas went. If the banker planned to merely turn down a man's loan request, he would belch. If he planned to give the poor man a lecture on how his kind would never see the color of his money and how he should never again be so bold as to ask for any of it, he'd rip a good one through the seat of his pants against the shiny seat of his leather chair. It was said that not even a big logging mule in a hard pull could match such powerful expulsions.

Heck had also learned from Grandpa Tennel that Blood Money was also crude in other ways. A person with limited schooling, he grew up under the influence of a cruel, greedy father, the richest man in the county, and one of the meanest to his family, the servants and everybody who did business with him. An only son, Blood Money inherited his father's vast land holdings, a gift resulting from his support of Texas's revolt against Mexico. The rest of it was bought for fifty cents an acre, or stolen from Mexican landholders and illiterate American settlers who had not filed a proper claim.

Squaring his shoulders, Heck pushed his way through the glass door and headed for Blood Money's secretary just outside his office. The banker was in his glass cell, leaned back in his high soft chair, patting his big belly as he talked to a man also dressed in a suit and tie. Heck felt terribly out of place.

He noted the secretary's pretty face, wavy brown hair and flat chest. She gave him a questioning look as he stopped in front of her, pulled off his hat and read her nameplate. "Hello, Miz Tucker. I've got to see Blood − I mean, your boss."

"Is he expecting you, young man?" Her eyes wandered from his head to his crotch.

"No, ma'am. But, then, I wasn't expectin' to be out a hundred dollars on hospital bills neither."

Her smile disappeared and she turned to glance through the glass behind her. "He's with someone right now, and we'll be closing in five minutes. Could you come back Monday?"

"I could, but I've got to see him now."

"Well, have a seat," she said to his crotch. "I'll see if he'll talk to you when he's through."

Heck sat down looking in awe at the castle-like proportions of the bank's interior. Everything in sight spoke of Blood Money's wealth.

All customers were gone and the front door locked before the secretary finally summoned him. Getting up, he headed for her boss's office, feeling more like a beggar than a borrower. Upon entering with hat in hand, he summoned enough nerve to speak first, being careful not to sound too much like an undeserving clodhopper. "Good afternoon, Mr. Vandergriff. I'm much obliged to you for seein' me."

"What do you want, boy?" Blood Money demanded, adjusting his steel rimmed spectacles to give him a look of annoyance. "Can't you see we're closed?"

Heck shifted his weight and cleared his throat. "My little brother's real sick."

"Why should that concern me? This ain't no hospital, and I ain't no doctor."

"I know that, Mr. Vandergriff," he said, swallowing hard as he fought to hide his fear of the man. "I've got to have one hundred dollars."

"Then get a job and earn it, boy. Don't bother me."

Knees shaking, Heck knew he had no choice but to finish what he'd started. "There ain't no jobs. And Doc Samuels just told me he'll most likely have to put Billy in the hospital, and it'll cost at least one hundred dollars." He paused, wondering if Blood Money was about to have a gas attack, and if so, which way it would move.

The banker looked at the sack in Heck's hand. "What's that?"

"Uh, lemonade," Heck said, glancing behind him.

For the first time, Blood Money took a close look at him. "Ain't you Crip Tennel's boy?"

Heck nodded, acknowledging another strike against him. "But I ain't – I'm not borrowin' it for him. Like I said, it's for Billy. And I don't want but one hundred dollars. I'll pay you back, honest."

"How?" the banker snapped, giving Heck another contemptuous look. "You just told me there ain't no jobs. You Tennels ain't got a pot to piss in. Never have, never will. None of you, that is, except your Uncle Tim, and he's barely able to pay his commissary bill every month."

Heck remembered Willa telling him the same thing that morning in so many words. He resented it as much now as he did then.

"And I know without askin', you ain't twenty-one yet. That's the legal age, you know. And you ain't got no collateral. You're wasting my time."

"But I've got plans for the future. You'll get your money back, I promise. With interest."

Blood Money's lips twisted into a crooked grin. "What you gonna do, rob a bank?"

"No, sir. But I appreciate the suggestion."

"Such impertinence. Get out of my bank!" He suddenly belched, loud enough to cause his secretary to glance his way. "I've got no money for Early Tennel or any of his kids." He punctuated his remark by breaking wind so loud Heck believed he might have ripped his pants.

Seeing his mission hopeless, Heck turned to leave the office straining hard to break one in the banker's direction. But his best efforts failed him, and he walked into the lobby angry and embarrassed. He was so upset he didn't even acknowledge the secretary's sweet "Good-bye" as he shuffled to the door to be let out.

Being talked to like a dog was something he could tolerate, seeing as how it had happened many times before at home, but Blood Money's treating his request for a loan like he thought Billy wasn't important made him mad enough to hit somebody.

*Damn! Blood Money got me so bumfuzzled. I clean forgot to ask him to postpone his orders about us paying rent. But there's no going back. Considering all that's gone wrong today, I'll be lucky if the front wall of the bank don't fall on me.*

# Chapter VIII

Heck was so angry he forgot to watch for his sisters on the way back to the hitch lot. He did see Slick Haskel wooing a pretty brunette in front of Yancey's grocery store next to the hitch lot. He could tell Slick's target for the day was a city girl, with skin clear and smooth, wearing a store-bought dress. Heck and Slick were the same age, but Slick was thinner and five inches shorter. Most girls liked his black hair and dark brown eyes. And apparently other things too, judging from the way their defenses melted in the face of his bold manner.

Heck never ceased to be amazed at how much Slick changed on weekends. In the country he always wore dirty rags and seldom bathed. But before coming to town on Saturday, he took a bath and put on a clean shirt and store-bought britches and slicked his hair down with rose water.

Slick told him several years ago that he'd been making out with girls since age ten, and started smoking Bull Durham cigarettes at eight. Slick was Frieda Haskel's only offspring, sired by one of her customers before she had an operation to prevent accidents, Ubis Sproggs took custody of him right after his birth, convincing most people that he was his father, but everybody was too afraid of the bootlegger to find out for sure.

"Hi, Heck," Slick said, placing his arm around the girl's waist. "This here's Beulah Mae. Beulah Mae, Heck Tennel."

Heck nodded. "Pleased to meet you, Beulah Mae."

Her eyes clung to his, but Heck was still so upset he hardly noticed.

Slick gave the girl a squeeze. "You'll have to watch Heck. Girls who know say he's the hottest lover in the whole county, and the best-hung. Besides me, of course."

Beulah Mae's brown eyes moved down Heck's body, then up again. "That's the kind of information a girl needs to know."

"I've been lookin' for you," Slick told Heck. "Thought you might want to take a ride out on Firetower Road with us. Beulah Mae's friend is dyin' to meet you, and she's as purty as a flower ripe for pluckin'. She's got long legs that could crack a man's ribs in a clinch. Ubis loaned me his hoopy, and I got a quilt to put over the bed."

Heck allowed his eyes to meet Beulah Mae's and wondered how many times she'd been out on Firetower Road with other boys. From her actions, he guessed it was one of her favorite hangouts.

Looking beyond Beulah Mae, Heck's eyes fell on a newspaper in a wire stand outside Yancey's store. Moving over to get a closer look, he read the bold headline, BONNIE AND CLYDE IN AREA. Bending down, he read the fine print.

> Bonnie Parker and Clyde Barrow, notorious bank robbers
> and killers who recently murdered two highway
> patrolmen and raided a state prison farm to break
> out fellow outlaw Raymond Hamilton, have reportedly
> come to Hispaniola County to visit relatives and lie
> low for a while.

The write-up ended with another poem sent to the paper by Bonnie. Slick and Beulah Mae read the article over his shoulder.

Slick said, "Looks like Bonnie and Clyde gave them law dogs the slip agin. But that ain't no reason for the likes of us to be scared of them. They don't bother poor folks. Just cops and bankers." He laughed.

"Yeah," Heck said. "I'll bet ol' Blood Money'll let out a real ripper when he reads that." He continued looking at the headline as he remembered the new Ford that ran him off the bridge. According to what he'd heard, it was the kind of car Clyde Barrow preferred. He also remembered Jake calling his friend "Clyde." The possibilities suggested by those facts caused him to become very nervous all of a sudden.

"What's the matter?" Slick asked. "You look like you just swallowed a turd in your milk."

"Never mind. I'll see you two at the musical tonight. Beulah Mae, bring your friend if she likes country music."

"Yeah, and let Willa kill her," Slick said, laughing.

Heck headed back uptown to look for his sisters and try again to unload the shine. In less than two blocks he came upon Marna and Elsie on Main Street talking to two dressed-up boys in a Buick convertible parked against the curb. Marna stood holding the hand of the driver, who appeared to be several years her senior. He must have just said something funny because all of them laughed.

Heck approached as the driver opened the door and slid his hand up his sister's leg. "Let's go, girls," he snapped.

"Just who the hell do you think you are, clodhopper?" the driver demanded.

"I'm their brother, lover boy." Heck felt the color rising in his face. "I don't let my sisters talk to anybody who treats 'em like trash."

The driver got out. He was tall and muscular. "Look at him, Eddy," he told his friend. "Wide shoulders, small brain, big mouth. Look at his horse nose, and those baggy ol' overalls. Ain't he a handsome dude?" He pointed to Heck's brogans. "Did you clean the cow shit from between your toes before putting on those boxcars, brave brother?"

The other boy laughed, but Heck ignored them both to take hold of Marna's arm and pull her away.

"You're embarrassing me, Heck." She jerked free, red-faced. "He didn't mean me no harm. The first cute boy I've met in this crummy town that's got a car, and you have to come along and mess things up."

"Yeah, handsome," the driver said. "Get lost, like your pretty sister wants you to. Me and Eddy were about to take 'em for a ride out on Firetower Road. Marna told me she wants to have a good time for a change."

Heck reached for Marna's arm again, but she stepped back. "I'm a grown woman, Heck Tennel," she said, loud enough to cause passersby to stop and watch. "How do you expect me to ever get a man if I don't go out with any?"

"You're only sixteen," Heck replied. "You have plenty of time for that. Elsie's only thirteen, for God's sake. Don't you know what them boys are gonna do if y'all go with 'em?"

"Anything would beat what'll happen to me out at that ol' shack today, tomorrow, or next year. I'm goin' with 'em, Heck."

"Oh, no, you're not. You're comin' with me. Both of you." He glanced cautiously at the growing number of spectators and began pulling his sister toward the sidewalk.

POW! A painful kick in the butt jarred him, and that was followed by a round of laughter from the spectators. Whirling, Heck glared at the grinning driver, now joined by his friend. His friend was tall and strongly built too.

"I say she goes with me, clodhopper," the driver said. "By the way she talks, sounds like she's been out there before. So why should that bother you, big brother? Saving her for yourself?"

Hearing more laughter behind him, Heck wondered: *Do city folks have any brains for thinking? I can't take them both on, but I'd sure punch the driver in the mouth if it wouldn't land me in jail, the cooling off place for poor boys who hit rich city boys.*

"I'm givin' you one more chance to get in your shiny car and leave my sister alone," he warned.

"Or else you'll do what, clodhopper?" The driver motioned to his friend who moved behind Heck. "I was minding my own business, talking to a grown woman there, or so she says. It's you that should be moving along."

"Do as he says, Heck." Elsie urged. "I don't want you to get in trouble. Make him come with us, Marna."

Marna moved close and said in a lowered voice, "Don't you know who he is? Come on. I'll go with you today. But next time, I'll do my courtin' when you ain't around."

Her warning calmed him enough to remember he had one more sale to make. It also caused him to remember that Doc Samuels had gone out to examine Billy. He turned to leave and POW, another kick in the butt, harder this time.

Whirling, Heck aimed a punch at the driver's face but missed when the second boy tackled him from behind. Losing his balance, he allowed the jar to slip from under his arm and smash to bits on the brick street, splattering glass and moonshine whiskey in a wide circle around him.

It sounded like the whole town was laughing at him now as he struggled to regain his balance and take another swing.

"Smell that, folks?" a voice from the crowd yelled, "That farm boy's a bootlegger. Somebody call the police."

The driver jumped out of Heck's reach and jumped into the Buick as somebody else called out, "Hey, Chief Heyduck, we got us a bootlegger here tryin' to start a fight. You'd better come quick."

"Damnation." Heck moaned, glancing down the sidewalk. "Marna, hitch up the mules and drive Elsie back to Grandpa's right now. When Daddy gets there, tell him I might be a little late gettin' to the musical tonight."

Heck took off as a policeman's whistle blew, racing down a side street past Pool's drug store, then down Kindle Street that ran toward the creek. Crossing the next street running north to south, he saw a police car as he darted down the alley between Bailey's clothing store and the newspaper office toward Lipan Street. The police car skidded to a stop behind him.

When he got on Lipan, he heard another car approaching him from behind. Figuring it was the High Sheriff himself, he ran faster. *I cain't let them put me in jail.*

The car moved up alongside him and a man said, "Jump in!" It was a familiar voice.

Glancing over, he saw Jake in the new Ford. He jerked the door open, jumped into the back seat and reached back to close the door as Jake made a U-turn and gunned it.

"Am I glad to see a friendly face," Heck said, pulling himself upright.

Jake quietly struggled to keep the car under control around the next corner. He headed east out of the business district and got on the main highway going toward Louisiana.

"What did you fall into this time, Mr. Saturday Night Musical?" Jake asked. "It smells stronger than river water."

"That was my last jar of shine." He crawled into the front seat. "Where we headed?"

"Hell maybe. Where do you want to go?"

"Anywhere except jail, which will happen if that cop back there catches us."

"No lawman can catch this Ford, Mr. Saturday Night Musical." Jake pressed the accelerator. "Where to?"

"Well, Marna — that's my sister — she can drive Daddy and Elsie home. So, after you lose that police car, I guess we can circle around and get back on the road that runs by our place north of town where I jumped off the bridge."

"Just stay away from home for a while. The city boys can't go out in the country looking for you, but they might get the sheriff to do it."

"But I've got a musical tonight."

"Don't you have a friend you can stay with for a few hours 'til things cool off? Cops are lazy. They won't make two trips to your place in one day."

Heck thought a moment. "Then I'll go to Nathan Meade's house. They won't bother me there."

Heck gave Jake directions and settled back in the seat to think about how quick a man sometimes has to change his best plans because of what somebody else does, and how serious his troubles would be if the sheriff ever found out he'd gone for a ride in Clyde Barrow's car. But he would ride in the devil's chariot itself to stay out of jail. Being behind bars would spoil all his plans. Billy would die and the rest of the family would starve to death.

# Chapter IX

Jake dropped Heck off at the end of the lane leading to Nathan Meade's cabin, turned around and sped away. Heck still didn't know for sure if his new friend was really Bonnie and Clyde's regular driver, but did know he'd be in jail now if he hadn't come by when he did.

Heck was relieved when he saw Mr. Meade's gray mare in the pen behind his little barn. Not wanting to risk getting shot, he stopped in the edge of the clearing to announce his presence.

"Mr. Meade," he shouted. "It's me, Heck Tennel. I'm comin' in."

The front door opened. "Anythang wrong?" Mr. Meade asked, looking up the lane behind him. "Where's your wagon?"

"Had to leave it when the police got after me."

"Police?" His eyes lit up. "What did you do, rob the bank?"

"Only in my dreams." Heck went inside and sat down in a hide-bottomed chair near the front window to tell his friend what happened in town. "I was wonderin' if it would be okay for me to stay here the rest of the day. Maybe the chief'll be tired of lookin' for me by then."

"Sure. Stay for a week if you want to. Heyduck can't do nothin' to you out o' town and Emmet Sloan knows better than to come in here."

The old man offered him a chew of Cotton Boll Twist, and when Heck declined, he bit off one himself and sat down near the open back door so he could spit. "I reckon that little run-in put you out of the whiskey-sellin' business."

"We sure did need the extra money." He told him about asking for a loan.

"You've got spunk, boy. I admire that in a man. But you gotta be extra careful in town now. Bein' out o' favor with the law don't help a poor man a'tall."

"Looks like the law ain't the poor man's friend no matter how hard he tries to behave hisself."

"That's the truth of it, boy. But don't fly off the handle and try to change anybody's peckin' order. That would be like throwin' salt in their eyes."

Heck stood up. "I've got to go out back before I bust."

While relieving himself next to a big pine tree, Heck allowed his eyes to pass over the area behind the cabin, a part of this place he hadn't visited since he was a little boy. It was covered with vines and tall grass except for a fenced garden spot. He counted twenty rows of vegetables, all green and clear of weeds. Mr. Meade's buggy mare also pulled his plows.

Heck stopped at the well and drew a fresh bucket of water. After cleaning his hands, he drank his fill from a gourd dipper. Going back inside, he said, "Been killin' lots of game lately?"

"Enough to smell up my skillet."

"I guess you mostly hunt in Panther Holler Woods, it bein' so close and all."

"I ain't particular where my meat comes from."

"With no jobs to be had, and with game gettin' scarce around the house, I've got to find a new place to hunt. I'd go into Panther Holler Woods if I wasn't so afraid of them panthers and that ol' miller's ghost. Must be lots of squirrel and coons in there, maybe a deer even. And fish."

Mr. Meade gave him a warning look that bordered on the unfriendly. "You'd best stay out o' them woods, boy." He turned and looked out the door as if suddenly reminded of a disturbing event.

*I suspect something very spectacular happened in those woods,* Heck thought, *something more unspeakable than the old miller murdering his wife and her lover. Could be that Mr. Meade had a hand in it some way, or knows something that Blood Money Vandergriff doesn't want spread around. If that's the case, it would explain why Sheriff Sloan and his lawmen friends stay clear of this place and allow Mr. Meade to do pretty much as he pleases.*

Heck was beginning to think what he said about Panther Holler Woods had made his old friend angry when Mr. Meade got up and took a metal pan out of the pie safe. "I know you're hungry, boy. Have a piece of this hot water cornbread and a slice o' sow belly."

Grateful for the offer, Heck took the food and began to eat. Mr. Meade returned to his chair and said, "You've got a good head on you, boy. Just don't quit usin' it because times is hard and things ain't goin' yo're way. Try to remember there are always some thangs beyond a man's reach. Knowin' what is and what ain't is the difference between bein' a boy and a man."

Heck nodded. "I'm gonna try real hard not to disappoint you, Mr. Meade." Swallowing a mouthful of food, he added, "You aimin' to play something special at the musical tonight?"

"Nope. Just the regulars. Don't reckon they'll ever get too old for my ears. But I ain't gonna play so many hoedowns. My bow hair is purt nigh wore out." He sighed. "And my bow arm ain't what it used to be neither."

Mr. Meade, an excellent fiddler, loved playing his old Amati only slightly less than sipping good whiskey and talking about the old days when he rode with Quantrill's Raiders as a boy. Going to his bed, he pulled out his battered black fiddle case, took out the instrument and tuned it. He slid a chunk of rosin back and forth over the remaining hairs in his bow and began playing "Sally Goodin'." After that, he played bits of some other old tunes, including "Leather Britches," and "Soldier's Joy," then tried some of the new ones he'd heard on somebody's radio or phonograph. He soon returned to the old songs and on the chorus of "Lorena," he got misty-eyed and turned away so Heck couldn't see his face.

He put his fiddle away and talked to Heck about the old songs and reels, naming the ones he'd like to play that night. He also mentioned a couple he'd like Heck to sing. Heck knew two of his favorites were "Lorena" and "Just Before the Battle Mother," but he never asked him to sing them at their parties. Heck was glad, because they were too mournful, not the upbeat, peppy music people like to hear when trying to have fun.

They talked some more about what happened in town, and about Jake and his mysterious friends. When the sun began to get low behind the trees, Mr. Meade said it was time to eat. He opened a can of pork and beans and put two glasses and two bowls and a crockery pitcher of buttermilk on his little table in the corner.

After supper, they went to the barn where Heck hitched the mare to the buggy to hasten their departure. The sun was sinking fast, causing him to be concerned about getting home in time to prepare the old sharecropper house for the night's event before dark. The more important reason to hurry, however, was to find out what Doc Samuels told Thelma about Billy. He believed he could even survive Sheriff Sloan dropping by, if only he could get some good news about his little brother.

## Chapter X

It was 6:40 by Mr. Meade's watch when they turned into Vandergriff Road and headed for the cut in the bank. Heck jumped out of the buggy as soon as they rolled into the front yard of the party house and headed for the porch where Elsie and Marna were already filling the lamps with kerosene. Early sat in his special chair at the end of the ramp leading up to the porch, whiskey jar in hand, watching him with accusing eyes. Heck, not engaging the stare, looked around instead for Billy and Amy.

"Are you okay, Heck?" Marna asked.

"Yeah, where's Billy?"

Marna shrugged. "Over at the house, I guess. What happened after you left us? We were afraid you got yourself arrested and throwed in jail after tanglin' with them two city boys."

"I'll tell you later," he said, heading for the main house.

He didn't see Billy or Amy on the way over, but did find his stepmother in the front porch swing, humming contentedly as she thumbed through an old issue of *Grit* newspaper-magazine. Sporting a clean dress and combed hair for a change, she was the picture of serenity for the first time in recent memory.

"I was afraid you was in jail," she said calmly.

"Because of something Marna and Elsie told you?"

"No, because they said you got with that good-for-nothin' Slick Haskel and some loose city girls. Slick's often locked up on Saturday nights. So naturally, I thought . . ."

"What else did the girls tell you?"

She raised her eyebrows. "There's more?"

Heck was thankful for his sisters' good judgment and would tell them so later. To Thelma, he said, "What did Doc Samuels say about Billy?"

She grew fidgety as if disturbed by the question or something she'd done in his absence. If caused by worrying about Billy, it was the first time he'd ever known her to show concern for her youngest child.

"Don't come runnin' in here pretendin' you didn't' see them extra set of car tracks out in the back yard. Well, I'll tell you what I told your daddy already after he pressed me on the subject. Them tracks was made by the Watkins salesman. And I want you to help me convince Early so there won't be no trouble."

He gave her a long, disbelieving look, not surprised that her first concern was not for her sick little boy. "I'm not in the habit of lyin' to protect anybody that does something bad, Mama. The best I can do is not tell Daddy those extra tracks were made by that philanderin' Homer Percy. And I won't even do that for you if you don't promise not to tell him about Doc Samuels comin' out to see Billy."

She stiffened. "How'd you know . . . I mean, that ain't so, Smarty Pants. It was the Watkins man."

"Mama, I came back to the house after we left to ask you to please go see the preacher about a part-time job at the church. God knows, we need the money. What I didn't expect to run into was something that could cause a killin' in the family."

"Don't you dare go judgin' me, Heck Tennel. You ain't lived in my skin the last ten years."

"I'm not judgin' you, Mama. I'm just tryin' to do what I think's best for the family with as little hell raisin' as possible. We're havin' a hard enough time without you carryin' on like that. People don't think much of us as it is."

"You've growed up, Heck." She studied him for a moment, as if seeing some part of him for the first time. "This family's only healthy boy is a full-growed man now."

"Billy's your boy too, Mama. Yours and Daddy's baby. And my little brother. He's important too. So are Amy and Elsie and Marna. You and Daddy talk about them like they don't count, 'specially Billy and Amy. That's not right, and I'm sick of it."

Apparently unmoved by his pleadings, she said, "Too bad God had to take Ross, your only full brother. He was strong and healthy like you. He could still be helpin' you support the family."

"Don't keep blamin' God for what happened to Ross. He died because Daddy wouldn't take him to the doctor in time. And the same thing's gonna happen to Billy unless I do something about it."

He walked to the edge of the porch to harness his desire to slap her. After calming down, he turned and asked, "What did Doc Samuels say is wrong with Billy?"

"That ol' quack," she said, starting the swing. "Asked me a lot of silly questions about his birthin'. Amy's too, just like it was my fault they ain't healthy. Wanted to know if they ate lots of vegetables and drank milk. I told him you always have a good garden and our cow ain't dry very long at a time."

"Get to the point. What did he say is wrong with Billy?"

"The ol' grouch said eatin' right will help Amy. But he said Billy's tonsils have to come out as soon as you can get the swellin' and the fever down, and come up with fifty dollars. He said he's anemic too, but some medicine might cure that."

"Anything else?"

"He kept listenin' to Billy's heart. When I'd ask him questions, he'd cut me off. Finally, after we left Billy's room, he told me something was wrong with Billy's heart. I think he said it didn't beat right, or somethin'. And it's got a sound it ain't supposed to have. I don't remember what he called it."

"A murmur? Did he say it had a murmur?"

"Yeah, that's what he said. See what goin' to the eighth grade did for you? It's got somethin' to do with a part of it not closin' and openin' right. Said you'd have to bring him in to the hospital for some tests before he'd know for sure."

"Did he say he could do anything about his condition if it checked out bad?"

"I don't remember, Heck. He said so much, my head was in a whirl. I ain't no educated woman, you know."

"Think real hard. Try to remember."

She sighed, shaking her head. "Seems I recall him tellin' me that if Billy's got real bad heart problems, nothin' can be done about it in this part of the country. Said he'd have to send him off up north somewheres."

A sinking sensation swept over Heck. "Lots and lots of money," he said, as if to himself. With a heavy sigh, he left the porch to look for his little brother.

He found Billy lying on his cot next to the window in their darkening room. "Hi, podner. How you feelin' this evenin'?"

Billy didn't raise up, but managed a smile. "'Bout the same, I reckon."

"Feel like comin' to the musical?" Heck dropped to his knees beside the cot.

"I'll just lay here by the window and listen. You and Mr. Meade and Grandpa make real purty music. Will you sing "Little Joe the Wrangler" for me?"

"You bet. Now tell me, how did Doc Samuels treat you?"

"Ain't never stood buck-naked before nobody but you and Mama before. And I ain't never been poked on like I was a sack of rotten 'taters neither."

"Well, maybe you won't have to go through all that again. Doc Samuels said he's gonna do lots of things that'll make you feel good real soon."

"But we ain't got no money for it, Heck."

"Don't you worry." Heck patted his brother's shoulder. "Ol' Heck'll take care of it. Just think good thoughts and before long, you'll be up boundin' around the place like a regular Charles Atlas."

"Really, Heck?" Billy smiled weakly.

"Sure. I've never lied to you, have I? But gotta go make the party house ready so we can play and get a few nickels in the hat."

Choking up, Heck leaned down and kissed Billy, discovering a fevered forehead. He forced another smile, telling him, "Listen up real good, now. I'll sing 'Little Joe the Wrangler' for you after we get warmed up good. I might even throw in 'When the Work's All Done This Fall'. That's another one of your favorites as I recall."

"You're a good brother, Heck."

Near tears, Heck walked back through the house and across the back yard on his way to the party house, feeling like he needed a big slug of Ubis's home brew. He helped his sisters finish filling the lamps and lanterns and place one in each room. Electricity wasn't available in the country, but Mr. Roosevelt promised it would be soon. Heck knew he couldn't afford it even if it could be had.

Heck felt his dad's eyes on him as he went about helping the girls. When his sisters left to get his guitar and the lemonade, Early called him away from double-checking the set up for Ubis Sproggs' weekly whiskey concession in the back room.

Still disturbed over what the doctor told Thelma about Billy, Heck joined his dad on the front porch of the party house, looking at him at last. Surprisingly, he didn't cuss him out or pull the razor strap from his back pocket. But Heck could tell he was having a hard time controlling his temper.

"What'n hell did you do with the money you stole out of my pocket?"

Heck searched his eyes for some positive changes which may have come with his renewed manhood. He was glad his dad had been able to prove to himself that he was still a man, and wanted to congratulate him, but to do so would reveal his presence during the event. He told him instead, "Your pocket, my money. I won't ask you exactly what you got for your share, including that twenty, or tell Mama you turned to another woman to get your nature back, if you won't ask me what I did with what I took."

Early's face paled, and his jaw muscles rippled, having never tolerated such brashness from one of his children, but he held his temper in check. "I remember something Papa told me once. He said, 'It's hard for a daddy to see when his boy stops bein' a boy and starts bein' a man.' But now that I do, I'll tell you this. I hope you don't live long enough to get in the shape I was in before I went to see Frieda today."

Caught off guard by being talked to like an adult, Heck was at a loss for words. His dad's penetrating gaze conveyed a message he could never put into words. This, their first ever lengthy eye contact, stirred Heck, convincing him something important had happened between them that day.

"It ain't fittin' for a man to live if he ain't really a man," Early said. "No matter what you or anybody else thinks about Frieda, she understands that. Today she made me want to keep on livin'."

Heck tried to think of something to say befitting the momentous occasion, but couldn't. He was on the verge of breaking down and telling him about Billy's serious health problems and the broken jar of moonshine when Mr. Meade and the girls appeared with the instruments.

Heck followed them inside with his father's words still ringing in his ears, but became sad again when he remembered what Thelma told him about Billy. *I need to make some money. And the quicker the better.*

He placed a glowing lamp on the apple box beside his dad's collection hat, and then lit one for the coffee/lemonade serving table in a back room. Here his sisters and the wives of farmers quenched their thirst and gossiped. Most of the men preferred sipping snuff glasses of Ubis' homebrew in the other back room, unless Sheriff Sloan's car was spotted driving up in the yard. If that happened, Ubis scrambled his goods out beyond the light in the backyard. The sheriff, an Episcopalian and a moderate drinker himself, had to enforce the liquor laws because most of the voters in Hispaniola County were Baptists.

While putting the last lamp in place, Heck sensed he was not alone, and upon turning found their neighbor Zeke "Loony" Toons watching him from the doorway. Loony loved slipping up on people, particularly city folks stopped in the woods nearby to do some courting. Indulging in his favorite pastime of catching couples in the act caused him to be run off or beaten up on more than one occasion. Called Loony by all who knew him because of his odd ways, he lived alone on a small farm up Vandergriff Road beyond the old Vandergriff home and Ubis Sproggs' place. He had no known relatives and no real friends other than Heck.

"Hi, Loony," Heck said.

"H-h-h-hi, Heck," Loony spoke with a stutter which worsened when excited or embarrassed, like when trying to talk to a girl.

The blue-eyed Loony was in his late fifties, skinny, and bald on the top of his head. What hair he had around the side and back was white, shoulder length, never combed. He seldom took a bath or shaved. This night, as usual, he was wearing worn-out overalls with only one strap hooked in front and both sides unbuttoned. His loose-hanging flour sack shirt was so faded one could barely see the original pattern, or make out the brand name.

"Walked up on any interestin' sights lately?" Heck asked.

"N-n-nope." His face flushed.

Loony told Heck a long time ago that he had never had sex with a woman. Some of the men in the area believed him crazy because he always played with himself instead.

"Where's your girlfriend?" Heck teased. "You can't dance without a girl."

"I-I-I ain't got one of them. C-can I-I come to your m-m-musical without one?"

"Sure, if you promise you won't steal some man's wife."

Loony slapped his leg and laughed, and was trying to respond when Marna walked into the room. He turned hungry eyes on her bosom, then her backside. Marna, accustomed to his weirdness, paid him no mind.

"Sis, anybody else out there?"

"Ubis Sproggs and the Banions."

"Enjoy the music, Loony." Walking past him, Heck went to each room, checking lamp wicks and making sure all the windows were raised. Neither of the back rooms had ceilings, so they were still very warm from the day's sun. The night air would cool them down.

He also checked the lantern over the back steps. Its light made it possible for the women to go to the outdoor privy without worry of stepping into an armadillo hole. The men knew not to use the privy, walking instead beyond the circle of light or stopping in the shadows of a large tree.

Others were arriving now, judging from the sounds in the front yard. Heck headed for the front room, passing Loony who had already sat down in the floor and leaned back against the partition wall. As was his custom, the eccentric old man would remain there until around eleven o'clock, patting his foot and alternately laughing and crying. He was too shy to talk to the other guests.

Heck's grandpa and Mr. and Mrs. Walt Banion were coming up the steps behind Mr. Meade. The Banions owned the dairy just west of Panther Holler Crossing. They came to the musicals once a month, but did not allow their two girls to accompany them. As a longtime member of Homer Percy's church, Mrs. Banion, who was strongly opposed to dancing and drinking, would never allow her girls to stoop that low. But since she couldn't keep her husband away, she came to make sure he didn't get drunk. Mr. Banion loved the back room where he sipped Ubis' moonshine and exchanged jokes with the other men who imbibed.

Heck greeted them all and took his grandfather's bass fiddle inside, placing it by his Sears-Roebuck guitar in the front room. Another car pulled into the yard, followed by the sounds of wagon wheels and mule hoofs walking on hard earth. Glancing into the back room, he saw Ubis finish putting snuff glasses on the old table, then hide a jar of shine under a tow sack on the floor. He always hid his main supply out back.

This exciting highlight of Heck's week made his otherwise dreary life tolerable. The exuberant singing would push aside all the trials and tribulations which had caused him so much concern during the week, allowing him to receive a hint of how good life could be and would be some day if all his plans worked out right.

It was now dark. The cry of katydids and the popping sounds of bugs flying against the outside lanterns bridged brief lulls in conversation. Still warm, the night air began cooling things down a bit.

Returning to the porch to push his dad inside, Heck heard a woman's voice out beyond the circle of light, and then saw Willa and her mother walk into view. Willa had made a half-hearted attempt at combing her hair, but the tangles weren't the worst part of her appearance. That dubious honor went to her faded, flowery dress, too long and too tight, and her white socks with men's slippers. The idea of approaching her repulsed Heck, but he had to find out if everything went okay in the field after he left.

"Hi, Heck," Willa called out. "Heard you got in a fight today."

"Shut up, Willa," he snapped, glancing around to see if his dad heard her.

"What's that?" Early asked. "A fight, you said?"

"It was nothin'," Heck said quickly. "Willa's just tryin' to stir up trouble, as usual."

Willa's knowing smile didn't disappear, and as she got closer her hungry eyes signaled her determination to get him out to the bushes before the night was over. She knew from past experience that his resistance broke down after a few shots of Ubis' moonshine. What she didn't know was, he had already made up his mind, that before letting it happen this Saturday night, he would find out what Beulah Mae's friend from town looked like. If she was as pretty as Beulah Mae, he'd have to figure out a way to meet her outside without Willa finding out and killing them both.

By the time he rolled his dad into the front room, several more couples had arrived, including Mr. and Mrs. Shorty McLean and Slick Haskel. Slick walked into the light between Beulah Mae and her friend, a tall, brown-headed girl. She was slender, had clear skin and some interesting curves, and did not appear to be uncomfortable among so many strangers. Heck saw Willa eyeing daggers at her. Sparks would fly if he so much as talked to the new girl unless he could find a secret way.

Returning to the front room to avoid having to greet the new girl in Willa's presence, Heck put his dad's old felt hat on the little table which also served as a support for his cut-off legs. He didn't approve of his dad using his condition to play on the sympathies of their guests, but never spoke up about the practice.

Most people came on into the front room, took seats and waited for the music to start, while others lingered outside to smoke Bull Durham cigarettes and talk. Mr. Meade removed his fiddle from its case and began rubbing the bow against the rosin stick. Grandpa Tennel picked the E string on Heck's guitar so he could tune to it. Heck could tell by Mr. Meade's color that he'd already taken a snort of Ubis' shine. As usual, no one seemed to notice his holstered pistol or the care he took hanging his tattered gray Stars and Bars hat on a nail just above his head. He almost shot a stranger one time for taking down the hat and tossing it out on the porch. A killing had been prevented only because Heck grabbed Mr. Meade's gun arm, giving the traveler time to escape out the back door.

"Evenin', folks," Heck said, turning around the room with a wave and a smile.

Those present returned the greeting, and somebody called out, "Let her rip, Heck."

Heck sat down next to Mr. Meade who led off with the lively, "Boil Them Cabbage Down." The party was on. Rebel yells and feet stamping in time with the music got everyone's blood flowing. Heck felt himself being lifted up and carried into another world.

Granddad Tennel fell in with them on the bass fiddle, and those still outside came in to watch and listen, occasionally glancing at Early who kept rhythm by beating his left leg stub against the box. Their expressions said they had been transformed as well.

What Mr. Meade's fiddling lacked in smoothness was made up by gusto, and he never played a short version of anything, or in any key except "D." He finally ended his first selection and began "Chicken Reel." At that point Ubis Sproggs sprang out of the back room, grabbed his heavy wife, letting out with a big "Eee haaa!" as he swung her around with the abandon of a man under the influence. In spite of enthusiasm for the dance, however, he kept watch on the serving room so as not to miss a sale. Heck believed the only reason Ubis hadn't hit him up for his share of the day's sales in town was because his dad had already paid him.

Ending the second number, Mr. Meade paused for a swallow of whiskey from a silver flask he pulled from his pocket. Slick and Shorty McLean took advantage of the break to follow Ubis into the back room. Mr. Meade began "Westphalia Waltz" and halfway through it, Slick reappeared and began dancing with Beulah Mae.

The new girl moved closer to watch her friend swing around the room with Slick, and for the first time, Heck got a look at her in full light. The glistening brown hair was curled on the ends, framing a smooth, round face and a turned-up nose that didn't have a single freckle on it. Her wide mouth wouldn't allow her to win any beauty contests, but her overall features formed a feminine quality he had never seen in Willa. Her eyes met his, she smiled and held his gaze without turning away, a look that told Heck she hadn't come along with Beulah Mae just to be stimulated by a ride in the night air. Her obvious boldness caused him to fall out of rhythm with his guitar for a few bars, a mistake he seldom made.

The McLeans joined Slick and Beulah Mae on the dance floor, and by the time Mr. Meade had to stop to rest his arms, everybody seemed caught up in the spirit of the party. Early didn't care that nobody had dropped any coins in his hat, thanks to Ubis slipping him a snuff glass half full of shine. With his manhood restored and some good moonshine under his belt, he was a changed man.

Heck's stepmother's reaction to her own renewal was more subdued. She sat between Marna and Elsie on a bench against the back wall quietly observing their guests with an expression of detached contentment. She appeared unconcerned that she was, as usual, being shunned by her women neighbors.

Mr. Meade pulled out the flask again, saying with unaccustomed loudness, "Another shot or two of this, folks, and I'll be ready to play 'Orange Blossom Special.' How about you, Ibsen?"

Grandpa Tennel nodded and said something that got drowned out by shouts of approval and applause from around the room. He had the voice of a sober man, always respected but seldom heard. Although no longer a churchgoer, he remained a devout Baptist at heart, never drinking whiskey except for medicinal purposes.

"I want to hear Heck sing," Willa shouted.

"Yeah, Heck," Slick said. "Show Ruby what you can do."

Heck looked at the tall city girl and she smiled. "All right," he said, beginning a song he'd heard Jimmy Rodgers sing over the radio at Mr. Slater's. A few bars into "Nobody's Darling," he took his eyes off Ruby for fear of becoming distracted and forgetting the lyrics. Even a glance at her during the chorus threatened his concentration, so he looked instead at the familiar faces in the room until he was finished. When he looked at her again, her gaze told him she was surprised a country boy could sing at all.

Willa shot Ruby another threatening look, causing Heck to suspect she might lunge across the room at any time and tear into the city girl, who up to that point had not sensed the danger she was in. Heck told himself to warn Ruby at the earliest opportunity.

Seeing the smiles and hearing the applause that followed his songs lifted Heck up like nothing else he had ever done. It made him feel important, appreciated and for a time, in charge of his life, which could be beautiful in spite of poverty.

He sang "When the Work's All Done This Fall," "Good-bye, My Little Darling" and "She's My Curly Headed Baby." Each number won him a vigorous round of applause, whistles and foot stampings, and it caused Ruby to move up so close he caught a whiff of her perfume. If Mr. Meade hadn't swung out on "Arkansas Traveler," Willa might have jumped her. Instead, she remained by the door, staring angrily at Heck and her new competition.

After the fiddle tune, Heck announced he was going to sing another song dedicated to Mr. Meade. At the start of "Pistol Packin' Mama," everyone loudly applauded, and his old friend smiled and saluted. When Heck was through, Mr. Meade began "Devil's Dream," and his audience clapped in time with its rhythm.

Mr. Meade had barely got rolling good when he looked through the door of Ubis' concession stand and abruptly stopped playing. Heck and his granddad gave him confused looks as they, too, stopped. All heads turned to the partition door, and an excited murmur ran through the room when they saw Sheriff Emmet Sloan standing there, so tall his black hat touched the top of the opening. Heck had never seen him look so big and threatening.

Ubis Sproggs stomped his foot so hard it made the floor shake. "Damn! Where'n hell did you come from?"

"Through the back door, Ubis. The one you always ran out of to hide this stuff when I came in the front." The sheriff held up a half empty jar of whiskey.

A hush fell over the room as everybody waited to see what the sheriff's next move would be. Calm and sure of himself in his customary black suit, white shirt and black string tie, he was a sight to put fear in the hearts of the worst of men.

Heck completely forgot about Ruby and his anticipated trip with her to the dark side of the yard. *Damn. The sheriff's come to arrest me.*

Sheriff Sloan said, "I'd haul you in, Ubis, if I wasn't here on more important business."

*I'm going to jail for sure.* Heck almost pissed in his pants.

Sheriff Sloan looked slowly around the room as if expecting to see a face he hadn't seen before. When his cold eyes stopped on him, Heck felt a fresh wave of panic sweep over him. He was unable to look at the fearsome man who had spoiled his musical, and might now put him in jail and spoil his life. To make matters worse, he sensed the big lawman was reading his every thought.

When the sheriff started walking toward him, Heck suddenly recalled a song he had sung at so many musicals, "He's In the Jailhouse Now." Taking on a whole new meaning, the lyrics pounded in his head like thunder before a storm.

Sheriff Sloan loomed over Heck like Goliath over David, exuding such an air of absolute authority that it made him tremble. He tried to speak, but his mouth was too dry. He wondered what Ruby thought of him now, cowering like a whipped puppy in front of his guests.

The sheriff said, "I have good information that tells me the man who hustled you out of town this afternoon was Clyde Barrow's driver."

A murmur ran through the room, causing the sheriff to look around as if he hoped somebody would speak up. Nobody did, so he turned back to Heck. "Bonnie and Clyde have ties in this area. Relatives, friends. They just killed two highway patrolmen up north a ways and robbed a bank. That means they're looking for a place to lay low 'til things cool off."

Heck stared at the sheriff, swallowed, and said meekly, "Then you ain't here to arrest me?"

"Spilled evidence makes for a weak court case," he replied. "But I'm sure Chief Heyduck'll be waitin' for you when you come back to town. Now, tell me about your new friend. How and where did you meet him, that sort of thing. What's his name?"

The question shattered Heck's momentary sense of relief. He didn't want to get Jake in a jam, but knew he would be in serious trouble if he lied and got found out.

"Well?" Sheriff Sloan moved closer. "He was driving a car like the one Bonnie and Clyde used when they robbed that bank. Are you going to answer my question here, or down at the jailhouse?" He pulled a set of handcuffs out of his side coat pocket, the sight of which sent a new chill rushing over Heck. He was so scared now he allowed his guitar to slide off his lap and slam against the floor, not bothering to pick it up.

Heck's daddy broke the silence. "Boy, was he the same fella who run you off the bridge this mornin'?"

"Bridge?" the sheriff snapped. "What bridge?"

Heck gave his dad an angry look for killing whatever chance he might have had of protecting the man who had given him twenty dollars.

Needing time to think, he leaned down and picked up his guitar, but nothing came to mind. Finally, he said, "It was a narrow bridge."

Slick snickered and others joined in until it seemed everyone in the house was laughing at him. Heck turned his eyes around the room to look at their faces when he failed to see the humor in what he'd said. The sheriff, apparently not thinking the remark funny either, leaned down and repeated the question. "What's the man's name?"

Eyes fixed on the handcuffs, Heck said nervously, "All I know is, his name is Jake. But he's a nice man, Sheriff. He gave me more money than I lost." He stopped, realizing he had said too much.

"Money? What money?"

*Way to go, stupid. Now you're in too deep to hold anything back.* Heck eyed the handcuffs and swallowed hard. "Jake gave me a twenty-dollar bill. I only lost three dollars and thirty cents."

"Where's the twenty now?"

"I gave it to my daddy."

A murmur ran through the guests as the sheriff turned his cold eyes to Early. Stepping toward him, he held out his hand. "Give it to me."

Heck saw his dad's face pale as he pulled his leg stubs off the box, shift nervously in his chair and throw a glance at his wife. Turning back to face the sheriff, his expression suddenly became defiant. "It's mine. You ain't got no right to take it away from me."

"I've got every right, Early. Could be part of the money taken in that bank robbery. If it's not, you'll get it back. Now, gimme, or I'll take you and Heck both to jail."

Early glanced again at Thelma, then at Heck. Lowering his voice, he told Sheriff Sloan, "I ain't got it. I spent it already."

"Where?" The sheriff's eyes didn't waver.

Early grimaced and squirmed. Leaning forward, he asked, almost in a whisper, "Can we talk about this outside?"

Sheriff Sloan held his gaze a moment then looked at his leg stumps. Sensing his sympathy, Early quickly added, "Heck can wheel me out. Come on, boy."

Sheriff Sloan gave the nod and Heck approached the back of the wheelchair. Turning to look at his confused guests, he forced a smile and said, "Only be a minute, folks. Mr. Meade, will you and Grandpa please keep the music goin' till I get back?"

When Heck started rolling his dad toward the front door, the sheriff walked over and glared down at the frightened Loony Toons.

"Loony," he said, "you've always been good to tell me about strangers seen in this neck of the woods. Have you run upon any lately?"

Stopping at the door to wait for the sheriff, Heck saw Loony's mouth move, but no words came out. Finally, the old bachelor stammered, "A-a-all naked behinds l-l-look alike, Sheriff. C-c-can't rightly tell which one b-b-belongs to a s-s-stranger."

The room exploded in laughter, ending just as quickly when the sheriff whirled, giving a warning look.

Slick broke the renewed silence. "You gotta give Loony a stamp, Sheriff, so he can put the county's brand on the locals."

There was more laughter, and the sheriff told Slick, "Stay out of this." Turning back to Loony, he asked, "What about a new Ford V-8? Not many of them around. If you'd seen one, you'd remember it."

Loony turned anxious eyes on Heck, and then lowered his head to stare at the floor, too frightened to say more.

"Sheriff," Nathan Meade said, "when bankers rob the farmers and other workin' folks, you lawmen stand by with folded hands. But when somebody poor like Bonnie and Clyde rob a bank, you cry foul, hunt 'em down and kill 'em like they was dogs. I, for one, don't care whether you catch 'em or not."

The statement caused a hush to fall over the room, and Heck could tell the old man's remark angered Sheriff Sloan. It got so quiet, Heck could hear the bugs buzzing around the lanterns outside.

The sheriff searched faces for signs of support, but nobody spoke. Turning back to Mr. Meade, he said, "Nathan, I'm aware of the sympathy the likes of you have for outlaws. But think about it, man. These two aren't fighting for a cause. They're cold blooded killers."

"That's the sad part," Mr. Meade said. "Sad because some good men got killed and lawmen like you don't get the message at all. But why pick on Heck and his papa? They ain't killed nobody or robbed no bank. Leave 'em alone and I'll make you a proposition."

"You know where those murderers are, Nathan?" the sheriff asked.

"Nope. But if you'll arrest a banker, I'll find 'em for you."

Some nervous giggles were heard, but everybody fell silent again when the sheriff looked around the room.

"That's the only kind of help you're gonna get out of these folks, Sheriff," a half-drunk Slick Haskel called out. "Better take him up on his offer."

"One more smart aleck outburst from you, Slick Haskel, and I'll arrest you for drunk and disorderly conduct."

Motioning for Heck and his dad to follow, the sheriff walked through the front door, tossing Ubis' jar of moonshine into the yard as he did. Heck heard Ubis groan when the jar smashed against the hard ground.

Behind the Banion wagon near the outer circle of light, the sheriff said, "Early, Heck, I know what hard times you've been having, but that won't keep me from arresting you if I have to. Now, Early, where did you spend the twenty?"

"Down at Frieda's, Sheriff. I've been havin' this awful man's problem, you see, and —"

"I'm not interested in your personal problems, Early. I've got enough official problems of my own right now. I just want that bill. When did you give it to her?"

"A little after twelve, but I don't want nobody in the family to know it 'cept Heck. He was with me."

Heck could feel the sheriff's eyes boring into him again as he turned to look back at the party house. He saw Willa sitting on the top step watching them. Inside, Mr. Meade and his granddad began "Little Brown Jug."

When the sheriff spoke again, Heck turned back to look at him in the near-darkness. "You two have got to stop selling Ubis' moonshine at your musicals. You're running an open saloon in there, for crying out loud. Keep that up, first thing you know somebody with clout is gonna start complaining, and I'll have to come back out here and arrest both of you. Tell Ubis his whiskey stays out in his hoopy. He can *give* anybody a drink that wants it, but he can't sell it."

"Oh, we will, Sheriff," Early said, nodding. "Yes, sir, we'll sure do that."

Heck gave his dad an accusing look, knowing he was lying.

The sheriff went on, "Now, about Jake, or whatever his name is. Tell me everything that happened at the bridge and in town this afternoon."

Heck recounted both occasions and Sheriff Sloan listened without interrupting. Afterwards, he told Heck, "One of those boys you had that run-in with, the driver, is the son of B.M. Vandergriff's mill foreman, but the fact that he's a regular asshole doesn't make what you did any less serious. The other one is Chief Heyduck's boy. So, if I were you, I'd stay out of town for a while. I don't know what the chief has in mind for you for not stopping when his man ordered you to, or for creating a disturbance."

"But I've got to keep runnin' my butter and egg route," Heck told him. "Most of my customers are in Milltown. That's in the city limits."

"Just make sure you don't sell anything besides butter and eggs. And stay out of town proper. As for me, I won't put you in jail for what happened this afternoon if you'll help me find this Jake. Which will it be?"

Heck glanced at the house and wondered if Billy was watching or listening. He thought about his sisters, and the fact that he had no prospects for work. He thought about the kind man who had given him more money than he'd held at one time in his life. And he remembered what Cracker said about life being a pisser.

"Well?" the sheriff said.

"I can't afford to have any more trouble piled on me or the family, so it looks like I'll have to do what I can."

"That's a wise decision, young man. Now, you're to notify me if you see Jake or hear from him again. And I don't mean the next day. You come running the minute you spot him. Clear?"

"Yes, sir." Heck nodded.

Sheriff Sloan turned and walked through the lighted area to his car parked on Vandergriff Road, and as he drove off, Heck pushed his dad back to the front porch and up the ramp. The music stopped when they entered the room, and all eyes turned on them. His granddad asked, "Everything all right, son?"

"Everything's fine." Looking around, he forced a smile and raised his voice to say, "Let's get on with the party."

Returning Early to his spot, Heck picked up his guitar, struck a loud "C," and began singing Billy's request, "Little Joe the Wrangler." Mr. Meade and Grandpa Tennel accompanied him from the beginning of the second verse and the guests appeared to relax as they listened to the song. When finished, he looked at Ruby and started "Be Nobody's Darling But Mine" as Willa squirmed and fumed. That one done, he glanced at Willa and began "Love Oh Loveless Love," and Ruby smiled. He then sang "Corrine Corrina."

Heck saw his mother giving his dad a long, accusing look, but his dad refused to meet her gaze. He looked at Ruby again, finding her eyes bolder than ever.

Mr. Meade began "Rose of Shannon Waltz" and when it ended, Heck stood up and told everybody he needed some lemonade. Heading for the back room where the angry Ubis Sproggs had already replenished his in-house supply, Heck didn't remember ever being more desperate for a shot of whiskey. He seldom drank, even at his musicals, but he'd never had a day like this one. More trouble than usual piling up all of a sudden had a very unsettling effect on him. And he didn't even know yet if anything happened after he'd left Mr. Slater's cotton field that would get Cracker hanged.

Willa didn't appear to be disturbed about anything other than the new girl with Slick, but Heck knew from past experience that appearances didn't mean much when it came to judging a tough, scheming girl like Willa. They needed to talk, but he'd have to go outside with her to do it. He didn't want to suffer the consequences of being in the shadows with her.

*I'll check on Cracker first thing in the morning. Right now, entertain the guests. Put your troubles on hold for a while. Reality will set in again soon enough. It always does after the playing and singing stops.*

# Chapter XII

Well known for his ability to curse, Ubis was living up to his reputation as Heck approached the serving table, and he didn't bother cleaning up his language when Slick followed him into the room with Beulah Mae and Ruby. Another whiff of Ruby's perfume helped Heck push the day's bad events to the back of his mind.

"You sing real good, Heck," Ruby said, pressing her shoulder against his.

"As good as Slick makes introductions?"

"Oh, hell," Slick said. "Names ain't important. You know she's a girl. That's all that matters."

"I'm Heck Tennel," He smiled at the new girl.

"And I'm Ruby Crenshaw. I already knew who you were, because I've seen you in town before. I like boys taller than me."

"And shorter, and fatter, and skinnier," Slick said, laughing.

Ubis touched Heck's elbow with a snuff glass. "Want a snort?"

"You bet," Heck said. He offered it to Ruby first, expecting her to decline, but she took it. After downing a gulp without so much as a frown, she gave it back to him.

Heck took a swallow and breathed in quickly in an attempt to put out the fire in his throat. He'd never liked the taste of whiskey or the way it burned going down. The only good part was the warmth it spread all over his body.

Heck didn't feel ill at ease with Ruby like he always was around other well-dressed city girls. Maybe it was because of the liquor and the fact she wasn't what he called the uppity type – those who turned up their noses if he dared to give them a friendly look.

He asked Ruby about where she lived, her school and her family. The more they talked, the more he was convinced she hadn't come to chitchat. Slick had told him about bold city girls, but he'd never believed any of them could be as brazen as Willa. Looking at Ruby close-up, he realized what a great improvement over Willa she was, dressed in her fine, store-bought clothes and white shoes. And her skin looked as smooth and soft as the tops of Frieda Haskel's breasts, causing him to suspect that she seldom saw the sun or felt a cold winter's wind. *Ruby's the kind of girl a man likes to squeeze real tight.*

His pleasant thoughts were suddenly interrupted when Willa barged into the room in a huff, glaring at him and Ruby. Judging by her flushed look, Heck knew she'd already sampled her dad's moonshine.

It was the first time Heck saw Willa wearing a brassiere. It made her breasts look as large as muskmelons, and Ruby's puny by comparison. The tight dress she wore caused her to look larger than usual in other places too, particularly her stomach. He blamed that on the fact that he was unaccustomed to seeing her in a dress, tight or otherwise.

A pleased expression swept over Willa's face when she saw him taking notice of the uplifted bodice. She pushed toward him, giving Ruby a contemptuous look in passing. Stopping, she told Heck in her loud, coarse voice, "Who's your skinny friend, lover?"

After Heck introduced them, she told Ruby, "I've been Heck's girl ever since his balls fell, honey. And I ain't givin' him up to no city whore that's so thin one of her bones would slice right through his belly if he got her in a serious clinch. Stay away from him. He's mine."

"Really?" Ruby's boldness wasn't diminished by Willa's outburst. "From the way you've been watchin' him tonight, I thought you believed he stole your last calf, you fat heifer."

Willa lunged at Ruby, but Heck caught her arm and held her back. "Calm down, Willa," he said. "No use gettin' riled up over nothin'.'

"Nothin', my ass. She's got the hots for you so bad I thought she'd catch the grass on fire comin' across the yard. I've been watchin' them looks she's been givin' you."

"Oh, so you're a mind reader too?" Ruby said. "What a shame, me misjudgin' you like that. I could've sworn you're good for nothing but choppin' cotton and shoveling cow shit."

Willa lunged at Ruby again and it took all of Heck's strength to hold her back this time. She slapped Heck's hand. "Let me go, dammit! I'll kick her where it'll do the most good."

Ubis Sproggs and Slick were laughing, thoroughly enjoying the show. Slick said, "Turn her loose, Heck. She's just lookin' after what's hers."

Unable to free herself from Heck's grasp, Willa growled at Ruby, "I never saw a giraffe in heat before. Do you plan on givin' it to Heck, or chargin' him your goin' rate?"

Ubis and Slick laughed louder, as did other guests who overheard the insult battle through the connecting door.

"What's the matter," Willa snarled. "Pussy cat got your tongue?"

Ruby's temper flared and Heck found himself grabbing her arm too. "Settle down, girls," he told them. "Willa, go back to the front room. Do something nice for a change, like takin' Billy and Amy some lemonade. Go on."

Willa jerked her arm free and straightened her dress. Calmer now, she told Ruby, "This ain't over yet, skinny Minny." She turned to leave.

"Be careful your padding doesn't fall down, heifer," Ruby said.

Willa whirled and came at Ruby. Again Heck stopped her.

"Come outside, skinny. We'll have a little contest to see who's padded." She began unbuttoning her dress. "Why go outside, by God? Start peelin'."

Heck caught Willa's hand on the third button as everybody laughed. "Stop. We're convinced."

"As if you need to be, honey. She's the one that ain't never seen 'em."

Red-faced, Heck pulled Willa's hands away from her dress. "Stop it, I said. Go on over to the house. I'll see you later. We need to talk."

Cursing under her breath, Willa clomped her men's shoes out of the room. Heck reached for the glass he'd put back on the table as Ruby moved closer to give him a perturbed look. "Slick didn't say I'd be competing with a wild cow tonight."

"Willa's lived a hard life, so she's had to be tough." He took another swallow of the moonshine. "Don't get into a fight with her if you can help it."

"I'd rather rassle you," she said, smiling.

"Whoo, damn, Heck," Slick said. "Let's all go outside."

Ruby appeared eager to hear his answer, but before he could give it, Grandpa Tennel and Nathan Meade entered the room. Not wanting his grandfather to know he was drinking, or about to go outside, Heck shoved the glass behind him. After Mr. Meade paid for his whiskey, he joined him, Ruby and Grandpa Tennel, telling Heck, "You done real good, boy, facin' up to the sheriff like you did. Anything happen outside you care to tell us about?"

Heck glanced at his granddad and shook his head. "Most of it was talk about the man that delivered me to your place."

Ubis leaned over the table. "Your dad didn't promise the sheriff he was gonna stop me from sellin' shine at your musicals, did he?"

Wanting to tell the truth, but not wanting another ruckus, he shook his head.

Mr. Meade said, "Looks like the sheriff believes your friend is one of the Hamiltons, Raymond maybe."

"Maybe," Heck said. He had read something about the Hamilton brothers, but didn't remember the details.

"Well, if Bonnie and Clyde are hereabouts, I can tell you why." Mr. Meade said, moving closer. "Hank Slater's wife is kin to Bonnie, and Clyde has relatives in the county too."

Heck was about to tell Mr. Meade how surprised he was that the Slaters could have such notorious kinfolks when his dad called to him from the front room. "Hey, Heck. You and Nathan come play some music. Folks in here want to dance."

As Grandpa Tennel walked away, Heck placed his glass on the table and told Ruby, "Later, okay?"

She smiled and followed them into the front room where Mr. Meade's first number was "Listen to the Mockingbird," played in response to a request from the Tarltons, farmers who lived on a farm past Loony's place, When it was over, he took another sip from his glass and started "Soldier's Joy." Later, when he led off with "La Goldendrena," those who had partners danced. Heck's stepmother, looking happy again, danced with Elsie. Up to that point, Thelma had been content with sitting unnoticed between Marna and Elsie, quietly watching Heck and the others play or listening to her neighbors chatter.

Heck kept an eye out for Willa for fear she'd come back, jump Ruby and do her serious injury. He spotted her coming in off the porch to fix her eyes on the city girl, and was relieved when she moved on through the room to join her dad. She had just disappeared into the back room when a movement in the front door caught his attention. Turning to see what it was, he fell out of time with Mr. Meade's lead as his gut tightened.

Jake Vest, smiling calmly, looked at Heck and nodded, then continued greeting people sitting nearby. He was more dressed up than when Heck first saw him, having put on a blue coat, a striped white shirt and a tie. He still wore the dress hat.

As the music faded and stopped, everybody turned their eyes on Jake, including those who had been dancing. He smiled and waved at them.

Heck held his gaze. *He doesn't look like a dangerous man to me,*

The appearance of anybody out of the ordinary at a musical had always been considered noteworthy, but no one as handsome or as well dressed as Jake had ever dropped by.

"Come on in, stranger," Early called out. "Welcome."

Jake entered the room, took out a roll of money from his pocket, peeled off a bill and dropped it into the collection hat. An excited murmur ran through the room as Early looked disbelievingly at the bounty.

"Looks like pickings have been pretty slim tonight." Jake nodded at the hat.

"You just threw in enough for my family to live off of for three months, stranger. Much obliged."

"My apologies for the intrusion." He took off his hat and looked around the room again. "My name's Jake Vest. I hope you don't mind my dropping by."

Heck heard whispered comments between some of his guests, as others remained silent, staring in awe at their unexpected stranger. The faces of the younger ladies, including Thelma's, flushed with excitement.

Realizing that both he and his new friend would be taken to jail if the sheriff should come back unexpectedly, Heck leaned his guitar against the wall and beckoned for Jake to follow him into Ubis' serving room. The strained silence ended when Heck and Jake walked out, then everybody started talking at the same time.

Ubis had a glass partially filled by the time they got to the table, and Jake took it, placing a five-dollar bill in the excited moon shiner's hand.

"The sheriff just left," Heck told Jake. "If he saw your car headin' this way, he'll come back."

"And what makes you think I'm interested in the whereabouts of your sheriff?" Jake calmly took a sip of the whiskey.

Heck hesitated, thinking he might be placing himself in serious danger if the outlaw really was Raymond Hamilton. Realizing he had said too much to back off now, he went on. "Because he thinks you're Bonnie and Clyde's driver. The police got a good look at your car today. He's searching for it, and you." He stopped, quickly adding, "Of course, nobody here is mad at Bonnie Parker and Clyde Barrow, or the Hamilton brothers either."

Jake's smile vanished and, for a moment, Heck feared he was about to get shot. "Well, if I see them, I'll pass on the message," Jake said. "In the meantime, do you think we could go join the party? I've been sitting on the ground out back listening to your fine music. I'd like a better seat. And to dance with one or two of those pretty ladies in there."

"Then your car's not parked on the road out front?"

"You want me to park where it'll get dusty?"

Heck glanced through the back door. "But your friends. . . "

"My friends are in there, I hope," he said, nodding toward the front room. "If I have any more close-by, they can take care of themselves." He pushed back his coat to show the butt of his pistol. "And so can I."

Heck threw a glance at Ubis who quickly turned away, pretending he hadn't heard what Jake said.

"Thanks for allowing me to join your party," Jake said. "Good people are hard to find. I believe things will be okay from now on if I don't get crossways with that big-busted gal that's lookin' for a fight."

Heck was relieved to know there was no longer reason to be afraid of the mysterious Jake, but he still realized that a shoot-out between Jake and the sheriff would get some innocent folks killed, and end his musicals forever.

Heck sighed. *Does every poor man with a plan have this much trouble making it work?*

# Chapter XIII

To everybody's surprise, Jake danced first with Heck's big-busted neighbor. Willa's face flushed red with excitement and her eyes lit up like a child's as she tried to follow Jake's lead, but her crude manner and simple attire emphasized her awkwardness. She'd never learned to dance, nor ever tried, but Jake didn't seem to notice, and when the dance was over, he thanked her and turned to Thelma as Willa continued to glow.

Thelma, rendered momentarily speechless by his invitation, took Jake's extended hand without as much as a glance at her husband. Heck couldn't believe how gracefully she fell into step with Jake's lead as Mr. Meade played "Over the Waves." The glow in her eyes almost made her look like a real lady.

Early, pretending not to care that his wife was tripping the light fantastic with such a young, handsome stranger, turned his attention back to the twenty-dollar bill Jake dropped in the hat. Thelma was giggling like a schoolgirl when they returned to her chair at the end of the number. Heck wondered what Jake's next move would be.

After bowing to Thelma, Jake turned to Marna, who timidly took his hand. After struggling through another waltz with her, he danced with Ruby and Beulah Mae, as if to prove he did not want to offend any of the ladies. His presence definitely added a touch of class to the musical that Heck welcomed. That fact, along with the beautiful old songs and music, caused him to forget what awaited him at the party's end.

By eleven o'clock, Jake was dancing only with Marna who, judging from her expression, seemed the happiest woman in the house, and the most envied. When Mr. Meade and Grandpa Tennel finally stopped playing to rest, Heck decided to take the opportunity to steal away with Ruby for a few minutes.

Leaning his guitar against the wall, he followed Slick and the two city girls outside, hoping Willa was in the back room with her dad and couldn't see them leaving. He didn't look back until reaching the outer fringes of the lantern's rays, and when he did, he saw Jake and Marna come down the steps and head for another part of the yard. His concern for his sister's welfare at that point overshadowed the relief of escaping Willa's notice.

The much cooler outside air didn't kill the effects of the last shot of moonshine he'd downed in the back room. He figured Slick and Beulah Mae could still feel their liquor too, because they had already begun smooching. The sight caused a strong stirring below as he moved over to take Ruby's soft hand and lead her further away from the light. She responded by squeezing his hand which really did arouse him.

He squeezed hers harder and said, "How do you like our country musical so far?"

"It's great." She moved closer, delivering another whiff of her perfume. "I'll bet that's not the only kind of rhythm you can play to make a girl happy."

He pulled her into his arms and kissed her hard on the lips, and she threw her arms around his neck, moaning softly. She was tiny compared to Willa, much softer and smelled a million times better − attributes that made him forget why he had stopped taking his coarse neighbor to the bushes. He had already let himself go too far to stop, or worry about the possibility of falling into another girl's baby trap. Besides, those frequent trips to the bushes with Willa over the last few years had kindled a fire in him that he couldn't put out or ignore, and at that hot moment it burned away reasoning.

He looked up long enough to see if they had an audience. Slick and his girl had disappeared. In the shadows across the yard, however, he saw Marna and Jake kissing. There was no sign of Willa, so he turned his attention back to Ruby.

Moving out further so Jake and Marna couldn't see them, Heck pulled Ruby into his arms again and kissed her longer this time. Both of them breathed hard as his hands slid down her slick, store-bought dress. Ruby groaned louder when he began exploring her most sensitive spots. His anticipation of the next move was making him shake when Ruby's trembling body was suddenly jolted forward by a blow to her backside.

Puzzled, Heck looked past her into the shadows and Ruby whirled in time to catch Willa's next kick in her crotch. She immediately doubled over with a grunt and fell to the ground.

"You city whore," Willa yelled. "Like I said, it ain't over between you and me. Maybe that'll put you out of commission for a while."

Groaning from the pain between her legs, Ruby struggled to straighten up. "You cow!" she screamed. "I'll get you for this."

When Willa stepped forward to deliver another kick, Heck jumped through the shadows to save Ruby and her big shoe slammed into his own crotch. Blinded by the pain, he clutched his groin and fell to his knees.

"Dammit, Willa. You ain't never kicked me there before."

"I'm sorry, honey." Willa threw her arms around him. "I didn't mean it for you. I just wanted to cool off the bag o' bones."

"Well, your aim ain't worth a damn," Heck moaned, shaking his head. "You've never done anything this stupid before. You might've ruined me for life, you know that?"

"I said I'm sorry." She reached for his crotch. "I'll make it well, sweetie."

"Don't touch me."

He hurt so bad he forgot what he and Ruby were about to do. He did turn to inquire about her injury, and heard another thud as she slammed her shoe against Willa's backside.

Willa screamed, whirled and lunged at her. They fell to the ground, rolling and scratching, shouting insults more vulgar than any Heck ever heard. Grimacing from the pain of his own injury, he limped over and began groping in the mass of flailing arms and legs for something to catch hold of to pull them apart.

Another figure loomed over them and Jake reached down and lifted Willa off Ruby. Heck found Ruby's arm and helped her to her feet.

Both girls continued kicking and hurling insults at each other, so loud that some of Heck's other guests came out on the porch to stare and listen.

"Let 'em duke it out, Heck," Slick urged.

Heck told him, "Take Ruby back to the house."

Slick caught hold of Ruby's hand, and when they were halfway across the yard, Jake released Willa to Marna who led her to where their mothers were waiting near the yard lantern. Willa cursed and fumed about not being allowed to put the city whore out of business for good, but she didn't pull away.

"You're something," Jake told Heck. "Few men ever have two young heifers fighting over them like that."

"Willa acts more like a bull than a heifer."

"Heifers sometimes go wild after being branded. And there's no doubt about whose brand she believes she's wearing."

"Problem is Willa's wearin' too many brands. I can tell Ruby has already been branded too, but at least she's got a little class."

Jake lit a cigarette, not speaking for a moment. "I've learned a lot about you and your family tonight. About your oldest brother dying, your dad's accident. How you're supporting the family."

"Marna talks too much. I'm not the only one havin' a hard time these days."

"I used to live on a farm."

"You don't look or act like a country boy to me."

"About everything me and my folks planted on that Oklahoma piece of dirt got eaten up by bugs, burned in a drought, or flooded. Then the bottom fell out of the cotton market. Too much cotton, they said. But shirts and socks didn't get any cheaper." He took another drag off the cigarette. "After the fifth year of nothing, I told my parents I'd had it. Went to Dallas, but couldn't find a good job. I was living under a bridge about to starve when I met some interesting people who knew how to make money fast."

Heck, awaiting an explanation and getting none, thought he knew. He said, "How many men have you killed?" and immediately wished he hadn't. Jake didn't respond and Heck was searching his mind for damage control when Mr. Meade began "Midnight on the Water."

Jake's voice was strained when he finally spoke. "I can't say I admire your delicate way of putting things, but the answer is none."

In view of the damage done already and his concern for Marna, he decided not to drop the issue. "How long do you think it'll be before you do have to shoot somebody, or get shot yourself?"

"In view of your low opinion of me, I hope you don't mind me dancing with your sister again."

"Let me say this first. I don't have a low opinion of you as a person. You're the nicest man I've met in a long, long time. I just don't approve of the way you make money. Now, about my sister. I don't mind at all. But I should warn you. She's awfully eager to find a husband. That makes her a sucker for a man with a smooth line and a handsome face. I don't want you or any other man to take advantage of her and ruin her life."

Jake thought a moment, then replied, "I may have lost faith in some things, but not in women, and how good the best ones are for the likes of us."

"I've got to get back inside." Heck touched his groin with a sharp intake of breath. "Looks like the party's over out here."

They walked into the well-lighted area, and, at the steps, Jake paused, asking Heck, "Do you sing requests?"

"If I know the words."

"My Mother Was a Lady."

His request caused Heck to suspect that Jake might be concerned about something he had lost. He nodded. "I'll do my best."

Heck rejoined Mr. Meade and his granddad that were playing "Red Wing." While singing Jake's request afterwards, he noticed his new friend standing very still next to Marna, closely following the words with a sober expression, his mind somewhere in another time. Everyone else had fallen silent too, listening with solemn faces.

Ending the song, Heck looked at one of the saddest sights he had ever seen: Loony with tears streaming down his face.

"How come you're cryin', Loony?" Slick asked.

"'Cause it was so p-p-purty."

As the ladies gave Loony sympathetic looks, Heck began "Waiting for a Train." Afterwards, he sang "She's My Curly Headed Baby" and "Strawberry Roan." Then Mr. Meade, tired but still feeling the whiskey, played a scratchy "Orange Blossom Special" and then "Great Speckled Bird." Heck sang the words of the song as best he could and everybody who had a partner danced. Heck watched Jake and Marna circle the room in each other's arms, getting closer with each round. When the song ended, they didn't separate.

Heck and his exhausted granddad played and sang "Will the Circle Be Unbroken," and Jake and Marna danced again, continuing into Mr. Meade's playing of "Shannon Waltz." When it ended, Mr. Meade and Grandpa Tennel announced they were too tired to play more and began packing up their instruments.

Heck, watching his sister and her dance partner, realized she might feel as he did about finding a proper mate who would make life better. *Much as I like Jake, Marna could end up on the run from the law, or worse. I can see she's already in love.*

Hoping to break the spell Marna had fallen under, he remained in his chair and sang "He's In the Jailhouse Now," fixing his eyes on Jake as he recited the lyrics. It wasn't the kind of song he usually closed with, but it seemed appropriate. As he sang, however, he wasn't sure who the words applied to most, Jake, for what he was doing to make fast money, or himself, for what he did in town that afternoon.

Regardless, he sensed a turning point in his life at hand, now that another of his musicals had come to a close. Forces beyond his control were pressing in on him more than ever, telling him that things were about to take a desperate turn. When it happened, another phase of his life, like the musical, would end as well.

# Chapter XIV

Their crowing Rhode Island Red rooster awakened Heck the next morning just after sunup. He felt his brother's forehead to see if the fever had gone down any. It had not.

He was still sleepy, having waited up until almost two o'clock for Marna to come in. After everybody left the party house at midnight, she and Jake went for a long walk up Vandergriff Road. Thelma and his dad went to bed as soon as they got home, apparently unconcerned about her welfare. When Heck finally heard their approaching footsteps and Marna's giggles, he slipped into the darkness of his room from which he could hear the murmur of their voices and the sound of them kissing. That's when he found himself wishing the sheriff had come back to the party and taken Jake away.

Grimacing from the tenderness in his groin, he sat on the side of the bed and thought about his own spoiled evening of courting. He walked outside with Ruby after Jake and Marna left, but when he tried to kiss her, she told him her sore places had changed her priorities for the night. To avoid the depressing prospect of her not coming to his next musical, he told her how sorry he was that she got hurt, and how much he counted on getting together with her after the party for some serious courting. The truth was he felt relieved over her not wanting to linger in the bushes, because he was too achy and drained by the day's experiences to perform.

He was glad for another reason too. After the whiskey wore off during the closing numbers, he saw himself about to take the same trap with Ruby as he had with Willa. *Maybe Willa's big foot did me a favor after all. Too bad I didn't get a chance to ask her about what happened in Mr. Slater's cotton field after I left.*

He wished he were already a famous singer and songwriter able to buy that big bottomland farm and find a proper girl to marry that would fill the empty spots in his life and make him a whole man. But wishing it true would never make it happen. Wishing alone never made anything happen.

Were his dad and Willa right about him expecting too much out of life? Even if his goals were high-toned and unreasonable, they would play second fiddle to his family responsibilities. But with no jobs to be had, bringing home the bacon was going to be a real problem.

He wondered how long Jimmy Rogers moved around in high social circles, and how wealthy he became before meeting the girl he wanted to marry. He surely couldn't do all that singing and yodeling unless he was a very happy man.

Heck lay back on his bed with a sigh and considered another immediate problem that the night's events brought to mind. How could he improve his life without allowing that woman-craving monster within to kick reason aside and make him scuttle all his long-range plans? It seemed every time he got to the point where good judgment prevailed, that demon threw up a roadblock and detoured him in the wrong direction. He guessed it was the problem every single young man had to battle during his prime. He had certainly gambled with his chances of ever becoming a winner by cavorting with Willa Sproggs. And just when it looked like he found enough backbone to turn down her favors, that new city girl cranked up his engine. It made him wonder if he would ever be fully in control of his life.

He walked out to the boy's privy behind the party house, and afterwards washed his hands and face in a pan of freshly drawn water on the back porch, all the time trying not to think about Miss Josephine coming to collect the rent. Facing the realities of a poor man's life after a good musical had always been a letdown. He wished he worked in a place singing and playing every day and night for a living.

And what about Cracker? He had to check on him, but couldn't leave before preparing breakfast for Billy and the girls, or before Miss Josephine came by. So he quietly built a fire in the stove, poured flour into a big bowl, and commenced making biscuits. After kneading the mixture, he pulled off portions of dough and patted each one flat on an aluminum pan he slipped into the oven. He put several slices of dry salt bacon and a sliced potato in an iron skillet and moved it over an open eye of the stove. Upon finding no eggs, he went out to a row of apple boxes attached to the side of the chicken house and collected the previous day's output.

The patch of sky above the openings in the trees was blue and clear of clouds, and a gentle breeze whispered through the tops of the tall pines. It was his favorite time of day, because it signaled a new beginning of sorts. He hoped getting a fresh start in his own life could occur in such an easy, natural manner.

Returning to the kitchen, he found the bacon and potatoes over the hot burning pine kindling about to scorch. He turned them over and checked on the biscuits.

After eating, he threw Spot some scraps from the previous day and went out back to feed the chickens. He had just sat down in a straight chair under a big Sycamore to watch the sun rise over the trees across the road when Marna came out of the house headed for the women's privy. She was smiling, and so wrapped up in her happy thoughts she didn't see him.

After returning to the porch to wash her hands and face, she spotted him under the tree and joined him.

"I'm in love, Heck," she said through an uncontrollable smile.

"Who's the lucky guy?'

"Very funny." She rolled her eyes. "Jake Vest, the nicest, best lookin' man I've ever met."

"And the most dangerous for you."

"What do you mean?"

"You heard what the sheriff said."

"What does the sheriff know? Have you seen Bonnie and Clyde around here anywhere, Mr. Smarty Pants?"

"Maybe."

"Really? Where?"

"Down at the bridge yesterday."

"How do you know it was them? Did they come up to you and introduce theirselves?"

"Nope."

"Then you're just like the sheriff, speculatin'."

"I guess I know about them and Jake because I haven't let love hamper my judgment."

"Humph." She placed her hands on her hips and gave him an angry look. "You just don't want me to escape from this ol' place and leave you with more than you can handle. Well, one of these days pretty soon I will. So you'd better get ready for it."

"Sis, don't work yourself into feeling so desperate to marry you hook up with somebody that'll cause you more misery than you'll ever see around here."

"I'd rather die than keep livin' here! Poor as church cockroaches, wearin' homemade sack dresses and wore-out shoes. A crippled, mean daddy that can't support his family, and a lazy, slouchy mother that don't care if I live or die. I'm tired of it, Heck. I'm leavin' the first chance I get."

"I'll tell the sheriff about Jake, and he'll arrest him when he comes back."

"You wouldn't dare, Heck Tennel. You do, and I'll tell Daddy about how you got Doc Samuels to come out here, and about your run-in with them city boys and the police."

She ran into the house, not waiting to see if her threat served its purpose.

"Pipe down, dammit!" Early yelled. "Can't a man find no peace and quiet around here?"

Heck watched his sleepy-eyed siblings appear one by one to wash their faces and use the privy. When Billy came back from the outhouse, he placed his sad eyes on Heck and walked over to him.

Heck tousled his brother's hair and pulled him into his lap. "How's my little brother this fine mornin'?"

"Why don't I feel good like you, Heck?'

"Remember what the doctor said? Bad tonsils. But like I told you last night, Doc Samuels is gonna take care of that real soon."

"Are you sure it won't hurt?"

"Not as much as they do now. And after we get that done, we'll find out what else you need to make you feel chipper the rest of your life."

"Daddy always says we ain't got money to waste on no doctor."

"Don't you fret about him or the money. Like I told you before, just trust me to take care of everything."

"Okay, Heck. But I heard Mama and Daddy fussin' agin last night. I guess they're feelin' bad too. You might need to get Doc Samuels to check them out."

"Don't worry about grown folks' problems, little brother. You'll have plenty of time for that after you grow up."

Billy's expression grew sadder. "I don't think I'll live long enough to be growed up, Heck."

For a moment Heck couldn't speak. Recovering, he pulled Billy up tight against him and said, "Yes you will. I guarantee it. You believe me, don't you?"

Billy nodded, but his expression didn't change. "Sure, Heck. You always keep your word." He put his arms around Heck, hugging him weakly. "You're real good to me. Amy said that if it wasn't for you, her and me'd already be dead, most likely, seein' as how Mama don't seem to care about us no more."

Fighting back tears, Heck patted Billy's shoulder. "But your mama does love you, my little buddy. She's your mama, ain't she?"

Billy didn't answer. Heck carried him to the wash stand, then inside to the kitchen table next to Amy. After dishing up their eggs, bacon and biscuits, he went outside and pulled a shiny metal cooler out of the cold well water to get their milk.

While they ate, Heck took a sponge bath in his room, put on a clean denim shirt, another pair of overalls and his best pair of tennis shoes. When he got to the kitchen, his dad was still in bed, and Marna and Elsie had finished breakfast and gone outside.

Everything was proceeding as usual following a Saturday night musical until Thelma came into the kitchen, decked out in her best dress and the only pair of Sunday shoes she owned. "I'm goin' to Sunday School and church," she announced.

After Heck got over the shock, he tried to talk to her about Marna and Jake, but she refused, telling him there was no use fretting about such a natural turn of events. She ended their short conversation with, "Every girl has to choose her bed sooner or later. It's one of them thangs a mother can't help her with."

After Thelma set out on foot for Homer Percy's church, Heck got his single shot Stevens .22 rifle and walked out back of the house with Spot at his heels in search of squirrels for lunch. He couldn't go so far that he couldn't hear Miss Josephine drive up. Soon as he talked to her, he'd go on through the woods to The Settlement and look in on Cracker.

He hadn't been allowed to count the money in his dad's hat after the party, but believed there was plenty for the rent with some left over.

He had been in the woods less than an hour, during which Spot hadn't hit one trail, when he heard Amy cry out. Turning his head to listen, he couldn't make out what she said, but the excitement in her voice caused him to fear something had happened to Billy. He started back to the house in a run.

Amy ran out to the back porch as soon as he entered the yard, frantically waving him inside.

"What's wrong? Is Billy okay?"

"It's Marna. She's run off!"

Stopping at the steps, he gasped, "Run off? Why? Where's Daddy?"

"On the front porch, chewin' and spittin'. He don't care."

Early sat in his wheelchair, calmly chewing a fresh cut of Brown's Mule with a crying Elsie standing close by. Heck asked him, "What's this about Marna?"

"She's run off with Jake," Elsie blurted out. "He come by and they talked. She wrote a note for me to give to you, then left with him."

"Is that true, Daddy?"

His dad spat a mouthful of tobacco juice toward the yard that left a trail of droppings from his chair to the edge of the porch. "Reckon she did. I ain't seen her."

"Why didn't you stop her?'

His dad shrugged. "Told you, I was asleep. Got woke up by Amy's bellerin'. Reckon she was gone by then."

"Elsie sweetheart, where's the note?"

She handed over a wrinkled piece of brown paper torn off a grocery sack.

*Dear Heck,*

> *I'm going to Oklahoma with Jake. I love him and he promised to marry me when the time is right. So bye. And bye, Elsie, Amy and Billy.*
>
> *Elsie, I hope it won't be long before you can find a husband and get away from that place.*
>
> *Amy, Billy, I hope you get better real soon.*
>
> *Heck, don't try to find me. Jake says he will bring me back sometime, don't worry. He said you're a swell guy and he's thought a lot about what you told him last night.*

*Love,*
*Marna*

Grim-faced, Heck sat down on the edge of the porch and read the penciled note again, more slowly this time.

"No use gettin' your bowels in a uproar over it," Early said. "It was bound to happen sooner or later. Girls do that."

Looking down the road toward Panther Holler Woods, Heck said, as if to himself, "Some Sabbath this has been so far. Mama's gone to see Homer Percy and Marna's run off with a stranger. What else you reckon could happen to knock us back a littler further on our heels? Maybe Miss Josephine'll tell us she likes men now, and one of 'em has convinced her to throw us out so she can burn down all these ol' houses."

Seeing his dad's look of concern, he realized his bad choice of words concerning his stepmother. He quickly added, "Mama's gone to church is what I meant."

"Well, if you ask me," Elsie spoke up, "Marna's better off. There's nothin' to keep her here. Who's a girl gonna get for a husband around these parts, that trashy Slick Haskel maybe, or some other ignorant farm hand? Heck, your friend Cracker would be a better catch than any white boy I know. At least he ain't afraid o' work."

"Shut yore mouth, girl!" Early snapped. "No daughter o' mine is gonna mention a nigger's name in my house in connection with the subject of beddin' down."

"Where's Billy?" Heck asked Amy.

"On his cot," she said. "He's hot."

"Get a pan of water and a towel, please. Did you give him an aspirin like I told you to?"

She nodded.

Regretting his gruff manner, he patted her head and said kindly, "Thanks, Amy. Me and Billy couldn't get along without a fine young lady like you to help us out. Now, bathe his face and arms with cool water while I go out back and kill us some meat for dinner and run a little errand. Tell Billy I'll come in to see him as soon as I get back."

Since he didn't know what time Miss Josephine would arrive, Heck decided to walk on over to Cracker's place. The rich old hypocrite would probably wait and come by after church. What a mockery of religion that would be.

Nearing the mule lot, he heard a car drive up in the backyard. Stopping, he turned to see Miss Josephine's black Cadillac sedan come to a stop near the back porch. Miss Cilla was with her.

There weren't many cars of any kind out in the country, nor in Two Rivers, so that long shiny car of hers always caused people to stop and stare wherever it was spotted. Studying the magnificent automobile now, he realized just how shabby the old house and premises looked, and how lacking his family was in worldly possessions.

He headed back to wheel his dad out in the yard, because Miss Josephine never got out of her car when she came by to discuss business. Miss Cilla did, on occasion, visiting with Thelma and the girls. One time she even accompanied Heck through his evening chores. She was a kind and understanding lady.

As her dad's hatchet lady, Miss Josephine managed all the family's businesses except the bank, and her arrogance clearly indicated she enjoyed controlling other people's lives. She also found great pleasure in the fact that employees of her dad's various enterprises were so afraid of her they would do her every bidding without complaint. She treated them all like peasants, firing whoever challenged her in any way.

Tall and skinny, she had short black hair, a protruding chin, and fierce eyes that accentuated her masculine features. Since Heck became old enough to know about such things, he heard she was a homosexual and, according to gossip, had been in a relationship with the family maid, Connie Blasingame, for many years.

Stopping at the edge of the yard, he leaned his little rifle against a tree and moved over to Miss Cilla's side of the car, tipped his cap, and spoke to both sisters. Miss Cilla greeted him with a smile, but Miss Josephine remained stone-faced as usual. Heck had never seen her smile.

"Is Early home?" Miss Josephine asked curtly.

"Yes'm" he said, leaning down and looking at her. "He's expectin' you. I'll go get him."

"You do that. I have other important business matters to attend to before church. It's God's day, you know."

Heck nodded and said to Miss Cilla, "Would you like to get out? It's cool in the shade."

Miss Cilla smiled. "Is your mother home?"

"No, ma'am, but Elsie and Amy and Billy are."

"Stay in the car, Priscilla," Josephine ordered. "Our business won't take long."

The two sisters watched Heck roll his dad down the back ramp and through the yard to the car. Approaching the Cadillac, Heck saw a third person in the back seat, but the car's rear panel kept him from seeing anything but part of a shoulder. It was small and low in the seat, so he surmised that person was a girl.

"Miss Josephine. Miss Cilla," Early said, removing his hat and nodding.

"Early," Josephine snapped, "I hope you have the money by now."

His dad groped around in the chest pocket of his overalls, coming out with the twenty-dollar bill Jake put in the hat. "Yes'm, but I was hopin'..."

"That we'd changed our minds? No way. We've already put it off too long, Early. You have several healthy children and a wife able to work, so paying your way through this world should be no problem. You know what the Good Book says about God helping those who help themselves."

"Yes ma'am." He handed her the twenty. "I appreciate you lettin' us stay here this long for nothin'."

Heck moved back to Miss Cilla's side of the car as Miss Josephine commenced her routine lecture on the merits of hard work and good money management while counting out his dad's change. Miss Cilla, pretending not to hear, leaned over toward the window and placed her blue eyes on him, apparently eager to visit for a few moments.

"How are you, Heck?"

He smiled down at her pleasant, pretty face that was always pale from lack of sun. Miss Cilla was 35, petite, no more than 5'3" tall. Her blue eyes always seemed to be smiling, her light brown hair wavy and soft-looking.

"I'm fine as a fiddle," Heck said, smiling. For as long as he could remember, Miss Cilla was the only refined rich lady he could talk to without feeling out of place. He went on, "I'd be finer if you'd come to one of our musicals sometime. We're never short of anything except class. A pretty lady like you would sure remedy that problem."

"Why, thank you, Heck," she said with a cautious glance at Josephine. "Maybe I'll surprise you one Saturday night." Half-turning toward the back seat, she told him, "Heck, I'd like for you to meet our niece, Charlotte DeHavilland."

Heck leaned down further to get a good look at the person in the back seat and froze, instantly captivated by the big brown eyes of a beautiful young girl with olive skin and long black hair. She was so small it appeared that the wide back seat had swallowed part of her. She smiled as his heart skipped a beat.

Momentarily flabbergasted, he recovered enough to jerk off his cap and blurt out, "Hi, pretty angel. I'm Teck Hennel – I mean Heck *Tennel*. Pleased to meet you."

Charlotte's smile showed even, white teeth between beautiful lips. "And I'm pleased to meet you, Heck Tennel."

Her voice was as soft and sweet as fiddle music, and she wasn't much longer than his guitar. Whistles blew and bells rang in every fiber of his body. *This is the girl I've been looking for. He wanted to say something appropriate for the momentous occasion but*, his tongue remained twisted when he said, "I-I-I'm real plastered, pleasured, to make your acquaintance, Charlotte. But I already said that, didn't I? Excuse my clumsiness. Are you a movie star or something? I've never seen nobody as pretty as you around these parts before."

He thought he heard Miss Cilla say something and giggle softly, but didn't take his eyes off Charlotte to find out if her remarks were directed at him. A shy smile crossed the pretty girl's face, and she replied, "Thank you, Heck Tennel."

Suddenly conscious of how he must look and sound to a refined young lady, he vowed to stop talking like an illiterate farmhand in the company of such class.

"Charlotte will be living with us from now on," Miss Cilla said. "She's from New Orleans."

Heck glanced at Miss Cilla and turned his eyes back to her niece. "And all this time, I thought angels came from some place other than New Orleans."

Charlotte glanced at Miss Cilla and dropped her gaze, making Heck believe he was coming on too strong and saying all the wrong things. He searched his brain for more appropriate words, but all he could think of was, "Would you like to get out and see my mules?"

*How stupid can you be? A pretty city girl ain't interested in dumb, ugly mules owned by a clodhopper.*

"I'd love to," she replied.

"You would? I mean, great!" He fumbled with the door handle, finally getting it open. Charlotte climbed out, straightening her white dress when she stopped beside him. The prettiest dress he'd ever seen had narrow black ruffles around the neck and short sleeves, and a black strip down the front of it under a row of velvet-covered buttons.

Not bigger than Amy, her waist was so tiny he believed he could reach around it with both hands. He had never seen a girl who excited him so.

Seeming not to have noticed his awkwardness, Charlotte asked softly, "Could I go out and touch one of them?"

He gave her a puzzled look. "Touch one?"

"One of your mules," she said, smiling.

He laughed. "Oh, sure. Come with me." G*et your act together, fool, before she starts believing you're the dumbest person she's ever met.*

"I love animals," she said, walking beside him to the mule lot. "I'm looking forward to having some of my own some day."

Miss Josephine called after them, "Where do you think you're going, Charlotte DeHavilland?"

"To see the mules, Aunt Josephine," she replied over her shoulder.

"Well, don't go too far. We'll be leaving soon. And be careful you don't get your shoes and dress dirty."

Charlotte gave Heck a cautious look as if she might be the one who was embarrassed now, but she seemed to quickly forget her aunt when they stopped at the pole fence near the barn. Maude directed her big eyes at them and flipped her ears forward. When she moved up close, Charlotte very slowly reached between the poles and touched her nose, immediately drawing back.

"It's so soft," she said, giggling. "Will he bite?"

"He's a she. Sweet ol' Maude won't bite nothin' but grass."

She looked around. "Do you have a horse?"

"No. Poor folks mostly have mules for plowin' and pullin' wagons." He wished he hadn't said poor. It was plain enough to see.

"Aunt Priscilla told me about grandfather's horses up the road on the old place. She said I could ride them sometime. I'm so excited."

She looked at the chickens inside a wire fence, and the cow, grazing in a small opening nearby. "I love chickens and cows too. I like everything about a farm."

Heck continued to be amazed by her appreciation for such simple things, suspecting he would wake up any second and find out it was a dream. Was she sincere, or just trying to make him feel good? How could a pretty, classy girl like her carry on so about country life, particularly livestock inside a pole fence behind a rotting old sharecropper house?

Continuing to feast his eyes on her, he said, "If you need any help when you ride Miss Cilla's horses, I'd sure appreciate it if you'd allow me to come up and do the helpin'. Mostly I just ride ol' Maude there to the fields and back, but I've rode, ridden, lots of horses."

"I'd love for you to come up and show me how."

Looking into her eyes up close sent Heck's brain whirling so much it made him dizzy, but he managed to say, "Just let me know when you'll be out to ride, and I'll be ready."

"Thank you. I will." Looking at the other houses, she asked, "Who lives in these homes?"

"Nobody. Sharecroppers used to. They raised cotton on the halves for Blood, uh, your grandfather."

She gave the Cadillac a cautious glance, and turned her eyes back to him. "Aunt Priscilla told me about your father. I'm so sorry about his accident. She told me you're supporting the family now."

Such a serious statement by someone unfamiliar with bad luck impressed him. "I thank you for your kindness. But I guess we ain't, aren't any worse off than most other folks around here."

"Aunt Priscilla also told me about how you play the guitar and sing at your weekly musicals. I've never known anyone who could do that. You must be very talented. May I come sometimes?"

"You'd come?"

"Of course." She smiled. "Why wouldn't I?"

He twisted his cap some more, wishing she wasn't with her aunts and could stay all day. "Like I told Miss Cilla, we've never had a fine lady like her, or you, to come. You do, and I'll sing a special song for you if there's one you like and I know the words."

"Do you know 'My Little Quadroon'? That's very popular in Louisiana."

"I only know part of it. But if you'll promise to come out next Saturday night, I'll learn the rest. How's that?"

"Sounds great. I'll try." Turning to look out into the trees, she told him, "It's so beautiful and peaceful out here. Someday I'm going to live in the country."

He was puzzled by a hint of sadness in her voice. He said, "Sometimes it's not so peaceful around here, I'm afraid. But I still like the country. I just don't like it the way it is here. That's why I've got this plan, you see. Some day I'm gonna own me a section of good land, a sturdy house and everything that goes with it, including a fine lady for a wife."

He couldn't tell if the look she gave him indicated admiration or pity. It caused him to become more tense as he wondered how, or if, she would respond to what he said.

"Aunt Priscilla said on the way out that you're an achiever, one who'll go far."

"She did?"

As Charlotte turned to look at the trees again, it suddenly occurred to him that he should mention just how he felt about her in case he never got another chance. With the kind of luck he'd been having lately, it wouldn't surprise him if something happened to keep from ever seeing her again. Miss Josephine might forbid Miss Cilla's bringing her out to his musical, or out to the old Vandergriff place even. He also feared never again feeling so confident in her presence. Steeling himself for rejection, he took the plunge. "You're the most beautiful and considerate girl I've ever met, Charlotte DeHavilland. I've just got to see you again real soon."

"Why, thank you, Heck. Maybe . . ."

"Oh, there can't be no maybes. I've just got to. I know you're a lady, and I respect you for that, but a man with any sense at all can't afford to let the gold horse on the merry-go-round swing by without at least tryin' to grab the reins."

"My goodness. You don't even give a girl time to catch her breath between compliments, do you?"

"You ain't, aren't mad?"

"After being flattered so? How could I be?"

She glanced at Josephine watching them from the front seat of her Cadillac. Miss Cilla was standing near the porch talking to Elsie, apparently unworried about their niece.

When Charlotte turned her eyes back to his, he thought he saw a sparkle in them that wasn't there before. "Aunt Priscilla has already promised to bring me out to the old home place this afternoon. We're going to live out here all next week so I can do some of the things I've always wanted to do on a farm. Maybe you can come by one day after work."

He thought his heart would explode with joy. "I'll do it," he said, bracing himself for another bold move. "Would I be rushing things too much if I came by tonight?"

"Well, I don't know," she said, glancing at her aunts. "But since Aunt Josephine won't be there, I'm sure it'll be all right with Aunt Priscilla."

He struck his left hand with his cap. "I do believe I'm finally beginning to live, by gollies. If I fell dead right now, I'd die a happy man."

"Hey, Heck," a voice called out from the road.

Heck cringed upon hearing the familiar sound, and for a moment hoped his ears were playing tricks. But no, unfortunately, his hearing hadn't failed him. Slick stood on top of the bank slouched down as if drunk, shirtless and barefoot.

"Oh, no," Heck whispered to Charlotte. "Looks like my chance of a lifetime just got shot deader'n last year's Johnson grass."

# Chapter XV

Fighting to control his temper in the presence of a lady, Heck shook his head in disgust as Slick moved into the yard and sat down under the big sycamore, not seeming to notice, or care, that he had company. Dreading what he might do next, Heck turned his back toward him in hopes he would leave.

Charlotte gave Slick a questioning look, but didn't comment on his unexpected appearance as Heck tried desperately to think of a nice way to explain away his crude neighbor.

"Hey, Heck," Slick said loudly. "Who's your fancy girlfriend?"

Everybody in the yard, including Miss Josephine, turned to look, but nobody spoke.

"Charlotte, please ignore him," Heck said. "If there's a God in Heaven, He'll make him leave."

"Who *is* that?" She gave Slick an amused look.

"One of my neighbors from up the road. He's what you might call, uh, a little rough around the edges. I'm sorry you have to see and listen to him."

"Hey, Heck," Slick persisted. "I've got somebody out here to see you." The remark was accompanied by a girl's giggle down in the road.

Heck closed his eyes and shook his head. "Oh, no. Anytime but now." Looking out at his unwanted neighbor again, he said, "Go away, Slick. I've got company. I'll drop by your place later." He wanted to use stronger language but couldn't under the circumstances.

"Ruby won't wait," Slick said. "She come out to party if you're up to it this mornin'. Says she ain't sore no more."

Angered to the breaking point, Heck knew he must remain calm and act in a respectable manner or lose whatever gain he may have made with the beautiful girl with him. How to keep the situation from getting worse? He couldn't afford to go out and punch a visitor in the nose in front of company. What a nightmare.

"It's a pity a man can't choose his neighbors." Heck smiled nervously at Charlotte. "Please forget what he said and try to ignore him. He still might go away."

"Question is, will *she* go away?" she teased.

"Oh, Ruby's not my girlfriend," He felt himself blushing. "She's a friend of Slick's girlfriend."

"Charlotte, get in the car this instant," Josephine shouted. "I've never heard such talk, and on the Sabbath. Shame on you, Heck Tennel, for causing my niece to witness such a vulgar display."

Heck gave Charlotte a worried look. "I'm really sorry about this. I hope you don't let it change your mind about me coming to see you."

"I won't mind if Ruby doesn't."

He was pleased to see she had taken the matter so lightly. Or had she? He'd hardly had time to figure out the true meaning behind some of the things the crude Willa told him from time to time. And now, having met a girl with culture and class, he was doubly confused.

Seething with anger over Slick's bad timing, Heck walked Charlotte to the car where he opened the door for her and Miss Cilla. He told Charlotte, "It's been a pleasure and an honor. I hope I'll see you again real soon."

He watched Miss Josephine turn the big Cadillac around and head toward the cut. *If Charlotte doesn't look back at me before they disappear behind the bank, all is lost. But if she turns and looks, I still have a chance of getting to know her better.*

He kept his eyes fixed on her pretty head all the way to the cut, but she didn't look back. He shook his head in disgust, promising himself to punch Slick in the nose as soon as the car was out of sight. Then, as the Cadillac turned from the cut onto Vandergriff Road, Charlotte turned, and for a brief moment, her eyes met his.

Forgetting his anger, he threw his cap to the ground and danced a happy jig around it. "She looked back. She looked back!"

"Have you gone loco?" his dad asked gruffly. "Well, before you go completely off your rocker, let me tell you what a fix we're in now."

Heck picked up his cap, still smiling. "There's nothin' you can say that'll make me feel bad now. Fire away."

"That horse-faced Josephine Vandergriff has got the gall. I've a damn good notion to burn all these ol' houses to the ground after what she said to me."

Heck looked out at Slick leaning against the sycamore just as his vulgar friend took another swallow from a bottle of whiskey. "What did she do now?"

"She said we got to start payin' rent on the party house too. Twenty dollars a month. Looks like Emmet Sloan didn't waste no time puttin' a bee in her bonnet about last night."

"Twenty dollars! That's more than we take in out there in six months."

"I know. And when I told her I didn't have the money to pay in advance, she said she'd lock it up if she didn't have the cash by noon next Saturday. And even if we pay, she said Ubis can't sell whiskey in there no more."

Heck shook his head. *First Slick and now bad news about the party house.* "So, we'll clean up one of the other houses."

"She'd still charge us rent."

"But why? They never use them old houses anymore."

"The ugly old witch said it's because we're usin' it for a business. Said it's only fittin'."

Heck struck his cap against his leg in disgust. "We need that ol' house more'n ever now, since there's no farm work."

Elsie's face lit up. "That must be why Mama decided to go to work."

"Your mama ain't never worked a day in her life," Early said. "What can she do?"

"She knows how to clean up Brother Percy's church, and the parsonage. She told me that's why she went to church this mornin', to check on the job."

*How could she have known? The preacher must've told her about the job on one of his visits.* Heck watched his dad's reaction, but couldn't tell if he believed her or not. His dad asked Elsie, "How much did your mama say the job would pay?"

"She said if it didn't pay but five cents, it would be more than she's worth around here. What did she mean by that, Daddy?"

Early spat a stream of tobacco juice to the side, keeping a suspicious eye on Elsie. "Has the preacher been out here anytime lately when I was gone?"

"No sir, not that I know of. But Amy said Mama usually sends her and Billy up the road to visit the Sproggses about dinner time some Saturdays so she can take a nap while we're in town. She don't know if anybody's ever come by durin' them times."

Early glanced at Heck, who quickly looked away, and went on as if to himself. "I never did trust preachers, 'specially with women that's got a weakness like your mama's."

"What weakness is that, Daddy?" Elsie asked.

"Elsie, sugar," Heck said, "go see if Billy and Amy need anything. Hurry now."

Early slumped down in his chair with a long sigh and said, "Thelma's gone, and she won't be back. I knowed somethin' was in the wind last night when she wouldn't let me prove my manhood was back. But even if she had've let me try, I doubt I could've done any good because she was in such a huff about somethin'."

Heck sensed his dad was right about Thelma leaving. But there was nothing he could say or do that would change anything. He wasn't angry, just numb.

"If I could walk, I'd get my twelve-gauge and kill 'em both," Early said, looking down at his leg stubs.

Heck looked out at Slick who sat calmly watching them and smiling as he listened. Slick thought everything was funny, even misery, if it was somebody else's.

Heck pushed his dad back in the house, then out to the front porch, without speaking to him. He promptly left to check on Billy. He found both him and Amy crying.

"Heck, you think Mama's really gone like Daddy said?" Amy asked.

"Why not? Everything else sure was shot to hell around here today." Immediately regretting his outburst, Heck knelt and pulled Amy into his arms. "She's not gone, honey. Daddy was just upset over his own problems. He didn't mean all that stuff. Mama'll be back."

After she and Billy stopped crying, Heck left to join Slick and Beulah Mae under the sycamore out back. By then, his anger toward his neighbor had been blunted a bit by the developments pertaining to his stepmother.

He found Beulah Mae lying on her back with her head in Slick's lap. Slick was holding a jar above her face, dripping moonshine into her mouth.

"Ain't this the life?" Slick said to Heck. He put the lid back on the jar. "Ready to get laid now, sodbuster?"

"Are you crazy? Why didn't you leave when you saw I had company?"

"Fancy city girls ain't for the likes of us, neighbor." Slick smiled. "Besides, them kind won't give a man a tumble. Ruby's the girl you need, now that Willa don't turn you on no more."

"Has it ever occurred to you there might be something more important in the world than gettin' laid? Damn." Heck heard a rustling in the bushes nearby and turned to see Ruby coming toward them adjusting her dress. Her eyes were as bold as they were at the musical.

"Loosen up, ol' buddy," Slick said, "You can start by findin' out if Willa's foot made a gelding out of you." He laughed. "You're gonna have to start hobblin' that wild heifer at your parties, otherwise you're gonna end up havin' a problem satisfyin' any woman. You'll be just like your ol' man."

"You've got big ears and a big mouth to match. If Miss Cilla don't let me see her niece again because of you, I'm gonna kick your butt."

Slick laughed. "You sure won't find no splinters in it if you do. Don't you know that every tumble you pass up while you're a young stud will end up bein' a splinter in your ass when you're old?"

Ruby stopped in front of Heck. Smiling sweetly, she said, "Hi. Feelin' okay today?"

He couldn't help noticing she'd left her blouse open at the top, and how sweet she smelled. "I'm not sure. How about you?"

"A little sore is all."

"Because of Willa's foot, or because I didn't give you what you was expectin'?"

"A little of both," she said, shooting him a seductive look. "Maybe we won't have any interruptions today."

Sensing his reluctance, Slick said, "Did talking to that city girl cripple your brain? Stop dreamin' and let Ruby fix up what's ailin' you."

Heck thought about what Doc Samuels said was ailing Billy. "A few thousand dollars would fix me up better," he said, as if to himself.

"Then go rob ol' Blood Money's bank," Slick said with a laugh. "Bankers and bank robbers are the only ones with money these days."

"Sounds like you talked to Jake last night."

"Sure, I talked to Jake," Slick said, stroking Beulah Mae's hair. "But not about what he does for a livin'. Didn't have to. Maybe he could give you some pointers on how to make lots of money. Then you can go to Dallas and buy yourself a honky-tonk and support that family of yours in high style and have yourself lots of women."

Slick handed the jar to Heck who offered it first to Ruby for a big swallow before he took two and gave it back to his neighbor who poured some of its contents in the lid and resumed the slow drip into Beulah Mae's mouth.

The whiskey warmed Heck's insides but it didn't take his mind off Billy, nor Marna running off, nor meeting the beautiful Charlotte. The lines of thought didn't fit well together and the more he tried to figure out a way to keep his personal problems from coming between him and Charlotte, the more frustrated he became. He wished Slick and the girls would leave and take the whiskey with them before he let it get in the way of good judgment.

Slick leaned down and kissed Beulah Mae on her lips, and placed one hand on her breast. When she began to squirm and moan, Ruby reached over and squeezed Heck's hand. Her clear message sent vibrations through him, arousing that monster within which he hoped to keep under control. *Am I gonna keep letting that monster pull me where my better judgment tells me not to go?*

Placing her arms around him, Ruby said, "I'll find out now if you're made of stone, Heck Tennel."

*What's a man supposed to do in a situation like this, tuck tail and run or do what a man's built to do?* After she tiptoed and kissed him on the lips, he found himself at last night's same point of no return before Willa kicked him.

"Did that take your mind off that cute little rich girl?" Ruby purred.

Heck's monster within wouldn't let him forget her if he wanted to. Taking her hand, he led her down the cut into Vandergriff Road and when out of hearing distance of the others, told her, "There's a place down the road a piece where we'll have privacy."

"Lead on, lover boy."

Fifty yards or so down the road, Heck led her back up the embankment into a stand of tall pines where the ground was covered with a thick blanket of pine needles. They were scarcely off the road when Ruby stopped, threw her arms around him and pushed her bosom hard against his chest. Feeling his passions rising to new heights, he pulled up her chin and kissed her and slid his right hand down over and around her hips to the spot in front where her legs met. She immediately began to groan like she was in pain, and when he laid her down on the pine needles she raised her knees and held out her arms. "Take me, Heck," she said. "Take me now."

The sight destroyed every chance he had left of changing his mind, but as he pulled down his overalls with the intentions of obliging her, Beulah Mae screamed from the other side of the pine grove. Hesitating, he turned in that direction and saw an irate Slick Haskel in a small clearing with his pants down shaking his fist.

"I oughta kill you, Loony!" Slick shouted. "What the hell do you mean, sneakin' around in here like that?"

Heck peered under limbs to find out if Loony was headed their way before proceeding with the urgent matter at hand, but all he saw were some shaking bushes between him and Slick.

"What's wrong, honey?" Ruby asked. "What are you waiting for?"

Heck was still looking through the woods with his overalls pulled down to his knees when he answered her. "Slick and Beulah Mae have a visitor," he said. "And I think he's headed this way."

"So let him come, honey. Don't leave me like this."

Heck hesitated, having never done it before an audience. Slick let out a string of cuss words on the other side of the pines and yelled, "Vamoose, you crazy ol' bastard. You're messin' up my girl's concentration. Git!"

Ruby rose up, grabbed Heck's hand and tried to pull him down. "Come on, honey."

"Listen," he whispered, pulling his hand free and turning to look in the opposite direction where he heard something else moving through the bushes.

"Now what?" Ruby fussed.

"I hear somebody comin' from over here."

Willa crashed through the underbrush no more than twenty feet from them, causing Ruby's priorities to suddenly change. Jumping up, she scrambled to get her clothes back in order while keeping her eyes glued on Willa. "You," she said. "Don't you ever go home to your cow stall?"

Willa charged Ruby. "You city whore," she screamed. "I'll really fix your saddle this time to where no man can't ride in it no more!"

Forgetting that his overalls were down around his feet, Heck lunged forward to catch Willa and fell. He tried calling out a warning to Ruby, but because the wind was knocked out of him, all he could do was move his mouth and watch.

Ruby tried to defend her half-clothed body, but Willa slapped her down and started kicking her, first between the legs, then in the side. Ruby flipped over in an effort to get up, screaming and cursing. Heck had never heard any girl beside Willa carry on so. He regained his breath and grabbed Willa's ankle, tripping her.

The injured Ruby sprang to her feet and lunged at the fallen Willa, but before she could kick her, Willa grabbed hold of her dress and jerked her back down on top of her. They were rolling and scratching like wildcats by the time Heck pulled them apart. In the process, he got a few scratches himself, and when he finally managed to push them out to arm's length, his overalls fell down again. When he released the girls to pull them back up, they started Round 2.

Jerking up his overalls and hooking one strap, he finally separated them again. By that time, he was so disgusted and spent that the monster within had died.

"You dumb hick," Ruby screamed at Willa.

"City clap bag," Willa shot back. "Bone wagon."

"Shut up, both of you," Heck shouted. "No use broadcastin' to the whole county."

"I thought everybody in the damn county was here already," Ruby snapped at him, crimson faced. She jerked free, tugging at her panties as she headed for the road at a fast walk. "I've had it. I'm leaving this crazy place forever. Come on, Beulah Mae."

Slick and his girlfriend joined Ruby. Neither spoke, but the glow on their faces told Heck they were both completely satisfied with the results of their trip to the pine thicket. When down in the road, Slick placed an arm around each girl and pulled them up close, reverting to his usual self, laughing and talking as they walked out of sight.

"You're mine, honey." Willa moved up behind Heck, placing her arms around him. "And because I interrupted your pleasure, I'm gonna do what's right. I'm gonna give you relief."

"Willa, how many times do I have to tell you? I don't belong to you." He pushed her away.

Undaunted, she reached over and unhooked his overalls. "You shoulda thought about that before you stuck your claim in me, Heck Tennel."

"That's the main problem, Willa. You've let too many other guys stake claims."

"Well, lover boy, you was the one who first set my fires to burnin'. But then you started havin' them big ideas on what you're gonna do with your life, you let me suffer. What did you expect? I love you, but I ain't got what it takes to fight off my woman's cravin'."

"Well, since I'm not gonna marry you, it's best we stop messin' around."

"But don't you miss messin' with me, honey?" She stepped closer, placing her hand on his crotch to squeeze him.

"Stop it, Willa." He stepped back, re-hooking his overalls. "You're worse than an octopus."

"And you're crazier about your nigger friend Cracker than you are about me, Mr. High-and-Mighty. Well, let me tell you something. If you turn me down this time after all them other good times you've had with me over the years, you'll be sorry."

"What are you drivin' at, Willa?" He never took her threats lightly.

"Ha. Wouldn't you like to know?"

He gave her a suspicious look. "Willa, did anything happen between you and Cracker after I left y'all yesterday?"

"You'll find out soon enough if you pass up this chance to make up."

He shook his finger at her. "Don't do something crazy, Willa. You did enough last night and here today to get even with me for not hittin' the hay with you these last few months."

Loony suddenly appeared behind Willa, grinning sheepishly. Turning at the sound, Willa said, "What's that crazy ol' galoot doin' here?"

Heck nodded a greeting at Loony. "You're lucky Slick didn't beat you up. It's risky business, interruptin' a man's romp in the pine needles."

Loony's eyes focused on Willa's bosom. "P-p-people's behinds are prettier'n horses' b-b-behinds."

Willa's eyes flashed. "Get outta here, Loony. Leave us normal folks alone."

Heck told him, "One of these days, Loony, you're gonna walk up on an armed man in a clinch and he'll shoot you."

"The sooner the better, if you ask me," Willa snapped. "Always snoopin' around, grinnin' like a hyena. Don't think I'm not wise to you hangin' out in the edge of the trees at our place watchin' me walk to the privy, pervert. Too bad you're so crazy you can't find yourself a wife so you wouldn't have to make out with your mare. Why, I bet you ain't bedded a woman in your whole miserable life."

Loony's face flushed red as he bared gapped, uneven teeth as he smiled.

"Loony," Heck said, "were you lookin' for me, or did you just come down here lookin' for new butts?"

Loony's smile disappeared. "S-s-storm's a'comin'."

Heck looked up through the trees. "Looks fair to me."

Loony shook his shaggy head. "It ain't gonna be one of God's s-s-storms. It's a d-d-devil s-s-storm."

"Humph," Willa said. "Talkin' in riddles again, the blabberin' ol' mare jumper. Run him off, Heck, so we can get on with our business."

Heck saw the fright on his old friend's face. "What's the devil cookin' up this time, Loony?"

"D-d-don't rightly know, 'cept it's gonna bring b-b-bad happenin's to somebody. B-b-but it's a'comin' fer sure, 'cause I heerd a f-f-fox holler three times yistidy." His scared eyes scanned the trees around them. Lowering his voice, he added, "A-a–and afore daylight this mornin', a panther screamed in P-P-Panther Holler W-W-Woods."

Willa waved a hand at him. "And pretty soon you'll be tellin' us you saw the ol' miller's ghost sittin' on your front steps eatin' possum. Run him off, Heck."

"Loony," Heck said, "nobody's heard the panthers so far this year that I know of." He looked at Willa. "Go on to the house and visit with Elsie and Amy. I'll be along in a little while."

"Guess I ain't got no choice now," she said, giving him a warning glance. "But you better not forget what I told you."

Heck and Loony sat down on a fallen tree trunk and Willa walked away through the woods toward the house. Heck didn't know if the old bachelor was predicting bad happenings because he'd seen the preacher with his mother or for some other reason, but he learned early on that the old man possessed an uncanny ability to foresee tragedy. For that reason, he felt compelled to find out the real meaning of his latest warning. Like other folks in the area, he had always taken a serious view of unusual happenings in the immediate natural world around them. A panther's scream was always seen with a sense of foreboding.

"Are you sure you heard a panther?" Heck asked. "A hawk's scream sounds mighty like a panther."

"W-w-weren't no dadburn h-h-hawk, nosiree. 'Twas a p-p-panther, pure and simple. They be g-g-gettin' awful restless agin."

Heck thought for a moment about recent happenings that might develop into something more tragic. *Did Loony sense something in Willa's threat or foresee tragedy in Charlotte's visit to the old Vandergriff place? But how could he know she planned to visit the place? Maybe he'd seen a vision about another bad turn in how he went about making enough money for Billy's doctor bills. Poor Billy.*

Heck studied the old bachelor's face and wondered if he was placing too much faith in what he'd said. *Loony seldom has good news.*

In an attempt to break the solemn mood that had settled over them, Heck said, "Maybe the old miller's ghost just wants you to fix him a mess of coon and collards."

Loony gave him a horrified look, jumped up and ran into the bushes. Staring at the spot where he disappeared, Heck mumbled, "Well, if that don't beat a cat a'hoppin'."

He thought some more about the old man's warnings and his hasty departure. Unable to come up with any plausible explanations, he stretched out on the pine needles and turned his mind to more pleasant things, like seeing Charlotte again. He had to think of some way to undo the damage done by the unexpected arrival of Slick and Ruby. If, after that, she was still willing to let him visit, he would have to conduct himself in a way that would cause her to feel as strongly about him as he did about her. Put his best foot forward and watch his Ps and Qs, as he once heard someone say – whatever that meant. Practice good manners, use good grammar. Not swear, or refer to her granddad as "Blood Money." *When I go calling the first time, I'll wear the white shirt Uncle Tim gave me Christmas before last, and the pair of overalls that ain't been patched yet.*

He believed he could improve his behavior and clean up his language enough to appear at least halfway respectable. Other than that, he didn't have anything to offer a classy girl like Charlotte DeHavilland. So what possible reason could she ever have for developing strong feelings for the likes of him?

If he found an answer to the question, he'd have to forget Loony's "Devil storm" warning, the storms raging within and all the other unpleasantness in his life. That should clear his mind enough to concentrate on winning over the girl who had existed only in his imagination until that morning.

*In spite of the trainload of bad stuff dumped on me so far today, I feel encouraged enough to believe that my life is beginning to make sense for the first time since Ross died and the responsibility for my family fell on me.*

Indeed, Charlotte DeHavilland had cast a ray of hope on the shadowy path of the downtrodden. She had pushed all his problems to the back of his mind and allowed him to think only of what surely would be his best night ever.

# Chapter XVI

By mid-afternoon Billy's fever dropped two degrees to one hundred, and Heck was able to coax his little brother into eating a scrambled egg and a warmed-over biscuit. He and Amy already missed their mother, and all of them missed Marna. The prospect of their never returning saddened Heck.

After feeding Billy, Heck rode Maude to Cracker's house with Willa's warning still ringing in his ears. He had seen no reason to rush over there after Slick and the girls left, because if anything bad had happened between Willa and his black friend, she would've jumped at the chance to tell him about it when she found him with Ruby in the pine thicket.

Underestimating Willa was risky business. Ever since leaving her and Cracker the day before, he felt to blame if anything had happened to his friend.

He found no one at Cracker's house, so went back home, doing chores until late afternoon when Miss Cilla's blue DeSoto sedan drove by en-route to the old Vandergriff house. Bursting with excitement, he went into the kitchen to help Elsie prepare a quick supper of beans and squash they canned the previous summer, and a pan of hot water corn bread. Since he didn't kill a squirrel that morning, they fried several slices of salt bacon. To make sure his dad didn't deprive Billy and Amy of their rations of whole milk, he drew the cooler out of the well and dipped out two glassfuls with a cup and took them to the kitchen table.

After eating and hearing Elsie promise to milk and gather the eggs, he sponged off in a foot tub in his room, eager to get up to the old Vandergriff house. He splashed rose water tonic in his hair, combed it down tight to his head and put on that new white starch-stiff shirt. He only had three pairs of overalls all well worn, but he put on the pair that hadn't been patched. He found some white socks with no holes above the shoe line and put them on with his best pair of tennis shoes.

Not wanting to explain his destination and receive his dad's inevitable ridicule, he told Billy he'd be back in a couple of hours and crawled out their window. On the road, the setting sun hit him square in the face, making him wonder if that was a signal from some higher power that a new light had entered his life at such a critical time. He hoped so.

The farm foreman's dogs set up a howl in the gathering darkness as Heck walked into the front yard of the old home a quarter mile away. The largest house in the area had screened windows and doors, inside running water and bathrooms. Aladdin lamps producing light as bright as electric bulbs had always given the place a city look at night. A wide front porch spanned the entire width of the house, and its freshly painted balustrade stood out in the fading light.

Curt Truesdale, Blood Money's unfriendly foreman who most likely acquired his low opinion of all Tennels from Miss Josephine and her dad, appeared at the door. He asked Heck in, but his somber expression wasn't welcoming. In the parlor, the foreman's pudgy wife promptly closed her magazine and went down the hall to announce his arrival to Miss Cilla and Charlotte. She returned presently to tell him "the ladies" would be in shortly, but didn't ask him to sit down.

Ignored by the Truesdales, Heck waited in silence by the door, turning his cap in his hands and hoping he wouldn't forget his manners when needed. After what seemed like half an hour, he worried that he had come at a bad time, or that Charlotte had changed her mind about seeing him again. Maybe Slick and Willa were right – girls like Charlotte weren't for the likes of him.

He had become very warm in his new white shirt by the time he heard footsteps coming down the hall. With pulse pounding, he fixed his eyes on the hallway door.

Miss Cilla appeared first, followed promptly by her niece. When Charlotte's eyes met his, he smiled and nodded, almost twisting his cap in two. Seeing her again was even more exciting than the first time.

"Miss Cilla, Charlotte," he said, smiling nervously. "I hope my comin' didn't put you to no trouble."

"Not at all, Heck," Miss Cilla replied. "We were about to come up front anyway." Miss Cilla was a woman transformed when not under the iron heel of her grouchy, domineering sister.

He had heard Miss Cilla's response as if from afar, because he had his eyes fixed on Charlotte whose beauty took his breath away. She was wearing a light blue dress with a white starched collar, and right away he noticed how the garment was tailored to best reveal just how mature she really was. That, and the way she had her hair pulled up into a bun on the back of her head, made her look like a grown woman.

She extended her hand in greeting, and he took it, minding not to squeeze or shake it like he would a man's. She said, "Would you like to sit in the swing on the porch?"

"If it's all right with Miss Cilla," he said cautiously.

Miss Cilla nodded her approval and he followed Charlotte out on the front porch, lighted only by the lamp's rays coming through the front window. A gentle breeze stirred the warm, humid air. *Good,* he thought. *Talcum powder won't keep a man from smelling bad for long when he's sweating like a field hand.*

Sitting down in the swing, Charlotte calmly smoothed her dress over her lap and pulled it down neatly over her knees. He sat down at the other end of the swing, frantically wondering what a city boy might say under the circumstances. He became aware of the sound of crickets in the darkness around the house, and the croaking of frogs on the stock pond out back. These usually comforting sounds didn't relieve the tension mounting in him. Why couldn't he think of something to say?

He felt her eyes on him as she waited for him to speak, so he looked out at the stars beyond the eaves of the roof and said, "It's a pretty night."

"Beautiful," she said. "And it's much cooler out here."

*Yes, but it's warming up fast.* Clearing his throat to make sure his voice didn't tremble, he told her, "This is a fine old place. I plan to have a place like this someday." To help relieve the tension, he pushed gently against the porch floor to start the swing.

"Grandfather's old place is just like I've always imagined it," she said.

"You haven't been here before?"

"No. We seldom visited Two Rivers, and when we did, we always went to grandfather's house in town." She looked up at the stars. "If I were him, I would've never left the country."

"Living in the country is okay if you ain't, aren't dirt poor like we are." *Stupid! Why emphasize something you're so ashamed of? She's not blind. She already knows that.* He tried to rectify his mistake by saying, "But it won't be like this much longer for my family, because I plan on making things better real soon."

She looked at him in the near-darkness, and he again racked his brain for something clever to say. He could see her features clearly because she was facing the light from the window. Her countenance reminded him of a pretty, fragile flower glowing with contentment and self-confidence – traits he wished he had, so he could stop fidgeting and communicate some brilliant thought. Concentrating on what to say and how to say it was complicated by her distracting beauty and his fear of making a fool of himself.

Finally, she said, "I've heard my grandfather say he's got no respect for a man without a plan."

*Darn. Wish she hadn't mentioned Blood Money. It messes up my concentration.*

"What kind of work do you do, Heck?"

"Farm work when I can get it. There's none in the fields right now, town either. But I don't plan to do farm work much longer."

He gave the swing another little push, because movement of any kind at that point helped to relieve his nervousness as he sat so near to the most delicate creature he'd ever known. The sweet fragrance of her perfume drifted over to him, making it even harder to keep a clear head.

"Have you had a good visit so far?" he asked.

"Yes, thank you. And I'm looking forward to staying out here the entire week. I've already fed the chickens and hogs. It was very exciting."

"I never knew a girl as pretty and refined as you that cared anything about farm chores." *Who am I trying to kid? I've never known a girl as pretty and refined as you, period.*

He immediately tried to overcome his blunder. "I mean, I've always associated nice ladies with good music, art and social teas, that sort of thing."

He was relieved when she smiled. "You're very kind," she said. "Let's see now. So far, I've found out that you're ambitious, you play and sing, and you're kind. And you live in the country. That means you're very different from all the other boys I've known up to now."

Her statement lessened the tension and gave his self-confidence a boost, but didn't prevent him from wondering about how many boys she had known. *And how well.*

"I don't reckon I've ever heard such nice things said to me before. What I hear mostly is, 'Hurry up, Heck', and 'How come you've got so many high fallutin' ideas, Mr. Know-it-all?'"

She laughed softly, raising her right eyebrow and cutely cocking her head to the side as she fixed her brown eyes on him. It made him want to grab her, pull her up tight against him and kiss her. Instead, he said, "I know I'm not handsome like the boys you've known in the city, and I can't dress as good as them either. I hope you don't hold that against me.'

"Ruby didn't seem to mind. Why should I?" She gave him a teasing look.

"That's something else I was hopin' you wouldn't hold against me," he said with a grimace.

"No need to apologize about that or anything." She touched his hand. "Relax. You have qualities that most girls admire."

"Really? You sure know how to make a fella feel as rich as ol' Blood . . . as the Rockefellers."

"Who knows? Maybe you'll be as rich as a Rockefeller some day. I know you'll be successful, but that doesn't require money."

She said things that gave him comfort, as if she might know what he wanted to hear, but the last part of what she said puzzled him. "How else could a poor man be successful?"

"I believe how people feel about themselves determines if they're successful. It's all in a person's state of mine."

That was pretty deep stuff to be coming from such a young, pretty girl, and it flustered him a bit. She was the first girl he had ever known that expressed herself in such a serious manner. *Beauty and brains. How lucky can a guy be?*

He said, "Then you must be a very happy person, because I can tell you're very comfortable with yourself. And I'm sure you've got everything else it takes to feel good too."

The hint of sadness appeared in her expression and she turned to look straight ahead. It was the same hint of sadness he noticed when they first met, and was still as puzzling. *Did I say something else wrong?* "Pardon me for being so bold, but I can't think of a thing in this world a girl like you doesn't have to make her happy. A fine home. Beautiful clothes. The best schools. Having a rich grandfather must guarantee you the best of everything."

She nodded, still not looking at him, and spoke in a sad voice. "Grandfather has been very good to me, and he was good to my mother until . . ."

"She's Miss Cilla's and Miss Josephine's sister?"

She nodded.

"Never knew they had a sister. Guess she moved away before I was born."

"She ran away from home to marry my father. Grandfather never approved of her choice of a husband, and when she eloped against his wishes, he refused to allow her back in the home until he found out she was very ill a few years back. That's when we started visiting him and my aunts in town."

"I'm glad. How's your mother now?"

"She died last week. That's why I came to live with my aunts and grandfather."

The news made him speechless for a moment. "I'm real sorry about that. I'm sure she was a fine lady like you. I'm also sorry you had to move, but since you did, I'm glad you picked Two Rivers for your new home. Is your daddy going to work for your grandfather now?"

She hesitated, causing him to suspect that he had pried too much into her personal affairs. Finally, she said sadly, "My parents divorced when I was six, and my daddy hasn't come to see me since. Aunt Josephine told me that's because he was no account, just like my grandfather said before mother married him." She sighed. "I think he must have got killed, otherwise I believe he would come to see me."

*Poor little rich girl,* he thought. "Oh, I'm sure he would. But try not to be too disturbed by what your Aunt Josephine tells you. She don't, doesn't have a very high opinion of lots of folks." *My family in particular.* "I didn't know bad things happened to rich folks too."

Her eyes met his as if she might be questioning his logic, then she smiled faintly and said, "Enough about me. Tell me more about yourself and your family. Tell me how long you've been having your musicals."

He talked and she listened. It felt good, finally meeting a fine young lady who had a real interest in his troubles and high hopes. The fact that she was beautiful made the finding even more outstanding.

When he finished, she said, "Aunt Priscilla told me you're a very responsible person. Now I know why she thinks so. She also told me you know all about farm animals. I'm looking forward to your helping me with the horses. We have an extra one you can ride if you'd like to."

"How about tomorrow? Is that soon enough?" *Slow down. You're rushing things.*

"Aunt Josephine'll be here tomorrow sometimes," she cautioned. "She doesn't like horses."

He detected something about the way she said it that suggested it wasn't a good idea for him to be there when Miss Josephine came by. He said, "I see. Well, how about me coming by tomorrow night? We can talk some more and decide when we'll ride."

"Tomorrow night is fine."

About to pop with joy, he gave the swing another gentle push. "Which school are you going to attend here?"

"Two Rivers High, beginning in September. It was so near the end of the school year in New Orleans, my teachers let me take finals early." She gave him another cautious look. "I'll be in the tenth grade."

"That's great," he said, too embarrassed about his educational shortcomings to tell her how long he'd been out of school. "I'd like to go back one of these days. I had to quit to . . ."

"I understand," she said, sensing his embarrassment. "But what you're doing for your family is much more important."

He wanted very much to hold her hand and tell her how good she made him feel, but figured that would be too bold on their first date. "And I don't mind it." He straightened his back. "I'm the oldest man in the family able to work, so it's what I'm supposed to do."

She didn't speak for a moment, but he felt her eyes on him when he turned to look through the window at the upright piano in the parlor. He could see the foreman's wife too, but didn't see him. When he turned his gaze back to Charlotte, she had one eyebrow raised again in that teasing look.

She said, "With a girlfriend who's crazy enough about you to walk from town to see you, I'm surprised you'd want to see me."

"You mean Ruby?" He felt himself flush. "She's not my girlfriend. Like I said this morning, she's just somebody Slick and his girlfriend brought to the musical." Thinking of his encounter with her in the pine thicket made him feel like a hypocrite. He wished it hadn't happened.

"Just the same, I'll bet you're popular with other girls who know about . . . things." Her gaze didn't waver, suggesting she considered the subject vital.

Heck had never wanted to kiss a girl more than he did at that moment and, except for his fear of being considered too fresh, he would do it. That might convince her she was the only girl he wanted from now on, worth more to him than all the Rubys of the world.

He finally answered her. "Some girls know too much about the wrong things. I'm gonna try to steer clear of that kind in the future. I've got plans, and them, those kind of girls pull a man down. I'm gonna make my life better, not worse."

She seemed pleased with his answer, and after they'd talked a few more minutes, he received her permission to use the telephone to talk to Doc Samuels about Billy. He didn't like to impose, but theirs was the only telephone close-by, and he was too concerned about his little brother to wait until he could go to town for a discussion in person.

Accompanying him inside, she pointed out the phone at the end of the hall and gave him a directory from a table drawer. After saying she'd wait in the parlor, she closed the hall door. *What a considerate person.*

Mrs. Samuels answered the phone and refused to call the doctor until Heck identified himself. He did, and moments later, the doctor said, "Yes?"

"Doctor Samuels, my brother Billy still has a fever, but it's down some. My mama said I was to call you as soon as he got better. I want to know when I can bring him in for his tonsil operation. And I want you to tell me about his heart."

Doctor Samuels told him to have Billy in his office for the tonsillectomy the following Saturday at nine o'clock. It would cost fifty dollars. He then proceeded to give Heck his preliminary diagnosis regarding Billy's heart condition. "We won't know for sure just what the problem is, or if anything can be done about it, until tests are run. The problem is with Billy's heart valves or in the chambers of the heart itself. The tests could cost as much as a thousand dollars, and payment would have to be made before the northern clinic admits him."

Not wanting to take a chance on Charlotte and the others hearing him tell the doctor he didn't even have fifty cents, let alone fifty dollars and had little hope of ever earning one thousand, he thanked him and hung up with a long sigh.

Miss Cilla and Charlotte gave him concerned looks when he walked back into the parlor. Miss Cilla asked, "Everything all right, Heck?"

He nodded, grim-faced. "I'd say things are runnin' about normal for us Tennels." He looked at Charlotte, forcing a smile. "I don't want to wear out my welcome on my first visit, so I guess I should leave now."

"It's early, and you haven't worn out your welcome," Charlotte said, getting up from the sofa.

Hesitating, he turned his eyes to the upright piano. Shiny mahogany, gold letters above the keyboard: CHICKERING. It was a much finer instrument than the one he'd learned to play at the church.

"Do you play?" Charlotte asked.

"What?" He looked at her.

"You were looking at the piano. I thought you might want to play it."

"Oh! Yeah, I play a little by ear," he said. "But right now I couldn't do justice to a fine piano like that. Guess I was just thinking of what it stood for more'n playing it. Music always makes me feel better when . . ." He stopped, realizing he was wandering. "Some other time maybe. Got to go now."

"Good night, Heck," Miss Cilla said as he left the room with Charlotte.

"Good night, Miss Cilla," he said, pausing. "Thank you for allowing me to come over." He nodded at the Truesdales who said nothing.

Stopping at the edge of the porch, he looked down at Charlotte by his side and wished his talk with Doc Samuels hadn't spoiled his evening. Fighting another strong urge to kiss her, he reached out and gently framed her face with his hands."

This has been the best day of my life, pretty lady. I've been needing a day like this for a long time. A very long time." He paused, wondering if it would be proper to be bolder about how he felt. "I need you every day in my life." She appeared to be impressed by his remark, or puzzled, he wasn't sure which.

"Heck, whatever's troubling you, I'm sure you'll find a way to work it out. I hope so, because I enjoyed your visit and hope you'll come back."

"A herd of wild horses couldn't keep me away." He kissed her cheek and released her, and they exchanged "Good nights" before he walked down the steps and across the yard.

Touching her and being with her following that telephone call had almost made things seem all right again, but walking into the valley of complete darkness between the trees along the road caused all his troubles to come crashing squarely onto his shoulders just like before.

He thought of Jake saying how he'd learned from some friends in Dallas to make quick money.

*Well I'm a long way from Dallas and not likely to meet Jake's friends on Vandergriff Road tonight, but if I did, and they made me the same offer, I'd be tempted to try it.*

His thoughts turned back to Charlotte and he realized the stupidity of doing something that would spoil his chances with her. But Heck remembered his Grandpa Tennel telling him on more than one occasion, "When the ox is stuck in the ditch, the man of the family has to get him out any way he can, and the how don't matter nearly as much as the doing."

Now that he'd seen a flickering of light at the end of the dark tunnel he'd been in for so long, he renewed a personal vow. *I'll pull that ox out of the ditch. I'll pull his horns, twist his tail and kick him in the butt. One way or the other that dumb ox is coming out of that ditch.*

# Chapter XVII

"I want Mama," Billy cried out during the night.

The second time Heck got up to check on him, his little brother asked, "Don't Mama love us no more, Heck?"

Amy cried too when she first went to bed, but finally fell asleep, tightly hanging onto her old rag doll.

In spite of his uplifting visit with Charlotte, Heck didn't sleep much himself, lying awake most of the night thinking about how his family was falling apart. Sometime before dawn, after a short nap and another check on Billy, he slipped out the window and headed for the parsonage, determined to bring the children's mother home. He would also stop and check on Cracker again, but thought it best to do that on his way back, after full daylight.

He arrived at the parsonage at first light. Judging by the darkened interior of the little house, no one was up yet. He knocked on the door anyway.

No response.

He knocked again, much louder. He stepped back then, not knowing what to expect of his mother or the preacher's wife, if Thelma had persuaded the Reverend Percy to let her stay the night. The preacher's skinny, flat-chested wife might not take kindly to the step-son of the woman who came to steal her husband.

"Heck!" A sleepy-eyed Homer Percy cracked the door and peered out around the yard behind him, as if expecting someone else. "What do you want at this hour?"

"Have you seen my stepmother?"

"Not so loud," The preacher grimaced, stepped out on the porch and closed the door. "You'll wake my wife." He glanced around again. "What makes you think I've seen Sister Tennel?"

"Because you were with her yesterday, for starters. Now, I won't tell my dad what a low-down, wife-stealin' backslider you are, if you'll quit stallin' and answer my question."

The preacher nervously licked his lips like Heck had seen him do many times during one of his hell-fire and brimstone Sunday sermons. He swallowed hard. "It was the Devil's doings, Heck. I went out there with the best of intentions."

"The road to Buckshot City is paved with men's good intentions too. That's where you'll end up if my dad finds out you visited his house while he was gone."

"Okay. Okay." The preacher shuffled his bare feet. "Thelma came to Sunday school and church yesterday, and afterwards I, uh, counseled her a while in the adult Sunday school room. Then she left."

"Where'd she go?"

"Said she was going to see an old friend of hers in town. Cotton somebody."

"Cotton Murphy?"

"Yeah, that's the name." As Heck turned to leave, the preacher asked him, "When are you going to start coming to church again?"

"You've got to be kidding." He headed for Two Rivers.

As far as Heck knew, this was Thelma's first contact with Cotton since marrying Early. In spite of the way it used to be between her and Cotton, Heck couldn't imagine a man being low enough to take in his best friend's wife. Then again, he still had a lot to learn about the ways of older folks.

Cotton lived alone in a two-room shack near the railroad track on the south side of Two Rivers, a section of town occupied primarily by Negroes. To Heck's knowledge, Cotton had never held a steady job, paying for rent and groceries with what he got from gambling and stealing, or what he could cheat out of the unsuspecting. Pulling two hitches in state prison for theft hadn't changed his lifestyle other than making him more careful. Heck once heard him tell Early, "I'm still waitin' for the Big Casino to come my way. And when it does, I'll set myself up for life in Californy, the land of milk and honey."

By the time Heck got to town, heavy thunder and bright flashes of lightning accompanied dark clouds blown in from the south. It was raining hard when he turned into the dirt street where Cotton lived.

The screenless door was open, but he didn't see or hear anybody in the front room. When he received no response to his knock, he stepped off the leaking porch. That's when he heard Cotton's voice in the back room, accompanied by the sound of splashing water. "I'm so hungry I could eat shoe leather, honey pot. Got to have a few bites of somethin' when I get through with this monkey bath you made me take."

"Them pantry shelves are empty," Thelma replied. "You should do somethin' about that, and you need to find a way to make some money, 'cause I didn't come down here so I could keep on bein' as miserable as a lizard in hot sand."

"Down, but not out, that's me," Cotton said, laughing and slapping his naked body. "Yessir. Cream always rises to the top. This ol' world can't keep a good man down for long, honey pot, 'specially now that you've wised up and come back to me after all these years."

"Don't honey pot me, lover boy. If you plan on beddin' me you gotta take me to nice places and feed me something better than your line of bullshit."

In a quandary about what to do, Heck questioned his notion that a bad mother is better than no mother at all. *Should I barge in and drag her out, or wait to see if she'll come back on her own? Sounds like she already might be having second thoughts about her move.*

The watery noise in the back room told him Cotton stood up in the tub. "Throw me that towel over there, honey pot. Do that, and I'll let you feast your eyes on my manly credentials some more, the likes of which I know you ain't seen for a long, long time."

"I've seen lots of naked men, big shot. Yours ain't no different from every other man's, 'cept it's a little more shriveled up at times."

"It ain't shriveled up neither. It's just restin' after a hard night's work."

"It's shriveled."

"Restin'."

Cotton popped the towel and she squealed.

He laughed. "Gottcha! You know, honey pot, you done the right thang returnin' to ol' Cotton. Knowin' you, I'm surprised you could stand doin' without a good tumble for so long. Now that you're back with me, I'll do you proud."

"Like gettin' caught stealin' again and bein' sent back to the pen? You can't do me no good in the pen, shrivel root."

"Thelma, ol' Cotton's done promised hisself he ain't never goin' back to the slammer agin, leastways not for no triflin' stuff. No, ma'am. The events of the last few days have sparked a good idea on how to hit the Big Casino. All I needed was somebody like you to come along and help me carry it out."

Heck started into the room but, upon seeing his stepmother naked too, jumped back, more confused than ever. A chair squeaked as one of them sat down, and he heard her say, "It wouldn't kill you to get a job. Heck works hard, and it ain't never hurt him none."

"Work? Wash out your mouth with lye soap, woman. That's for folks that don't know how to use their brains. But even if I got lame-brained and decided to go to work, there ain't no damn jobs. If you ask me, a man would be better off in the pen these days if he could take a woman with him."

"Sounds to me like you may want to go back."

Cotton patted some naked flesh, causing Thelma to say, "Watch it, buster."

"Hell, no, I don't want to go back. Got me a woman now. When a man's got a good woman, all's well with the world. I jus' hope Heck don't bring Early down here with his twelve-gauge Winchester and mess up everythang."

"I ain't goin' back to Early, even if he does kill you. I can't do no good with no cripple. It's awful, lookin' at them naked leg stumps. His manhood ain't never been the same since the accident, and it went totally to pot a few years back."

*Thelma must not've told Cotton about giving Homer Percy a tumble. Wonder if he'd run her off if I rushed in there and spilled the beans.*

Cotton said, "You mean that special trip to Frieda's didn't do him no good?"

After a pause, a surprised Thelma replied, "Is that what he done? I wondered what he meant Saturday night when he mumbled something about havin' a good day 'til he tried it with me. He accused me of not helpin' him like a real woman should."

"Well, honey pot, my money says you've still got it all. So, jus' don't you fret about me workin'. I've got me this here plan."

"You can't plan nothin', 'cause all your brains are in your pecker."

"They ain't neither. The way I got it figured is, the reason so many folks is poor, is because there's them that's got more'n their damn share. The problem, you see, ain't got nothin' to do with the amount of money in the damn country. No, sir. It lays in how it's spread around. Any idjit can see that. So all we've got to do to improve our situation is get us a cheap pistol and relieve some rich bastard of his cash, spread it our way."

"You mean, like rob somebody?"

"Sure. Bonnie and Clyde do it all the time. They're in these parts now, so if we dress like them and don't let nobody see our faces real good, they'll get blamed for it and we'll be in the clear. Hell, your hair's about the same color as Bonnie's, and you're about her height. Just wear somethin' loose so nobody'll see your big belly or fat butt."

"Fat butt, my ass. What about your beer gut? How would you hide that?"

"Hell, honey pot, the dumb bastard bein' robbed will be so damned scared he won't notice the little details. And after we make our big haul, we'll take off to Californy and live out our days like fat cats in a cheese factory."

Thelma laughed.

"What's funny about goin' to Californy?"

"Nothin'. I was just thinkin' about how I can help you pull it off and get even with a scrawny preacher at the same time."

"How you figure a preacher can help us do anything?"

"Because I know one that works where there's lots of money. That dried up wimp Homer Percy had the gall to turn me down yesterday for his bony wife. Told me to hit the road, he did. And after I give him the best he's had since marryin' that hag o' bones."

"Honey pot, you ain't about to get religion all of a sudden, are you?"

"No, simpleton. You know that prissy Homer Percy, don't you?"

"Only in passin'. I ain't on speakin' terms with no preachers."

"Durin' the week he works as a teller at Blood Money Vandergriff's bank. I ain't sayin' I'll help you yet, mind you, but if I do, I would walk up to his cage and give him a note tellin' him I won't tell Early about him and me gettin' together if he'll hand over a handful of fifties."

Cotton laughed. "Early would splatter his ass with buckshot for sure."

"And Homer, knowin' that, would hand over the money."

"If we wuz dressed up right, Homer could tell the law that Bonnie and Clyde done it so's not to give you another reason to squeal on him. Even if the law wouldn't buy his story, they sure as hell couldn't send me back to the pen for just askin' for money. But maybe I ought to take a borrowed pistol, just in case."

"No pistols. It'll be my way or not at all."

"Okay. Okay. But we'd still have to dress up like Bonnie and Clyde, so people'll show us some respect. Then, everybody but the preacher will think it really wuz them outlaws, and he wouldn't dare tell nobody the truth for fear of Early blowin' his ass off. Honey pot, you're a genius."

Heck heard steps, then Cotton's voice. "Don't pull on it so hard. It ain't proper to walk up to a sleepin' tiger with a yank like that. Be patient. It'll perk up agin in a little while."

Too embarrassed to stay, and convinced Thelma wouldn't go home with him if he asked her, Heck started toward the door, stopping short when his foot hit an empty beer can. He waited in half-stride to see if anybody noticed.

"What was that?" Thelma asked in a frightened voice.

"My God, you don't reckon it's Early, do you?" Cotton replied. "Open the back door so I can make a quick getaway just in case."

"Open the door for you?" she snapped. "What about me? One blast could get us both."

Heck was going out the door when Cotton peeked around the doorframe. "Heck, is that you?"

"Oh, my God," Thelma cried out, scrambling for her clothes. "Is Early with him?"

"Naah," Cotton said. "It's just Heck. What you doin' here, boy?"

Turning to face Cotton, Heck said, "I came for Mama. But I heard enough to know she's not plannin' on comin' back."

"You ain't gonna tell Early, are you?"

"You're supposed to be his best friend, for cryin' out loud. Do you know any reason why I shouldn't?"

"I'm too young to die is the first reason that comes to mind," Cotton said. "Ain't that good enough?" He was so scared he'd forgotten he was naked. "Now, come on back and let's talk this over man-to-man like."

The rain pounded on the tin roof so loud that Heck had to step closer to Cotton to be understood. "You're disgusting, both of you. Why should I let a little thing like your dyin' stop me?"

"But your step mama come to me," Cotton pleaded. "I didn't go drag her out of your daddy's house."

"It'll take a better reason than that to keep me from tellin' what his best friend did to him."

"I'll give you a hunderd dollars," Cotton blurted out.

Heck held his gaze as he thought about all the good he could do with that much money, the first being Billy's tonsillectomy just a few short days away. He said, "I wouldn't mind seein' you scare the preacher's shorts off, but I don't want any part of holdin' up no bank."

"Oh, you heard," Cotton said, shaking his head. Then his face brightened. "But it won't be no robbery. It'll be more like makin' that sorry preacher pay for what he done to your step mama in your daddy's house. We ain't gonna hurt nobody. And you can just consider your hundred as a loan if it'll make you feel better. Pay me back when you're able."

Heck again recalled how much Doc Samuels said it would cost to have Billy's tonsils taken out and about that legal loan he was denied by Blood Money. The banker treated him like trash just for asking. Getting one hundred dollars of Vandergriff money would be true justice.

Sensing interest, Cotton moved closer to press his case. "Nobody'll see you. You don't even have to go in the bank. I know you can drive a shiftin' car, 'cause Early told me your uncle Tim showed you how. Just drive us to the back door and wait for us while we make our, uh, withdrawal. Then you can drive us away from there and we'll go our separate ways. What do you say, Heck? Us poor folks gotta stick together, right?"

"You've got a car. Drive yourself over there."

"In that ol' jalopy? Shit, it probably wouldn't run all the way to the bank, let alone get us out o' town. Besides, everybody'd take one look at her and know it was me. Bonnie and Clyde wouldn't get caught dead in a wreck like that. I've got to borrow me a Ford V-8 or at least a Model A for this job."

"You mean steal one, don't you? I'm not goin' to jail for drivin' a stolen vehicle."

"It'll be borrowed, boy, not stole. I got connections."

Heck looked at the rain. "That's all I'd have to do, drive you there and pick you up?"

"The Lord's truth. How about it?"

"There'd be no guns?"

"You musta heard what Thelma said about no guns allowed. Are you in?"

"Put on your clothes while I think about it."

Cotton disappeared into the back room and Thelma appeared in the doorway. "How'd you know where to find me?"

"Why am I surprised that your first question wasn't about your sick little boy and your cryin' little girl."

Her face flushed. "I gave 'em life. No mother can do more'n that. I didn't ask your daddy and God to give 'em to me in the first place, and I sure didn't ask him to give 'em to me sick."

"I came to get you because Billy and Amy cried nearly all night for their mama. I can see now it was a waste of time."

Cotton reappeared, dressed only in a pair of shorts. "It ain't no waste of time if you make a hunderd dollars."

Thelma said, "Heck, it looks to me like you'd want to make some money if you're as concerned about Billy and the girls as you pretend to be. You help us out with the drivin', and I'll go back to see 'em."

"You'd come back home to stay?" His face brightened.

She hesitated, and then said, "Sure." She exchanged a knowing look with Cotton.

Heck nodded, telling Cotton, "All right. When do you need me?"

"In the mornin'. Be here a few minutes before twelve. That'll give Blood Money's big shot customers time to get through with their business and out of our way."

Heck sighed. "I'll be here."

Disgusted with Thelma's conduct and his having to resort to such desperate measures for money, Heck left, walking in the rain through back alleys and side streets to Panther Holler Road. He stopped several times as he thought of what he had promised to do, urging himself to go back and tell Cotton he had changed his mind. He even started back once, but visions of his sick little brother made him reverse course.

The rain stopped by the time he reached the road leading into The Settlement. To his surprise, Ubis Sproggs came driving out with Slick, and when the hoopy pulled to a stop beside him, Heck saw Ubis' shotgun leaning against his leg.

"Squirrel huntin'?"

"Nigger huntin'," Ubis declared.

"Yeah," Slick said, patting the shotgun. "Did you see Cracker runnin' down the road between here and town?"

"Why are you lookin' for Cracker?"

"'Cause he raped Willa, that's why," Ubis said. "And now I'm gonna kill him."

Heck's heart jumped up in his throat, and for a moment he couldn't speak. He recalled Willa's threat and immediately blamed himself for not trying harder to find Cracker.

Glancing at the shotgun and the half-empty jar of moonshine on the floorboard, Heck asked Ubis, "What makes you think he raped her?"

"'Cause she told me he did, by God."

"And where did this so-called rape take place?"

"In Hank Slater's field Saturday, if it's any concern of yours."

"Willa waited this long to tell you about it? Don't that strike you as a little odd?"

"Nope," Ubis snapped. "I was at my still all day Sunday, and I didn't get home before she went to bed. Now, quit askin' dumb questions and tell me where he goes when he needs to hide out from the law and white folks."

"He's not at home?"

Ubis and Slick laughed. Ubis patted the shotgun and said, "Not any more, he ain't."

"You shot Cracker?"

"Shot at him is more like it," Slick said. "He run off, the coward."

"You shot at Cracker before you even asked him if he did it?"

"Why should I bother listenin' to him lie?" Ubis snapped. "Willa's word is all I need."

"Where is Willa now?" Heck asked.

"Question is, where's Cracker? You ain't told me yet where I might find him."

"You won't have to find him if I can talk to Willa," Heck told him. "I'll make her tell you the truth."

"I don't take kindly to you callin' my girl a liar, boy. 'Specially when you're doin' it to protect your sorry nigger friend."

In fear of being shot himself, Heck said, "Oh, I ain't claimin' Willa's a liar. She's just all mixed up because she's mad at me. If I can talk to her, I can save everybody a lot of grief."

Ubis reached over and poked his finger into Heck's chest. "Boy, you stay away from Willa 'til this is over. I don't want you makin' her all kinds of promises just so she'll change her story about your nigger friend."

"At least let the sheriff handle it," Heck pleaded.

"We're on our way to town now to tell the sheriff," Slick said, laughing. "Unless we see Cracker on the way."

As the hoopy began moving away, Ubis shouted, "Just make damn sure you don't find that nigger before we do and hide him out. That'd put you in trouble with me *and* the law."

The old hoopy groaned and rattled away in the direction of Two Rivers, and Heck watched until it was out of sight. Disturbed and angry over the unexpected developments, he said out loud, "Damn it, Willa. This is the meanest thing you've ever done."

He headed for The Settlement at a fast walk, clueless about how to keep his friend from being shot or hung, if he was still alive. What a mess.

The door of Cracker's house stood open, and no one was inside. When Heck came back outside, however, he found that his presence had not gone unnoticed. Several women and two old men were watching him from neighboring yards. He spoke to those nearest him, but received only hostile glares in response.

Walking around to the back yard, he heard someone call out his name. Turning, he saw Cracker's mother coming from behind a bush.

"Is Cracker all right? Where is he?"

Cracker's younger brothers Tinker and Liga came out of the house next door and their sisters followed them. The mother's eyes were filled with fear as she approached. "You gotta do somethin', Mr. Heck. That white man done shot Cracker."

"Cracker was hit?" Heck said.

Tinker said, "He's hit, all right. We seen some blood out yonder in the edge of the woods after them white folks left."

"Where exactly did you find the blood?" Heck asked, turning toward the trees.

"Yonder, by that scrub oak." The mother pointed. "He run thataway with that mean ol' white man tryin' to catch him. Ain't no white man in the world gonna help my boy now 'less you do."

"First, I need to find him and see if he's hurt bad," Heck told her. "Where's his dad?"

"He left last week to look for work," she said, absently wringing her hands.

"Well, you take your family somewhere away from here 'til I can straighten out this mess," Heck said. "Ubis Sproggs'll be back in a little while with the sheriff. I'll let you know if I find Cracker."

She gave him the unique look of concern mothers have for their children. "Mr. Heck, do you think Cracker done raped Miss Willa?"

"I don't think so. But that Willa comes on strong to a man sometimes. I won't know for sure what happened until I find Cracker."

"Be careful, Mr. Heck," she said as he moved toward the scrub oak. "As soon as the word gets out, every white man in this part of the county'll be lookin' for my boy with a gun or a rope."

Heck found a few drops of blood on some weeds near the scrub oak, but none on the ground as he moved deeper into the woods. He kept going, looking for signs and stopping to call Cracker every hundred feet or so. No answer.

He continued his search until near sundown, repeatedly calling his black friend's name in vain. He looked for signs of someone's passing that way, but didn't find any. Concluding that his friend's wound was not life threatening – otherwise he wouldn't have been able to walk out of the area – he returned to The Settlement.

Locating the mother in a house next door to her own, he said, "I think he walked away. If you've got a flashlight, I'll keep lookin'."

"Ain't got nothin' but a coal oil lamp," she replied.

"That won't work. I need something that'll throw a light out a ways. It's awfully dark in them woods. Know anybody that's got a good flashlight around here?"

"No, suh."

"And I don't have one at home either. Where are your boys?"

Liga and Tinker walked out of the house to join them. "We gonna walk up the road and call him. If'n he's still around, he'll answer us."

"Then I'll go with you," Heck said.

"Ain't no need of that, Mr. Heck," the mother said. "You done all you could already, and I thank you kindly fur that. When the boys find him, I'll tell him about you lookin'."

"But he's my friend."

"He knows, and we does too. Now, go on home to yore own fam'ly. They couldn't make it without you, and they won't have you if'n some mad white folks shoot you for lookin' for my Cracker. And the sheriff'd put you in jail fo' messin' in his business. He's already been by with a warrant for Cracker's arrest."

He hesitated, considering the implications of her statement. "I'll stay as long as it takes."

"Without no light?" She shook her head. "My boys'll do the lookin' now, and I'll do the doctorin' if they find him and he needs it. But sounds to me like he lit a shuck out o' the county, like you said. If he did, he'll be all right."

"Well, okay, but I'll be back at first light."

Tired and hungry, Heck walked home with his mind in a whirl over the newest complications in his life. Willa had never pulled any punches when she made up her mind to have her way, but up to now she'd never gotten anybody killed. It was bad, very bad.

He ate a supper of cold corn bread and black-eyed peas that Elsie had left on the table next to a coal oil lamp. After eating, he picked up the lamp and went in to check on Billy who was lying down, but not asleep. He was about to lean over and check his forehead, when Amy came into the room.

"Where's Mama, Heck?" she said, yawning.

Heck didn't like having to lie to Billy and Amy about their mother, but at least part of what he had decided to tell them would make accepting the loss easier. He told them he'd seen their mother and she promised to come back home to stay as soon as she finished a job she had started in town. Elsie, standing in the doorway, lamp in hand, gave him a look as if to say she knew better.

Elsie said, "I already told Billy he could sleep in mine and Amy's room on his cot, but he was waitin' to see if that would be okay with you."

Heck looked at Billy. "Sure, if that's what you want to do."

"Elsie's been actin' sorta like a mother to me all day," Billy said sleepily. "But that don't mean I love her more'n I love you now."

Heck looked at them a moment, not wanting to leave them. His conscience got some relief when he felt Billy's forehead and found the fever gone. "Since you'll be with Elsie tonight and feelin' better, would it be okay if I went out a while to visit somebody?"

Elsie nodded. "He'll be fine. Amy too. Go on up and visit that little city girl."

Heck kissed Billy's forehead, telling him, "I'll go, podner, if you'll promise me not to cry while you're with Elsie, and will try real hard to get a good night's sleep."

He patted Amy's head and kissed her cheek. "And you too, little lady. Okay?"

"Okay, Heck," Amy said. "Don't worry none about us. We'll be fine, 'cause we know you ain't leavin' us like Mama did."

"Can I come back and sleep with you tomorrow night?" Billy asked.

"You'd better," Heck said. "It would be too lonesome in here all by myself."

Choosing not to join his dad on the front porch, he went out back and drew water for a sponge bath, convinced his leaving for a while would cause no problems at home. When he finished, his dad still didn't ask to be wheeled inside, preferring instead to sit in the fading light of day to chew and spit. Heck was glad. He had seen and heard enough ugly things for one day. Now that his presence wasn't required at home, what he wanted and needed was some time with the girl who had opened the door to a kinder world. To get through the door, he knew he had to maintain his high wire balancing act long enough to do what he had to do. That wire, narrow as the hair in a mule's tail, was swaying in a strong ill wind. If he toppled off before entering that door, he'd fall into something he couldn't wash off.

# Chapter XVIII

Moving at a brisk walk, Heck arrived at the old Vandergriff home in about twenty minutes to find the front and side rooms brightly lit. Through the parlor window he saw the foreman and his wife sitting by their radio, but saw neither Charlotte nor Miss Cilla. That caused a sinking feeling to sweep over him when he remembered Charlotte telling him about Miss Josephine coming out. He was afraid the bossy aunt had ordered them back to town after finding out he had visited her niece the night before.

He was relieved when he got closer and spotted Miss Cilla's DeSoto sedan parked under the open shed in the back yard. It was barely visible in the outer fringes of light from a back room. Walking across the porch, he knocked softly and stepped back to wait.

"Come on in, Heck," Mrs. Truesdale called out in a pleasant voice. "Miss Charlotte's expectin' you."

Mrs. Truesdale looked up with a pleasant smile when he stepped inside, but her husband glared at him without even as much as a nod. That look told Heck the man didn't want him there any more than he did the previous night.

"Have a seat," Mrs. Truesdale said. "I'll tell her you're here."

Mrs. Truesdale came back momentarily, and Heck waited, cap in hand, very much aware of the growing tension in the room. He tried to ignore the foreman's presence, but felt his eyes on him.

Moments later Charlotte appeared at the parlor door and Heck jumped to his feet. When her eyes met his, he was disappointed to see the same hint of sadness he'd noticed the night before. But her expression brightened as she drew near, and she smiled and said, "Hi, Heck."

"Hi, Charlotte. Sorry I'm late."

She raised her eyebrow and tilted her head to give him that teasing look again. "I thought perhaps you'd decided to go see somebody else instead."

"I was hopin' you'd forgot all about her by now." Glancing at the Truesdales, he asked, "Is it okay if we sit out in the swing again?"

"Sure," she said, moving past him to the door. The sweet fragrance given off by her passing swept away the tension in the room.

Sitting down beside her in the swing, he feasted his eyes on her pretty face in the light from an Aladdin lamp that had been placed on a table by the window since his last visit. "I was afraid you'd gone back to town when I didn't see Miss Cilla's car out front. That would've made my day a total loss."

She gathered up her spreading blue skirt, very carefully straightening it in a way he remembered from the night before. She was the neatest, most organized girl he had ever known. Her black hair was again pulled back into a bun that allowed him to see her pretty ears and her slender white neck. Still operating under the "look but don't touch" rule he imposed on himself, he found the desire to kiss her almost overwhelming.

"It's good to see you again," she said. "How's your day been up to now?"

"Not so good, I'm afraid, but not a whole lot worse than some others I've had lately. How about yours?"

"A great day. There's so much to do on a farm. I'd like to live out here the rest of my life."

Her enthusiasm pulled him up, allowing him to push bad news out of mind for the moment. "I'd like that too," he said. "We could sure use the community improvement that would bring."

She laid her hand on his wrist, but quickly withdrew it. "Thank you, Heck. But I'm afraid no girl, especially me, can live up to your grand expectations. I'm just an ordinary person really."

"Not in my eyes, you ain't, aren't. Being with you makes me feel richer than a Rockefeller with two sections of bottom land." He glanced through the window and slid closer to her. "Until I looked into your pretty eyes yesterday, all I knew about paradise was what I'd heard from the local preacher. He never did do justice to anything he talked about."

"You're very kind." She smiled, but seemed a bit overwhelmed.

*How great it would be to take her for a walk up Vandergriff Road where we wouldn't have a parlor audience.* About to ask if she would go, Willa popped into mind. He couldn't take a chance on running into her on the road. Even though the Sproggs house was a quarter of a mile away, she might be out on the prowl.

Charlotte asked him about Billy and he told her the appointment with Doctor Samuels was on Saturday.

"If he hadn't been feeling much better, I couldn't have come tonight. Elsie, bless her heart, is helping me look after him now. She's lettin'

Billy sleep in her room, and she's a good little cook." He didn't want to tell her about Thelma leaving. He had enough strikes against him as it was.

"Aunt Priscilla told me what Aunt Josephine said to your father about the rent on your party house. We're both sorry. Will you still be able to have a musical this Saturday night?"

"It don't, I mean, it doesn't look like I will. And those other ol' houses are too rotten and full of rats."

"What a shame. It sounds like fun, your musicals. If you're able to keep having them somewhere, I'll ask Aunt Priscilla to bring me sometimes when Aunt Josephine is out of town."

"Great. But I should warn you. Some of the people who come are a little rough around the edges, like that Slick Haskel you saw down at our place yesterday."

"But at least your friends are real people, not fakes and imposters."

He wasn't sure what she meant, but suspected there was an important message in it. "But none of your friends are as crude as Slick and . . ." He almost said Willa, which would put a real damper on things. "I'm sure all your friends are very nice people."

Her eyes held his for a moment, but she didn't answer immediately. Turning away, she said finally, "I've never had any real friends. When I got old enough to go on trips with my friends, or to private parties, my mother wouldn't allow it if she knew boys were going to be there. And she wouldn't allow a boy to come see me, even when she was home."

"Then New Orleans must've been full of very unhappy boys," he said with a nervous smile.

She glanced at him and smiled faintly, not totally erasing that hint of sadness in her expression.

"Charlotte, with so much to offer, and so much to look forward to, you can afford to take your time and be choosy in the boy department."

"I don't have much to look forward to, really. With my father out of the picture, and my mother . . ." She stopped, suddenly on the verge of tears.

A wave of guilt swept over him for allowing the conversation to engage a subject that would make her cry, but he couldn't think of anything to say that might undo the damage. Because she was sad, all of a sudden he was also sad and shocked. *How can such a pretty creature have anything so wrong in her life to make her sad? Probably because her mother just died. Yeah, that's it.*

Recovering, she went on in a rather melancholy tone, "I haven't done much living so far, but I suppose my mother did enough of that for both of us in the years before she died."

Another puzzling statement, Heck thought. He still couldn't think of something appropriate to say, but did find himself questioning his long-held belief that all rich folks' lives were bright, continuous parties. He said, finally, "As I said before, I didn't know Miss Cilla and Miss Josephine had a sister before I met you."

"Grandfather disinherited her a long time ago and never changed his will."

"He disowned his own daughter?"

She nodded. "Does that shock you?"

"Sure. Don't see how any man could disown his child, no matter what." He smiled. "But don't you worry. Miss Cilla will make up for all that. She'll show you lots of interesting things to do. She's a good person."

"Yes, she is. In fact, she's always seemed like a mother to me. When I'm with her, I feel wanted, and loved."

"I love you."

The words just jumped out, sounding like something somebody else said. Embarrassed, he clamped his mouth shut and gave her a questioning look, wondering if she'd make him go home for being so bold.

In the lamplight he could see that the remark startled her, but she said nothing. With her large brown eyes fixed on him, she sat quietly studying his expression. He held his breath, waiting for her response. Would she ask him to leave and never come back?

She said, finally, "But you just met me. How . . ."

"How could I, so quick?" He was afraid to say more, but already committed, decided to stay the course. "When a man's struck by lightning the first time, he knows right away what it was." He smiled. "If the shock don't kill him, that is."

When she appeared to relax, he figured it was safe to press his case, so went on. "I suspect the people you're accustomed to aren't so outspoken about their true feelings, and I'm sorry I jumped the gun like I did. But I never figured there was anything wrong in telling the truth at any time." Emboldened by getting away with so many impulsive statements, he squared his shoulders and added, "And I'm not gonna apologize for saying what I've never said to another girl."

To his surprise, she placed her hand on his and said, barely loud enough for him to understand her. "I'm flattered, Heck. But I'm only sixteen."

"Which gives me more time to prove I ain't, I'm not lyin'.'" He placed his other hand on hers. "Shoot, around here, girls your age are considered grown women. Many get married by the time they're fifteen." He held up his hand, hastening to add, "Now, I'm not saying that's the way it should be, mind you. A fine young lady like you should finish her education and go to socials and do all them, those, things that make her life full and interesting. No real lady should ever be rushed into doing anything that's worth waitin' for."

She gave his confidence another boost by not pulling back her hand. "This is overwhelming. I've never been told so many nice things before by anyone, not ever."

Heck found himself doing something even more daring. He pulled her into his arms and kissed her pretty lips, long and hard.

He immediately released her and moved back, realizing his error. "Miss Cilla'll kill me," he whispered. "And I wouldn't blame her a bit. A man is supposed to have better control of his nature than that."

Embarrassed by his behavior, Heck anxiously watched as Charlotte made a nervous effort to straighten her hair, then her dress. *Will she tell me to leave now, or just run back into the house and let me worry about whether I'll ever be allowed to see her again?*

She glanced through the parlor window, then at him. The radio was still playing inside, so Heck believed no one had heard what he had told her.

After regaining her composure, she said, "Speaking of lightning." She took another deep breath. "My goodness!"

"To show you my intentions are honorable, I'll stay down at my end of the swing 'til I leave. But in all fairness, I should warn you. I could be ten miles away, or a hundred, and I'd still want to kiss you again. I guess it's something I could do the rest of my life and never, ever tire of it."

Breathing faster than usual, she turned her eyes to the window, then back to him. "You don't have to sit *that* far away."

Interpreting her remark as a sign of approval of sorts, Heck quickly slid to the middle of the swing and took her hand. "I don't want to do anything that would make you tell me to hit the road and not come back."

"I may be inexperienced, but I think I know the difference between a phony and somebody who's sincere."

"Then you'll let me come to see you again?" He smiled, pressing her hand.

"If you want to."

He squeezed her hand harder. "I want to, and I will. And nobody except you can stop me, ever."

She gave him a questioning look, as if she might know of someone who could. Then she appeared to relax and they talked about all the things to do on a farm as large as her grandfather's. He asked her about New Orleans, and she wanted to know all about Two Rivers. When the grandfather clock in the parlor struck ten, someone turned off the radio and Miss Cilla appeared at the door to tell Charlotte it was time to come in.

They walked to the front steps with him still holding her hand. Looking up at him, she said, "If you're not busy in the morning, come up about nine and we'll ride horses."

"A herd of Hoover hogs and ten hungry panthers couldn't keep me away. I'll be here with a shine on my nose and bells on my toes." He thought about Cracker, and knew he couldn't come if they still hadn't found him. But thinking about what he promised Cotton he'd do to help him and Thelma at the bank was the most unsettling of all.

"You're funny."

Telling himself it was no time to think negative things, he pulled her into the shadows near the banister. This time he asked if he could kiss her, and when she didn't say no, pulled her into his arms and did it.

She was trembling when he released her, and he was breathing considerably faster, but he made himself step back. They exchanged good nights and he moved down the steps, allowing her hand to slowly slip from his.

Skipping down the graveled driveway by the light of a half moon, he turned into Vandergriff Road and began singing, "I'll Be All Smiles Tonight." Finishing that, he began to whistle "You Are My Sunshine." After that, he did a quick two-step, ending up in a waltz in the loose sand between the ruts.

About halfway home he became silent between the high red banks under tall timber, and the further he walked, the more the darkness pressed in on him. All the unpleasant things he had pushed aside for a while came rushing back and he stopped. *Should I go up against Ubis Sproggs and walk to his house now and to talk to Willa?*

Deciding it was worth the risk and would allow him more time to keep his date with Charlotte the next morning, he retraced his steps, walking briskly past the darkened Vandergriff house to the Sproggs place. He was encouraged when he saw only one lamp burning, that being in Willa's room. It meant her dad was already in bed.

Four barking hounds jumped off the front porch and raced toward him. "Dang dogs," he said. "Shut up! Go away!"

He'd started around the house to Willa's window when he heard the front door screen creak open and a gruff voice shout, "Who's out there?"

Not wanting to get shot, Heck stopped dead in his tracks. "It's me, Mr. Sproggs, Heck Tennel. I came to talk to Willa."

The door banged shut and the dim outline of Ubis Sproggs and his shotgun appeared at the front corner of the house.

"I already told you, you ain't gonna talk to Willa. Unless you can bring me that nigger, I don't want to see you around here 'til I do what's got to be done."

"You already shot Cracker. If he's not dead by now, I'm sure there's no reason for you to finish him off. Please let me talk to Willa and straightened everything out."

"How come you're so damned worked up about that nigger? I never knowed no Tennel to be a nigger lover. Now, git, before I forget about you bein' my neighbor and sprinkle your hide with a load of buck shot."

Turning, Heck headed back to the road and home, telling himself, *I'll find a way to talk to Willa in the morning, as soon as I make sure Cracker ain't seriously hurt.*

Mr. Sproggs' question about his interest in Cracker was still ringing in his ears. That made him recall the time Cracker pulled him, half-drowned, from a deep hole in Morales Creek where he'd been grappling for catfish and got this arm caught under some roots. Even if they weren't friends, he owed Cracker for that, no matter what his neighbors thought.

*But Cracker is my friend. He does the same kind of work I do, eats the same food, and sweats the same way. We even bleed the same color blood when cut. I sure didn't jump back into the creek and suck some more water into my lungs because I didn't want my life saved by a man with black skin. Besides, it was my fault if anything happened between him and Willa. If I'd convinced Willa to leave with me, Ubis wouldn't be aiming to kill him.*

Walking alone in the darkness, with only the sound of his footsteps for company, it occurred to him how hard it had become of late to find peace of mind for more than a few minutes at a time. It was like sitting in the shade of a small tree on a very hot day. Every time he settled back and tried to cool off, the shade moved.

He sighed. His shade had been moving too fast for too long.

# Chapter XIX

Getting up at four the next morning, Heck slipped quietly out of the house and walked to The Settlement to see if Cracker had come home.

He approached the front door in almost complete darkness under trees blocking most of the light from the half moon. No lamps burning inside indicated everybody was either asleep or had abandoned the place after the sheriff came by. He knocked anyway, and to his surprise, a shadow moved toward him in the darkness. Not knowing who it was, he moved back a step and asked, "Did Cracker come home?"

"No, suh," came the reply. It was Cracker's mother. "The boys couldn't find him. I'm afraid he's dead, Mistuh Heck."

"Or too scared to come home. I'm gonna try to find him again. See you later."

Waiting in the edge of the woods for sufficient light in the trees to walk by, he moved in beyond the area he had searched before, calling his friend's name every hundred yards or so. Approximately two hours later by the sun, he again concluded that Cracker had been able to walk away and therefore was not seriously injured. He returned to The Settlement, reported to Cracker's mother and headed home, thirsty and hungry. Looking at the sun, he judged it to be about eight o'clock.

He refused to tell his dad where he'd been except to say he had gone for a walk. Not taking the time to eat for fear he'd be late for his date, he washed his hands and face, put on a clean denim shirt and went into the girls' room to check on Billy. His little brother, looking at an old magazine with Elsie, was relieved to see him, and wanted to know if he was leaving again.

"I was plannin' to, but won't go if you're feelin' real bad." Heck touched his forehead. No fever.

"He's okay," Elsie said. "He didn't cry as much last night. I fixed him two eggs for breakfast."

"Great, thanks," he told her. "I've never met a girl like the one I'm going to see. I don't like leavin' you again so soon, but I'm afraid Miss Josephine'll make her go back to town and I won't get a chance to see her again. I hope ya'll understand."

Elsie smiled. "Guess love's got you in the same fix Marna was in, huh?"

"Maybe, but I'm not runnin' off with nobody."

"It's okay, Heck," Billy said. "Mama'll probably be home sometime today,"

Heck and Elsie traded anxious glances, and he told them, "After visiting my new girlfriend, I'm going to town and see if I can make us some money." He tousled Billy's hair. "We'll need it Saturday, right podner? Be back as soon as I can. Love ya."

Heck made it to the Vandergriff place in record time and Miss Cilla answered his first knock to ask him in. Telling him they'd just finished breakfast, she asked, "Won't you have something? Charlotte prepared the food."

Famished, but feeling much like a beggar, he accepted her kind invitation and proceeded down the hall into the dining room where he saw scrambled eggs, biscuits and pan sausage in white platters on a large, linen-covered mahogany table. Turning to Miss Cilla, he asked, "Did Charlotte eat already?"

"Yes. She's dressing and will be in shortly. Have a seat and help yourself."

He was eating when Charlotte walked in smiling, looking refreshed and relaxed. "Good morning," she said, motioning for him to keep his seat when he moved to get up.

"Mornin', pretty lady," he replied. "Hope you don't mind me eating here."

"Why should I?" She sat down opposite him and pushed the biscuits closer. Her presence lifted his spirits, but he was concerned about her seeing him as a moocher.

Sensing his discomfort, she said, "I'm so pleased you could eat here, because it's the first time I've prepared a complete breakfast. Mrs. Truesdale and Aunt Priscilla are teaching me how to cook. It's something I've always wanted to do. I hope you like it."

"It tastes great. You're gonna make some lucky man a fine wife." He immediately wished he hadn't said it, because it sounded like he was only thinking of her as a domestic. "Sorry. I didn't mean to get so carried away so early in the mornin'. A fine lady like you will be much more than just a fine cook to the lucky man she decides to marry."

She smiled. "I'll stoke the fire and warm the coffee."

"Please. Could you just sit with me while I eat? It would be such a comfort."

"Of course." She smiled, and rearranged the plates. "It's the first time someone special has eaten at my table. Outside of family, I mean."

Seeing that hint of sadness in her eyes again, he said, "And it's the first time I've been lucky enough to have somebody special like you to sit with me while I eat. It's a winning combination, somebody special and smackin' good vittles."

Her smile swept the sadness from her eyes. Continuing to eat, he realized this was the first time he had ever sat down to a meal served in genuine china and eaten with real silverware. He likewise had never before used a starched cloth napkin. The elegance of it all added a certain quality to what had always been merely a procedure of absolute necessity in his family. But the richest of all things present was the understanding, supportive girl with the brown eyes and swept-up hair sitting across the table from him.

If she resented anything he said or did the previous night, she didn't show it. Ever since she sat down, he'd noticed certain radiance about her expression that he hadn't seen before.

Finished eating, he said, "Thank you. Your breakfast was delicious. I'll help you put up the leftovers and wash the dishes."

She stood up. "If we had time, that's what I'd like to do. But because it's getting late, Mrs. Truesdale will do that. Thanks."

Heck accompanied her to the barn and saddled three horses, a paint mare and two brown geldings, and led them back to the house where they were joined by Miss Cilla. Mounting, they rode out to the road and turned toward the Sproggs place. He was very relieved when he saw neither Willa nor her parents.

*This is my lucky day.* A ways up the road, they passed Loony Toons' little house. They were riding three abreast with Charlotte on the paint in the middle.

When they turned to go back, Miss Cilla reined her horse to a stop and climbed down. "I want to walk a while," she said. You two go ahead." Soon they were out of her sight down the road.

To his surprise, Charlotte rode well. That told him she had ridden somewhere many times before. Having a gentle horse helped. She was embarrassed, however, by her lack of proper riding attire. Her dress slipping above her knees kept her hands busy pushing it down. Heck tried to avoid ogling, as he knew it wasn't the proper thing to do, but when they rode at a gallop and her dress flew up to her thighs, he found it impossible not to steal a few glances.

Not wanting to risk the wrath of Willa, he took hold of the bridle of Charlotte's paint and kicked his into a gallop. Charlotte gave out a whoop and grabbed the saddle horn as her mount surged forward. Relieved to find the Sproggs had not returned, he pulled the horses to a walk after passing their house.

"Wow!" Charlotte exclaimed, pushing her dress down. "That was fun, but a little frightening. I've never ridden at full gallop before."

"Sorry I didn't warn you so you could've leaned into it. That saddle horn has saved many a rider." He laughed.

The return trip was much too short, and while unsaddling the horses at the barn, he found himself wishing he didn't have to drive Thelma and Cotton to the bank. His obligations to his little brother left him no choice, however. He'd do anything for Billy.

They walked to the front porch hand in hand. Seeing neither Truesdale around, he was preparing to pull Charlotte into his arms and kiss her when Miss Cilla walked into the driveway, still leading her horse. They accompanied her to the barn, where he unsaddled the shiny chestnut gelding.

Heck glanced at the sun on the way back to the house and guessed it to be at least nine-thirty. *If I leave now and run part of the way, I could be in town by eleven. Plenty of time to get to Cotton's place and set up for my chauffeuring job.*

Noticing his growing nervousness, Charlotte said, "Did you enjoy our ride?"

"You bet. I enjoy being with you anywhere, anytime." He squeezed her hand. "But I have to go now. Gotta see if I can pull an ox out of some very deep mud."

"Excuse me?" She gave him a puzzled look.

"I won't burden you with my problems, pretty lady." He patted her hand.

"Is there some way I can help with whatever's bothering you?"

"They're my problems. I'll solve them."

"When will you come again?"

"I'm not sure. Tomorrow sometime, I hope."

When they stopped by the shed where Miss Cilla's car was parked, he turned and said, "I'll be thinkin' about you every minute I'm gone."

She smiled, but he saw that hint of sadness return to her eyes. "Be careful, okay?"

He nodded, pulled her into his arms and kissed her, and this time she relaxed against him. He wanted to do it again, but knew he had to leave.

She walked with him to the driveway, waving as he moved out of sight beyond the tall trees along the road.

Arriving home at 9:50, he checked on Billy and Amy, telling them he was going to see their mother again. At least that wasn't a lie. Elsie had rolled their dad out on the front porch where he was sipping on a jar of moonshine when Heck passed him on the way out.

"Where you goin'?"

Heck didn't stop or look back when he answered him. "Where I can earn some money I've got to have."

"Well, just don't forgit, half of what you make is mine."

It was an hour's walk to town, which meant he wouldn't get to Cotton's house in time to get set up for their trip to the bank unless he ran part of the way. Run he did, slowing to a fast walk when needing to catch his breath. He reached Cotton's in record time. Breathing hard, he walked into the back room of the little shack and stopped short, shocked by the sight before him.

Cotton and Thelma were dressed up like they might be going to a funeral or joining a circus side show. Cotton sported a frayed blue suit, rumpled white shirt, blue tie and a white snap-brimmed straw hat. Thelma wore a bright red dress, white shoes and black hat. They both looked in pain.

Giving them the once-over, Heck asked, "Where'd you get those clothes?'

"Borrowed 'em, where else?" Cotton shot back, pulling at his collar. "You didn't think I'd go in no bank lookin' like white trash, did you?"

Heck said to his stepmother, "I'm doin' this to pay for Billy's tonsillectomy Saturday, and because you promised to come home. That'll make Billy and the girls happy."

Thelma gave him a contemptuous look. "Humph. Kids. What do they know about livin'?"

"They know they love you, Mama. Billy and the girls need you whether you need them or not, more than ever, now that Marna's gone."

"Gone? Gone where?"

He told her about Marna leaving with Jake. "She left me a note, sayin' how Jake promised to marry her. At least her arrangement is gonna be legal and proper." He looked at Cotton.

"Well, good for Marna. She saw her chance and took it, just like I'm doin'."

"But Marna didn't have any kids to think about. The least you can do is live at home 'til Billy's over his sickness and the girls are a little older. If you're so hot natured you've got to get out of line every now and then, do it on the sly, like you did Saturday."

"I ain't wastin' another day out there in that ol' shack with a cripple. You and Elsie'll just have to do the best you can without me."

Heck folded his arms on his chest. "Then you'll have to drive yourself to the bank, because if you won't keep your word about comin' home, I'm pullin' out."

Cotton, suddenly worried, nudged her.

"Oh, all right, dammit. I'll go back." She shook her finger in his face. "But I ain't sayin' how long I'm stayin'."

Cotton pulled at his collar again. "Y'all quit jawin' and let's take care of business. This garb is crampin' my style."

"And exactly what style do you have, lover boy?" Thelma said. "I ain't seen any."

"Very funny, honey." His eyebrows rose. "Did you notice that rhyme? Poet and don't know it. Ain't that proof enough of my style?"

Heck looked at Cotton. "Everything's still the same, right? No guns. Just a note."

"That's what I said, no guns. But I'll have to find one if you told your daddy about me and Thelma."

"I didn't tell him," Heck said. "But how long do you think you and Mama can live like trash in a town as small as Two Rivers without him finding out?"

Cotton pulled at his collar again and glanced at Thelma. "Let's haul ass. It's eleven-fifteen already." He stopped at the front door and peered out cautiously. "The coast is clear. Heck, bring the car around to the front. Honey pot, you ride in back with me."

Instead of a Ford V-8 in the back yard, Heck found a rusty Model A sedan which he doubted could make the round trip without falling apart in the street. He eyed a sagging front bumper, and bent fender that would probably rub the tire, a broken headlight, mashed-in door, and the right rear fender was missing. A piss poor excuse for a getaway car. *They'd stand a better chance fleeing the scene on foot. If it don't break down between here and there, I'll probably be arrested for driving a stolen junker.*

To his surprise, the old car had an electric starter, but he almost ran the battery down before turning the motor over enough times to get it started. Then it spit and sputtered something awful, smoking like a grass fire. He drove it alongside the house into the street and Cotton and Thelma quickly climbed into the back seat.

"I thought you said a V-8," Heck said, pulling away.

"It's a car, ain't it?" Cotton said. "Just as good as the first one Bonnie and Clyde used startin' out. My friend's car supply was runnin' a little low."

Heck drove back streets to Main. Crossing it, he turned into the street that would take them to the bank's rear entrance. When they got to within half a block of it, Cotton leaned forward.

"Stop here. We'll watch the back door for a few minutes to make sure the coast is clear. I'd hate to rush in there and butt heads with Bonnie and Clyde. A fella could get killed doin' that."

Heck turned off the motor and fanned gas fumes from his face as he looked at his passengers in the rear view mirror. They were slumped down in the seat, hats pulled low over their eyes, looking more like scared rats than bank robbers in moth-eaten garbs the folksy Barrow-Parker duo wouldn't be caught dead in.

"What's that wet spot on your pocket?" Thelma demanded. "You didn't pee in your pants, did you, lover?"

"Not that I know of," Cotton said sheepishly. He ran his hand into his pocket and pulled it out wet. "That dang water pistol's leakin'."

"*Water* pistol?" Thelma laughed like somebody goosed her in the ribs.

"I thought you said no guns," Heck said.

Cotton grunted his contempt. "A water pistol ain't no gun, you weed-choppin' hayseed."

Thelma stopped laughing. "You can't scare nobody with a water pistol, lame brain. So what are you plannin' to do with it, spray my note so I can stick it to Homer Percy's pretty face?"

"You said yourself everybody's gonna be too damn scared to notice anythang," Cotton said. "It looks real enough. Nobody'll believe we're Bonnie and Clyde if they didn't see a gun, silly. I can't kill nobody with it."

"Not unless you drown 'em," Thelma said, cackling again and slapping her thigh.

Thelma stopped laughing and they both sat up straight when they spotted Homer Percy come out of the back door of the bank. "What's he doin'?" Cotton asked. "We can't make no withdrawal if he leaves."

"Look at that prissy walk," Thelma said. "Don't know how I ever worked myself into a lather over him."

"Where do you reckon he's goin'?"

"Who knows?" she replied. "Probably just runnin' an errand for Blood Money, or steppin' out to get a new bottle of rose water, the sissy. We'll wait."

Only two other people were in sight besides the preacher, a customer coming out of the bank and an old man crossing the street to the alley that led over to Main Street. A car drove past, but the driver appeared not to notice them.

Ten minutes dragged by, causing Heck to question the wisdom of taking part in such a crazy caper. Cotton and Thelma remained slumped down in the back seat, with him grumbling about being miserable in the suit.

"There's the little prick," Thelma said as the preacher walked from around the corner of Smith's drug store that adjoined the bank's east wall. Heck and his passengers slumped down more in the seats until he disappeared inside the bank.

"Let's go, honey pot," Cotton said. "Hold that bandana over your face, like you're blowin' your nose or somethin'. We don't want nobody to recognize you."

"This'll be fun," Thelma said. "We'll make that little wimp shit in his britches for sure."

Opening his door, Cotton told Heck, "Wait right here 'til you see us comin' out the back. Then drive over real quick and pick us up. Got that? And another thang. Come inside and give us a signal if you see a policeman."

"Okay," Heck said. "But how are you gonna keep the preacher from tellin' the police Mama robbed him? He'll recognize her when she gives him the note."

He got no answer as they moved away from the car, disappearing moments later inside the bank. Glancing around for a police car, Heck slumped down in the seat to wait, but not so far down he couldn't see out.

"Oh, no!" he moaned when he looked into the rear view mirror and saw Sheriff Sloan's deputy Squeeze Usrey drove into view at the end of the block.

He fell across the seat until he heard the deputy drive by. After waiting for what seemed an eternity, he rose up and peeked over the dashboard, feeling much like a chicken thief checking on the farmer.

Squeeze had pulled to the curb up ahead to talk to Blood Money's secretary.

"Damn," Heck moaned. All of a sudden that one hundred dollars seemed very far away. A *lot further away than the county jail at the end of Main, my next stop if Squeeze sees Bonnie and Clyde look-a-likes run out of the bank and hop in the car I'm driving.*

Keeping his eye on the deputy, Heck slowly opened the door of the sedan and got out, intent on warning Thelma and Cotton of the danger at hand so they would nix the "withdrawal" and leave through the front door. Afterwards, he would walk away from the stupidest stunt of his life.

Squeeze was so occupied with the secretary he didn't notice Heck cross the street and approach the glass rear door of the bank.

Heck saw one customer at a teller's window and two others in the middle of the lobby suspiciously eyeing Thelma and Cotton as they moved up to Homer Percy's cage near the rear entrance.

Fearing himself too late. He thought: *I can't let Billy and my sisters' mom go to the pen.*

Glancing at Squeeze again, Heck pushed the door open, entered the bank lobby and began signaling Thelma and Cotton. Unnoticed, he helplessly watched Thelma hand the startled preacher the note as Cotton pushed his hand into his wet pocket. Heck beckoned again, but they didn't see him. Homer Percy read the note and turned unbelieving eyes on Thelma.

When Heck glanced through the glass door and still didn't see Squeeze, he tried again to catch his stepmother's eye and warn her. He moved closer to Homer Percy's cage just as the preacher said, "I can't do this. It would be stealing."

Cotton leaned over the counter and said, "Yeah, but it won't hurt as much as gettin' yore friggin' head blowed off by Early's twelve-gauge Winchester. That's what'll happen when I tell him what you done to his wife, unless you fork over a handful of them twenties and fifties to Bonnie."

At the sound of "Bonnie" everybody within earshot whirled and froze.

"Psst!" Heck beckoned. Neither of them heard him.

Visibly shaking now, the preacher picked up a handful of money. Holding it out of Thelma's reach as he glanced around, he leaned forward and told her, "Everybody's watching. I'll go to the pen for sure."

"Not if you tear up my note and tell 'em you was robbed by Bonnie and Clyde, lame brain," Thelma snapped. "Now, hand over the damn money."

Increasingly frightened and at the same time emboldened by his new-found sense of power, Cotton suddenly whipped out the water pistol and pointed it at the befuddled preacher.

"I ain't leavin' empty handed, by God," Cotton snarled. "Give her the damn money before I fill you full o' water – holes."

"Who are *you*?" Homer Percy asked.

"Clyde Barrow, by God," Cotton said from behind his bandana, loud enough for everybody to hear.

A murmur ran through the place as the other tellers ducked out of sight and customers ran for the front door. A woman screamed in one of the offices.

"Oh, my God!" Heck moaned, heading for the door. He looked back to see the preacher heap more handfuls of money into Thelma's hands. She whirled and headed out. Cotton, suddenly a control freak, waved the water pistol around as he backed away, shouting, "Everybody freeze. Clyde Barrow ain't never shot nobody that wasn't tryin' to git him, so don't try nothin' unless you wanna get blasted!"

As fleeing customers stopped and threw up their hands, Heck backed out the door and looked for a hiding place, relieved he hadn't been spotted. Just as he stepped behind a shrub, Thelma and Cotton came charging by.

"We done it, honey pot," Cotton said. "Must be at least five hundred dollars in that stack o' bills."

Upon seeing the deputy's car, they screeched to a halt. Heck had never seen such frightened faces on two human beings.

"What now, money pot, I mean honey pot?" Cotton's voice wavered. "The damn law's here and Heck ain't nowheres in sight."

"Run, idiot," Thelma said, taking off in the direction of the empty Model A. Cotton ran after her, glancing back to see if Squeeze had spotted them.

"I dropped a twenty," Thelma said over her shoulder. "Pick it up."

"Pick it up yourself, honey pot," he yelled, pulling ahead of her. "I'm haulin' ass and ain't stoppin' 'til I'm clean out o' Texas!"

"The bank's been robbed!" yelled a man running out the back door. "Bonnie and Clyde robbed the bank."

Squeeze scrambled for his starter switch and burned rubber making a U-turn. Heck moved slowly from behind his cover and calmly walked in the opposite direction, not daring to look back for fear he'd be recognized.

He turned north at the end of the block, then west on the next street to head for Panther Holler Road, frequently glancing back for signs of pursuit. He saw none, but knew the sheriff would be coming out to arrest him if Squeeze arrested Cotton and Thelma.

# Chapter XX

Heck saw no one in Cracker's house when he walked into The Settlement, only angry faces pressed against windows in the other houses. His knock on the door unanswered, he walked around, closely examining the ground for signs that his friend had come back after all.

Knowing Cracker could have gone home and passed out, he peered through each window but didn't spot him or any member of his family. Turning, he looked toward the bushes out back and saw Liga beckoning to him.

"Did you find Cracker?" he asked Liga, as he approached him at a fast walk.

"Sho' did, but he's too bad off for me to move him."

"Then why didn't you walk to the nearest phone and call an ambulance?"

"No, suh. Cracker said that would get him hung fo' sho'. You got to help him where he's at."

"Let's go."

Heck followed Liga through the woods about a quarter of a mile to a ravine where Liga pointed. "He's down there."

"Come on," Heck said, running down the slope.

At first sight of Cracker lying in the leaves, Heck thought he was dead. His eyes were closed and he didn't respond to his name.

"Liga, was he conscious when you left him?"

"Just barely," Cracker said, opening his eyes to look up at them.

"Cracker," Heck said, kneeling to look at the fresh blood inside his friend's right thigh. "What are you doin', resting? You can't chop no cotton out here in this ditch."

"Heck, that mean ol' Ubis Sproggs done shot me bad."

"Heck leaned closer to examine the thigh, then turned his eyes to a less severe wound in the same leg near the ankle. "We've got to take you into town to see Doc Samuels."

"No! I'd rather die right here than get hung for somethin' I didn't do."

"Then you didn't rape Willa?"

"Miss Willa done lied on me, Heck. Reckon how come she done a crazy thang like that?"

"Did you even try to do anything to her after I left? You know, touch her, or tease her."

"No way. She touched me though, just like I tol' you she done befo'. But I jus' kept choppin'."

"What happened after that?"

"I heard her holler, and when I turned 'round, I saw her flat on her back with her dress pulled up high, claimin' she stumped her toe and fell down."

"Was she hurt?"

Cracker rolled his head from side to side. "She was hurtin', but not because of no stumped toe. She was temptin' me. 'Bout that time, a little voice in my head told me, Nigga, you gonna get hung if'n you stay 'round here, so I throwed down my hoe and run outta that field as fast as I could."

"Then you've got nothing' to worry about. Your two friends can back up what you tell the sheriff."

"Can't neither. Them niggas run off when they seen Miss Willa comin' up to me with the devil in her eye."

Heck shook his head in disgust. "I *told* Ubis Sproggs you didn't rape Willa, but he wouldn't listen to me." He looked at the bloody thigh again. "That wound needs doctorin' bad."

Taking out his pocketknife, Heck cut away the leg of Cracker's overalls and pulled it off over his foot. "Buckshot," he said, leaning closer. "You're lucky the blood dried quick, otherwise you'd already be dead. But it's still oozing out a little. I've got to stop that and clean the wound. If I don't, you'll bleed to death or die of infection."

"Do what you can, Heck, but in case I pass out agin, you got to promise me you won't take me to town fo' any reason."

"I'll promise that if you'll promise me you won't die." He turned to Liga. "Gimme your shirt."

Heck tore off one sleeve of the garment and wrapped it around Cracker's thigh above the wound that was less than six inches from his crotch. He told Cracker, "If that buckshot had been just a little higher, you could still look at the girls when you get well, but that's all."

The tourniquet tightened, Heck cleaned the wound the best he could with another piece of the shirt. After wiping away the freshest blood, he could see the damage had been done by a single buckshot passing through the leg.

"I'm leavin' the old dried blood so's not to start serious bleedin' again," he told Cracker. "I'll need some soap and water, and more rags for bandages before pullin' off that dried stuff to clean the wound."

"Liga, git to hoppin'," Cracker said.

"And Liga, bring me a bottle of rubbin' alcohol," Heck told him. "If your mama don't have that, bring coal oil. Run both ways. And tell you mama to send me some clean white rags."

Liga left, and Heck leaned down to press a rolled-up piece of shirt against the thigh. "After applyin' some pressure for a few minutes, I'll take off the tourniquet." He felt Cracker's forehead. "You've got fever. As soon as Liga gets back, I'll do the best I can for you, but I can't give you any guarantees. One thing's for sure. As soon as I clean you up, I'll have to take you somewhere safe, out of the weather where I can doctor you better and get you something to eat, and some water."

"Don't take me back to no house in The Quarters, 'cause the High Sheriff'll find me there fo' sho'." He rose up, looked at his leg and fell back, breathing hard from the effort.

"Credit me with havin' a little sense," Heck told him. "I'll have to take you where the sheriff will least expect to find you. A white man's house would be ideal."

"Are you crazy? No white man would even let me in his yard for a drink o' water with the word out that I raped a white woman. One sho' ain't gonna take me in the shape I'm in."

"Shut up and let me think. Let's see now. I can't take you to my house, not after that stupid trick I pulled this mornin'. Both Ubis and the sheriff could be watchin' my place."

Cracker closed his eyes with a groan. "There ain't no use in botherin' yo'self 'bout takin' me anywhere 'cause there ain't no place for me to go 'cept this here ditch. When I die, just shove some leaves over me."

Heck pretended not to hear as he searched his brain for a way to save his friend. Moments later, he snapped his fingers and leaned down over Cracker. "I know just the place. It's set back off the road in the woods and nobody ever goes in there. The owner lives alone, and he's got a hay barn you can hide in out of the weather. I'm takin' you to Loony Toons' place."

Cracker's eyes popped open. "You can't do that. Mr. Loony's the one that's always blabbin' to the law about everything and everybody. That would be like takin' me straight to the sheriff hisself."

"Not if we go about it right. We've got to offer Loony something he wants real bad, or never had."

"What's that, brains?"

"A woman."

Shaking his head, Cracker said weakly. "Yo're crazy."

"And you're nearly dead already, so what have you got to lose? Willa will lay down with any man, but since she's the one that got you shot, we can't ask her to help us." He leaned down close to Cracker's face. "You know some Negro party girls. Who's the big light-skin one you're always talkin' about?"

"You mean Tiny Lucy?"

"That's the one. Do you think she'll give Loony a roll in the hay if I promise her five dollars?"

"'Spec' so, but . . ."

"Then she's the answer to our problem. I'll send Liga for her soon as he gets back."

Cracker closed his eyes. "You done some crazy thangs, Heck Tennel. But this takes the cake. Tiny Lucy's a good-time girl, so she won't see you askin' her as no insult or anything like that. And I know she's hit the hay with whites befo', 'cause she's always told me about how they ain't got enough spark. Any man plannin' to party with her better pack his suitcase, 'cause he's gonna end up a long way from where they start their romp. She goes plum' wild. She'd kill that ol' man."

By the time Liga got back, Heck had removed the tourniquet and used it to bind two pieces of rolled up cloth against the entrance and exit wounds to stop the oozing blood. After telling Liga to go round up Tiny Lucy for Cracker, he removed the two pressure bandages and used an alcohol-soaked clean cloth to clean both wounds, disregarding Cracker's painful grunts and frequent flinching. After covering them with a piece of cloth delivered by Liga, he cleaned and bandaged the lower wound.

Upon seeing that Cracker had passed out or gone to sleep, Heck settled back in the weeds to wait for Liga to return with Tiny Lucy. He lay down and tried to go to sleep, but couldn't, because it had become too hot in the ravine where there was no air stirring, and no shade. *I hope Squeeze didn't catch Cotton and Mama.*

Realizing he couldn't endanger Liga by involving him in their plan, he pulled out his pocketknife and began searching for poles and vines suitable for a travois that would allow him to transfer Cracker to the old bachelor's house by himself.

While collecting the things needed and constructing the crude carrying device, he again thought about Cotton and Thelma. *How could they get away from Squeeze on foot? And if they got caught, how long will it be before they tell Sheriff Sloan about me driving them to the bank? Man, what a day this has been.*

He had just finished tying a mat of small vines between two hardwood poles when Liga returned with a tall, obese mulatto woman who looked to be in her late twenties. Her big bosom rolled and bounced as she walked, and she was perspiring profusely.

Giving Heck a questioning look when she stopped at the top of the incline she searched the immediate area and asked, "Where's Cracker? Liga said he wanted me bad."

Heck pointed at his friend lying in the leaves near his feet.

She jumped back with a gasp. "He don't look in no condition to be needin' me, white boy."

"He needs you, all right, more than ever before. Come on down."

Grunting and mumbling, Tiny Lucy eased down the incline to approach Cracker's still body. "He looks dead to me," she said. "The only one that can do anything for him now is the undertaker."

Heck pulled the travois closer. "He's not dead, but he will be soon if you don't help us."

"Humph. I heard that white trash mighta shot Cracker after Miss Pussy Willa squealed on him. But I ain't no nurse."

"Liga didn't tell you what we want to do?"

"No, suh, but bein' as how there ain't but one way I've ever helped Cracker, I figured he wanted to party."

"Liga," Heck said, "you can go back to The Settlement now. Tell your mama we're movin' Cracker to a safe place where we can better take care of him. I don't want you or anybody in your family to know where, because Ubis Sproggs or the sheriff would beat it out of 'em. Thanks for your help. Now, get away from here." He watched the brother disappear and then turned to Tiny Lucy.

"This is how you can help me and Cracker." He told her about Loony and his hay barn, the only safe place they could hide Cracker until he got Willa to change her story. He explained that Loony wouldn't allow it unless they gave him something he'd always wanted but never had, a woman. He told her that if saving one of her own kind from a racist killer like Ubis Sproggs wasn't reward enough, he'd give her five dollars to make Loony happy.

When he was through, she continued staring at him with her usual stoic expression, finally saying, "You say that ol' man over there ain't never been wid no woman?"

Heck nodded.

"Then I might kill him. I ain't one o' them lazy, sportin' women that jus' lays back like a wet dish rag the way white girls do. A man's got to be in top shape and full ready for a wild ride when he takes me on."

"There's no better way for a man to die. Will you do it? If he'll agree, that is."

"I don't much like foolin' wid no ol' man, 'specially no ol' white man. I have to do too much to get 'em cranked up."

Feeling he might lose his only chance of moving Cracker to safety, Heck decided to sweeten the pot. *So it's a little crazy. But no risk, no gain.* "Loony doesn't have a family, Tiny Lucy. No kinfolks anywhere. So, by playin' your cards right, you could end up owning his house and farm, and all that virgin timber on it." He thought he saw a glow of interest in her dark eyes.

"You ain't jus' messin' wid my mind now, is you, white boy?"

Heck shook his head. "The only way you'll ever find out if what I'm tellin' you is the gospel is to help us. How else will you ever get your hands on a home and farm before you die?"

She held out her open palm. "Show me the five."

He shuffled his feet and glanced up the grade to make sure Liga hadn't come back. He looked at Tiny Lucy. "I, uh, you'll have to wait 'til we get Cracker to Loony's."

"Humph. You ain't talkin' to no fool, you know."

"Only a fool would turn down a once-in-a-lifetime chance at a place like Loony's."

She looked down at Cracker and thought some more. "All right. But don't go sickin' the law on me if that ol' man turns us down, or takes me on and kicks the bucket while I'm fixin' him up. It'll be bad enough jus' havin' to clean him and put up with his white folks ways o' sportin'."

He nodded. "Let's go."

Tiny Lucy refused to help place Cracker on the makeshift carrying device, so he finally did it by himself and dragged him out of the ravine. With a pole in each hand, he headed toward Loony's place in a slow walk. Tiny Lucy brought up the rear, puffing and mumbling.

Heck dared not allow himself to dwell on what the consequences of actions would be if Charlotte or his neighbors found out. He didn't even want to think about what he'd do if Loony panicked and ran them off. He couldn't, because all the problems he'd encountered lately had pushed him to the point where there were no options.

He would think about mending fences with Charlotte and everybody else after saving Cracker. What everybody else thought wouldn't matter anyway if Sheriff Sloan found out he was the one who drove Thelma and Cotton to Blood Money's bank.

*The way my luck's been running, I'm sure that if anything can go wrong, it will.*

# Chapter XXI

It was around three o'clock by the sun when they finally arrived at the edge of the clearing around Loony's little house. Cracker had been awake for most of the trip, grunting in pain when the poles bumped over a rough spot. They'd traveled under the cover of heavy timber, avoiding all roads and lanes except to cross them when necessary.

Exhausted, Heck lowered the travois to the ground and fell down to stretch out on his back in the leaves. "I need a cool drink o' water."

"We'll both be wantin' sunshine piped in to us in jail if'n the sheriff finds out what we're doin'," said Tiny Lucy who plopped down nearby, exhaling loudly.

She mumbled something else Heck couldn't understand but was too tired to ask about. He did turn his head to see perspiration streaming down her face into her lap. Tiny Lucy was almost six feet tall and weighed no less than two hundred fifty pounds, but in spite of her great strength she refused to help pull Cracker through the woods, saying that wasn't part of their agreement. Afterwards, she complained about the heat and the business missed by being away from The Settlement for so long.

"Where am I?" Cracker asked, raising his head to look around. Surprised to see Tiny Lucy, he said, "How come *you're* here?"

"Questions, questions," Heck said. "We're at Loony Toons' place."

"How come?"

"You don't remember me sayin' I'm takin' you to a safe place? Relax."

"What if he ain't home?" Tiny Lucy asked.

Heck rose up to look through the woods toward Loony's barn. "His mare's here. I'll find out for sure."

"Are you gonna tell me what you're up to?" Cracker asked.

Ignoring him, Heck walked out of the woods into the clearing and around the end of the house on his way to the front porch. That's when he heard Loony talking to himself.

The old bachelor jumped when Heck came into view, almost upending a pan of dry peas he was shelling. Loony's jaw began to move as he attempted to overcome his fright and speak. "Y–y–you scart me, Heck. W–w–w–what you c–c–comin' from that direction fer?"

"Hi, Loony." Heck glanced back toward Cracker and Tiny Lucy, then stepped up on the porch and pulled a rope-bottom chair over next to the old man. "Something happened that caused me to come see you in a hurry. After all, you're one of my best friends. You consider me one of your best friends, don't you?"

"You bet." Loony nodded.

"What are friends for if they can't help each other out now and then, right?"

"R-r-right."

"Well, I've come to do you a favor. And I hope you'll do me one in return."

"Huh?" Loony appeared to be thoroughly confused now.

Heck leaned closer. "You remember that time you told me how you'd never had a woman, and how you'd never met one that would as much as say howdy?"

"Y-y-yeah." Loony blushed, dropping his eyes.

"I've brought a woman out here that's ready to take you on. Imagine that, Loony. Your very own woman, givin' you a tumble like few men have ever had."

Loony raised his head and looked around the clearing. "I d-d-don't see no dadburn woman." He looked at Heck. "B-b-but I see the d-d-devil d-d-dancin' in yore eyes, Heck Tennel. Yore pullin' my l-l-leg, ain't ya?"

"I am not. There's one out there, and she's an expert. Name's Tiny Lucy."

Loony was thoughtful a moment, then a knowing look swept over his face. "I-I-I heerd of her f-f-from Slick. But she's c-c-colored. S-s-s-she won't mess around with m-m-me."

"She ain't no more'n a deep tan. Why, I've seen you got nearly that dark after working your fields all summer. Besides, what's that got to do with it? God made all women the same way for a purpose, didn't he? And this one's better than all the rest because she's here, and she's hot to trot."

"H-h-how come? I ain't never done n-n-nothin' fer her."

"The 'how come' brings us to my problem, Loony. You know my friend Cracker Washington Carver. Well, he got himself shot for something he didn't do, and I want you to let me put him in your hayloft a few days 'til he's well enough to travel again. You don't have to do a thing for him yourself. I'll do all the doctorin'. Just let him stay in the barn and not tell anybody about it."

"H-h-how come he's shot?"

Heck told him, and when he did the old man became so frightened he could barely speak. "I don't w-w-want to give that U-U-Ubis Sproggs no excuse to come bustin' in here and shoot me t-t-too."

"He won't if you don't tell him Cracker's here. Think of it, Loony. Besides givin' you what you've always wanted, Tiny Lucy will clean your house, wash your clothes and cook you some of that Southern food you love so much."

"S-s-she will?" The worry lines on his face vanished.

"Yep. And this is probably the last chance you'll ever have to get yourself a woman that'll do all that for you in one day. And if you play your cards right, you might get her to stay on. Wouldn't that be great?"

Loony turned anxious eyes around the opening again, and his fingers began to shake so much he couldn't shell the peas in his hand. He asked, "How come she'd do that?"

Sensing victory, Heck signaled for Tiny Lucy to join them, and when she came into view, Loony focused hungry eyes on the large bosom approaching the porch. But his excitement was overcome by an expression of fear.

Approaching Loony to take the pan from his lap, Tiny Lucy said, "Gimme them peas. Never know'd a man that could shell peas right. It ain't a man's job no how."

Blushing, Loony feasted his eyes on the big woman towering over him. It appeared to Heck he had forgotten about Ubis Sproggs.

Not wanting to break the spell Tiny Lucy had cast over Loony, Heck left the porch to pull Cracker to the opening running through the center of the barn at ground level, then up the steps into the hayloft.

Rolling his friend off the travois into the hay, Heck told him, "Rest easy. We're finally here. I'll get clean rags and some of Loony's rubbing alcohol and clean your wounds again. And aspirin for that fever." Glancing at his thigh wound, he added, "All that bouncin' around made you start bleedin' again. How do you feel?"

"Real bad, Heck," Cracker said. "And I'm wearker'n a hay fart."

"That's because you've lost so much blood. Unfortunately, that didn't make you any lighter. Do me a favor. Before you get shot next time, try losing a few pounds."

Cracker fixed his eyes on Heck. "Can I ask you somethin'?"

"Shoot."

"How come you doin' this? It ain't right, you getting' in trouble on my account 'cause o' somethin' Miss Willa done said. You gonna have every white man in the county mad at you too, includin' the High Sheriff."

"Don't fret, friend. Nobody knows about it but the four of us."

"Everybody'll know as soon as the sheriff finds out what you done. You'll end up in jail wid me."

"Well, at least they won't hang me. Now, quit thinkin' and get some rest. I have better things to do than stand here listenin' to you ramble. If it'll ease your mind, I will tell you this. I'm gonna talk to Willa as soon as I catch her with Ubis not around. I'll make her tell the sheriff the truth."

"Heck," Cracker said when he started to leave.

"Now what?" Heck turned.

"I know what you're tryin' to pull off between Tiny Lucy and Mr. Loony on my account. That means you're crazier than I ever thought you was. And besides bein' crazy, it ain't right, and you know it."

"Cracker, I'm not necessarily doin' it because it's right. I'm doin' it because it's the only way I know to save your life. Now which way do you want it, for me to do what's proper, or for you to be dead?"

"You puttin' it that way mixes me all up."

"I figure it's not nearly as wrong as a man gettin' shot for somethin' he didn't do."

Cracker mumbled a few words Heck couldn't make out before saying, "I ain't never know'd of no white man goin' out on a limb to save no black man like you're doin'. Jus' want you to know how much I 'preciate it."

"Well, don't get too grateful yet, because you still ain't out of the woods by a long shot. Excuse my choice of words. But if my plan does work, you'll have to give Tiny Lucy some of the credit. Just don't sample the merchandise and mess up her concentration after I leave."

"Don't worry. Ain't strong enough to even think about a sample." Cracker shook his head and settled back on the hay. "Always said you was half devil. Never knowed what you was gonna do next, and never could tell you nothin'. I'll probably die anyway."

Heck shook his finger at Cracker. "You'd better not die on me, Sportin' Man." He laughed. "That's what Tiny Lucy told me she calls you, Sportin' Man. She said on the way over here she'd be real sad if you was to kick the bucket. I'm leavin'. Be back in a few minutes."

As Heck approached the front porch, he heard Tiny Lucy tell Loony, "There, the peas is shelled. You got any more chores I can do? I'll bet your house is a mess. I'll give it a good cleanin', then I'll give you a nice bath so we can see how tough the slats are in your bed tonight."

Loony uttered a series of stammers and grunts.

Changing course so as not to interrupt anything, Heck went around the house and entered through the rear door. He searched all four rooms, found what he needed to dress Cracker's wounds, and returned to the barn.

Besides the new bleeding, the thigh had become more swollen, causing Heck to recall what he heard Doc Samuels tell his grandpa one time about that kind of problem: if infection sets in, apply cool packs to keep down the fever. He'd also said that if the infection isn't stopped, blood poisoning would set in and the patient could lose the limb or die from gangrene. A grim thought.

Cracker was asleep, but woke up when Heck started swabbing the wound with alcohol. "What you doin', settin' me on fire?"

"Lay down and be quiet, unless you can tell me where I might find a bucket of ice."

Cracker settled back and mumbled, "Bucket of ice, my foot." Looking at Heck, he said, "It's bad, ain't it?"

"It ain't good. How about some scrambled eggs and a drink of cool well water? You got to be starvin'. It'll perk you up."

"Ain't hungry. Just cold and achy-feeling."

"You've got to eat, and drink something. Doctor's orders." He finished cleaning and dressing the wound and left to prepare some food.

When he got to the kitchen, he spotted Tiny Lucy in the front room, cleaning and putting things in order. He heard her say, "What a mess, Mr. Loony. What you need is a regular housekeeper. You know, one that lives in one room of your house or out in a shed in the back yard where she'll be handy."

Heck stopped gathering wood from the wood box to hear Loony's answer. He was beginning to think the old bachelor was too timid before he finally said, "I d-d-don't know no w-w-woman that'll do that. N-n-never knowed a w-w-woman that wasn't a-a–a-f-feared of me, or thank I was t-t-tetched."

"Lordy mercy, You ain't really touched, are you, Mr. Loony?"

In the process of building a fire, Heck missed the rest of their conversation. He scrambled enough eggs for everybody, and fried several slices of salt pork he found in a barrel. He cut up a couple of unpeeled Irish potatoes and dropped them into the bacon grease.

The food was about half-done when Tiny Lucy's large frame filled the door leading from the front room. Glaring at him, she said gruffly, "If you'll wait 'til I get through cleain' up this pig sty, I'll do that."

"I wouldn't want an heiress-to-be getting her hands greasy."

She grunted and mumbled as he turned back to the stove, telling her, "You concentrate on Loony. I'll feed Cracker."

"Well, don't get so busy you can't bring me a tub o' water from the well. That ol' man's long overdue for a bath."

By the time he was through cooking, Tiny Lucy had finished cleaning the two front rooms. Heck didn't see Loony, but judging from the talk he heard, it sounded like he was helping Tiny Lucy.

Heck took Cracker a jar of water, some eggs, potatoes and bacon, then came back down to Loony's wash shed where he found a number three wash tub which he delivered to the living room. Loony, silently sitting in his old rocking chair, too overcome by all the unexpected developments to move or speak, seemed out of place in his own house because it was now clean and orderly.

Going to the well, Heck drew a foot tub full of water that he brought inside and poured into the larger container. He repeated the process until the wash tub was about two-thirds full.

Loony silently observed the process without comment, obviously too cowed to ask the purpose of the water. Finally overcome by curiosity, he asked meekly, "W-w-what's that fer?"

Not wanting to upset him further, Heck said, "That's my bath water."

Going back to the loft, Heck found Cracker had eaten the food and drunk some of the water. Looking down at his friend, he said, "Feelin' better?"

Cracker nodded. "A little."

"All you need now is rest." He moved the water to within easy reach. 'Take a long nap while I go up to the Sproggs house and see if I can talk to Willa without gettin' shot myself."

"Be careful, you hear?"

Heck nodded, went down the steps to the hall of the barn and out. Approaching the back porch, he heard the sounds of splashing water from the front room.

"Set still, Mr. Loony. How can I give you a bath with you jumpin' 'round like a skinny ol' grasshopper?"

Peeking through the window, Heck almost laughed out loud at what he saw, Tiny Lucy forcing Loony to sit in the wash tub as she scrubbed his face and neck with a large soapy rag. His waving arms and feet pushing against the floor to get up were no match for her shoving him back down.

"Now, stay put!" she ordered. She picked up a bar of lye soap, vigorously rubbed the wet cloth against it, and began scrubbing his back.

"I-I-I-It ain't f-f–fittin'," Loony protested. "Oh. That hurts! You scrub t-t-t-too hard."

"Got to. You're the dirtiest white man I ever seen. When did you bathe last?"

"D-d-don't rightly remember. Wooo. That's c–c–cold."

"I'll be warmin' you up soon enough," Tiny Lucy said gruffly. "You'll be wishin' you had some o' this cold water splashed on you then."

"B-b-but it ain't decent, bein' s-s–scrubbed by no woman."

"Yo' mama was a woman. She bathed you when you was a baby, didn't she?" Tiny applied more pressure to the wash cloth. "And from the way you looks and smells, I'd say you ain't had a proper bath since."

"B-b-b-but I'm growed up now. And naked as a j-j-j-jaybird."

"You sho is," Tiny Lucy said, scrubbing under his arms. "Jus' like you wuz when the Good Lawd sent you screamin' and kickin' into this rotten world. And jus' like you gonna be when you leave it. That oughta tell you somethin' 'bout what God likes. If'n they was anything wrong wid bein' naked, he'd a' birthed you wid clothes on. Now, hush up and be still!"

"B-b-but you ain't gonna wash my p–p–private parts."

She rubbed the soap against the cloth again, giving Loony a hard look. "Who said I ain't? They's part of yo' body, ain't they? No different from other men's parts I seen, 'cept they's awful pale and puny lookin'."

She began to scrub again, this time moving down his belly, and when she touched him where no other woman had, he almost jumped out of the tub. She pushed him back down, splashing water on the floor around them and resumed the bath.

As Heck moved away from the window, he heard her say, "I'm about there. Mr. Loony. Now, don't that feel good?"

Heck walked through the woods along the road down to the edge of the small clearing behind Willa's house in hopes she would come outside alone. After waiting what seemed like an hour, the only person he saw was her mother, who near sundown went into the garden and pulled up some onions. Finally deciding everyone else was gone, he returned to Loony's barn, checked Cracker's wounds in the fading light and bedded down. He didn't remember ever being so tired.

Seeing no light and hearing no sounds from Loony's little house when he returned, Heck had no way of knowing if Tiny Lucy had introduced the old bachelor to man's greatest pleasure. If she had, he hoped it hadn't killed him like she feared it might. If so, Cracker would lose the only safe haven available to him and most likely die on the run or be hung. If either happened, Heck would soon be known as "Jailbird" Tennel.

Lying there on the hay in a sea of darkness with no sounds to disturb thought, his mind whirled over his newest dilemma. *How could Willa and her dad do such a thing? Guess some folks get a certain joy out of making others bend to their will. One thing's for sure. Being right or wrong don't amount to a fiddler's fart in determining the final outcome of anything. Seems if a man's interested in deciding his own fate, it's not enough to just be right. He must have power, and to gain power, he has to be rich. Able to count the rich people he knew on one hand, he made comparisons and decided they all had one thing in common: they owned lots of land and other property.*

Only the sounds of Cracker's breathing and the katydids cut through the still night as Heck thought about Charlotte. I w*onder if she's in bed too. Hope she don't find out about that stupid bank stunt. Should I go ahead and tell her about it before somebody else does, which might cause her to see me as an unworthy person after all? Hope I don't lose her.*

His solitude became more disturbed when it suddenly occurred to him that Thelma and Cotton might be bedded down in the pokey. That being the case, the sheriff would be looking to serve him with an arrest warrant. Perhaps he was waiting for him down at the house. *Billy and Amy might be crying again. I hate that. I'd hate not being able to keep my promise to Billy about the tonsillectomy. Need to find another source of money for the operation and make another appointment with Doc Samuels.*

Finally, a little after Loony's rooster crowed at midnight, Heck fell into a troubled sleep.

# Chapter XXII

B efore dawn Heck felt his way over to the stairs, moved slowly down the steps and out to Loony's privy in the dim light of the half moon. Later, on his way back to the barn, he paused to look skyward and saw stars forecasting a clear day.

Loony's house was still dark. He moved closer, hoping to hear something indicating the old bachelor was all right. Silence. He didn't dare go inside. Instead, he sat down on the back steps and waited for the sun to come up, and when it did, went back to the hayloft to check Cracker's wounds. His friend was awake.

"You ain't wised up and gone home yet?" Cracker asked.

"Glad to see you're well enough to ask dumb questions. How do you feel?'

"Cold. My leg feels like it's been chopped on with a dull ax."

"Take these." Heck gave him two aspirin and the jar of water. "I'll tell Tiny Lucy to fix you some breakfast before I leave, if she's still here." He examined the wound.

"Where you goin' after that?"

"To check on my family. I'll be back unless the sheriff grabs me. If you hear Ubis Sproggs' hoopy or the sheriff's car drive up in the yard, cover yourself with hay."

The thigh wound was still swollen, but no more than when he last checked it, and there was no new bleeding or additional redness. He re-wrapped it.

"You'll live."

"I got to go to the privy, Heck," Cracker said, frowning. "How'm I gonna handle that up here?"

"I'll throw you a bucket and part of Loony's Sears-Roebuck catalog from his outhouse. When you're not using it, bury it in the hay. I'll tell Tiny Lucy to bring you a pan of water and some soap. See you later."

On his way to the privy, he heard dishes rattling in the kitchen, and saw Tiny Lucy through the window standing over the makeshift sink next to the stove. Getting part of the catalog, he found a syrup bucket in a shed and returned to the barn. From the top of the stairs, he said to Cracker, "Here's to your good health, Sportin' Man. Have fun." He tossed the items to his friend and went back outside.

Stopping at the wash table on the porch, he washed his hands and stepped through the back door. "How's Loony?" he asked.

She glanced at him on her way to the stove. "Sleepin' like a new-born baby, jus' like I always leaves 'em."

"I was afraid he might die with a heart attack."

"He was still breathin' when I looked in on him on his mattress on th' flo'."

"I was afraid his slats wouldn't take the strain." He looked at her huge body. Smiling, he added, "Hope you didn't have too much trouble gettin' his horse out of the stable."

"For a while, I thought his horse was dead. But I know a few tricks that'll make any ol' tired nag come chargin' out."

"I've gotta go home now, so will you take care of Cracker 'til I come back? For starters, you can take him some breakfast, a wash cloth and a pan of water. And some soap."

"You expect a lot fo' that five dollars I ain't seen yet, white boy." She shoved a couple of sticks of wood into the stove's firebox and gave him a stern look.

Heck smiled. "Why work yourself into a lather about a piddlin' five dollars when there's so much at stake here? What did Loony think about you bein' his full-time housekeeper?"

"He didn't say yea or nay. I can tell that he ain't used to decidin' on such big thangs. He's jus' like a chil'."

"Too scared or too bashful. My guess is he'll never ask you to do that on his own. So you'll have to keep bringin' up the subject, or just straight out tell him. You can see he needs you. I really feel sorry for the ol' feller. Always have."

She pulled up one huge breast to scratch under it. "Humph. That sounds like some mo' of your slick talk. You want me to feel sorry for him too."

"Well, if you're as good as you claim, ol' Loony'll be beggin' you to stay when you build up his strength with a good breakfast."

She lifted an eye off the stove and poured some coal oil on the sticks and dropped a struck match on them, slamming the lid down on leaping flames. "I could think better about thangs if I knowed you'd draw me a tub of water befo' you leave, and fill up the wash pot. I could also use a pile o' firewood out there." She looked at him. "He do have a wash pot, don't he?"

"You're sly, Tiny Lucy," he said, smiling. "You can hear that whistle on your ship blowin' loud and clear on its way to your landin'. Why, I'll bet ol' Loony couldn't run you off if he tried. And I expect you've already picked out which one of his beds you're gonna put in that storage shed out back. With a little fixin' up, it would be a pretty good place to live."

She waved a big arm at him. "Go on. Get outta here, Mr. Slick Talk."

After drawing the water and piling up some dead limbs near the wash pot, Heck ate part of the scrambled eggs and biscuits Tiny Lucy had prepared and set out for his house. It was still so early no one was up at the Sproggs place, and he didn't dare stop to wake up Willa because her daddy's hoopy signaled his presence. Talk would have to wait until Ubis went to his still later in the morning.

He approached the Vandergriff home place with caution, ready to jump up on the opposite bank and walk home through the woods if he saw the light on in Charlotte's room. He didn't dare let her see him in dirty clothes, or before he decided how to tell her about what he'd done the day before. He knew he had to tell her, because he never wanted to give her any reason not to trust him.

At home, he climbed the embankment near the barn and watched the premises for a while to find out if a deputy was waiting for him. All clear, he walked across the back yard and into the hall, finding everybody asleep except Billy who had remained in their room after Amy had pulled her cot in next to his. When Heck saw his spotted terrier lying on the foot of his cot, he knew why the little dog hadn't announced his arrival.

"Heck. Where you been? Me and Amy was worried about you."

Amy woke and sat up on the side of her cot. "Did you find Mama?" she asked sleepily.

Sitting down on Billy's cot, Heck pulled both of them close and kissed their foreheads as he tried to think of something encouraging to tell them about their absent mother. He didn't want to lie, but felt the whole truth would be worse. "I sure did find Mama. She's fine, and sends her love. She promised me she'd be comin' back home real soon."

"She ain't never comin' home," Amy said, tears welling up in her eyes. "That's because she don't love us no more."

"Sure she does. But even if she didn't, I love you enough for her and me both." Heck hugged her tighter. "And Elsie loves you and so does Marna, and you love each other. I'm gonna see to it that both of you get everything you need, regardless. Now, how about some breakfast?"

"I ain't hungry," Billy said.

Heck tousled his brother's hair. "You will be when you smell that bacon, podner."

Elsie got up, and while helping with breakfast, said, "I told 'em they could sleep in my room, but Billy was afraid you might come in and he'd miss you."

After breaking the eggs into a bowl, she went to the well and got three glasses of milk. Later, when the eggs, bacon and biscuits were done, she persuaded Billy to join them.

Heck and Elsie were washing dishes and Amy and Billy had gone out in the back yard when their dad yelled from the front room. "A man can't git no sleep around here with all that bangin' and clatterin' goin' on back there. You kids better be quiet unless you want me to lay the razor strap on you!"

Heck and Elsie exchanged glances, but neither spoke. Moments later, Early yelled at them again. "Well, since you woke me up and it's daylight already, one of you can at least come in here and roll me out to the privy."

Heck promptly left the kitchen to attend to his dad's needs. On the way back to the house, Early asked a lot of questions about the previous day. Heck merely told him he spent it looking for a way to make some money. "Daddy, did anybody come by looking for me?"

"Ubis and Slick a couple of times."

"Nobody else?"

His dad eyed him suspiciously. "Nobody else, but if you're hidin' your nigger friend Cracker Carver, Ubis won't be the only one lookin' for you. The sheriff'll get you for sure."

Meeting his terrier in the hall, he picked him up to pet him. "Ready to tree a squirrel, Spot?" The dog barked and licked his hand, eager to do his bidding. "We'll go huntin' real soon."

He placed Spot back on the floor, wheeled his dad to the end of the dining table, and went to the well to draw bath water which he poured into a foot tub. Taking it back into his room with what was left of a bar of P & G soap from the back porch, he bathed and put on another faded denim shirt and a clean pair of overalls. After brushing off his tennis shoes and combing his hair, he told his dad he was going to the old Vandergriff place because Heck didn't want him to suspect he'd gone up the road for any other reason in case the sheriff came by.

His dad turned scornful eyes on him. "Just who do you think you are, anyhow? Do you really believe you can do any good courtin' the granddaughter of the richest man in the county? I swear, you're worse than Ross was with your high ideas and pipe dreams."

Not wanting to endure another lecture on how he'd never be anything but a farm hand, Heck stepped off the porch on his way to the cut. Behind him, his dad called out, "That gal ain't your kind. You ought to be out lookin' for work instead of wastin' your time with her."

About half-way to the Vandergriff place, Heck met Ubis and Slick. Ubis braked to a stop and fixed his fierce brown eyes on him. "Have you seen that nigger yet?"

"You mean Cracker?"

"You know damn well I mean Cracker. Where's he at?"

"How should I know?" Heck shrugged. "Workin', I guess. Why don't you ask the sheriff? Maybe he found him."

"He ain't found him neither," Slick said, laughing. "I don't know who's madder at you, the sheriff or Ruby. Ruby said . . ."

"Clam up, boy," Ubis ordered. "We got more important thangs to talk about than loose women." He turned his eyes back on Heck. "Where you goin' so early all spruced up?"

"Up to the Vandergriff place."

"What's the likes of you doin' up there? Ain't no work there."

Heck didn't answer him.

"Have you seen Loony?" Ubis queried. "We just left there. A nigger woman doin' his washin' told me he wasn't home, which I thought was kinda queer. And another thang puzzled me. I ain't never knowed of Loony payin' nobody to do his housework, black or white."

Heck shrugged, breathing a sigh of relief.

Slick snickered. "Did you hear about ol' Blood Money's bank bein' robbed?"

"Uh, no. Who robbed it?"

"Bonnie Parker and Clyde Barrow that's who, by God. Clyde stuck a pistol in Homer Percy's face and got fifty thousand dollars as clean as a whistle. Then him and Bonnie lit out and ain't been seen since."

"Fifty *thousand?*"

"That's what Homer Percy said he handed over, and you know preachers don't lie. Emmet Sloan's hoppin' around like a short-legged rooster in a pen o' tall hens. He can't look for Cracker no more 'til he rounds up Bonnie and Clyde."

Heck's face lit up. "Really?"

"We gotta go," Ubis said, revving the T-Model's motor. "Me and Slick'll find and kill that nigger while the sheriff's busy lookin' for them bank robbers."

Fanning away thick exhaust fumes, Heck called after them, "Y'all better be careful on the road. Them two bank robbers are real killers." He laughed and watched as they disappeared in a cloud of smoke and dust.

*Fifty thousand dollars? My-o-my. I never woulda believed the preacher so clever. That much money in his pockets might give him enough courage to leave his skinny wife and head for California. He might even run into Cotton and Mama on the way. Life is full of little surprises.*

Heck didn't see the foreman and his wife when he got to the Vandergriff place. Charlotte and Miss Cilla gave him a warm greeting and Miss Cilla asked him right away if he'd eaten breakfast. When he told her he had, she asked him into the dining room for coffee.

Heck followed them down the hall, sitting beside Charlotte while Miss Cilla brought him a cup of hot coffee and poured her niece a cup of hot chocolate.

Charlotte was wearing a dark blue dress with a wide collar trimmed in white that contrasted sharply with her olive complexion. She had her hair pulled back again, making it hard for him to believe she was only sixteen. None of her dresses he'd seen so far were as tight as Willa's, but that didn't keep him from seeing her womanly figure when she turned a certain way.

He suddenly felt ashamed for sizing her up like she was a prize mare and for comparing her in his thoughts to the likes of Willa and Ruby. So many other things about her were just as beautiful as her face and body.

Meeting his gaze, she asked, "Did you have a good day yesterday after you left?"

"Crazy is more like it," he said. "How about you?"

She nodded. "But Mr. Truesdale wouldn't show me the rest of the farm and the cattle. He said Aunt Josephine wouldn't approve, too risky and too dirty."

"I haven't worked on this place in a long time, but I know it well enough to show you around, if it's all right with Miss Cilla." He looked at her aunt at the end of the table.

"There's heavy dew," Miss Cilla said. "You'd both get wet."

"We'll stay on the horses," Heck assured her.

Miss Cilla gave her approval, and he and Charlotte went to the barn where he saddled the paint and the horse he rode the day before. After giving her a leg up, he mounted and led the way to the back pastures. It was a clear day, and very still.

They passed the Truesdale's garden where he identified each vegetable: English peas, now wilted from the warm spring sun, carrots, onions, young sweet corn, field peas barely six inches high, turnips and collards, potatoes and beans. Later, as they approached a large crop of young field corn no more than a foot high, he told her what that was.

"What does Mr. Truesdale do with it?" she asked.

"Feeds it to your granddaddy's cows mostly. But it can be eaten by humans when it's young and tender."

"How long before it's ready to eat?"

"About three more months, if it rains."

"And if it doesn't?"

"It'll be stunted, about half-sized."

"What's that planted between the rows?"

"More peas."

"Cow peas?"

"Human peas," he said, smiling. "They'll feed only the vines to the cows."

"You know everything about farming. I admire that."

He sat a little taller in the saddle, unaccustomed as he was to such flattery. "It's common knowledge in these parts," he said. "Nothing to brag about."

"I wouldn't like you if you were a braggart."

He wanted to again praise her knack for saying the right things, but told himself to keep his feelings in check today. He said, "Knowing that you like me makes me proud. I'm gladder still that you were kind enough to tell me. Compliments are a rare commodity where I live."

She touched her heels to her mount and the paint began walking faster, causing Heck to do the same thing to catch up. Going through an iron gate to by-pass a cattle guard, they rode out into a large meadow with grass that came up over the horses' fetlocks.

"Oh, my!" Charlotte said, pulling her horse to a stop. "It's so beautiful here. So peaceful."

"It's pretty because Mr. Truesdale keeps the weeds sickled down."

"What's a sickle?"

"A blade that slides inside a metal track to cut grass and weeds. It's all part of a two-wheel mower that's pulled by a pair of mules, or horses."

She gave him another admiring look, then gazed off into the distance. "What kind of cows are those?"

"Hereford cross. Your granddad and Miss Josephine have several registered Hereford bulls. The cows are mixed breeds. For good calves, it doesn't make much difference what kinda cow you've got, just as long as you've got a big, strong breedin' bull." He gave her a cautious look, suspecting he'd been too plainspoken. If she was embarrassed, she didn't show it.

He watched her turn slowly to look in all directions. Strands of her hair had slipped from the bun, framing her pretty face like some he'd seen in cameo broaches.

So far, she had managed to keep her dress tucked in around her knees to make it look more like a pair of bloomers. It was the only part of her that hinted of disorder.

"This is such a wonderful place," she said. "How many acres do you think are in this part that's been sickled?"

"About fifty. There are two more pastures. They rotate the cows to get a cutting of winter hay off each one every summer." He almost told her they used the different pastures to isolate the bulls from the cows at times, but thought that might be considered too vulgar.

She looked toward the trees along the banks of the Morales on the west end of the meadow. "The place is so large."

"I'm going to own me a big piece of land like this someday." He sat up more erect in the saddle. "A man never amounts to much unless he owns land. But everybody tells me I'm crazy for thinkin' I can do it."

"It doesn't sound crazy to me, Heck Tennel. I believe you can do it."

If she kept saying things that made him feel so good he thought he might bust. Or break the promise to himself about reining in his natural urges.

It wouldn't be easy to talk about less pleasant subjects at a time when things were going so good, but before losing his nerve or getting sidetracked, he decided to explain what he'd done in town and at Loony's barn. He figured he owed her that.

"Charlotte, there's something I have to tell you. It's like this, you see. A man as poor as I am has to make do with what he's got, and when he ain't, doesn't have all he needs, he sometimes has to do things he'd rather not do."

She fixed her intense brown eyes on him again, apparently sensing his sudden change of mood. "I don't think of you as being poor, Heck."

His face brightened a bit. "Thanks, but I am. And that's the pure truth. Except when I'm with you, that is."

She smiled, holding his gaze.

"Most things a workin' man does, he does to make ends meet. That needs no explainin', I reckon. But some other things are done because he's got no choice in a matter, if he stands for anything. I mean, at times there just ain't, isn't a nice way to do what he's got to do, whether it's for family or a friend. That's when he bends the rules a bit, which often puts him crossways with the powers that be. Am I makin' any sense at all?"

"A little. I'm sure it will when you decide it's time to be more specific. In the meantime, I know you'll do the right thing about whatever's troubling you. You don't impress me as someone who's afraid to take a stand just because somebody doesn't agree with you."

Continuing to be amazed by the grown-up things she said, he found the nerve to continue. "I never couldn't've put what I was tryin' to say in pretty words like you do. And you're the first girl I ever knew that I could talk to about serious stuff. Besides Miss Cilla, that is. But she ain't, isn't a girl. I mean, she's a woman. But you're a woman too. I mean . . ."

"I know what you mean," she said, smiling. "Let's ride some more and enjoy this beautiful day and this place."

He followed her across the meadow toward the cows, relieved that she had given him a reprieve. Riding slowly through the herd, she said, without turning, "Aunt Josephine called last night and told Aunt Priscilla we'd have to get back to grandfather's house in town on Sunday in time for church."

"I'm sorry about that. Not the church part, but you having to leave."

"Me too, but Aunt Josephine always gets her way."

"I know she and your granddad don't have a high regard for me, but I want to keep seeing you. If you want to see me, that is."

"Things have been easier for me since I met you. Yes, I want to keep seeing you. Aunt Priscilla and I will be coming out to the farm from time to time."

"Great. But if you don't get to come out for a long while, I'd like for us to stay in touch. Since we don't have a telephone, will you write me?"

"Sure. What's your address?"

"Don't send it to my house. Between my dad and our gossipy mail carrier, your Aunt Josephine and your granddad would find out about us for sure. I don't want to cause you any embarrassment."

She was thoughtful a moment. "I know a special place where we can hide our letters. I'll show it to you when we get back to the house."

"It had better be big, that special place. Otherwise, I'll have it runnin' over in a week."

She smiled, kicking her horse into a slow lope as she rode away with her skirt billowing. Urging his mount into a gallop, he caught up with her to ride no more than two feet from her stirrup. *Riding a good horse across a green meadow with the wind square in my face alongside the girl I love. Life has indeed become much kinder.*

After riding the other meadows at a slower pace, they reined their horses back through the iron gate toward the barn. They had talked about less serious topics on their return, laughing most of the way.

Heck unsaddled the horses, and when he was finished with rubbing them down, Charlotte asked him to follow her. She led him past the house along the gravel driveway, then into the woods east of it without comment. After going through about a hundred yards of heavy underbrush, they came upon the crumbled remains of a little log house.

"Aunt Priscilla told me this was once occupied by my grandfather's slaves. Later, it was the servant's quarters. When she told me, I just had to find it. Almost everything has rotted and fallen down except the chimney."

What used to be a yard was overgrown with vines, tall grass and trees. Between where they stood and the chimney, in a spot brightened by filtered sunlight, was a small patch of jonquils in full bloom. The sunny flowers seemed out of place among the ruins of a house no longer fit for living. Heck vaguely remembered the old place from earlier days of roaming through the surrounding woods, but he had never seen the flowers. They struck him as some kind of desperate plea from a dark past.

"Aren't they beautiful?" Charlotte stooped to pick one of the blossoms.

He nodded and picked another, placing it in her hair over her left temple. "There. That's the side your heart's on. Beauty for the beautiful."

"Thank you, sir." She curtsied.

Charlotte very carefully stepped through the flowers to the vine-covered chimney made of mud bricks. Above the firebox level, the chimney narrowed into a single flue that had cracked, causing it to lean as if tired. On the side of the wider part, the mud and grass mortar had fallen from between some of the clay bricks, leaving wide cracks in that part of the structure.

Reaching up to arm's length, Charlotte pulled out a loose brick from the chimney's sidewall. "See?" she said, turning. "We can put our letters in this hole."

He joined her and reached up to place his hand in the cavity. It was located at the point where the brick in the chimney's inner rear wall curved forward to join the flue to form a narrow cavity between them and the back wall.

She said, "I'll find a metal box and put it in there so our letters will stay dry."

"It's a good hiding place," he said, returning the brick to the slot. "I'll check it every day after you go back to town. But when you make a delivery, be sure to watch out for black widow spiders and rat snakes."

"You're kidding, right?"

"Rat snakes don't bite. Just wear a glove in case there's a spider in there."

She looked so feminine and vulnerable in her fright he was overwhelmed by the urge to hold her. Reaching out, he pulled her close and kissed her. She didn't resist, so he kissed her again.

"I know I'm no prize catch for any girl right now, and you may think I'm rushing things. But I'm afraid if I don't make my case before you go back to town, I might lose you to one of those rich city boys. What I said last night just slipped out, but since then I've thought it through. I meant what I said then, and I'll say it again. I love you." Holding her out so he could look into her eyes, he added, "I care for you more than I thought I could ever care for any girl, because up to last Sunday, a girl like you wasn't anything but wishful thinkin' on my part. Ever since then, when we're together, I feel like a whole man, and life makes sense all of a sudden. You're my every dream come true."

"You're good for me too, Heck," she said, moving up close to rest her head on his chest. "I was very frightened when I came to live with my aunts and grandfather. You've made it easier for me. All of a sudden, my life got exciting and interesting too." She raised her head to meet his gaze. "But how can you be so sure, so soon?"

"Because of the way you make me feel," he said. "And for a lot of other reasons I can't think of a way to describe. All I'm asking for is enough time to prove it. By the time I do that, I hope to be somebody you'll be proud of, and you'll be out of school. That's when I want you to marry me."

She turned her head, and when she looked at him again, there were tears in her eyes. "Those are the kind of beautiful things all girls want to hear, Heck. You're the most real, down-to-earth person I've ever known. Up to now, I thought all people were frivolous and unpredictable like my mother and father and the crowd they ran with. You make me feel safe and wanted. You also make me laugh, and you're gentle and considerate."

"That's music to my ears." He smiled. "But I won't be satisfied until I hear you say that you love me."

"But I . . ."

He placed his fingers over her lips. "I know, I know. I'm pushing you, expecting too much too soon. I ain't, haven't proved anything yet. But I will, and I don't care how long you make me wait."

"I was just going to say that I'll give you the time you've asked for. But you must understand that I'm not in control of my life at this point. I don't know what plans Aunt Josephine has for me before I reach legal age. For that reason I can't give you a definite answer on anything now, except that I won't see any other boys."

"Fair enough. Right now I'm not in complete charge of my life either, because certain people and events are trying to push me where I don't want to go. But nobody can stop me from loving you. Just wanted you to know that."

"I do believe you, Heck. I have strong feelings for you too, but things have happened so fast that I can't think straight right now. So, please be patient with me. Believe me. What you've said makes me very happy."

He kissed her again and held her hand as they hop-scotched back through the flowerbed, being careful not to step on the jonquils. Out of the woods on the way to the driveway, he said, "I'll be tied up tomorrow with some things I have to do. So, can I come back tonight?"

"Please do. I want to hear you play the piano and sing." She studied his face a moment. "All of a sudden you look worried, like you did back there in the meadow. Is there something else you'd like to tell me?"

He glanced around to make sure they didn't have an audience. "I started to tell you out in the pasture, but was afraid I'd say something that would spoil my chances with you. Charlotte, I feel bad, knowing I haven't told you about certain things."

"Then tell me now."

"You remember me mentioning my black friend Cracker?"

She nodded. "Yes."

He told her about Willa's charges against Cracker and how he had defied his neighbor Ubis Sproggs and the sheriff by helping him. "White folks around here won't take kindly to what I've done if they find out. The rape of a white woman by a black man has always been a killin' offense in these parts. That's why I've got to find Willa and get her to tell her daddy and the sheriff the truth. The sheriff's looking for Cracker, and so is Mr. Sproggs. I'll be in lots of trouble if they catch me helping him before I can talk to Willa. I hope you understand."

He couldn't tell from her expression whether she approved or disapproved. "I've heard of similar things happening in Louisiana, but I never knew about them firsthand. I don't understand how some people can be so brutal and inhumane to others. But I do admire what you're doing to protect an innocent person. Please be careful."

"I will, and I'd feel better if you'd say you won't hold it against me."

"How could I? But what if Willa demands something in exchange for changing her story? Based on what I've heard and what you've told me, I know she's quite a rounder." She hesitated, giving him a concerned look. "And I also know she's in love with you."

Her statement surprised him. How could she possibly know that? Besides, he never believed Willa capable of loving anybody. He said, "Love means different things to different people, I guess. I know Willa as well as anybody, but I can't explain her. Never knew she had any tender feelings about anything or anybody. I never loved her and I never told her I did. I don't even want to be around her any more. If she can't understand, that's her problem."

The look of concern and confusion on her face caused him to wonder if he had been too frank in his remarks. "Please, Charlotte, tell me you at least half-way understand, and that you won't let anything Willa does or say come between us."

Her expression remained noncommittal for a few moments. Finally, she said, "I realize how difficult it must have been for you to talk to me about her. No, it doesn't change my feelings toward you. It proves you believe my opinion of you is important. That's the part that counts."

"I appreciate your kind words. But while we're on the subject of dumb things I've done, let me tell you about another . . ."

"Charlotte," Miss Cilla called out from the front door. "Telephone."

"I've got to go in now," she said. "See you tonight. In the meantime, don't worry about Cracker or Willa making a difference in our relationship, okay?"

He watched until she disappeared inside the house and wondered if she would have been as understanding if he'd told her about the bank episode. Maybe he was saved by the bell. *You'll have to come clean with her soon and find out for sure.*

Keeping his ear tuned for the sound of Ubis Sproggs' hoopy, he walked through the woods along the road to Willa's back yard, stopping short when he saw Ubis' T-Model parked beside the house. He apparently had come home the back way from his still.

Disappointed, he sat down in the bushes hoping Willa would come outside. About a half-hour later she did. Unfortunately so did Slick and her dad. He heard her tell Ubis, "I'll sign the damn thang, but you should let me talk to Heck first like I wanted to."

They all got into the hoopy and drove off toward Panther Holler Road. Concerned about what Ubis required her to sign, Heck continued walking through the woods to Loony's place, pausing at the edge of the clearing to make sure the sheriff or his deputy didn't have it staked out. Detecting nothing out of the ordinary, he started out across the yard, but stopped upon seeing a stranger coming out of the back door. The man looked vaguely familiar, but Heck couldn't immediately place him. His jaw dropped as he continued to stare in disbelief at the sight before him.

"I'll be a catfish's whiskers," he muttered. "And I'd stopped believin' in miracles."

Clean-shaven, with his hair neatly trimmed and wearing a clean shirt and khaki pants, Loony was a man reborn. He spotted Heck and waved, smiling sheepishly.

"H-h-hi, Heck."

"Is that really you, Loony?" Heck said, moving closer.

"It's m-m-me, all right."

"You look like a million bucks. That Tiny Lucy knows how to take care of a man." He nudged Loony with his elbow and winked. "But it wasn't the shave and haircut that put that gleam in your eye, right?"

"Y-y-you're a devil, Heck." Loony blushed.

"Guess you'll be needin' some new slats in your bed after last night. Hope it didn't bang you up too much when the mattress hit the floor."

Loony's face turned a deeper red as his grin broadened. "S-s-still got good s-s-slats. Tiny Lucy made me p-p-put the dadburn m-m-mattress on the f-f-floor fust off."

Heck laughed, slapping his leg, and Loony laughed too. It sounded strange, hearing him laugh like other folks. Heck told him, "That should put an end to you sneakin' around in the woods lookin' for excitement."

Loony's grin disappeared, and he suddenly looked sad. "I r-r-r-reckon I'll have to p-put my bed back on the s-s-s-slats, 'cause Tiny Lucy's leavin' today."

"She won't if you play your cards right. It's just like farming, Loony. You've planted your seed, so now you need to weed and fertilize so you'll have a good crop. Fix up a place for Tiny Lucy to live in. Tell her you'll take care of her in your will if she'll take care of you now. You've got no family, and no close friends but me. Tell her you'll do that, and I'll bet she'll stay out here the rest of your life."

"Y-y-you thank so, Heck?"

"Of course."

Loony's expression turned somber again, and he said, "M-m-most folks won't think it's p-p-proper, me keepin' a c-c-colored lady on my place. I m-m-might get tarred and f-f-feathered."

"All the rich folks do it, don't they? They call 'em maids. If they can, why can't you? Now, I've got to look in on Cracker. Don't forget. If Ubis Sproggs or the sheriff comes by, tell 'em you haven't seen me or Cracker. Got that?"

Loony nodded. "G-g-got it."

"And ask Tiny Lucy about what we just discussed."

Heck found Cracker awake propped up in the hay.

"Mornin'," Heck said. "Feel like choppin' a little cotton?"

"I feel better," Cracker replied. "But I was afraid the High Sheriff grabbed you."

"I see Tiny Lucy's been takin' good care of you." He looked at the empty bowl near his friend. "And speakin' of care, you ought to see Loony."

"I seen him, and I overheard that hare-brained plan you laid out to him just then. Besides not bein' right, yo' plan would sho' mess up the sportin' life of lots of colored dudes, if Mr. Loony rakes up enough nerve to make her that offer and she goes fer it."

"Well, try not to get too upset. He hasn't asked yet, so she hasn't had a chance to say what she'll do."

"If she does agree to stay, the white folks out here would run her off, and no tellin' what else. Mr. Loony wouldn't come out much better. They ain't gonna put up with no colored woman livin' wid no white man."

"She doesn't have to live with him, dummy. She'd just have to live on the place. Like I told Loony, rich people always let their colored help do that, and some of 'em get something from the women besides help around the house. It would be a shame to take away the only thing that's ever put a spark in that lonely old man's life."

Kneeling, Heck removed the thigh bandage. "It looks a little better. I know you're gonna live now."

"Tiny Lucy said to tell you to put some of this on it." Cracker handed him a can of Cloverine salve. "Did you talk to Miss Willa?"

Heck coated the entry and exit wounds with the salve and applied clean patches. "Nope. But I will, soon as I can. I expect to have everything cleared up by tonight. Did you take any aspirin this mornin'?"

Cracker nodded, and Heck stood up, stretched and looked out the loft door to see what Loony was doing. He was surprised when he saw Tiny Lucy heading toward the trees in a fast walk. He called out to her, "Hey, wait up, Tiny Lucy. I want to talk to you."

"What's she doin'?" Cracker asked.

"Leavin', looks like," Heck replied, heading for the steps.

"I told you she would. That ol' man ain't got no money."

Running down the steps and out to where Tiny Lucy was waiting for him, Heck said, "Where ya goin'?"

"Home, o' course."

"I, we were hopin' you'd stay around here for a few more days at least."

She gave him a contemptuous look. "And what would I wear? I ain't even got a change o' clothes that I needed after bathing last night. I'm goin' home and get my thangs and tell my folks I'm okay, if'n that's all right with you."

"Then you're comin' back?"

"You ain't deef. But o' course you know that neither whites or colored'll look kindly on the 'rangement, even if Mr. Loony does fix me up somethin' to live in outside his house. But I aim to see after him and Cracker while he's decidin', if he wants to do that."

"Thanks, Tiny Lucy." He patted her shoulder. "Cracker thanks you too. And I can tell by the strut in Loony's step that he's happy as a Banty rooster in a pen full of young pullets. He'll fix up his storage shed for you, I guarantee."

She turned toward the woods at the edge of the yard, waving her arms and mumbling something. The only thing he made out was ". . . slippin' 'round in the woods like a chicken thief."

"Remember now," he called out after her, "if anybody asks you about me or Cracker, you haven't seen us."

She kept moving, throwing up her hands to show her disgust upon hearing his orders. Feeling uplifted, Heck went inside to warm a pot of peas and some turnip greens he found on the back of the stove. He dished up hefty servings of both and joined Cracker.

They had just begun to eat when a car drove up out front. Heck scrambled to the end of the loft to take a peek.

"Holy chit'lins," he exclaimed. "It's the sheriff. Quick. Let's get you under the hay."

"I'm gonna hang fo' sho' now."

Heck pulled Cracker to the side of the loft where the hay was thickest and buried him. He threw a double handful over their food, dived under and pulled several armfuls over himself.

Cracker sneezed.

"You want to get hung?" Heck whispered. "Cut that out."

"But this stuff's dusty, man," Cracker whispered back.

"I don't care if it's full of giant tarantulas, shush or we'll both end up in jail."

Heck heard the sheriff call Loony's name a couple of times while walking through the house and again from the back porch.

"Out here, Sheriff." A trace chain rattled near the barn.

Sheriff Sloan's booted feet tramped across the yard.

"Who are you? Where's Loony?"

"R-r-right chere. I-I-I'm Loony."

A long pause. "By God, it is you," the sheriff said. "What happened? Did you get religion or something? You don't look a day over forty."

No response.

"I've got an arrest warrant for Cracker Carver. Thought maybe you might've seen him."

Heck held his breath.

"N-n-n-nope. Ain't seed 'im.'

Heck breathed again.

"Then who made all those tracks in your yard? A man living by himself doesn't leave that many footprints around."

Heck's lungs froze again. *Damn. I shoulda pulled a bush over 'em. Don't fail us now, Loony.*

"Oh, them t-t-tracks. I had a c-c-colored woman come do the wash. She b-b-brought some h-h-help with her."

"Why'd she go out to the barn, to clean that too?"

Cracker whispered, "Loony's gonna spill the beans for sho', Heck. Run while you still can."

"Shut up!"

"S-s-she got some of my w-w-work clothes out'n the shed," Loony said. "A-a-and I got her and her h-h-helpers to clean up around the p-p-place."

Heck could tell by his stuttering that Loony was really scared now.

After a long pause, the sheriff told Loony, "Well, I did notice how clean your house was. You could use her more often."

"I m-m-might at that."

"I can't find Heck Tennel either. Got a bone to pick with him too. Figured if I find one, I'll find 'em both. Have you seen Heck?"

"N-n-not since the m-m-musical Sadidy night."

"How about a new Ford? Have you seen one, or that Jake fella that ran Heck off the bridge?"

"N-n-nope. But I heerd a panther night 'fo last."

"Panthers," the sheriff grunted. "Well, I'm going to take a look around, just in case them two slipped in on you."

Heck and Cracker heard the sheriff poke around in a nearby storage shed, then in the stalls on both sides of the barn downstairs. Moments later he walked along the hard ground directly under them, paused and started up the steps to the loft.

Heck's entire body began to tremble at the sound. They were both bound for jail, or worse.

# Chapter XXIII

Each clump of the sheriff's boots on the stairs made Heck's heart pump harder. By the time Sheriff Sloan entered the hayloft, he was too weak to run even if he wanted to.

"That cleanin' woman cooked some mighty powerful greens," the sheriff mumbled. "I can smell 'em all the way up here."

Heck held his breath. When he started feeling dizzy, he exhaled slowly and took in more air in short, noiseless gasps. He almost sprang up out of the hay when he heard a sudden sneeze nearby, convinced that Cracker had given them away.

"All this hay. Phew." The sheriff sneezed again. "There's nobody up here." He headed down the stairs.

As soon as Heck heard footsteps on the ground, he pushed the hay off his face and took a deep breath and listened. He heard the sheriff say, "Loony, if you see those two, send me word, you hear? I'll be back tomorrow if I don't hear from you."

The sheriff's car pulled out of the yard and Heck burst out of the hay spitting and gasping and knocking it out of his hair and mouth.

"Cracker, you can come out now."

Cracker flung the hay aside and sat up sneezing and wheezing. "How does a cow eat that stuff? I been dyin' to sneeze, and when the sheriff stopped at the top of them stairs, I nearly messed in my pants."

"At least that would've kept him from smellin' the greens. I thought we were goners for sure." Heck stood up and brushed off more hay. Going to the end of the loft, he looked down to find Loony hitching up his mare to a plow.

"Thanks, Loony," He waved down at him.

"S-s-storm's comin'." Loony hooked the second trace chain, gave him a warning glance and turned back to the mule.

Recalling that the old bachelor had given him the same warning two days before, Heck returned to the center of the hayloft wondering what it meant, if anything. He retrieved the bowls of food from under the hay and pulled everything out of them that crawled or didn't look good enough to eat, and placed one in Cracker's trembling hands.

"Relax," Heck told him. "The sheriff won't look up here again, even if he does come back. Eat up. I've got to go into town to see if I can find a man who owes me a hundred dollars. Tiny Lucy'll be back tonight."

Outside, Heck saw Loony plowing some young peas in the garden as if nothing out of the ordinary had happened. Not wanting to disrupt the old man's apparent peace of mind, he crossed the yard and entered the woods to head for the Sproggs place. He had to talk to Willa. He and Cracker wouldn't be so lucky next time.

Ubis' hoopy wasn't back yet, so Heck figured Willa wasn't either. Disgusted over not being able to talk to her, he decided to talk to the mother.

Going to the back door, he knocked lightly. Mrs. Sproggs appeared, wiping her hands on her flour sack apron as she cautiously approached the screen door. She was short and obese and had one crossed eye. The skin on her face was coarse and freckled like Willa's.

"Heck! Boy, the sheriff just left here. He was lookin' for you."

"I've got to find Willa." He glanced at the road through the trees.

"She said she wanted to talk to you too, but she ain't here now. Had to go to town to sign somethin'."

"I want her to tell the sheriff the truth before Cracker gets hung and I get put in jail. Cracker didn't rape her."

"She said he did, that's all I know about it. And Ubis said he was gonna kill Cracker, so I don't guess you'll have to worry 'bout him gettin' hung."

"Will you give Willa a message for me?"

"I reckon there ain't no harm in that."

"Tell her I understand her problem and I'm willin' to make things right. But tell her I won't do anything until she tells the sheriff the truth."

"I will. But that Willa has a mind of her own. Guess you know that better'n anybody."

He tried not to look at her bad eye as he said, "Tell her I'll be back in the mornin' at sunrise, to meet me in the trees behind your barn so I can get things right between us and save a man's life. But don't say nothin' to her daddy unless you want her to get a beatin'. Okay?"

She nodded and he left, this time crossing the woods toward the road that ran through The Settlement some two miles away.


"Where's my boy? Is he all right?" Mrs. Carver had spotted Heck approaching her house and had run out on the porch.

"I came to tell you he's fine," he said, nodding. "But I can't tell you where he's at right now. Don't want to get you or a special friend that's helpin' us in trouble with the law."

"But can't I at least see him? As his mother, ain't I got that right?"

"Yes ma'am, you sure do, and I wish you could, but this way is better. I'll have this mess straightened out by tomorrow." He looked at her. "You still trust me, don't you?"

"Yessuh," she nodded. "Jus' please take care o' my boy."

"We'll let you know as soon as I talk to Willa. Bye."

Going back out to the main road, he headed to town at a brisk walk, jumping into the bushes when he heard a car coming. It was Mr. Banion on his way home from the Two Rivers milk plant. As soon as he passed, Heck jumped back in the road and resumed his trip to town.

The first stop in town: Cotton's little house. Heck knocked loudly, but got no response. After a second knock, he pushed the door open and stepped inside. On the floor in the front room he found Cotton's borrowed suit and the red dress Thelma wore to the bank. The sight gave him some relief, because it told him they had at least made it this far without being arrested.

"Cotton!" he called out. "Mama!"

Receiving no answer, he went into the back room. Empty. Out back, he saw that Cotton's T-Model hoopy was gone. Convinced they'd abandoned the place, he walked along the side of the shack and sat down on the porch with a big sigh, disgusted and confused.

*What now?* He spotted an old black woman peering at him from around the corner of the shack next door.

"Hey, there. Have you seen Cotton?"

The woman studied him a moment as if she might suspect him of being a bill collector. "He the one that lived there?"

Heck nodded.

"Yassuh, I seed him, but I ain't likely to agin."

"Why's that? Did he get put in jail?"

"No jail. He left for Californy."

"California! Was a woman with him?"

"Yassuh."

Heck found himself looking up the dirt street as if expecting somebody, or something, to suddenly appear with a clue as to what he should do. When he looked back, the old woman was gone.

He walked through some tall weeds to the railroad tracks that ran north and south through the ghetto. He would follow them out to the mill and go to his granddad for advice.

"Hi, Grandpa," he said, noticing it was quarter to four by the living room clock.

"Heck," He glanced at the door behind him. "Where you headed by yourself?"

"Jail, seems like, or the poor house. But before I leave, I'd sure like a glass of water if you can spare one."

His granddad gave him a concerned look and followed him into the kitchen to watch as he drew a glass of water from the tap. "Heck, I'm really worried about you," he said softly. "The sheriff came by lookin' for you, but he wouldn't tell me why. You in trouble, boy?"

"Maybe, but don't worry. I haven't done anything wrong. Just stupid. It's funny what a man will do for money when he ain't got, doesn't have any." He told him about Billy's appointment with Doctor Samuels that Saturday, and how bad he felt about not being able to take him. He explained about driving Thelma and Cotton to the bank for a promised hundred dollars. "Nothin' went right. Now they've both skipped without givin' me a cent."

"Thelma and Cotton." His granddad's expression was grave. "They got back together after all these years. I never saw a crooked bush that made a straight tree."

"Billy and the girls will never stop cryin' now."

"I'm sorry for you, Billy and the girls," his granddad said sadly. "I'm especially sorry for Billy. Come on, let's go back to the livin' room and talk it out."

Heck followed his grandfather into the front room and sat down on the sofa opposite him in his rocker.

"Things are past talkin', Grandpa. I said all I knew to say to those two yesterday. I tried to get Mama to come home. And I've talked to Blood Money about a loan. I asked all over town last week about a job, but didn't find one."

"Well, if Cotton and Thelma made it out of Texas, they likely won't be arrested and made to tell how you helped 'em at the bank. So it looks like you're in the clear there."

"Lord, I hope so. I sure could use a break for a change."

"I've managed to save four dollars." His granddad's voice was soft and kind. "It's yours if you want it. Tim may have a spare dollar or two."

"Thanks, Grandpa. But you and Uncle Tim need that money. Besides, it wouldn't be nearly enough."

His granddad sighed. "Things will be getting' better soon in the way of jobs accordin' to what Mr. Roosevelt tells us. He started some programs that'll put men to work. Maybe Billy can hold his own 'til you get one of those jobs and put a little aside for doctor bills."

"Billy's problems won't wait. Even if they would, a man should help himself, not bank on others to do things that are his to do."

"I admire your spunk, boy, but don't become so desperate that you start doin' wild things like Bonnie and Clyde did for so long. I guess you heard about what happened to them."

"You mean all that fuss about how they held up Blood Money's bank?"

"That's only part of it. They were ambushed by a bunch of lawmen and killed earlier today in Louisiana. It happened somewhere just across the state line."

Heck felt a sudden chill rush over him. Leaning forward, he asked, "Was anybody with them, like a driver maybe, or another woman?"

"Don't know. A neighbor down the street that's got a radio told me about it. He didn't say nothin' about nobody else. Why do you ask?"

Heck got up and paced the floor. "You remember Jake, the stranger that came to our musical? I'm afraid he might've been drivin'. If he was, Marna could've been with him." He told his granddad about her running off with Jake.

"Early's family is breakin' up, and all on account of that weak wife of his. I warned him about her a long time ago."

Heck stopped at the window and gazed out across the tops of the little houses at the smokestacks over the mill. *What should I do now? What can I do now?*

"Heck, I know you'll find a way to provide for Billy and the girls with their mama gone. But there ain't no short cuts. What happened to Bonnie and Clyde is proof enough of that."

Heck's mind was in such turmoil he figured a response would contradict his grandfather. It was true that bank robbers got killed, but it was also true that hungry people starved and sick people died without having done anything bad. So what is a man to believe about which fork in the road he should take?

"I've always believed in you, Heck. You're strong of character, like Ross. Just don't let hard times make you give up believin' in yourself, or in people in general. Will you promise me that?"

"I'll try, Grandpa." He glanced at the mantel clock. "Gotta go."

His grandfather accompanied him to the door, saying, "Be careful. Don't do nothin' that'll hang around your neck like a ragged horse collar the rest of your life."

Bidding his grandfather good-bye, Heck walked down to Peach Creek where he turned north through the woods toward Loony's place.

In order to save time, he cut through Blood Money's back meadow, pausing there long enough to look toward the big house and wish he could talk to Charlotte. She always seemed to know his feelings and what to say to make him feel good.

He found things the way he'd left them at Loony's place. The swelling in Cracker's thigh had gone down some more and he had no fever. Encouraged, he said, "I told you you'd live, Sportin' Man."

"So how come you got such a long face? You ain't got yo' self in more trouble on my account, have you?"

"If a man's already standin' up to his knees in cow manure, how can another inch or two matter?"

Heck went to the kitchen and built a fire in the stove. He was cooking supper for Cracker and Loony when Tiny Lucy walked through the back door unannounced, huffing and puffing and sweating profusely. She dropped a sack of her things on the kitchen floor and turned her fierce eyes on him.

"Lawdy!" she said. "I should come up the road like white folks and respectable people. Them briars don't care what they scratch. Now, you get outta th' way. I'll do the cookin' 'round here. I ain't never seen men folks that could cook nothin' worth eatin'."

Upon hearing her voice, Loony came in off the front porch still wearing the clothes he had plowed in. He stopped in the doorway to stare at Tiny Lucy's large backside, but said nothing.

Turning, she said, "Don't jus' stand there gawkin' like a goat on a pile o' garbage. Go take a bath and change clothes. We're gonna be eatin' in a little while and I don't wanta smell nothin' that ain't in my plate."

Loony blushed and grinned, but didn't move.

"I come back to take care of you, if you'll fix me up a place out back," she said, holding his gaze. "Do you understand what I'm sayin'?"

Loony's pleased expression gave her his answer even before he spoke. Finally, he said "Yes'm," and meekly walked though the kitchen on his way to the well.

It was nearing sundown by the time they finished eating. Heck took a plate of food to Cracker, and when Tiny Lucy moved to the front porch, he sponged off on the back porch with a piece of cloth from an old shirt and that thin bar of P & G soap he retrieved from the kitchen. Throwing out the bath water, he dried off and put his clothes back on and headed for the Vandergriff place in a fast walk as the sun set behind the big trees along the road.

Miss Cilla answered his knock and asked him in with a pleasant smile. He didn't see Charlotte, but the Truesdales were just coming into the room from the hall. Both had on nice clothes as if they might be going out.

Mr. Truesdale placed hostile eyes on Heck and told Miss Cilla, "Your sister and Mr. Vandergriff won't like it when they find out the sheriff has been by their old home lookin' for criminals."

Heck held the man's gaze. "I didn't know you had criminals in your family, Mr. Truesdale."

"I don't, smart aleck. It's *you* the law's been lookin' for. You and your nigger friend."

"Curt!" his wife said with a glance toward their employer. "Miss Cilla can handle this."

The foreman glanced at Miss Cilla. "But it's her I'm worried about. Her and that sweet little orphan niece she's got with her."

Miss Cilla smiled. "You and your wife can go on to town now. Charlotte and I will be just fine." To Heck, she said, "I'll go tell Charlotte you're here."

As the Truesdales walked out, Curt turned and held the screen door open. "You'd better enjoy your last visit to this house, boy. After tonight, you ain't comin' back."

Heck watched them move out into the yard as he considered the somber prediction about this being his last visit. *Whatever he has in mind to do, I'm sure it won't be in my favor.*

After they drove off in Miss Cilla's car, Heck went out on the porch and sat down on the swing where he felt a gentle breeze stirring the night air. It was a clear night, so clear that the stars seemed close enough to touch. He was looking at the dark outline of the trees across the road when Charlotte came through the front door.

"Hi," she said. "Penny for your thoughts."

He stood up. "Hi. You'd be cheated, because a penny is worth a lot these days."

She sat down beside him and her nearness immediately lifted his spirits. Wearing a white dress with a red strip around the hem and collar, she was prettier than ever.

"Mr. Truesdale doesn't take kindly to me coming here," he said. "I hope his feelings aren't contagious." Correct grammar was coming to him easier, now that he'd found good reason to make the effort.

"Don't worry about Mr. Truesdale. I might have been bothered too when the sheriff came by looking for you if you hadn't already told me why you helped your black friend."

"Can the foreman keep me from coming here as long as it's okay with you and Miss Cilla?"

"I hope not. Depends on what Aunt Josephine has to say about it. Aunt Priscilla said she believes he's going to town now to give her a full report. She tried to stop him by telling him things were going well out here for both of us. She didn't want him to say anything about . . ."

"Me?"

"About anything she and I are doing to enjoy ourselves. Aunt Priscilla has always resented her sister's domination. Being out here is the happiest I've ever seen her."

"Do you think Mr. Truesdale will do what she wants him to do?"

"No. He made it clear that he takes his orders from Aunt Josephine."

Heck started the swing with a gentle push of his foot. "I sure needed to be with you a while, because that always makes things better for me."

"Did you talk to Willa yet?"

"No, but I'm supposed to meet her in the morning. Then me and Cracker will both be in the clear."

"I'm glad. That'll free you to start doing those other things you want to do."

He was building up his nerve to tell her about what happened at the bank when she placed her hand on his arm. "I want to hear you play and sing. Will you do that for me?"

"I'd jump off the high end of the barn and dance Yankee Doodle on a mean bull's back if you asked me to, I reckon. But I must warn you, I just play by ear in major chords. Nothing fancy."

She took his hand and led him through the parlor to the piano, pushing back the keyboard cover as he pulled out the bench. When she sat down beside him, a whiff of her perfume almost made him forget what he'd come inside to do. Playing for an audience could be unnerving enough, but having Charlotte as that audience would make it even harder. For starters, he couldn't think of anything to play.

"Any suggestions?" he asked.

"How about 'When the Red, Red Robin Comes Bob, Bob Bobbing Along'?"

"I think I remember the tune, but not the words. Does it go something like this?"

He found the C chord and began to play, slowly picking out the melody with his right hand at first, then picking up the beat with his left as he brought the tempo up to normal. He grimaced at a couple of sour notes, but Charlotte didn't seem to notice. After he played it the second time without any errors he stopped and she clapped her hands.

"That was pretty," she said. "Now sing a song."

Pleasing her made him swell with pride, and forget a few missed fingerings. He told her, "I usually have my guitar to beat rhythm on when I sing. I might really mess up on a piano."

"You'll do fine."

"Don't say I didn't warn you." He ran through a D chord and began "Brown Eyes," singing all the verses as he remembered them. Those he didn't, he improvised. He ended with, "I'll never love blue eyes again."

Perspiring, he gave her a questioning look and hoped he hadn't damaged her opinion beyond repair by such a bad performance.

To his surprise, she placed her hand on his arm and said, "That's a beautiful song. And you sing it with such feeling."

"Every time I hear it from now on, I'll think about how pretty your eyes are, up close like this." He wished he'd thought of something more elegant to say, but more than anything else, he wished he could kiss her. He knew that wouldn't be proper under the circumstances, but the way she was holding his gaze caused him to have second thoughts. He didn't see the slightest hint of sadness in her expression that he noticed on previous occasions.

Taking a deep breath, he forced his concentration back to the piano and played "Red Wing." After that, he played and sang "Just Before the Battle Mother," a song that Mr. Meade had taught him, and after catching his breath, "Goober Peas" with some embellishments Charlotte found humorous. Her soft, sweet laughter was prettier than any music he'd ever heard, and her eyes sparkled like dew on a field of flowers in the bright morning sun.

She brought him a glass of water. After taking a drink, he sang "Be Nobody's Darlin' But Mine." Her smile disappeared as she listened intently, inferring that she detected a message in the song meant for her. To brighten her pretty face again, he sang "I'll Be All Smiles Tonight."

"Thank you," she said, smiling. "Pretty songs and music make life sweeter, don't you think? And from watching you, I'd say they do as much for the singer as the listener."

"You have such a nice way with words. If it'd been me trying to describe music, I would've said it makes every night seem like Saturday night. It perks up a man and brings out the best part of him."

Still wanting to sing something more befitting the occasion, he began playing "Beautiful Dreamer" and she sang the words, moving up so close that he could feel her shoulder against his side. When they finished, a gentle clapping of hands in the hall entrance signaled that Miss Priscilla had joined them.

"Miss Cilla, I hope all the racket didn't bother you too much."

"To the contrary, I'm enjoying it," she said, stepping over near them. "Nobody's played this old piano in over twenty years. It's full of dust and a bit out of tune, I'm afraid."

"Oh, is that the problem?" he said. "I thought it was me."

They all laughed, and Miss Cilla said to Charlotte, "Don't you want to play something for Heck now?"

Heck gave Charlotte a surprised look. "You know how to play proper music?"

She nodded. "A little."

He grimaced. "Then my fumbling must've sounded awful."

"Don't be so hard on yourself," she said. "I liked what you played and the way you played it."

"Well, I want to hear some real talent now." He slid down to the end of the bench.

Miss Cilla nodded, and Charlotte moved to the center of the bench to place her small hands on the keys, running the chord of F. Heck marveled that such tiny hands could reach an octave.

She began "Flow Gently Sweet Afton," and he became very still beside her, alternately looking at her pretty face and her small hands moving so expertly over the ivories. He soon found himself in a euphoric state, having passed through that portal leading from grim reality to a kind and loving world. It was a place he had always sought but never found, until now.

Next she played "There's An Old Spinning Wheel in the Parlor." At the chorus the second time, he began singing the words: "There's an old spinning wheel in the parlor, spinning dreams of long, long ago. Spinning dreams of an old fashion garden, spinning dreams of an old fashion beau . . ."

He abruptly stopped when car lights swung into the driveway and disappeared as a car moved past the house into the back yard. Upon seeing the flash of light on the wall in front of her, Charlotte stopped playing and gave her aunt a frightened look. That hint of sadness again appeared in her eyes.

"They're back already?" Charlotte said to Miss Priscilla.

"Maybe it's best you and Heck wait out on the swing until I talk to them."

They had no sooner sat down on the swing when the back screen door squeaked open and slammed shut. Hushed voices came from the kitchen. Heck could tell by Charlotte's worry lines that she was very concerned about what was being said, and her sadness disturbed him.

"Maybe I should've gone and talked to Miss Josephine," he said. "I could've told her how good it was of her to let you come out here and what a good time you've had." He paused, and added, "Never thought I'd be thankful to her for anything." He quickly added, "No disrespect intended."

"None taken," she said. "I know how cold and uncaring Aunt Josephine can be at times. That's why I've never understood why Grandfather has always been so fascinated by her. She's not at all like Aunt Priscilla."

He placed her hand on his. "Or you," he said. He gave the swing a little push as a whippoorwill in the woods sang out with "Chip-fell-out-of-the-white-oak" a couple of times. That's when he noticed there was no longer a breeze moving across the porch, and the only sound he heard was the steady chatter of the katydids.

The tranquility about them was shattered by Mr. Truesdale's heavy footsteps coming through the house. He appeared just inside the front window nearest them where he leaned a chair against the wall and sat down.

Nodding toward their observer, Heck whispered to Charlotte, "I wonder if he'll jot down everything we say in shorthand, or just take a chance on remembering it."

She smothered a laugh, shaking her head. He didn't care if the foreman had heard what he said, because his presence reminded him of how tired he was of people who seemed to take pleasure in holding him back.

Leaning closer, she whispered, "This is ridiculous. Come with me." He followed her into the shadows at the end of the porch. "Help me down. I know a place where we can talk in private."

He jumped down, reached up to take hold of her hand, and slid his arm around her as she stepped off the porch. Only a dim glow of light through a back bedroom window was visible now, not enough for him to walk by in unfamiliar territory.

"We'll go sit in Aunt Priscilla's car," she said. "No eavesdroppers out there."

With no light on the back porch, the DeSoto was only a dim shadow under the flat shed. It was so dark Heck couldn't see the ground as they walked past the back corner of the house. While groping their way hand-in-hand, toward the car, Heck's right foot caught on something, causing him to fall hard.

"Are you all right?" she asked, giggling.

"Just had some of the wind knocked out of my sail is all. But I don't think this croquet hoop will ever be the same."

"Sorry. I should have warned you."

When they reached the car, she told him, "Don't open the front door. The dome light will come on if you do."

Groping for the back door handle, Heck found it and they climbed in. "Ahh," he said. "This is a lot softer than Maude's back."

"You have a girlfriend named Maude too?"

He laughed. "Maude's my mule."

"Oh."

"I'll roll the windows down so the breeze can get in." He lowered the rear windows, then leaned across the front seat to open those up front, amazed at how hot it had become all of a sudden. He sat down and placed his arm around her. "Now, this is the life," he said. "Yessir. The way I feel now, I don't care if cotton drops to a penny a pound and all the wells go dry."

"You shouldn't say that," she warned. "It might bring bad luck."

"Oh, I don't have to worry about any new bad luck. With all that's already come my way, it would have to wait in line so long I'd have a way figured out to beat it before it got a good hold on me."

"You're one surprise after another." She laughed. "You can be so serious one minute, then funny the next. Are you always that way?"

"I'm always serious with you." He pulled up her chin and kissed her.

Catching her breath, she said, "My goodness."

"Just think," he said, squeezing her hand. "When you marry me, you'll have to put up with a lot of kissing, hand-holding and goggle-eyed lookin' all the time. Why, I'll probably ask you to shut down this entire farm someday and have it dedicated as sacred ground, the place we first went horseback riding together."

"You might be tired of me by the time we can get married. Or disappointed to find me just an ordinary person, pretty much like the other girls you've know."

"What other girls? I've already forgotten them. And from now on there are no other girls as far as I'm concerned."

"But what if . . ."

"I never play what if. It's too uncertain. When I set my sights on something, I don't make any allowances for what ifs. I'm harder'n a snappin' turtle to pry loose from whatever it is I've latched onto."

"A snapping turtle? What's that?"

"The meanest, toughest, strongest and ugliest critter God ever created. He'll bite through your boot or your boat to get hold of you. Why, one time, a big one snapped a thick limb in two I was pokin' him with. Then he grabbed onto my ax, and wouldn't turn it loose 'til it thundered."

"Oh, my. Are you really like a snapping turtle?"

"Only with certain things," he said, kissing her cheek. "I'll always be gentle with you, like I was when I was usin' Miss Priscilla's fine china."

She snuggled a little closer, causing his head to spin like a top. He took a deep breath and said, "It sure is warm tonight."

"Want me to get you some lemonade?"

"Only if you can bring enough to pour all over me."

She laughed. "You're so funny."

He wondered if she suspected the real reason he was so warm. Pulling her tightly against him, he kissed her again.

"But you get serious so quick," she whispered.

"No quicker than the first time I saw you. I almost swallowed my Adam's apple."

"You weren't bad looking either."

"You're just being kind. I know I'm not much to look at. And that day I was wearing them, those overalls and that ragged ol' cap. An awful sight. That was the first time I ever hated overalls."

She was quiet a moment, then said, "I've had my fill of pretty faces and pretty clothes, and behavior that's too proper. They go together, it seems. I find comfort in your sincerity and your predictability. Your straightforwardness. And you're tall and strong. I could tell right away that you weren't conceited like a lot of boys I've known casually. I could also tell you don't think you're handsome, but I think you are."

"You sure know how to make a fella feel like he's somebody." He tightened his grip around her. "And as long as you believe I'm okay, I don't care what other people think. I'm more convinced than ever that there's hope for this ol' country boy after all. A good woman does that for a man. Up to last Sunday morning, I was beginning to wonder if I'd ever meet that kind of woman."

After a brief pause, she said, almost apologetically, "I'm not a woman yet."

It suddenly became warmer in the car and he kissed her again, longer this time. And he found his hand sliding down her arm, then over to her breasts. They were full and soft. A little voice inside his brain screamed, *Watch it. You're going too far too fast.*

She didn't push his hand away, and the monster within wouldn't let him stop. Kissing her again, he continued to caress her, but upon approaching the point of no return, he released her and moved back. After several deep breaths, he told her. "I was just about to make a woman out of you. Did you know that?"

She responded with a sigh and, instead of moving away, leaned closer and laid her head against his chest. "I know," she whispered, seemingly unworried about the matter.

His heart pounded so hard he could hear it thumping in his ears. He said, cautiously, "Have you ever wondered what it'll be like when your husband makes a woman out of you?" That little voice within said, *There you go, wading into deep water again.*

Instead of changing the subject like he expected her to do, she snuggled closer and said, "That's something all girls think about."

*Oh, my God. I should change the subject, talk about something else.* "But don't, uh, all nice girls want to wait 'til they're married to make the, uh, changeover? Or do you think maybe some of them want to jump the gun, so to speak?"

"They believe it's important to become a woman with the man they love," she said without hesitation. Her voice was soft, dreamy.

His pulse raced faster, and the tension in his body built to the point of explosion. *Oh my. What's a man supposed to do in a fix like this with a nice girl?*

Taking another deep breath, he asked, "Do you love me just a little bit already?"

"Yes."

Unable to restrain himself any longer, he pulled up her chin and asked, "Question is, how you feel right now?"

"All mixed up, strange. I've never felt this way before . . . like I'm floating, and weak all over. I don't know whether it's love or something else."

With his pulse pounding even louder now, he found himself easing her backwards on the seat and moving his hand to her bosom again, then down further, gently exploring. She sighed and became limp, making no move to stop him.

In spite of the pounding urgency driving him, he proceeded slowly, finding out immediately that she was giving him what a woman can give a man but once. Noting her discomfort, he moved more gently, pausing each time she made sounds that indicated he might be hurting her. When she placed her arms around his neck, he proceeded with more vigor, pulling her tight against his chest, kissing the top of her head and telling her how much he loved her.

Moments later he collapsed on top of her, kissed her lips and cheek and told her again how much he loved her. Removing himself from over her, he fell back in the seat to catch his breath. Upon recovering, he sat up and lifted her from the seat to hold her.

"Oh, Heck," she whispered. "I do love you. I do."

As soon as his energy was sufficiently restored, he helped her with her clothes and rearranged his own. When he settled down beside her again, she was sobbing softly.

"It's all right." He pulled her into his arms. "We're the same people we were before. Nothing's changed, except I love you more. I'll never let anything, or anybody, come between us."

She stopped crying and placed her arms around his neck. "Promise?"

"Promise."

"And you won't want to stop seeing me, now that . . ."

"Charlotte, sweetheart, I'll never get tired of you. I want to see you more than ever. And until we're married, I'll control myself. I don't want to do anything else that might cause you problems, ever."

They jumped when a flashlight's beam swept across the back yard, momentarily lighting up the car. Looking toward the house, Heck saw that it was coming from the back porch. He told Charlotte, "I think somebody's looking for us."

A woman's voice called out. "Charlotte. Where are you, sweetheart?"

"It's Aunt Priscilla. We must get out of the car quickly. If Mr. Truesdale hears her and comes outside, I'll be in serious trouble with Aunt Josephine."

Heck stepped out of the car and held out his hand to assist her. "Too bad," he said. "We needed time to talk. I've got lots more to tell you."

Standing up, Charlotte straightened her hair and clothes. "Out here, Aunt Priscilla. I'm coming." She squeezed his hand. "I'm sorry we didn't have more time too."

Curt Truesdale joined Miss Cilla on the porch with a lamp. He immediately took the flashlight from Miss Cilla and placed its beam on their approaching faces.

Heck walked on limber legs, and Charlotte's face was still flushed when they walked into the bright circle of light. The foreman gave Heck an angry, knowing look and snapped off the flashlight when they stopped at the steps.

"It's time to come in, Charlotte," Miss Cilla said. "You can see Heck again tomorrow."

"Yes, ma'am. I'll just walk around to the front with him."

Once in the darkness at the end of the house, Heck stopped, pulled Charlotte into his arms and held her tightly. "I love you so much. I hate to leave you."

"And I love you. I just wish I was old enough to manage my own life. If Aunt Josephine finds out about us . . ."

"How could she? Nobody'll ever know about what happened tonight except you and me. Before long, I'll improve my situation so much even Miss Josephine will take a liking to me. Soon after that we'll get married."

"I do believe you, Heck." She laid her head against his chest. "I just hope you don't get tired of waiting for me."

A lamp was placed on the front porch, lighting the area around them. Looking through the parlor window, Heck saw the foreman walking in from the front porch and said, "Somebody really wants me to leave."

"When will you come back?" She looked up at him.

"Tomorrow sometime. Remember what I told you back there."

"I will."

He kissed her again and backed away, slowly releasing her hand as he walked away, and when he looked back, saw her silhouetted against the porch lamp. She was still and her shoulders slumped, as if suddenly tired. The sight of her standing there so alone made him want to go back and hold her, reassure her, but he knew he could not.

# Chapter XXIV

Heck walked out his back door at first light the next morning and headed for the Sproggs place. Elsie promised him to fix breakfast and take care of their dad's morning needs.

The clear mental picture of Charlotte standing alone in the driveway as he walked away had kept Heck awake until sometime after midnight. He doubted the memory of it would ever fade as long as he lived. He was also troubled by a sense of guilt at having lost control of his urges in the back seat of her aunt's car. But while lying in the dark before going to sleep, he had attempted easing his conscience by telling himself the act was not wrong because they loved each other and planned one day to marry. *She approved, and afterward told me she loved me in a way that sounded more convincing than before the deed was done.*

In spite of his attempts to right it in his own mind, however, he still found himself hoping he had not done anything that would sadden or bring her shame.

He reached a spot behind the Sproggs' barn by the time the sun was high enough to light up the woods around him. Shortly thereafter, he heard noises inside the house, then the squeak of the back door as someone came outside. It was Willa.

"Over here," he called out in a loud whisper, waving.

She changed course, heading directly toward him. Coming into the bushes, she threw her arms around him, squeezing with the strength of a man, blurting out, "Honey, I'm so glad to see you I could scream. Kiss me quick. I'm about to cum."

"Wait a minute." He tried to push her away, but she held on. "Ain't it a little early for that?"

"Early, my foot," she said, reaching for his crotch. "It ain't never too early or too late for a tumble with you, lover boy. Now, quit stallin' and get on with it."

"I didn't come down here to do that." He wiggled out of her clutches. "I came to talk to you about Cracker. I want you go with me to the sheriff's office and swear he didn't rape you."

"How do you know he didn't?" She gave him a teasing look.

"Be serious, Willa. Cracker has already been shot and nearly killed by your daddy because of what you said. He'll get shot dead next time or hung, if you don't change your story."

"Well, since you come to make things right between us like you told mama you would, I guess I'm willin' to talk to the sheriff."

He sighed with relief. "Let's go."

"Soon as you say you're ready to make an honest woman out of me."

"What are you talking about? What have you got up your sleeve now?"

"It ain't what's up my sleeve, lover," she said, slapping her belly. "It's more like what I've got in here. I'm pregnant, dummy."

Her words shook him like the kick of a mule. "You're what?"

"You ain't deaf, Heck Tennel. And you ain't blind."

Numbed by her unexpected announcement, he looked at her belly. "I noticed you'd put on a few pounds," he said. "But I thought it was because you'd been having trouble pushin' back from the table." He made some quick calculations. "But I haven't touched you in nearly five months."

She hugged her belly. "Then I'm five months gone, stupid."

"Even if you are, how do I know it's mine?"

She slapped him. "Damn you, Heck Tennel. You know I wouldn't stoop that damn low."

"You lied about Cracker," he said, rubbing his face.

"That didn't take no skin off my nose, or yours either. I had to do something to pull you down off your high horse."

"But you live in the same house with Slick Haskell. I know you've done it with him, because he told me you did, lots of times. And according to him, you've been with other guys too."

"Men talk," she snapped. "Lies. Slick's my half brother, for cryin' out loud. And he's a liar, just like them other braggin' clodhopper ding-dongs. Oh, I've been tumbled a few times with another boy or two, but not before you got me started. You know what an appetite I've had since then. You cut me off and made me suffer every time you had one of your dreamin' fits. But I ain't let nobody else touch me since I decided it was you I really love. That was over a year ago."

He sank to his knees, too shocked to think clearly. He said, finally, "This pregnancy business. Was that what you were drivin' at over in Hank Slater's field last Saturday?"

"Of course."

"Then why didn't you just out and tell me?"

"Because, lover, I knowed how you felt about bein' trapped. Like a stupid goose, I had hopes you'd marry me because you cared for me like you seemed to back when it all started between us."

"In the beginning, you always told me you were taking care of things afterwards so you wouldn't get pregnant. Was that a lie too?"

"Well, I either lied or slipped up, didn't I? But it don't make no difference, considerin' the shape I'm in."

He stared at her in numbed silence, his mind suddenly bombarded by the fears of never being able to break away from what he'd always been, or marry the girl he needed and loved. He stood up, suddenly angry, and told her, "I won't let you do this to me, Willa."

She patted her belly. "You already done it to me, buster. And now, by God, you're gonna marry me."

"But I've already said I don't love you."

"Well, who'd believe it, considerin' how you was havin' your way with me for so long. Now, you make things right with me and your kid, or my daddy'll be huntin' *you* with his twelve-gauge shotgun."

He remembered last night and all the things he told Charlotte, both before and after the act. Frustrated, he closed his eyes and wished his head would stop spinning. *What can I do to get out of this jam?*

Looking up, he told her, "I can't marry you. I've already told another girl I'm going to marry her."

"Who, that city whore, Ruby?" Her eyes flashed her anger. "I'll put her out of whack for sure now. She won't ever be able to do you no good, married or not." When he became too absorbed in his own thoughts to answer her, she continued berating him. "It don't make no difference what you promised, or who you promised." She pointed to her belly. "You made your deal with me first, so I've got first claim, lover boy."

Heck turned to look out into the woods, recalling again how forlorn Charlotte had appeared when he left her in the Vandergriff driveway. He remembered his promises to her, and why he made them.

Willa moved around to check his face. "You don't look so good. You ain't comin' down with somethin', are you?"

He didn't bother to respond as that little voice within calmly talked to him. *Remember how stubborn an ox in a deep ditch can be. First things first. Don't lose sight of your goals in life. You can deal with this dilemma later, in a way that won't ruin your life forever.*

He looked at Willa. "Even if I were inclined to marry you, I wouldn't do it before you talked to the sheriff and cleared Cracker. In the meantime, if you tell your daddy about this and get me killed, I guess you'll never know if I would've married you, will you?"

"Oh, all right. I'll talk to the sheriff." Agitated, she threw up her hands. "But if you don't want Daddy to know about it, how do you expect me to talk to the sheriff before your precious nigger friend gets shot or put in jail? Daddy'll beat the tar outta me if I refuse to tell him what made me change my story."

"Walk to town with me now. Let your daddy find out about it from the sheriff."

"Walk to town in my condition? No way, lover boy."

"Then I'll bring the sheriff to you. Just keep quiet about this 'til he gets here."

He whirled and walked away, angry at Willa and fate, angrier at himself for doing what he did five months ago that was now threatening to ruin all his best-laid plans. If he allowed it to happen, he would be admitting that Willa, his dad and Slick were right all along when they told him, "Heck Tennel, you're doomed to be what you've always been."

*No way,* he vowed on the long trek back to his house. *I'll marry nobody but Charlotte DeHavilland. Right away, if she's willing. We'll figure out how without Miss Josephine's approval. I've loved her from the time I first saw her, and she loves me too. She said so.*

Plodding down the road, he formulated a plan to elope. *I'll take Charlotte to that justice of the peace across the line in Louisiana that Slick told me about, the one who asks no questions. Once married, I'll be safe from Willa's scheming ways forever and Miss Josephine can't undo what's been done. We can leave Hispaniola County, even Texas, if necessary to find a job so I can support my wife and family. I'll work hard at making Charlotte happy, because she's the most important thing in my life, now and will be forever. If it turns out I'm the father of Willa's baby, I'll find a way to take care of that responsibility when the time comes to measure up.*

# Chapter XXV

The spring in his step returned as he continued toward Panther Holler Road. He could get to town quicker by following the main roads, and if the sheriff or his deputy came by looking for him, so much the better. That would save him a long walk.

Curt Truesdale's dogs began barking and came charging out to the edge of the embankment when he neared the driveway. Even though it was full daylight, he saw a lamp still burning in the parlor, and as he watched, someone passed between it and the front window. Moments later Charlotte appeared, and he turned into the driveway, dreading what he must tell her.

Beaming, she met him on the porch to take his hand. He embraced her and started to kiss her, but stopped when Miss Cilla and Mrs. Truesdale appeared at the front door. He asked her, "Are you okay?"

"I'm fine. Want some coffee?"

He was relieved to find she bore him no ill will, nor was burdened by feelings of guilt or loss. Giving Miss Cilla a cautious look, he said, "No, thanks. I've got to get to town in a hurry." Studying her pretty face a moment, he added, "You're truly a beautiful sight for a man's eyes, any hour, any place. Sorry I can't stay."

"Can't you at least sit on the swing with me a few minutes before you go?"

Because he thought he detected a note of concern in her voice, he nodded and said, "I'd love to."

When he looked to see if Miss Cilla had any objections, she and the foreman's wife had disappeared. They sat down.

The hint of concern he had detected in her request did not match the glow in her eyes and he was glad. He also found relief in the contented expression he saw in her face that had not been there before. It seemed to suggest the presence of inner contentment he had always sought for himself. He was a long way from that now.

Knowing they didn't have an audience, he leaned over and kissed her, and she moved closer, pressing her thigh against his. She said, "It feels so good, sitting next to you. How's your friend?"

"Fine. I'm on my way to talk to the sheriff now. I'll tell him he can tear up his warrant."

"Then you saw her?"

She said it as if she had been hoping it wouldn't happen. He nodded, and his expression became sober when he recalled what Willa said. He wanted to tell Charlotte about it but decided to wait. Soon, but not now.

"You look worried," she said. "Is there something you want to talk to me about?"

Screwing up his courage but fearing the consequences of rejection, he leaned closer and said, "Charlotte, will you marry me, now?"

Her dark eyes opened wide. "Now?"

He nodded and took her hand. "I'm afraid if we put it off until everything's just right, something will happen that'll cause me to lose you."

"But like I said before, I'm only sixteen."

"You're a sixteen year old woman now. I know where there's a justice of the peace that'll marry us. He won't ask about your age, or anything, which means your family won't have to be there. After it's all done, nobody can do anything about it."

She opened her mouth to speak, but all that came out was, "Oh, my."

"Please?"

"I don't know. This is so sudden."

"I love you, Charlotte, and last night you said you loved me. I'll find a good job somewhere right away. Like I told you already, I've got this plan, and as soon as I save enough to take care of Billy's health problems, I'm going to start working on it. And after I'm a success, I'll be able to take care of you in the style you're used to, and I can buy that big piece of land I've always wanted. But rich or poor, I promise I'll always be good to you."

Her eyes told him she was excited, but also afraid. "I believe you, Heck. And I'm not worried about how your support would compare to my grandfather's. Believe me, I'd welcome the chance to get out on my own, away from Aunt Josephine. But I can't get married without Aunt Priscilla's blessing."

"Do you think she'd tell her sister?"

"I don't know. She might be afraid not to. She's already told me that Aunt Josephine threatened to have grandfather disinherit her for things she's done in the past."

"I don't want you to do anything that would cause you to be unhappy later, so will you ask her approval?"

"I'll ask her today," she replied, nodding. "As soon as she and I are alone."

Heck was about to speak again when the sound of an approaching automobile caused them to look toward the road. They exchanged anxious glances when Miss Josephine's big Cadillac swung into the driveway. She braked to a stop in a shower of gravel, jumped out and marched toward the front porch in a gait that indicated she was very upset about something. Her flushed face and the anger in her fierce eyes suggested to Heck that it had something to do with him and Charlotte.

"Oh, no," Charlotte said. "That look tells me I'm in trouble."

The grim-faced Josephine began shaking her finger at her niece before reaching the steps. "Get in my car, Charlotte DeHavilland!" she shouted. "I'm taking you home this instant. I would've come last night if I hadn't been out of town when Curt Truesdale called me from father's house."

Josephine rushed up the steps and charged across the porch. Fixing angry eyes on Heck, she railed, "The very idea. My niece cavorting with white trash behind my back and on her grandfather's farm."

Heck stiffened, and an angry, sinking feeling swept over him in the face of such insults. Glancing at Charlotte, he saw how pale her face had become when she said, "But Aunt . . ."

"Don't you Aunt me," Josephine snapped, waving her arms like a wild woman. "Get in the car. Your stupid Aunt Priscilla can bring your things. Where is my simple-minded sister anyway?"

"What's the matter, Josephine?" Miss Cilla said from the front door.

She whirled to face her sister and pointed at Heck. "He's the matter. And you. How could you let anyone in our family associate with such trash?"

Heck was too furious to speak for fear he'd say the wrong thing in front of Charlotte. But how else could he strike back except with words? Perhaps it was his early training to respect women and one's elders that restrained him or the fear that the very poor have of the very rich. One thing was certain. At that moment, he hated Josephine Vandergriff more than he had ever hated anyone or anything.

Recovering from her initial shock, Charlotte stood up and said, "Heck is not trash, Auntie. He's a nice boy, and I love him."

Josephine's jaw dropped. "Love?" she shouted. "What do you know about love? You're just a child. I'm ashamed of you. Where's your pride? You're half Vandergriff, for God's sake."

Barely able to control himself, Heck stood up next to Charlotte, trying very hard to remain outwardly calm and not do or say anything to make matters worse for her and Miss Cilla.

"You nitwit." Miss Josephine turned on her sister again. "Don't you have any respect for our family's reputation? Don't you know our niece is particularly vulnerable right now?"

Miss Cilla, with a pale, frightened face, meekly said, "I agree with Charlotte, Josephine. Heck is a good boy. Just because he grew up poor is no reason . . ."

"He's as sorry and worthless as his father and stepmother," Josephine said heatedly. "He's got no future whatsoever." She turned to Charlotte. "I said, get in the car, damn it!"

Unable to hold his tongue any longer, Heck said, "Miss Josephine, if you'd just listen to me a minute, I . . ."

"And what makes you think I'm interested in what white trash has to say? Let me tell you this, trash. If you've done anything to harm my niece, I'll see to it that you go to the penitentiary for life."

Shaking from held-back emotion, Heck looked at Charlotte and saw tears in her eyes. The sight almost sent his anger to the boiling point, but he contained it.

Charlotte said in a trembling voice, "Aunt Josephine, will you please listen to me? I love Heck, and I'm going to keep seeing him regardless of what you think about him."

"Like hell you are. Get in the car."

Taking Heck's hand, Charlotte told her, "I'm going to marry Heck, Aunt Josephine."

An expression of utter disbelief swept over the woman's face as she looked at her niece. Too overcome with shock to speak, she exchanged anxious glances with her sister, also speechless. Before either recovered, Heck leaned over and told Charlotte, "That's great. You'll never be sorry."

"*Marry?*" Josephine, almost choking on the word, grabbed Charlotte's arm and began pulling her toward the front steps.

The sight of his wife-to-be receiving such rough treatment swept Heck's inhibitions aside and sent him into action rescuing her. But when he jerked Charlotte's arm free, the aunt lost her balance and stumbled backwards toward the edge of the porch. Heck grabbed for her, but missed, and Josephine fell off the high porch into the flowerbed.

As the aunt lay helpless on the ground gasping for air that had been knocked out of her, Heck jumped down and attempted to help her, but she shoved him away. Catching her breath, she screamed, "Don't you dare assault me again, trash."

Mr. Truesdale came running around the corner of the house and gave her a hand. When she got to her feet, she cried out, "My arm. Something's wrong with my arm!"

Heck could tell by the way her right arm dangled that it was broken. He moaned, "Oh, my God. Just what I need, another problem."

Josephine raised her good arm and pointed at him. "You'll pay for this, you filthy piece of shit! Leave Vandergriff property this instant, and don't you ever come back for any reason."

"Charlotte, dear," Miss Cilla said, placing her arm around her sobbing niece. "Perhaps it's best that you get in the car before there's any more trouble. You and I will talk later. We'll work things out."

Gasping with pain, Josephine shouted at her sister, "You will *not* work things out later. I'll see to it that our niece never comes into contact with this fortune hunter again."

Angry and frustrated over his helplessness at not being able to do or say anything to ease Charlotte's unhappy state or defend himself against the powerful woman, Heck took Charlotte's hand and walked her to the big car.

Leaning down close to her ear after rolling down the window and closing the door, he told her, "I'm sorry about being here at the wrong time and causing you so much trouble. But I'm happy you said you'd marry me. I'll figure out a way to see you real soon so we can decide on the when and the how."

Josephine walked toward the car assisted by Mr. Truesdale. Her face was white now, her mouth set in a grim line against the pain. Arriving at the passenger side of the Cadillac, she shouted, "Charlotte, don't dare listen to one more word from that good-for-nothing. Truesdale, get in and drive."

Charlotte looked at Heck, confused and afraid. "Remember our special message place? I'll have Aunt Priscilla put my note there saying when and where we can meet."

"I'll check it every day." He moved his lips without speaking to form the words, "I love you."

She tried to smile, but began to cry instead as her moaning aunt climbed into the front seat and Curt Truesdale ran around to the driver's side and jumped in. He started the motor as Josephine fussed at her sister. "Father and I will talk to you about what you let happen out here as soon as I get my arm attended to and speak to Bob Norton. Get Charlotte's things and come home. Now!"

Heck whispered to Charlotte, "I'll start checking that special place tonight. Send me a photo in your first letter if you can." He glanced at her injured aunt. "Don't let her whip you down."

Josephine half turned. "What are you two whispering about back there? Get away from that door, trash."

Heck jumped back as the car lurched forward, and watched it run through one of Mrs. Truesdale's flowerbeds near the woods in Curt's hurry to get out of the yard. Swerving into the road, he sped away in a cloud of dust, barely giving Charlotte time to steal a look back at him and lift her hand in a shy farewell. The Cadillac roared out of sight behind the embankment.

Heck waved back, but feared his gesture too late to be seen. With his arm still extended, he remained still, not taking his eyes off the spot where he last saw her face.

When he heard Miss Cilla approaching, he slowly lowered his arm as she said, "I'm so sorry this happened, Heck." Her kind voice was strained. "Someday, some way, God willing, I'll do my best to make amends for what Josephine did and said here today."

"Thank you, Miss Cilla. I thank you for everything you've done for me through the years, and for always treating me like I'm somebody. And I'll always be grateful for making it possible for me to be with the only girl I'll ever love. You're a mighty fine lady."

"I don't feel so fine right now, Heck." She smiled faintly, wiping a tear from the corner of her eye. "Truth is I'm ashamed. I'm ashamed because I've never been able to stand up to Josephine when she's on one of her rampages. I've always told myself that next time I won't allow her to run roughshod over me. But when the next time comes, I always lose my nerve."

"You did all you could. But would you consider doing me just one more favor?"

"I'll do anything for you, Heck."

"If you bring out any notes from Charlotte, will you take mine to her? She'll explain our arrangement."

She nodded. "Of course."

He looked at the dust settling from Miss Josephine's hasty departure and shook his head in dismay at being so low in someone's eyes and called such vile names. Would he ever overcome all the handicaps that caused some folks to think of him in such a way?

The heavy silence was suddenly broken by the distant scream of a hawk circling somewhere over the trees across the road. Or was that a wildcat's scream in Panther Holler Woods? So, maybe it meant a devil's storm had arrived, just as Loony predicted.

# Chapter XXVI

Kicking lots of rocks and dirt clods on the way home didn't lessen Heck's anger. Josephine Vandergriff's stinging insults had hurt worse than similar verbal abuse by Ol' Money Bags at the bank, but the worst was seeing Charlotte cry, knowing he was unable to do anything about it. *How can I live if that witch makes good on her threat to never let me see Charlotte again?*

Under normal circumstances, he could think through his problems and chose a workable solution, if there was one; but in view of what happened at the Vandergriff house and a couple of other recent developments, he was finding it harder to believe in the righteous and reasonable approach.

His mind churning, he didn't see Squeeze Usrey until the deputy stepped out from behind the big sycamore in the back yard. Heck froze, too scared to run. Squeeze walked toward him, a chubby hand on the butt of his pistol.

"Don't run from me, boy," Squeeze warned. "I'll shoot you in the leg if you do."

Squeeze had a reputation for being trigger-happy. Some folks said he shot first and asked questions later because he hated lawbreakers. Others claimed it was because his big belly made it impossible for him to catch anybody in a dead run.

"What do you want?" Heck asked, looking around for the county car.

Squeeze spat a mouthful of tobacco juice and reached in under his potbelly to hook his thumbs on his gun belt. "I'm taking you in. The sheriff wants to talk to you."

"Well, I want to talk to him, too," Heck said, relieved. He looked at the house, but didn't see his sisters or Billy. "How long have you been hidin' our here? Does my family know?"

"I ordered them to stay out of sight if they didn't want to see you get hurt. You've been hard to find, so the sheriff told me to sit on your place 'til you come home."

"I was on my way to see the sheriff so I could tell him Willa is willing to tell the truth now. She wants to tell him Cracker Carver didn't rape her. Since you're here, why don't you just go on up to the Sproggs' place with me so she can tell you?"

"My orders was to bring you in." Squeeze shook his head. "The sheriff didn't say nothin' about me talkin' to nobody else." He took hold of Heck's arm. "Let's go."

"Don't I get a chance to talk to my family first?"

"Nope. I'm too hungry and thirsty. Come on."

Heck looked at the house again and saw the frightened faces of Billy and Amy pressed against a window. He forced a smile, waving to them as he was escorted down the cut. Squeeze led him to Panther Holler Road where he'd hidden his patrol car behind some bushes on the top of the embankment.

Sheriff Sloan was waiting for them in his office, looking particularly authoritative in his black suit and hat. He motioned to a chair without speaking, and Heck sat down. Squeeze moved up behind his chair.

"Like I told Squeeze," Heck said, "I was on my way to see you when he arrested me. I had just talked to Willa Sproggs. She's ready to tell you Cracker didn't rape her."

The sheriff seemed unimpressed. "That's not what she said in her sworn statement to the D.A."

"Then she lied to the D.A. Everything she said about Cracker was a lie. She did it to get even with me."

The sheriff caught his deputy's eye and nodded, and Squeeze promptly left the room. He turned back to Heck. "And why would she want to do that?"

"Well, uh, you see, she and I had this thing going on between us for a long time. I broke it off and that made her mad." He told the sheriff what happened in Hank Slater's field. "So she lied about my friend Cracker to get back at me."

The sheriff's expression indicated he still wasn't convinced. After studying Heck for several moments, he asked, "So why does she want to change her story now?"

"Because I told her I wouldn't talk to her about our situation until she did."

"But if she's that anxious to get back together with you, how would I know she's not lying this time?"

"Because this time it's the truth. Bring her in and talk to her. You'll see."

"Then, I suppose, you'll tell me where to find Cracker so I can talk to him too."

"Yes, sir." He again tried to swallow that lump that wouldn't go away.

The sheriff got up, opened his office door and said to Squeeze, "Go out and get Willa Sproggs." He returned to his chair and again fixed his cold eyes on Heck. "Even if she comes in and crawfishes on her charges, you still won't be off the hook, young man. Not by a long shot."

The statement caused a tightening in Heck's belly. "I won't?"

The sheriff opened a drawer, pulled out a twenty-dollar bill, held it up and said, "This twenty your dad gave Frieda was one of the bills taken in a bank robbery Bonnie and Clyde pulled last week."

Heck sighed with relief. "Well, since Bonnie and Clyde were ambushed and murdered by lawmen yesterday, I guess that takes care of that, right?"

"You keep up with the news pretty good for a boy who has no radio and doesn't take a newspaper. How'd you know the law killed them?"

"Grandpa Tennel told me. One of his neighbors has a radio."

"I see." The sheriff nodded. "Well, your friend Jake passed the bill to your dad, so it's him I'm looking for now. Since he wasn't with Bonnie and Clyde when they were waylaid, I figured he must have branched out on his own. I want you to help me find him."

Although gladdened by the news that Jake and Marna weren't with Bonnie and Clyde, Heck didn't want to help the sheriff find his brother-in-law-to-be. "But I don't know where he's at, Sheriff."

"You know he's with your sister. You'll hear from her pretty soon and, when you do, you'll know his whereabouts."

"I doubt it." Heck's trembling insides made it hard to think straight. "Marna probably won't ever write, because she's mad at me for things I said about Jake."

The sheriff took a Lucky Strike cigarette out of a pack on his desk and lit it. "She'll write. And when she does, you're to give me their address. Is that clear? You'll do that or face charges for harboring a criminal and receiving stolen merchandise." He exhaled a cloud of smoke. "Now, let's talk about something else."

"There's *more?*" His insides began to quiver.

"Let's talk about the robbery of our bank."

Heck suddenly felt faint. *Oh, crap. I'm going to jail after all.* "But everybody said Bonnie and Clyde pulled that robbery."

"That doesn't mean I believe it."

Heck braced himself for more bad news; most likely that Thelma and Cotton had been incarcerated and had spilled their guts. He searched his brain for a way to find out just what the sheriff did know about the "robbery" without divulging his firsthand knowledge of it. He said, "Homer Percy was the one that got robbed. Haven't you talked to him?"

"No. The preacher disappeared as soon as the bank closed. So I figured you could tell me who did it, since you were there. And while you're at it, explain what part you played in that little caper."

*My God, he knows. But how?* Heck wished for a shot of Ubis Sproggs' moonshine. Working around that lump in his throat, he finally managed to say, "It's not against the law to go in a bank, is it?" His voice sounded like it was coming from somebody else.

Sheriff Sloan leaned forward. "And why would you go in a bank at that particular time? Why go at all? You've never had a dime in it, or done any business there. But you tried to, according to B.M. Vandergriff. He told me about you hittin' him up for a loan. Said you acted real desperate. Desperate men rob banks, or help somebody else do it."

Suddenly made a little braver by anger over being put upon again by the rich and powerful, he said, "Seems like desperate is my middle name lately. Is that a crime too? If it is, you could arrest ninety percent of the people in Hispaniola County."

"Now, don't you start gettin' smart with me, boy," the sheriff said, blowing smoke at him. "Answer my question. What were you doing in the bank? Mr. Vandergriff's secretary said she saw you get out of that jalopy and go inside, then exit the back door, just ahead of the ones that did it."

Self-preservation, his marriage and the welfare of his family took first priority now. He must do or say anything that would keep him out of jail. Squaring his shoulders, he told the sheriff, "Well, there's no denying I was in the bank earlier to ask Blood Money Vandergriff for a loan, but that was because I needed money for my little brother's tonsil operation."

"Go on." The sheriff's eyes didn't waver.

"Go on?" Heck gave him an inquisitive look. "There's nothin' else to say. He turned me down and nearly ripped his britches in the process."

"Stop beatin' around the bush. Why'd you go back to the bank on Tuesday? Give me a straight answer or you're going to the lock-up on a charge of accessory to robbery."

Heck's new strength brought about by his responsibilities and hurt pride vanished, and fear took control again. It wasn't easy to be brave or lie in the face of certain disaster. *I could tell the sheriff I'd gone back to the bank to make another plea for a loan, but all he'd have to do to prove me a liar would be to telephone Blood Money. A lie would just pull me deeper into trouble. Looks like I don't have but one choice and that's to tell the truth and hope his blood's not all ice water as some claim. Cotton and Thelma lied to me, didn't they? Then ran off and left me hanging to dry. Why should I worry about protecting them? More important things are at stake here.*

Looking the sheriff squarely in the eye, he said, "It was Cotton Murphy and my stepmother that took that handful of twenties from the preacher. But it wasn't robbery. It was more like an unfriendly withdrawal."

Surprise swept over the sheriff's face. "You aren't lyin' to get yourself off the hook, are you?"

"No, sir. It was them all right."

Sheriff Sloan studied him so long that Heck began squirming in the chair. "Cotton Murphy's nothing but a petty thief, crap shooter, loafer and whore chaser," he said. "Not enough gall to rob a bank. And Thelma, well, I recall her and Cotton being a hot number before she married Early and I ran for sheriff, but nothing recent. True, her reputation is nothing to brag about, but as far as I know she's never been arrested for anything. How come she'd do something like that all of a sudden?"

Heck told about catching her and the preacher in the front room at home, and about how she'd gone to Cotton's the next day after the preacher sent her packing. "She meant to leave home for good, and didn't care how much it hurt Billy and the girls as long as she got back at Homer Percy. She knew he worked in the bank,"

"You seem to be very well informed about what two old lovers were up to."

"I overheard her and Cotton talkin' in his shack when I followed her to town. She made it clear she was stayin' with him and that he had to make some money and show her a good time. The disguise for the robbery was Cotton's idea. He figured since Bonnie and Clyde had been seen in the area, it wouldn't be hard to convince everybody they did it. But Thelma talked him into using her idea about scarin' the preacher into givin' them some money by tellin' him she'd tell my daddy about him comin' by to see her if he didn't. She gave Homer Percy the note, and she's the one that took that handful of twenties from him."

There. He'd told the truth. He would soon know if the truth would set a man free, like the old saying said it would. It was high time something moved in his favor for a change.

The sheriff, apparently still not convinced, said, "How do you know it was twenties she had?"

"Because I heard 'em tell the preacher what to give 'em, and what they said when they ran past me. Mama dropped one."

"You must have good ears. I'm sure they were really hot-footin' it by then."

"Yes, sir. Like they were runnin' barefooted in hot coals."

"So why didn't they hop in that jalopy that Squeeze said was parked behind the bank? The one you got out of. Why in the world would you drive them over there? Who were you trying to get even with?"

"Nobody." With his voice breaking, he added, "I was tryin' to get a hundred dollars for Billy's operation. Cotton promised me that much just to drive 'em over. I'd already been turned down for a loan. Couldn't find work. I'm afraid my little brother is gonna die if I don't get my hands on a lot more than that."

Ashamed to be seen tearing up, he quickly wiped his eyes, hoping the sheriff hadn't noticed. He made himself settle down and speak more calmly as he told what Doctor Samuels said about Billy. But he became excited again when he ended with, "But Cotton ran out on me. I didn't get a cent of the bank's money, I swear. Now Billy can't have his operation, and I can't send him to that hospital for tests."

The sheriff got up and walked slowly around the room. "What did you do after Thelma and Cotton ran out of the bank?"

"Walked away like a whipped dog."

"Do you have any idea where they are now?"

Heck shook his head. "No, sir, I sure don't."

The sheriff sat back down and asked, "You said they gave the preacher a note. Homer told me the guy pointed a pistol at him and that he gave him and the woman fifty thousand dollars in twenties, fifties and hundreds."

"It was a water pistol and there couldn't have been more than three or four hundred dollars in that stack."

Heck couldn't tell if the sheriff was about to laugh or cry. Instead, he turned his chair to face the wall behind him, and for a moment his body shook as if he might have taken a sudden chill. Moments later, he swiveled around wearing his former stern expression and said, "I must say, your tale is a little weird and hard to believe, but if it's a lie, it's original, by God."

"Am I going to jail?"

"I don't know. I'll have to talk to Bob Norton about it. Driving the car over there makes you an accomplice, which means you're as guilty as the ones that went in and took the money."

"Even if I didn't say anything to the preacher, or get any of the money?" Heck felt a weakness sweep over him again. "The law works in funny ways."

"If what you told me checks out, and if Bob Norton approves, I won't have you put in jail as long as something new doesn't gum up the works. However, I'm not bound by that promise if you won't give me your word to help me get both Jake and Cotton. Thelma too. And if Willa backs up what you told me about Cracker Carver, I won't have to put you in jail for harboring him."

Heck saw a faint ray of hope in what he said, but still felt under the gun. He felt very uncomfortable in the sheriff's presence and wanted to leave, but knew he couldn't before Willa arrived. He wanted to make sure she told the truth this time.

Squeeze and a frightened Willa finally arrived, and she stopped at Heck's chair, giving him a worried look. "You ain't goin' to jail, are you, honey?"

"I will if you don't tell the sheriff the truth."

Wearing the same old faded dress and brogans she had on when he talked to her earlier, she looked terribly out of place, and, for the first time in Heck's memory, tired and subdued.

Sitting down in the chair next to Heck, she told the sheriff. "I might as well tell you the truth, I guess. Cracker didn't rape me. But he touched me."

When Heck gave her a disbelieving look, she turned back to the sheriff and added, "All right, all right. He didn't even touch me. It was me that touched him."

"Where were the other colored boys who were working out there with you?" The sheriff's expression indicated his skepticism.

"They run off before Cracker did," Willa said, looking at Heck. "Will Heck still have to go to jail if you find out he's been hidin' Cracker?"

"No," the sheriff said. "But I don't know about you. It's a violation of the law to lie in a sworn statement that results in false charges against a person."

Clearly frightened by his remark, she said, "But I didn't know that. Don't seem like it ought to be against the law for a girl to do what she's got to do to get her man back. That's woman's law. It's been around lots longer than yours."

"Wouldn't be surprised if it hasn't," Sheriff Sloan said, apparently amused by her remark. "Anyway, I won't put you in jail this time. But I warn you. If you pull something like this again, I will. Take her home, Squeeze, and tell Ubis Sproggs the rape charge is dismissed."

Willa turned at the door and gave Heck an anxious look, "When are we gonna have that talk?"

"Real soon. I'm not through here yet."

When the door closed behind them, Sheriff Sloan said, "I'll tear up the warrant on Cracker and have Norton dismiss the rape charge against him. But remember what I said about letting me know about Jake, Cotton and Thelma. If I don't hear from you soon, I may bring another arrest warrant with your name on it."

Heck was planning on doing some deep thinking about his problems on the walk home, but found Squeeze and Willa waiting for him in the outer office. Outside, he reluctantly slid into the front seat of the patrol car with the deputy to avoid another confrontation with Willa. Squeeze immediately asked him where Cracker was, but Heck refused to tell him because he didn't want to get Loony and Tiny Lucy involved. Besides, he wanted to stop at his house first to prove to Billy and the girls that he was all right.

Willa wanted to get out at his place too, but he told her he'd talk to her later in private. She gave him a suspicious look and said, "Heck Tennel, you'd better not back down on your promise to me."

With her implied threat ringing in his ears, Heck walked up the cut into the yard where he was greeted by his happy sisters, Billy and his terrier. After allaying their fears of his going to jail, he and Elsie prepared a meal of beans and squash from the previous year's canning and a pan of hot water corn bread. They were hungry, but he was still too shaken up by the morning's developments to eat more than a few bites.

Early remained silent after Heck told him the sheriff talked to him about Cotton getting into more trouble. He didn't dare give all the details for fear of a beating with the razor strap for not telling him sooner about Thelma and the preacher. Their dad had become withdrawn early in the week, a condition brought on apparently by his finally coming face to face with the reality that he wasn't man enough to hold onto a woman any more. He smelled strongly of home brew.

Heck looked forward to taking Cracker the good news, and then later that night checking the special place for a note from Charlotte. If one was there, he hoped it would tell him when and where he could meet her to plan their elopement.

Just the thought of being married to Charlotte for the rest of his life put a whistle on his lips as he set out for Loony's place. His whistling stopped as he approached the old Vandergriff house and recalled the sad events surrounding Miss Josephine's visit. Noticing Miss Cilla's car gone and no sign of the Truesdales, he believed everybody had left.

Turning his mind back to the prospect of receiving a note later, he began whistling "I'll Be All Smiles Tonight" and headed up the road.

When he got close to Willa's house, he climbed up on the red embankment and walked the rest of the way through the woods. He wanted to tell Cracker the good news and talk to Charlotte again before meeting with Willa.

Still not convinced that she was carrying his baby, he didn't want to jump the gun and burden himself with supporting the results of some other man's good times. He had always believed there was nothing worse than a man getting run over by another man's baby buggy. Even if Willa proved it was his, he still couldn't marry her because he would already be married. But he would work out something regarding child support if it was proved that he was the father, because he never wanted it said that he failed to measure up in any way. He had never lied, gone back on his word, or failed to honor his moral obligations. Grandpa Tennel and Ross taught him those rules for living, and his conscience wouldn't allow him to betray them now.

Life might be a pisser like Cracker said, but right now it was more like a puzzle. Solving the puzzle would require lots of study and planning and a few lucky breaks. He wouldn't allow his hopes to be dampened by the fact that Lady Luck had not been kind to him to that point in this life.

# Chapter XXVII

Cracker wept when Heck told him the rape charge was being dropped. Embarrassed by his emotional display, he told Heck, "Has anybody told Mr. Ubis 'bout this? I don't want him shootin' my other leg or anywhere in between."

"Squeeze took Willa home. He said he'd tell him."

"Well, if it's all the same to you, I'm getting' outta this barn before that crazy white man finds out about Mr. Loony and Tiny Lucy. I don't want to get caught in the crossfire when he starts blastin' them."

Heck reached down to help him rise, but Cracker got up on his own and walked to the end of the loft and back with only a slight limp.

"Tiny Lucy's cookin' sure perked you up in a hurry," Heck said.

"Been walkin' around to build up my strength in case I got a chance to walk home and get back to work. There ain't nothin' more useless than a nigga wid' out work, unless it's one wid no work and a busted leg."

"Think you're up to walkin' home? Unless you've lost some weight, I'm not about to take you back like I brought you over."

"I'll roll home if I have to. I sho' ain't got no cravin' to be bounced back on that rig you brought me in."

"Think you can make it down the stairs on your own?"

"Sho' can."

Heck went down the steps ahead of Cracker in case he misstepped. It was slow going, but they finally made it. Approaching the back porch, they saw Tiny Lucy standing in the door watching them. "Where's Loony?' Heck asked.

"Takin' a nap." She gave Cracker the once over. "How come you crawled down for God and everybody to see?"

"He wants you to rub his good leg," Heck said

"Don't pay no 'tention to him," Cracker said. "He's jus' tryin' to stir up trouble. I'm goin' home."

"Willa finally talked to the sheriff," Heck said. "He's a free man again."

"Hallelujah," Tiny Lucy said, waving her arms. "What's the sheriff gonna do to Pussy Willa for causin' all this trouble?"

Cracker sat down in an old wooden chair against the white wall as Heck went to the well for a drink of water. He scooped the gourd dipper into the bucket, held it out and asked, "Care for a shot?" Cracker nodded, and Heck took him the water, returning to the well for another dipperful for himself.

Looking at Tiny Lucy, Heck asked, "Have you got a cold 'tater I can eat on my way home? I'm awful hungry all of a sudden."

She disappeared and came back with a large sweet potato.

"But it ain't peeled," he said with a twinkle in his eye.

"You ain't paralyzed," she said sharply.

"Don' pay no 'tention to his lip," Cracker said. "He's jus' tryin' to start somethin' as usual."

"Ready to go home to your mama?" Heck asked his friend. "I'll get my wagon."

"Ain't waitin' fer no wagon," Cracker said. "I'm walkin' home."

Peeling the potato, Heck took a big bite and told him, "Always said you can't keep a good man down for long. I'll go with you just in case."

There was about two hours of daylight left when they walked into The Settlement. Mrs. Carver, seeing her son, began to jump and shout, causing others to come outside to find out what all the racket was about.

Heck happily announced to everybody within earshot that charges against Cracker had been dropped, and then sat down by him on the porch.

"Cracker, after resting few a minutes, I'm going home. I'll check on you later to make sure everything's been straightened out with the D.A. It might be a good idea to stay in close for a few days to make sure all the folks know you're in the clear. I'll tell everybody I see."

"Guess we're even now, so you won't be havin' to bother wid me no mo'." Cracker turned solemn eyes on Heck as his mother and brothers gathered around.

"Even?" Heck frowned.

"Yeah, I jerked you outta the creek, and now you done saved me from gettin' hung. You don't owe me nothin' no mo'."

"Didn't know we were keepin' count. But it don't matter, 'cause I'm gonna be your friend as long as you can stand me. Anyway, I figure I came out way ahead. And I know Loony did."

Cracker's dark eyes held his for a moment as if seriously considering his statement, but he didn't respond.

Heck told him, "Sportin' Man, whether you like it or not, I'll most likely be around pestering you for the rest of your days."

"If bein' bull-headed makes a man live a long time, you probably will," Cracker said, extending his hand. "But yo're my true friend and I thank you for everythang."

"Just don't call me if you get crossways with another wild woman." Heck shook his hand.

Heck left for home. Feeling good that everything had turned out all right with Cracker, he would now focus on other pressing matters and hope they turned out as well.

When he reached the parsonage, the place looked deserted, confirming what the sheriff had told him about the preacher. A man well established in a community needs a good reason to run away, and Heck figured Homer Percy had at least two: Early Tennel's twelve-gauge Winchester shotgun, and a big bundle of money he claimed Bonnie and Clyde took.

*Wonder where Thelma and Cotton are now. She won't never come back home to stay, but she could at least visit Billy and the girls from time to time. Maybe she'll write them.*

Arriving home in the fast-fading light, he petted his happy terrier on his way to the barn to check the cow's udder to see if Elsie had milked. She had. He then gathered the eggs. Finding the pig's water trough empty, he filled it with two bucketfuls of freshly drawn water.

He'd noticed his dad silently watching from his wheelchair on the back porch, but neither of them spoke. Heck could tell by his expression that he was upset with him about something. That wasn't unusual, but Heck knew he would at the very least receive a severe bawling out if his dad had heard about what he did for Cracker. He just hoped to avoid the razor strap.

"Daddy, did Elsie slop the pigs today?"

Early continued glaring at him, not speaking until he was on the porch. "You disgraced this family, Mr. High an' Mighty."

"What did I do this time?"

"You goddam smart aleck. I told you to stop hobnobbin' with that nigger. And don't try to deny it, 'cause Willa come down here and told us all about what you done. You should be out lookin' for work 'stead of lookin' after that worthless nigger."

"Where's Willa now?" Heck changed the subject, knowing it was pointless to defend his actions.

"She went back home. She said you two got some plannin' to do."

When Elsie and Amy came out of the deepening shadows in the hallway, Heck asked, "Where's Billy?"

"On his cot," Amy said, glancing at her dad.

"Well, I'll cook some supper," Heck told her. "I'll fry up something that'll put us in a better mood."

"You ain't leavin' this porch 'til you explain yourself," Early snapped.

"I did what I thought was right, Daddy. No more, no less." With that he whirled and stamped into the darkening dogtrot, turning into the kitchen, the first room on the left side of the opening. He grabbed the matches and lit a lamp, anxious to get through with the meal and go check his and Charlotte's secret mailbox.

After frying several slices of fatback to flavor the warmed over corn bread and peas, he got a quart of milk from the well cooler and sat down to eat with Billy and his sisters. Their dad, still angry over the way Heck had brushed off what he considered a serious breach of white man's ethics, didn't join them.

After Elsie and Amy told him they'd wash the dishes and clean the kitchen, Heck took down a coal oil lantern from a nail in the dog trot and walked past his dad on his way to the cut. Since he didn't want his dad to monitor his movements, he didn't light the lantern until reaching a spot on the road opposite the old Vandergriff servant's quarters. He lit it, adjusted the wick, climbed the embankment and moved through the underbrush toward the old chimney.

Locating the remains of the house, he worked his way around to the chimney and removed the loose brick, then slid his hand into the space. It was empty.

Disappointed, he replaced the brick with a sigh and stood still in the darkness pondering the implications of no message from Charlotte. *Maybe I'm rushing things,* he thought. *Maybe she wrote a note and Miss Priscilla couldn't deliver it for some reason.*

Back out on the road, he blew out the lantern and walked on up to the Vandergriff house in hopes that Miss Priscilla had returned. A half moon dimly illuminated the clearing around the house, but not enough for him to see the carport behind it. All the windows were black. Since it was still early evening, no lights meant no one was home.

He studied the big house for several moments, recalling time spent there with Charlotte before Miss Josephine arrived. *Definitely the best hours of my life.* It was the place where he started believing life could be good, and that all his efforts at living by the rules were finally being rewarded.

His pleasant thoughts were suddenly interrupted when Truesdale's dogs set in to barking and charged out to the road. He turned and headed toward home.

Tired, but not wanting to go to bed, he left the darkened lantern at the cut and walked on out to Panther Holler Road where he turned down the hill leading to the Morales Creek Bridge. At the top of the hill, he stopped and peered through the darkness at the crossing where he lost his week's wages.

Standing alone in the silence gave him the feeling that might come over a man who suddenly discovers he is the only person in the world. A man's mind couldn't help but turn to profound thoughts in such a place. *Why can't a person, willing and able to work, not find a job of some kind? How come I labor for such meager earnings – when I find work – while a few make much more than they'll ever need? What makes some people so cruel, or under any circumstances think of love as a bad thing?*

A small cloud passed from in front of the moon, and for a moment there was enough light for him to see all the way to the point in the road where it leveled off to approach the bridge. If not for the looming presence of the fearful Panther Holler Woods, it would be a very calming sight to behold.

Looking up at the stars between the clouds, he wondered if it was true what preachers said about God sitting up there somewhere watching every individual on earth. Homer Percy told him one time that He kept vigil day and night with his little black book in hand, writing down everything a man does, good or bad. Heck had always felt that if that were true, He must be very, very busy. And if the preacher was right, He probably already knew whether he would get a letter from Charlotte, and if he would soon be married to her as planned.

Brother Percy had also told him back when he was still going to church every Sunday that God was all-powerful, the maker of all things, human and non-human. If that was true, He had made good people like Charlotte, Miss Cilla and Grandpa Tennel, and all wonderful things like music and good food. The part of Brother Percy's theory that Heck had the most trouble accepting was the part that said He had also created folks like Blood Money Vandergriff and Miss Josephine, and bad things like weak heart valves and bad tonsils.

A mosquito biting his neck brought him back to more earthly considerations, and as he slapped at it, a heavy cloud drifting over the moon left him in complete darkness. Feeling terribly alone all of a sudden, he turned to go back to the house, walking slowly like a weary laborer who'd plowed or picked cotton from sunup to sundown.

He could probably sleep when he got to the house, in spite of worrying about his not being able to pay for Billy's scheduled tonsillectomy. *You should again make the rounds of the surrounding farms looking for work. If you don't find any, put on your best shirt and check with all the store owners in town. Even the Vandergriff commissary. If lucky, you'll find a job of some kind and save enough in a few months to pay for Billy's operation. Then, after you and Charlotte get married and move to a big city, like Dallas or Houston, a good job will come easy. That's when you can pay for those tests Billy needs. After that, you can begin working on your long-range plans in music and that bottomland farm.*

He'd already told himself he would again check the special place in the old chimney in the morning and tomorrow night. Surely he would have some good news by then.

About halfway to the house, he stopped, suddenly paralyzed by a loud, blood-curdling scream from somewhere from within the big woods behind him. He tried to run, but couldn't, and felt so faint he could hardly stay on his feet.

"Good Godamighty!" he muttered. "A panther's comin' to get me!"

Coaching his legs into action, he ran toward the house as fast as he could, and after what seemed like an eternity, arrived at the top of the hill. He fell down, weak and out of breath. Shaking, he rose up and fixed his eyes on the dark void at the bottom of the hill and wondered if the panther was stalking him, licking his chops, preparing to pounce.

He had been too frightened by the scream to judge how far the creature might have been from the bridge, or if it was actually between him and the fence already.

The thought of becoming a beast's feast gave him the strength to get back on his feet and head for the bank in front of the house. On the way, he was given some relief in knowing that no one witnessed his cowardly behavior.

He recalled Loony's warnings about a Devil's storm and wondered if the panther's scream was another omen of impending tragedy. He might never know, but one thing was for sure. After tonight, he would never again make fun of the old man's predictions.

# Chapter XXVIII

Heck cooked breakfast for the family and as soon as there was enough light, went out back to milk. He had his head pressed into the cow's side while performing the chore when he heard a car pull up the cut into the back yard. Excited over the prospect of it being Miss Cilla with a message from Charlotte, he squeezed harder and faster. Finished, he got up from the milking stool.

"Heck Tennel, you're under arrest," said a stern male voice behind him.

Heck jumped so he almost dropped the milk. Turning toward the ominous messenger, he found himself looking into the grim face of Sheriff Sloan. Staring at him in shocked disbelief, he said, "Sir?"

"I said, you're under arrest."

"What for?" Heck felt sick to the stomach. "Willa didn't change her mind, did she?"

"This has nothing to do with Willa."

"Then what's this all about?"

"I have a warrant for your arrest on charges of rape, felony assault and bank robbery." He held up a paper.

Heck felt the bucket slip from his hands and heard the precious milk spill. "Is this somebody's idea of a joke? I've never raped a girl, and I haven't assaulted anybody. And I've already told you what happened at the bank."

"It's no joke." The sheriff walked into the milking stall and pulled handcuffs from his belt. "The complaining party spelled it all out."

"Who told you such lies about me?" Heck moved back.

"Bob Norton filed the bank robbery charge after receiving a visit from Josephine Vandergriff who filed assault charges against you for attacking her. And as her niece's legal guardian, Miss Josephine also had you filed on for statutory rape. You were indicted last night by an emergency meeting of a special grand jury. Hold out your hands."

Heck stepped back. "I will not. I didn't hit Miss Josephine. And I don't believe Charlotte told anybody I raped her."

"She didn't have to. She can't give consent under the law, because she's a minor."

"This is crazy. Charlotte and me are gonna get married."

"You weren't married when you had sexual intercourse with her in the back seat of Miss Priscilla's car. And don't try to deny it, because Curt Truesdale showed me some blood and dried fluids on the upholstery."

"I want to talk to Charlotte."

"What that little girl might have to say won't make a bit of difference, boy. I already told you she's under age."

"That's stupid."

"That's the law."

"It's a stupid law. Miss Josephine ain't under age. The flap about me assaulting her is a lie and she knows it."

The sheriff extended the handcuffs again. "I didn't come out here to try the case, boy. That part is up to the jury. Now, hold out your hands."

"I'm no criminal and no wild animal. You ain't puttin' them damn things on me."

Sheriff Sloan kept coming until Heck found himself against the end of the stall.

"What about my family? They'll starve without me here to work. And my little brother will die. Ain't there a law against that?"

"Your personal problems aren't my concern. Hold 'em out."

Sensing the inevitable, Heck fixed his eyes on the handcuffs. "Please don't put them things on me, Sheriff. Not in front of my sisters and my little brother."

The sheriff reached for his right arm, pulling it forward to snap the metal around his wrist. "It might keep you from doing something foolish. It's for the good of both of us." He cuffed the other wrist, took his right arm and led him out of the cow stall into the back yard.

Elsie and Amy were watching them from the back porch, their eyes wide with fright. Billy walked into view, and at that point, they all began crying.

"What's he doin' to you, Heck?" Amy screamed.

"Sheriff, you can't take our brother away from us," Elsie cried. "Our mama run off, so we ain't got nobody else to take care of us."

Heck heard his dad yell, "What the hell's goin' on? Somebody wheel me out!"

Amy and Billy joined Elsie in the yard and watched in disbelief as the sheriff pushed Heck into the back seat of his car and walked to the driver's side without comment.

Early, still on the front porch, peeked around the corner of the house. "Will somebody come help me so I can find out what the hell's happenin'? What's he done now, Sheriff?"

"I'm arresting him on three felony charges, Early. You can talk to him down at the jailhouse. I strongly advise you to get him a lawyer." He climbed into the car.

"I warned him about his high fallutin' ways, but he wouldn't listen," Early yelled. "I knowed it would get him in serious trouble."

Elsie ran around to the driver's side of the car and screamed at the sheriff, "I thought you wuz supposed to take only bad people to jail. Our brother's a good person."

"Your brother has violated the law," the sheriff told her, starting the car. "What he needs now is a good lawyer."

"We ain't got money for no damn lawyer," Elsie shot back. "We don't even have enough for groceries next week or the rent."

Angry and embarrassed, Heck raised his manacled wrists to wave at Billy and his sisters as the sheriff swung the car around and down the cut on his way to town.

Too numb to speak, Heck rode in sullen silence, feverishly searching his brain for a way out of his newest dilemma. He couldn't believe it was a violation of the law for a boy and a girl to do what comes naturally when they love each other and both are willing. He did believe Josephine had made good on her threat to keep him and her niece apart. It reminded him of what he and all other poor people learned early in life: Nobody dares get crossways with a rich and politically powerful family like the Vandergriffs. Now that he was arrested, he was prison-bound for sure.

He looked at the sheriff and tried to think of something to say that would help his situation. Although frightened and angry, he was still rational enough to realize that it was a time for a cool head and cold reasoning rather than headed words. With that in mind, he asked, "Have you talked to Charlotte?"

"Briefly," he said, not taking his eyes off the road.

"What did she think about Miss Josephine's rape complaint?"

"She was shocked. Cried a lot. At first, she wouldn't admit to having sex with you, but when I told her about the evidence we found, she told us what happened."

"Did she tell you we're going to get married?"

"She did. But Miss Josephine won't give her consent. So you can forget getting out of this jam that way."

"I wouldn't be doing it to get out of a jam, Sheriff. I'd be doing it because I love her and *want* to marry her. Where's Charlotte now?"

"Incognito."

"What the hell does that mean?"

"She's being hid out somewhere 'til the trial. She won't be allowed to talk to you, to reporters or anybody else."

The shocking news killed his only hope. Miss Josephine would now have her way for sure. Shaking his head in disbelief, he asked, "What do you think my chances are of beatin' this?"

The sheriff glanced at him in the rearview mirror. "About as good as a spoonful of shaved ice in a bowl of hot chili."

The prediction of doom made it even harder to remain calm and think, but Heck made himself settle back against the seat and try. It didn't take much brainpower to conclude that the only way he could stay out of the pen was to escape before he was put in jail. But how? Handcuffed in the custody of the High Sheriff himself. It wasn't possible.

The lawman began watching him more closely in his rearview, as if trying to read his thoughts. He also increased his speed, making it impossible for Heck to jump out.

The church parsonage coming into view up ahead gave Heck an idea. Highly excited about what might be his last chance to escape, he leaned forward and calmly said, "If you want to talk to the preacher, there he is."

"Preacher? Where?" The sheriff applied the brakes, glancing around.

"At the parsonage." Heck pointed. "I saw him go in the back door."

When the car stopped, Heck jumped out, running as fast as he could toward the woods along Settlement Road.

"Stop!" Sheriff Sloan yelled, scrambling out of the car. "Stop or I'll shoot!"

Heck jumped across the ditch, heading for the thick timber.

*BOOM!* A shot rang out. Heck ducked as a bullet zipped by his ear.

Entering the cover of the trees, *BOOM*, one slammed into his left side like a red hot branding iron, knocking him down. He rolled over, stunned and unable to get back on his feet for a moment.

Hearing the sheriff approaching, he climbed to his feet and began running again. The underbrush closed in around him.

*BOOM!*

*BOOM!*

# Chapter XXIX

Running for dear life, Heck soon found himself dizzy and short of breath, staggering on rubbery legs, grinding his teeth against the throbbing pain in his side. He didn't hear the sheriff running through the brush behind him anymore, but didn't dare slow down and look back. Whatever life he had left was ahead, behind him a miserable existence in the pen.

The little Settlement houses had just come into view through the trees when his legs collapsed and he plunged face down into the leaves, too weak to turn over. The fear of passing out and waking up behind bars did shock him into turning his face to breathe.

Unable to hear anything besides his heart pounding, he made himself roll over, sit up and look back for the sheriff. Nothing. He probably returned to his car and left for the nearest telephone to call for reinforcements since he had no two-way radio in his vehicle. He would return shortly to search the immediate area with the assistance of his trigger-happy deputy Squeeze Usrey and his bloodhounds. The local constable would come too, along with courthouse loafers looking to bring excitement into their otherwise boring lives.

Still gasping for air, Heck looked down and found the side of his shirt soaked with blood. Unsnapping his left gallus and raising the crimson fabric, he saw a deep gash along his ribs about six inches below his armpit, bleeding badly.

Fighting panic, he grabbed a handful of dirt and leaves to press against the wound, holding the makeshift poultice in place with his arm and watched it until convinced the blood wasn't seeping through. He lowered his bloody shirt.

His ribs ached fiercely, but since he could still take a deep breath, didn't believe they were broken. The bleeding had to be stopped and the wound cleaned, however, plus he had to find someone with equipment that would cut away the handcuffs.

He knew only one person who would take him in and protect him from the law under the circumstances, but he was afraid he couldn't make it alone to Mr. Meade's cabin before the sheriff got back with a posse and Squeeze's dogs.

Climbing to his feet, he held his breath and again listened for sounds of pursuit. All he heard was the stirring of a gentle breeze through the tops of pines and his heartbeat. He headed for Cracker's house, and after stopping twice to regain his breath, arrived at a spot in the edge of the trees that allowed him to see it.

Sinking to his knees, he studied the row of houses and that part of Settlement Road he could see beyond them. He tried to remember if anybody had an anvil and a ball-peen hammer, but didn't recall ever seeing one there. *I'd seriously consider tradin' my left thumb for a drink of cold water right now*

Getting up, he moved to where he was opposite Cracker's house. Seeing Liga playing mumblety-peg near the steps, he whistled softly and called out, "Liga, come here, please. It's Heck Tennel."

Liga came running out to him and stopped short at the sight of blood. "Oh, Jesus. Mister Ubis done shot you too."

"Where's Cracker?" he asked through clenched teeth.

"'Round back o' th' house." Liga pointed.

"Go get him. And Liga, don't tell anybody else I'm out here, not even your mama."

Liga left in a run and Heck lay back in the leaves.

Moments later, Cracker appeared and stared down at him with frightened eyes before dropping to one knee at his side. "Who done this to you? Was it Mr. Ubis?" He saw the handcuffs. "How come you got them on?"

Heck shook his head. "No time to explain. I want you to get 'em off and help me over to Nathan Meade's cabin before I pass out. Think you're up to it?"

"But you needs a doctor." Cracker looked at his side.

"I'll need a jailhouse key if you don't stop jabberin' and take me to a hammer and anvil."

"Ain't nobody here got nothin' like that," Cracker said.

Heck sighed, grimacing against the pain in his ribs as he looked down at his blood-stained shirt. "Mr. Meade ain't got an anvil either. So maybe you'd better take me over to Loony's first. I remember seein' one in his barn." He climbed to his knees, determined to resume his flight.

"You ain't in no shape to go nowhere, and I ain't in no shape to drag you that far." Cracker jumped up and grabbed his arm. "Come in the house and let Mama doctor you some. I'll see what I can round up in the way of a cuttin' tool."

"That would get you and your whole family in bad trouble with the sheriff."

"So it was the sheriff that slapped that iron on you. What you done now?"

"I'll explain later. Got to go before the law gets back." Looking at Liga, he said, "You haven't seen me, understand? They'll track me to this spot with their dogs, but if I keep goin', they won't know I stopped." He stood up and turned to leave.

Cracker again grabbed his arm and began walking beside him, steadying him. He told his brother, "Liga, don't say nothin' about this to Mama or nobody. When the law comes by, tell 'em I went fishin'."

As they set out through the timber bordering Settlement Road, Heck said, "Let's go down to the branch and walk in it as far as we can. That'll knock the hounds off my scent."

Cracker, not yet up to par himself, soon broke out in a sweat as he strained to keep Heck from falling. He shook his head, mumbling, "Never thought I'd see the day when I'd be helpin' a white man run from his own law. What's this crazy world comin' to?"

They'd gone about a hundred yards when Heck stopped and sank to his knees. "Can't make it to Loony's. Too far."

"I don't reckon my sore leg could make it that far neither. Ain't we a pitiful sight?" Cracker kneeled down beside him, breathing heavily. "But if we don't get away from here, we'll end up in the graveyard fo' sho', me shot by the sheriff fo' helpin' you, and you bled dry."

"That would make Miss Josephine happy." Heck breathed hard. "Well, I ain't gonna die and give her the pleasure." He told Cracker about the charges she had the district attorney file on him, and about driving Thelma and Cotton to the bank. "You're the only one that can help me get to Nathan Meade's place. But you got to promise, if I pass out, you'll drag me the rest of the way."

Cracker nodded. "This really puts a kink in the cow's tail. You done got yo'self in a real fix this time, Heck Tennel."

"You make it sound like somethin' I wanted to happen."

"The wantin' ain't got nothin' to do with it. You're in a fix, and that's the Lord's truth. The same shape I was in, and I didn't have nothin' to do wid dat neither."

Realizing he wouldn't last much farther before passing out, Heck looked around to get his bearings in the fog gathering around them. Should he go on or just lie down and bleed to death out here in the woods where he wouldn't get anybody else involved in his problems?

"No!" he said out loud, causing Cracker to jump. "Billy and the girls are depending on me. And I'd never see Charlotte again."

"Huh?" Cracker gave him a puzzled look.

Heck climbed slowly to his feet, and Cracker jumped up to brace him.

"What we gonna do now?" Cracker asked. "If you can't walk to Mr. Loony's, how come you think you can make it anywheres else?"

Heck looked out across Settlement Road. "It's not far to Nathan Meade's place straight through the woods in that direction." He nodded. "No lawman will come in there looking for me. Let's go."

"And what makes you thank th' law won't go in after you there?"

"Don't know for sure, but I do know they won't. Guess it's because he's got somethin' that can't bear to be told on the sheriff or some big shot in town."

After Cracker got him across Settlement Road, Heck had him go back and wipe out their tracks with a pine top. Meanwhile, he checked his wound again. No blood was dripping through his shirt, but the dirt poultice was mushy. He had to make sure it didn't fall off and cause him to leave a blood trail for the sheriff or Squeeze's dogs to follow.

Cracker helped him up and they headed for Panther Holler Road, moving in short, faltering steps through the tall weeds and bushes under the big timber. Cut off from any breeze, it was sweltering in the undergrowth.

About one hundred yards later, Heck felt so dizzy he fell down, pulling Cracker with him. Turning Heck over on his back, Cracker said, "Let me go get a doctor. Yo're as white as my mama's sheets."

"No doctor, no jail," he gasped. "Get me back on my feet."

Cracker pulled him up and they lumbered on, slowly, stopping often to catch their breath. Finally, Panther Holler Road came in view up ahead.

Stretched out on his back, gasping for air, Heck's nose twitched, detecting a very foul odor. Looking at Cracker, he said, "Do I stink that bad, or do I smell a skunk?"

Cracker crinkled his nose. "Well, it sho' ain't me. So if it ain't you, it's got to be a polecat." Looking off to his right, he pointed. "There it is, upset as an ol' wet hen."

Heck rose up on one elbow. "Go get him. I've got an idea."

"You crazy? I ain't even getting close to that animal."

"I ain't askin' you to eat him. Get a stick, or a rock. Knock him in the head. We'll use him to cover our tracks."

Reluctantly, Cracker searched around until he found a dead limb. Snapping off a big piece of it, he gave Heck a final look of disapproval before crouching down and starting toward the pungent mass of black and white fur. About ten feet from it, Cracker drew back the club and let it fly, knocking the animal down, but not out. When he approached it, the skunk jumped up and limped out of sight.

"Catch him," Heck yelled. "Don't let him get away."

Cracker disappeared and came back shortly empty-handed.

"Where's that skunk?"

"In a hole in the ground. And that's where yo're goin' too, if'n you don't let me get you some real help."

Together they began moving toward the main road again. Reaching it, they stopped, looked and listened. Convinced no one was coming, Heck nodded. Cracker supported him across the opening, laid him down and erased their tracks.

Resuming their trek through a wild plum thicket, Heck said, "After leaving me at Mr. Meade's place, go back and get the skunk out of that hole. Tie a vine around his neck and drag him over our trail all the way to your place."

"What if that critter don't wanta come outta that hole? What if −"

"Don't what if me. I've watched you do worse things. Punch him with a stick, or smoke him out."

Cracker gave him another questioning look, but didn't choose to argue the point. Heck beheld the clearing around Mr. Meade's cabin and was glad to see the old bachelor's gray mare in the lot. His old friend seldom went anywhere and never had company except for Heck or Grandpa Tennel.

Heck sagged to his knees as his head began spinning. Without looking up, he told Cracker, "If I pass out, just drag me over to Mr. Meade's front door. Tell him what happened. Then run back . . . get that . . . skunk . . ."

Everything went black, and the last thing he felt was his face hitting the ground at Cracker's feet. His last thought, *Please, God, don't let me die.*

# Chapter XXX

The next sensation registering in Heck's brain was a sharp pain in his injured side. Relieved to find himself still alive, he immediately tried to rise up, but fell back when the pain became more severe. That's when Mr. Meade's deeply furrowed face appeared over him.

His vision, still fuzzy, tried to focus on the old man's squinting eyes behind spectacles with small, oval lenses. It was the first time Heck had ever seen him wear glasses or look so worried.

He again tried to sit up, but Mr. Meade's hands on his shoulders gently pushed him back.

"Be still, son, while I finish washing out that gully in your side and put somethin' on it." He moved Heck's left arm out of the way and turned his attention back to the wound.

"I'm not dead or in jail. Thank God for that."

"No, you ain't dead. But for a while there I wasn't sure which way your cards was gonna fall."

Heck's anger soared when he recalled the sheriff's accusations and being shackled. Raising his hands, he found his wrists still manacled, but the connecting chain cut.

"I have some bolt cutters," Mr. Meade said. "But they won't go through the thicker stuff. We'll work on that after you get to feeling better."

"I've never been treated like some kind of wild animal before. It was awful, havin' those things put on me in front of my little brother and sisters. I'm much obliged to you for getting' 'em apart. And for takin' me in." He flinched when Mr. Meade dabbed his wound.

"Don't forget how it felt to have that steel slapped on you, boy. Maybe rememberin' it'll keep you out of future fixes."

With his eyes focusing better, Heck looked around to find he was lying on a cot under a window in the front wall of Mr. Meade's cabin. It was warm and very quiet. There was only one other window, that being in the back wall. There didn't appear to be enough light for Mr. Meade to see how to clean and dress a wound, but his old friend kept at it. The alarm clock on a little shelf told him it was eleven thirty-five.

Mr. Meade continued with an alcohol-soaked white cloth, occasionally touching a more sensitive spot, causing him to flinch.

"How does it look?"

"Mean. But that dirt poultice you packed on it kept you from bleedin' to death. I've cleaned it up the best I can without knockin' off the dried blood. I'm gonna put some healing salve on it, and a clean bandage, and if it don't get infected, you'll see lots more winters. But you're lucky. You would've died on the spot if that bullet had gone through you instead of bouncin' off your ribs."

"Some luck is better than no luck at all, I guess. Up to then, it hadn't been one of my best days." He told him about the three arrest warrants and jumping out of the sheriff's car.

"Your colored friend told me part of it. Was wonderin' if you'd get around to givin' me a full account."

"Where's Cracker?"

"Went fishin', I guess."

"Fishin'?"

"Yep. Said somethin' about tellin' somebody he'd gone fishin'. Borrowed one of my fishhooks and a cane pole for an alibi."

"He didn't say anything about catchin' a skunk?"

"He did, for a fact. Said he had to catch one. I thought maybe he was touched until he told me what for. I saved him the trouble by givin' him my own special recipe for messin' up a hound's sniffer."

"What's better than a stirred-up skunk?"

He dropped the bloody rag in a pan beside the cot. "Pepper. I had a big box of Watkin's red."

"Has the sheriff been in here lookin' for me?"

"Nope." He glanced at Heck. "It's like I told you before. No local lawman's gonna come in here."

Heck noted an air of defiance in the old man's statement. Studying him a moment, he asked a question he'd always been too afraid to ask. "Why, Mr. Meade?"

The harsh expression on his old friend's face indicated he shouldn't have asked. It caused Heck to recall his friend's reaction when asked about trapping in Panther Holler Woods that bordered the back of his property. In an attempt to make amends, he said, "I apologize for bein' so nosy. It's none of my business."

Perhaps something about the request for forgiveness or just plain sympathy brought him around, but his eyes remained defiant, and he didn't smile when he said softly, "Boy, I give my word not to ever tell what happened in Panther Holler Woods way back yonder because of the harm it would cause a certain prominent party in the county. But since you're my friend and you're in this mess because of the actions brought agin you by those prominent people through their lackeys Emmet Sloan and Walter Norton, I will say this much. The present sheriff and D.A. won't let me be bothered because they know I'll keep my promise as long as I'm left alone and the prominent person in town holds up his end of our bargain. They're bound by promises they had to make too. Had to, to get elected and prosper. Now then. It's best you don't ask no more questions about the matter or repeat what I jus' told you. Will you give me your solemn word as a Southern gentleman not to ever speak of it as long as I'm alive?"

"Yes, sir." Heck nodded, relieved to be off the hook, but disappointed that the old man wouldn't give him any of the juicy, hair-raising details of what happened in Panther Holler Woods. *It probably had something to do with the old miller murdering his wife and her lover. Grandpa Tennel mentioned once that along about then Blood Money Vandergriff took over ownership of all the timber and land in Panther Holler Woods.* "I've always been too afraid of Panther Holler Woods to hunt or fish there. And that tall fence has been around it for as long as I can remember."

"Fear's a good thang sometimes. It's best you didn't go pryin' around in there, boy. Let the past rest in peace."

Heck nodded and for a moment studied the weathered face that suddenly appeared older and wearier. "I'll let it be. But I'll never forget what you did for me today. For a while there, I sure thought I was a goner. You're a real friend for puttin' up with me after what happened between me and the sheriff."

Mr. Meade closed the salve and picked up another white piece of cloth. "Stay on your good side a few more minutes. I'm about through."

"Any chance at all of the sheriff changin' his mind and come in here lookin' for me? Miss Josephine has some mighty convincin' ways."

"Not nearly as convincin' as her daddy."

His remark didn't surprise Heck. He wanted to hear a more detailed explanation, but didn't dare press the issue. "What's that smell?" He sniffed the air. "Is something burnin'?"

"Your bloody clothes. I'll get you a clean shirt and pants d'rectly. Some of mine are too small for you, but I've got some here that'll fit good enough, I reckon. The church sends me other folk's discards now and then."

Mr. Meade told him to raise up his shoulders, and when he did he wrapped a strip of the cloth around him, fastening it in front with a safety pin. Stepping back, the old fiddler gave the bandage a pleased look and told him, "I've seen men shot up worse'n you that lived to talk about it." He took the pan into the lean-to kitchen.

Heck wanted to ask him if the ones shot up worse than him were outlaws from the old days, but decided he had already pried too much into the old man's private affairs. He rose up on his right elbow to test his strength, then swung his feet off on the floor and sat up. Glancing down at his flour-sack shorts, he got to his feet, but had to press his legs against the cot to keep from falling.

"Whoa." His old friend reappeared and grabbed him. "What you tryin' to do, bust somethin' open? Lay down."

Heck sank on the cot and took some deep breaths in an attempt to clear his spinning head. "I need to leave. There's something I've got to do."

"I'll do it, if I can. What is it?"

"I have to find out if the pretty girl all this fuss is about sent me a letter yet."

"Is that all? I'll hitch up my mare and go out to your mail box."

Heck shook his head. "It won't be in our regular mailbox. And nobody but me is supposed to know where it's at."

"You trusted me with your life. 'Pears that's a bit more important than a letter."

"It's not to me."

"I reckon I can savvy that. You wouldn't think it now, but a long time ago I loved a pretty little girl that much, and she said she loved me." He turned his tired eyes toward the trees out front and was silent a moment. "It was a dastardly act by a coward that took her from me."

Heck found himself waiting again for more details, but instead of giving them, Mr. Meade said, "If that letter's where an old man can get at it, I'd be glad to fetch it for you. And I won't tell a soul where I got it."

Heck was reluctant to further impose, but realized he had no choice. He told him about the secret hiding place, and the importance of nobody seeing him go to and from it.

Mr. Meade's blue eyes indicated empathy for Heck's predicament. "I'll go by way of Settlement Road. By comin' in from the other end of Vandergriff Road, I won't have to ride by yore place." He studied Heck a moment and added, "I'll go that way, that is, if you don't want to send word to your folks about you bein' alive and well. They'll most likely be mighty worried once the word gets out about what happened between you and the sheriff."

"I've thought about that. I'm not as concerned about Daddy not knowin' as I am about Billy and the girls. I'd like them to know I'm okay, and that I'll see 'em as soon as I can."

"But if I tell them, I don't see how they could keep from tellin' their daddy who gave 'em the news."

"You're right. I can't afford to let that happen. My dad's weak. He's likely to blurt out anything if he's under the influence when the law comes by lookin' for me. He's mad at me for a bunch of things, helpin' Cracker bein' the most outstandin'." He told him about that. "Just check on the box for me for now. Later, after I'm able to move around, I'll get word to the kids."

It was agreed, and Mr. Meade strapped on his old Smith & Wesson Scofield revolver and pulled shut the hinged board shutters over the windows, latching them from the inside. He locked the front door from the inside as well, and headed for the back entrance where he stopped to tell Heck to not make a sound in case somebody did come by, and not to open the door or window for anybody. He added, "There's a bucket in the corner if you have to take a pee." He locked the door behind him.

Heck heard the horse drawn buggy pass by on the way to Panther Holler Road. He hoped Mr. Meade pushed his mare into a trot once he got out on the main road, because he was anxious to know if Charlotte had sent him a note.

He tried to relax in the increasingly warm room, but the events of the day, and week, wouldn't let him. It was still hard to believe he had been charged with three criminal offenses and was now a wanted man. *Was Bonnie and Clyde's first brush with the law brought about by good intentions gone wrong? Is there no turning back for a poor feller like me who has no friends in high places?*

What to do now? He was no match for the forces that had placed him in such a predicament, and he didn't have money to hire a good lawyer who could even the odds. Giving himself up in an effort to convince the district attorney to drop the charges was no option. That would get him hard time in state prison for sure, because Miss Josephine was not a forgiving woman.

Besides being warm, it was quiet in the cabin with the only sound heard being the ticking of Mr. Meade's old alarm clock. *Tick tock, tick tock. My life is ticking away, with no hope of returning to normal in the near future. If only I could see Charlotte, talk to her. That would make things better.*

He became so absorbed in his thoughts about the latest tragedies in his life and whether there was a letter for him in the old chimney, he forgot about his aching side. He now became aware of the throbbing pain in the spot where Mr. Meade had done all the scrubbing. He rose up to look for the clothes Mr. Meade told him about, but pain pushed him back down.

He rose up again, more slowly, and stood up, holding to the chair for a moment before heading for the battered chest of drawers in a back corner of the cabin. He finally found a wrinkled shirt, socks, and some overalls large enough for him and returned to the cot to put them on.

Afterwards, aching and spent, he sat with head bowed on the side of the cot, trying to think of a way out of his most recent troubles and about how he would take care of Billy and the girls without losing his war with Miss Josephine. *Unless I win that war, I can't take care of anybody. But how? Charlotte's my only acquaintance with ties to the rich and powerful, but the sheriff said she couldn't do anything without Miss Josephine's approval.*

He came up with lots of questions, but no answers. Sighing, he thought about Billy again. *Poor Billy. What will happen to him and the girls now?*

*That ox in the ditch has gotten a lot bigger and meaner and sunk down to his ears in the mud. Cracker was right. Life ain't no Saturday night musical.*

eck found a crack in the shutter through which he could see the front lane. Almost two hours had passed and he was beginning to think Mr. Meade had been stopped by the sheriff, or couldn't find the chimney, when he saw the mare's head appear at the turn in the lane. He pressed his eye closer to the narrow opening and watched Mr. Meade drive past the cabin to the barn without even as much as glancing his way. Did that mean he hadn't found anything behind the loose brick?

Heck didn't move until his old friend unlocked and entered the back door, then lay back down when he saw no letter in his hand.

After flooding the cabin with the afternoon sun by opening the shutters, Mr. Meade said calmly, "I see you found some clothes. I hope you didn't bust something loose gettin' 'em on."

Disappointed over not receiving a letter, Heck said nothing.

"You look like a whipped hound that ain't been fed in a week. You ain't feelin' worse, are you?"

"About the same, I reckon. I'd feel better if there'd been something for me in that box."

"You mean a letter like this'n?" He pulled something from his back pocket.

"There was a letter!" Heck's eyes sparked as he sat up on the cot. "Thank you very much."

Tearing off the end of the white envelope, he unfolded the sheet of matching stationery and saw a beautifully written letter.

*Dearest Heck,*

> *Aunt Josephine and the sheriff asked me a lot of personal questions, and at first, I told them nothing had happened between us, as I didn't consider it to be any of their business. But in view of what Mr. Truesdale and the sheriff had already told the district attorney, they didn't believe me.*
>
> *Aunt Josephine was beside herself when I told her again that I wanted to marry you. She vowed to never give her consent. That's when I decided to tell her what really happened, thinking it would cause her to change her mind. But she only*

*became more furious. She told me I would be sent out of state immediately to a girl's boarding school up north somewhere.*

*I'm sorry about all those horrible things Aunt Josephine said to you and about the charges she had filed on you. She has tried to convince me she, as my legal guardian, did it all for my own good. She and Aunt Priscilla had a violent argument about it. Aunt Priscilla begged her to allow you to visit me and let us get married, but she wouldn't hear of it. Aunt Josephine told us both I was never to see you again or write you.*

*I don't know the name of the private school or its location yet, but as soon as I get there, I'll write Aunt Priscilla, and she'll pass my address on to you. I may even get to send you one more letter before I'm taken away. Please write. Leave your letters in our secret place and Aunt Priscilla will pick them up. This is how we will stay in touch until you're able to come to see me, or until I become of age and can live where I please.*

*Aunt Josephine said I will not be allowed to return to Two Rivers except to testify at your trial. How horrible that makes me feel. I have told everybody concerned that no wrong was committed; if so, why wasn't I charged too? But I cannot deny what happened between us any more than I can say it was not done for all the right reasons. I'm so sorry I am the cause of the injustices done to you, because you are the first person to ever make me feel truly loved, and the first to make me feel good about life.*

*Love,*
*Charlotte*

Heck looked at the letter, both numbed and encouraged by what she said in it. "Well, Miss Josephine," he said, "you and Blood Money won the first round. But the fight's not over yet."

He gave Mr. Meade an embarrassed look for having spoken out so. Mr. Meade's expression was solemn, and for a moment it appeared he might say something, but instead he turned and walked out the back door.

"Did you run into anybody on the way?" Heck asked when he returned.

"The sheriff, and Squeeze, on the north end of Settlement Road. You sure ruffled their feathers, boy."

"Did you talk to 'em?" Heck became tense, anxious to get his answer. "Did they ask you any questions?"

"They did, for a fact. Wanted to know where I was goin', and if I'd seen you."

"What did you tell 'em?"

"Nothin' that you need to worry about, boy. Told 'em, that if I was you, I woulda lit a shuck down to the Natchitoches River bottom where Cotton Murphy was hidin' out at a fishing camp gettin' ready to high-tail it out of the state with your step-mama."

"Huh?" Heck saw a mischievous twinkle in Mr. Meade's eye and the hint of a smile on his lips. "Oh, yeah. I sure would."

"After the sheriff left to take Squeeze back to town to get another dog to send down there, I drove around a while, then cut through the woods on an ol' loggin' road. While over there, I saw Loony and a big colored woman in his back yard, but they was so busy washing they didn't see me. Pulled into the trees and walked past the Vandergriff house on the other side of the road 'til I got opposite that slave cabin. Heard your pa yelling at the kids down the road at your place, but didn't go see what all the fuss was about."

"I'm obliged to you for getting' the letter and for doctorin' me. But I can't stay and take a chance on gettin' you in trouble too." He closely watched Mr. Meade's expression to gauge his true feelings on the matter.

"That's crazy talk, boy. You've got no place to go." Mr. Meade poured himself a glass of water from a bucket on the table and sat down near the cot. "Hide out here where the sheriff and Miss Josephine won't look for you. But just 'cause they don't dare come in here, don't mean they won't post a deputy out on the main road to watch who comes and goes. And if they see me leave, some greenhorn lawman fresh on the job might come snoopin' around my house. In case that happens, I've got a special place where you can hide." He pointed to a large wood box near the stove. Just raise it up and get in the hole I dug under the floor. There's hay in it for nappin' and a jar o' water. It latches from the underside."

"Thanks. Something you learned in the old days?" He immediately wished he hadn't asked.

"Old days, new days. Some thangs never change, boy. If a poor man finds hisself in a corner and he ain't got no friends in high places, he does what he has to do."

"Yes sir. I reckon I know the feelin'."

"You'll feel like bein' up and around in a day or two. But even a frog knows where he's gonna jump next, which means you've got to do some plannin'. If you'll stay with me tonight, I'll check that box again for you tomorrow."

The sincere look in his friend's eyes comforted him - - the way he felt in the presence of Grandpa Tennel. "Okay, but I'll be leavin' as soon as I'm able." He shrugged. "Trouble is I don't know how or where I'll go. Got no money, no job, no nothin'."

"With your spunk, you'll find a way to do what you've got to do. You don't need no money for travelin', so don't fret about that. The T. & N.O. pulls out of Two Rivers every Saturday, Monday and Thursday night about eight. It's always heavy loaded, so when it goes up Old North Church Hill 'bout a mile from here, it ain't goin' no more'n five miles an hour. It's a poor man's dream when he has to make a little trip if he's down on his luck and don't cater to farewell parties."

Heck looked at him with an added sense of appreciation. The old man's eyes had that sparkle in them again, like he might be remembering some escapades in his youth, pitting himself against the law.

"Hungry?" Mr. Meade got up.

"Starving. My stomach's about to eat my backbone."

"I'll scramble us eggs and fry some pork belly. You just rest easy."

Turning to look through the front door, Heck found the day's light fading fast. Up at his house, it was supper time too. He wondered who would fix the meal, and if Billy's fever had come back.

Mr. Meade came over and pulled a dingy white curtain across the front window and closed the door. "Don't want to take no chances." Noticing Heck trying to read Charlotte's letter again in the darkened cabin, he lit a kerosene lamp and sat it on the chair beside the cot, then went into the lean-to kitchen and fired up his little kerosene stove.

Heck re-read the letter and returned it to the envelope with the same sense of loss as before, but more determined to go see Charlotte as soon as she sent him her new address.

Supper done, Mr. Meade placed a bowl of scrambled eggs, warmed-over biscuits and bacon strips on the little table in the center of the room and said, "Feel like comin' over to set with me, or do you want me to brang it to you?"

Heck slowly walked over and sat down, then put some food in a chipped blue plate. The biscuits and cold coffee made it all taste mighty good.

Little was said as they ate; Heck was too worried about Billy and the girls, and too angry at Josephine Vandergriff to engage in idle chitchat. But the wheels of his mind were churning out questions: Would Charlotte be able to slip another letter out to him before being taken out of town? How would she feel about him after settling in that northern school? Would she still want to write? If she did, would Miss Josephine prevent Miss Cilla from delivering her letters to the old chimney? If some did get through, who would pick them up if he left?

When he was finished eating, Heck pushed back his plate and asked Mr. Meade if he had some writing paper and something to write with. Momentarily he was handed a Big Chief tablet and a cedar pencil. Heck asked, "Will you take my letter out to that box tomorrow when you go to check it?"

"You bet." A twinkle appeared in his eye. "You can write it while I feed my mare and take care of other night chores before it gets too dark to see how."

Putting on his battered gray hat, Mr. Meade left, and Heck turned his mind to answering Charlotte. Full of words, but not knowing how to begin, he merely stared at the tablet for several minutes. Finally, he began to write.

*Dearest Charlotte,*

*I'm sorry for all the embarrassment and trouble I've caused you, and I'm real upset about your Aunt Josephine sending you away. I never realized that being in love can be so hard on folks. But as soon as you write me from that school you're being sent to, I'll write you, I promise. And as soon as I make arrangements to take care of my sisters and little brother, I'll come to see you.*

*I'm real confused about why the law is chasing me like I'm some kind of dangerous criminal. I hope you don't hold it against me for doing what I had to do to stay out of jail. I did it for Billy and the girls' sake and I couldn't bear the thought of being sent where I couldn't see you. Don't worry about me. I can make out some way as long as I know you have strong feelings for me. You have given my life a meaning it never had before. I will never be happy again unless I can be with you.*

*I'll write more next time. Until then, try to think about me now and then, and keep on being sweet and beautiful. Regardless of what happens, don't be sad. That would put wrinkles on your pretty face and make your days long. One snapping turtle in the family is enough.*

*I consider you to be my wife already under God's law, so that makes us a family, right?*

*Love,*
*Heck*

Thinking through what he should say and writing it down tuckered him out, so he was glad when Mr. Meade came back in the house and told him it was time to blow out the light and "fly up." Full of pleasant thoughts for a change, he went to sleep.

A new sun was breaking the horizon behind the trees on the east side of the cabin when he woke up. He felt stronger, but his side ached something fierce when he sat up on the cot to look at Mr. Meade who was already in the lean-to kitchen lighting the kerosene stove.

"Your color is better," Mr. Meade called out to him. "Want some breakfast?"

"Sure do. But first I've got to make a trip out to the privy."

"Just move easy, and don't strain too much doin' what you got to do.'

After going to the outhouse and washing his hands at the well, Heck moved slowly back into the cabin, sitting down at the table to rest. About thirty minutes later, Mr. Meade served him a breakfast of fritters, bacon and hot coffee. It was good, but he ate with a sad face, depressed over hiding out like a common criminal and the dismal prospects of having to abandon his family.

Respecting his feelings, Mr. Meade said little besides announcing that he would take his letter to the secret stash before it got hot, and in case somebody saw him leave or was bold enough to check out his cabin, he should remember the hiding place under the wood box.

The sun's rays were just topping the trees when Mr. Meade locked up and left with the letter. Alone in the quiet cabin again, Heck soon found himself nodding off, but fought to stay awake and alert to possible visitors. Using the chair as a crutch, he got up and searched the cabin for something to take for his aching. Upon finding a tin of St. Joseph's aspirin, he took two and lay back down.

Around mid-morning, Heck heard the buggy coming back down the lane and rose up to peek through the narrow crack beside the window shutter, eager for more mail. Mr. Meade drove on by the cabin toward the barn without looking his way as he did before.

It took his friend forever, it seemed, to unhitch his horse and come inside. A sinking feeling swept over Heck when he saw nothing in his hands but his hat.

"This'll perk you up." Mr. Meade pulled a white envelope out of his back pocket. "It took me longer this time because Miss Priscilla was just pullin' up when I got in sight of her old place. I waited in the woods 'til she left."

"Thank you very much." Heck reached for the letter.

Opening the envelope, he found a small photo of Charlotte and a letter written in a beautiful, but different hand. He looked at the signature on the bottom: Priscilla Vandergriff. *Miss Josephine must've already sent Charlotte out of town.*

Mr. Meade spoke, but Heck was too concerned about the letter to know what he said. He only was aware of him leaving the room to go into the lean-to. Heck took a deep breath and began reading.

*Dear Heck,*

> *Josephine and her friend Connie left with Charlotte yesterday afternoon, refusing to tell me their destination. Charlotte slipped me the enclosed photo before she left, telling me to place it in my first letter. Poor Charlotte. She was very sad and crying when she told me good-bye as they drove off.*

> *Even though I tried, I was powerless to stop Josephine and Father from carrying out their vicious plan. Charlotte asked me to go live with her, and I agreed, but they forbade it – assuming I'd take her to a place unknown to them and inform you of our whereabouts. I must admit, they were right about something for a change.*

> *Josephine told Charlotte she will not be allowed to write you.*

> *My sister is banking on the out-of-mind-out-of-sight theory.*

> *Charlotte told me, however, that she will never forget you and still will write you through me even though I'm under threat of losing my inheritance if I intercede further, I'll bring*

*her letters to your secret place if Josephine does not intercept them. The postmaster in Two Rivers is a close political friend of Father's, so a plan on Josephine's part to reroute them could be easily carried out.*

*I'm happy you escaped custody, and hope you were not injured in any way when you did. But how long can you stay in this area, and avoid being arrested if you do? I worry about you, Heck, and hope and pray that Josephine and Father will come to their senses soon and revoke the terrible burdens they have placed on you.*

*If you leave Hispaniola County, please have someone you trust come by and let me know. That person can pick up Charlotte's letters sent to me, if they get through, and forward them to you.*

*Charlotte and I love you.*
*Stay safe,*
*Priscilla Vandergriff*

He reread the letter, admiring the beautiful face in the photo. It was a good likeness, but in her eyes he saw that hint of sadness he'd seen before. He sighed, shaking his head over his loss.

"Bad news?" Mr. Meade said as he came back in the room.

"Just a temporary setback." Heck continued looking at the picture. "It looks like it'll be a while before I receive any more letters."

"Too bad. But you do need to put your mind on matters at hand. Now, I don't mean to rush you into makin' your next move, but it ain't too early to start givin' it some serious thought. Even the best and the smartest of them that get crossways with the law sometimes wind up gettin' caught eventually. And Emmet Sloan might get up enough nerve eventually to send somebody from outside the county bustin' in here lookin' for you when he knows I'm gone. In my way o' thinkin', you'd be better off goin' clean out of state. Real soon. Once the law takes after a man, it won't bend the rules to allow for a man's special problems."

"I can't leave before figuring out how I'm gonna take care of Billy and the girls. And I need to stay around until I find out if Charlotte's able to send letters to Miss Cilla."

"I admire your spunk, boy. Don't ever let nobody take that away from you." He shook his head. "Your pride either. A poor man's pride has always been his first line of defense."

Heck placed the letter back into the envelope. "If I do leave, I'd need a good friend here that I can mail money to after finding a job. Somebody'll that take it to my family."

"I have a mailbox, and I'm willin'."

"If I mailed you enough money, would you see to it that Billy has his tonsils out and gets those tests he needs? You could give the grocery money to Elsie. She's old enough to handle that."

Mr. Meade nodded. "I'd be glad to as long as I'm able."

Heck looked through the front door at the trees between him and Panther Holler Road, thinking back. He told his old friend, "Two Rivers and Hispaniola County have never been very friendly towards me and my family, but I'll miss it just the same. I'll miss it in spite of knowing that big shots like Blood Money Vandergriff and his cronies will always look upon my kind of folks as nothin' but axle grease for their money-makin' machines." His eyes blurred with tears. "But I can't leave Billy and my sisters. What in the world will become of them and our helpless, crippled daddy?"

Mr. Meade came over and placed an arm around Heck's drooped shoulders. "I know it ain't easy, boy. But a real man does what he has to when there ain't nobody else around to take on his burdens. You know the law is watchin' your family. If you even so much as try to see 'em, here or anywhere else, you'll end up in the pen for sure. You don't want that to happen, do you?"

Heck shook his head and wiped the tears off his face with the back of his hand.

Mr. Meade's voice was soft and kind. "As soon as you're in a safe place, and in a shape to do 'em some good, you can write 'em through me. And as soon as you pull out, I'll make a special trip over there to tell 'em how much you love 'em and how much you hated to leave 'em."

"You've been a real friend, Mr. Meade. What can I ever do to pay you back?"

"By not flyin' off the handle and doin' somethin' foolish that'll land you in more trouble than you're in already. A long time ago, you might remember me tellin' you about what happened to the Dalton brothers, the Youngers and Jessie James. Same end come to Pretty Boy Floyd and John Dillinger. Look what just happened to Bonnie and Clyde. Most of them was pretty good boys once, but they used bad judgment, and quicker'n lightnin', it was too late to quit. It's like that with the law, no matter how much a man may want to quit later on. So keep a cool head on your shoulders. Think thangs out. Time changes 'most everythang."

Heck nodded, looking at the photo. "Even people, Mr. Meade?"

"Yep."

"That's the part that worries me the most."

# Chapter XXXII

The seventy-nine-year old Heck spent a restless night in Cracker's spare bedroom. But unlike all the others when he'd been unable to sleep, it wasn't old wounds alone keeping him awake. Rather, the memories of his youth that recent events so vividly rekindled.

He loved Miss Cilla dearly and appreciated what she did for him in the past, but he had misgivings about her trusting Norton to carry out her "last wishes." In spite of that, however, he still believed she meant well by having him tracked down and urged to return home. But, when all was said and done, coming back had forced him to remember too many disappointments.

Over the years he'd managed to push the old memories into dark corners of his mind. Not forgotten, just stowed away. What's past is past, he kept telling himself. Lost chances are just that: chances. Nothing is real unless a man can hold on to it; otherwise, he'll drive himself crazy second guessing how things might have worked out.

If he got himself arrested at his and Charlotte's secret place now, he would lose the only things of value he fled with, his freedom and his pride. Mr. Meade was right many years ago when he told him how a poor man's pride is his first line of defense. He couldn't allow himself to be arrested now and lose it in his final battle with Josephine and Blood Money Vandergriff.

Upon hearing the clatter of dishes in Cracker's kitchen around sun-up, Heck shaved and dressed, joining his host who had just placed cups and saucers on the dinette table.

Cracker's eyes lit up when Heck walked into the kitchen, but his expression became solemn when he saw how tired he looked. "Hard night?"

"Does it show that much?"

Cracker nodded, pointing to a chair. "A cup of my Louisiana coffee with chicory will help pull you up. How do you want your eggs?"

"Shelled and cooked," Heck said, sitting down.

Cracker shook his head. "I see lack of rest didn't kill the devil in you." He filled their cups. "What time are you supposed to be out at the old Vandergriff place?"

"Ten, if I go."

Cracker sat down, studying Heck. "Still afraid Miss Josephine will reach up out of her grave and latch onto you?"

"Something like that."

"Appears to me, if that lawyer wanted to tip off the law, he'd have done it already. Why wait 'til you show up out there?"

"Because he won't know for sure I'm who I claim to be until I walk out to the old chimney and pick up that box."

"I see. Well, my gut feeling tells me Miss Cilla wouldn't do anything to pile more hurt on you after all these years."

Heck took a swallow of coffee. "I'd be more inclined to risk it if you'd take me out there in your car. I could duck down out of sight and let you drive by and look things over real good. As we used to say, make sure the coast is clear."

"Okay. But while you're hunkered down, who am I supposed to be on the lookout for besides the lawyer?"

"Cops. And Blood Money's ghost." He shook his head, and his eyes sparkled when he turned them back to Cracker. "Wouldn't it be a kick in Blood Money's butt if I did go out to his old place and was able to walk away? I'll bet you five to one that mean old bastard and Miss Josephine would turn over in their graves so hard the ground would shake worse than the floor in that old cropper house in thirty-four when Mr. Meade played a hoe-down and everybody danced."

Cracker went to the counter top and broke eggs into a bowl, and gave him a thoughtful look before replying. 'You haven't changed a bit, 'cept for aging around the edges. You're still just like a snappin' turtle, never lettin' go of nothin'."

Heck drank his coffee in silence as he watched Cracker prepare breakfast. Finally, he said, "You've done well, Cracker. I'm proud to have you as my friend. Truth of the matter is, you and Nathan Meade and Miss Cilla were the truest friends I ever had, back then or since."

Cracker glanced at Heck before placing link sausage in another pan. "As I recall, you used to take lots of heat for being my pal in the old days. And these days, lots of my people say a black man can't have a real friend who's white. I always told them, it's because they've never had one like I had."

"Why, thank you, Cracker. That's a real compliment. Any members of your family still live around here?"

"Everybody's dead except Tinker. He lives in California."

"Golden California." He laughed. "Remember Tiny Lucy? Whatever happened to her? Did she stay with Loony?"

"She did. He fixed up his tool shed real nice for her. She still lives out on his place, but in the house now. She took real good care of Mr. Loony for ten years before he died. It was sad, the way all the white folks refused to go to his funeral. They wouldn't let us bury him in the cemetery at the white folk's church. So my brothers and I helped Tiny Lucy bury him out behind his barn next to his mare after I said a few words over him."

"Poor Loony." Heck shook his head. "He must've died about the same time Mr. Meade passed away."

"About five years later."

"I sent money to Mr. Meade for Billy and the girls. At least, that's what I thought at the time. Didn't know better until hearing it from Willa when she and my daughter met me one time up in Seattle."

"I didn't know you kept seeing Willa."

"I didn't. Never slept with her after we married to give her baby a name. Oh, we got together about once a year for three or four years so I could see my daughter. She'd already divorced me by then and was living with another man. After our daughter Sissy started to school, she wrote me every year until she was ten. Sent the letters through a friend." He wiped his eyes. "Sissy was a sweet child until she got old enough to take on her mother's ways."

"You did the right thing, Heck, giving your child a name."

Heck grunted. "Sometime I'll have to tell you about marrying the wrong woman in Louisiana."

"Oh, yeah." An expression of sudden recall swept over Cracker's face. "In all the excitement, I clean forgot. Before he died, Mr. Meade gave me something to give to you in case you ever came back."

Turning down the flame under their breakfast, Cracker left the room in a fast walk, returning shortly holding an object wrapped in an oily rag. Heck took it and unwrapped Mr. Meade's old .38 pistol, complete with holster and belt, both scratched and worn.

"Well, I'll be," he said. Breaking it open, he spun the cylinder and found it still loaded. "Thanks. I may have need of this if I go out to the Vandergriff place."

"You ain't that crazy, are you? 'Cause if you are, I'm not going."

Heck pushed the old gun back into its holster, saying grimly, "But there were times back there when . . ."

Cracker stirred the eggs and sausage, sliding them into a white bowl. Giving the pistol a cautious look, he placed them to the table.

They ate in silence for the most part. Cracker kept glancing at Heck, as if he wanted to ask a question but was afraid to. Finally, after refilling their coffee cups, he said, "Because we went through so much together, I'm hoping you don't mind me bringing this up. You haven't told me a thing about what happened to your family. Or Miss Charlotte. Would it help any to talk about them now?"

Heck didn't respond until he'd finished his eggs and sausage, as if the subject might be too painful to discuss while eating. Finally, pushing back his chair, he sighed and said, "I traveled to lots of towns in several northeastern states looking for Charlotte after I got a job in Kansas City. That's the area she was sent to, according to Mr. Meade's sources. I used my vacation for three years doing that. I went by, or called, every boarding school for girls I found in each town's telephone directory. But I never found her."

"That's a shame. Then again, if you had, Miss Josephine and the law most likely would've found you. Right after you left, word got out about her offering a ten thousand dollar reward to the person that found you and brought you back for trial. She was determined to make you pay for what you did, even if she died first. She was a laughing stock for a while after you left, being so powerful and all and not able to get her way with a simple country boy like you. The fact that folks were on your side in the matter galled her too. She wanted you real bad."

"And she might still get me, if I'm not careful," Heck said. "Anyway, Elsie and Mr. Meade couldn't find out any more about where Charlotte was sent either, because Miss Cilla never found out herself. And if she ever wrote me through Miss Cilla, I guess her letters were intercepted and destroyed, because the girls here never sent Marna anything from her. Marna was our go-between for lots of years." He sighed. "Maybe Charlotte changed, like Miss Josephine predicted. Maybe she never wrote me at all. Who knows?"

Cracker opened his mouth to respond when Heck added, "Some things just don't improve with the telling."

"Maybe it depends who you do the telling to. You've never discussed it with me. And I'll bet five to one you've never talked it over with The Man either."

"Don't be too sure about that, you old reformed clodhopper. Foxholes and bullets do strange things to a man, no matter how cynical he gets."

Heck helped with the dishes, then went to the bathroom. He rejoined his friend in the living room, eager to leave and find out what awaited him at the old Vandergriff house. He said to Cracker, "Ready, chauffeur?"

"If you are. And, if I may say so, I think you've made the right choice in the matter."

Cracker backed his Ford Taurus out of the drive and they headed for Josephine Vandergriff Road. When Cracker turned north on it near the old church site, Heck studied the place until they'd passed it, wondering what happened to the old building and the schoolhouse that stood nearby.

"Anybody ever hear from Homer Percy after I left?"

"Not that I know of." He looked over at Heck. "Heard your stepmother slipped back in at one time, her and that trash she left with. I was out of town but heard they raised a ruckus when somebody discovered them in Panther Holler Woods looking for that old miller's gold. They got away again, though, and I was told she didn't go by to see her family any more, and they didn't even know she was here 'til after they were chased out of town. Nothing more about them after that. How about you?"

Looking straight ahead, Heck said, "One can of worms at a time, okay?"

Heck felt himself becoming more anxious as they drew near the row of old sharecropper houses on Vandergriff Road. What before had been only mixed feelings, now boiled into an inner storm.

Turning into Vandergriff Road finally, Cracker said, "I don't see any sheriff's cars up ahead, so I'll stop and give you a chance to get a good look at your old home."

Heck leaned over to look past his friend at the remains of the old houses, now nothing more than sagging, rotting scraps of wood and rusty tin. Pine trees fifty feet tall grew where once there were floors and the back yard of the one they lived in was a mass of vines and weeds growing beneath more trees. The barn and chicken house had disappeared within the heavy undergrowth.

First studying the crumpled remains of the house they lived in, then the one where they held their musicals, Heck found himself overcome with emotions so strong he could neither move nor speak. When he felt tears welling up, he turned to look out at the woods on the other side of the road to prevent Cracker from seeing a part of him he had never seen before. Moments later, he turned again to look at the first mass of rotting scraps of lumber and said, "Billy might still be alive if I could've stayed with him."

"As I remember it, you had no choice."

Consumed by his memories of the place, Heck took a while responding. "Mr. Meade got him his tonsillectomy like he said he would, but right after that he wrote and told me he was feeling poorly and that I would have to start sending the money to my dad. Daddy was supposed to take Billy for some tests, but Elsie wrote me through Marna that he spent it mostly on whiskey and Frieda Haskel. I wrote him through Marna lots of times and begged him to bring Billy and the girls up to live with me, but he refused. Appears he didn't want his income cut off, which would've happened if they'd left him. He didn't even write Marna in time for me to come to Billy's funeral." He turned away again when he teared up.

"Don't do it, Heck. Don't take it all on yourself. You did everything you could. It was God's will."

"Don't say that," Heck snapped, turning. "If that God you preach about has anything to do with who lives and dies, how could he be so unmerciful as to let an innocent little boy like Billy die?"

Cracker's hands clenched the steering wheel and his jaw muscles tightened, but he didn't respond. He kept his eyes straight ahead, not looking at Heck.

"Sorry, old friend," Heck said, calmer now. "Please accept my apology. I had no call to jump on you for somebody else's mistakes. Billy died because I left, and because Dad was weak. He didn't love Billy or the girls." He climbed out of the car, shut the door and walked to the rear of the road. As he stared at the remains of the old houses, a gentle breeze moved through the weeds and trees like whispered words from the dead past. The sight brought a lump to his throat like the one he had that time he placed his arms around his little brother and promised to never let him down.

He walked to the driver's side of the Ford and said, "Hope you're not so mad at me that I'll have to walk the rest of the way."

"It's all right, Heck," Cracker said. "I'm not angry. Finish your visit."

"Thanks."

Turning to study the remains of the place where music was made by his grandfather, Mr. Meade and himself, he told Cracker, "Truth of the matter is, I've never stopped blaming myself for what happened to Billy, poor little fella. I've always believed he would've beaten the odds if Josephine Vandergriff hadn't . . . if I hadn't left. I should've tried harder to find a way to get him away from Dad, but Mr. Meade and Elsie both warned me not to come back for any reason."

"The law wouldn't have allowed you take him away from his own daddy, Heck. Besides, what would you have done with him and your sisters while you were away in the war?"

"I wouldn't have enlisted for starters. I could've found a way."

"Did you ever find a way to see Billy again before he passed away?"

The question caused him to choke up and return to the rear of the car to be alone with his thoughts. Standing there, out of Cracker's view, he did what he'd sworn not to do: he wept openly. Minutes passed as he lingered there, weeping and fighting to control pent-up emotions that had been held back for so long. Finally, he stopped the flow of uncontrolled sentiment. At that moment Heck became aware of the stillness about him, hearing the buzzing of a passing bee and the wind whispering through the pine tops. Dabbing his eyes with his shirt sleeve and clearing his throat, he returned to the side of the car.

Cracker said, "I'm sorry about puttin' my foot in my mouth."

Heck forced a smile. "You owe me no apology, friend. It was me that got out of line." He looked out at the remains of his former home. "At first, I wrote Billy and the girls every week through Marna. She sent my mail to Mr. Meade. I didn't try to get Billy and the girls to live with me right away, because I figured he'd be better off staying here with Doc Samuels who understood his problem. But when Mr. Meade got sick, I sent Marna down to get the three kids. That's when I learned Dad wouldn't let them leave. He called the sheriff and the law backed him up. Evidently they thought I'd come down myself and give them a chance to arrest me on those old warrants."

Heck sighed and looked across the road at some cut-over pines. "The second time I sent Marna for them, the law put her in jail because she wouldn't tell them where I was, or Jake. Wouldn't have let her out if Jake hadn't sent a lawyer down." He walked back to the passenger's side. "Let's go." He slid down in the seat as Cracker headed for the old Vandergriff house.

"Let me know if you see a sheriff's car," Heck said. "But don't stop if you do, because that'll catch their eye. Just drive on by, normal like."

"Yes suh, boss man," he teased. "Cracker the chauffeur at your service."

"I see you've got a little touch of the devil left in you too."

In a more sober tone, Cracker said, "What finally happened to your sisters, Heck?"

"When Dad died, they went to live with Marna and Jake in Tennessee. Got married. Still there."

Continuing slowly up the road, Cracker said, "I hate to disappoint you, but I don't see any police cars."

Heck peeked over the dash as the old Vandergriff house came into view. "I see a car parked in the yard."

"You didn't expect the lawyer to walk five miles, did you?"

"But he's not supposed to be out here this early."

"He's no earlier than you are. Want me to stop or keep going?"

Heck studied the clearing for a moment. "Pull in."

Shocked at the run-down condition of the old house, Heck sat up straight as Cracker swung into the weed-infested driveway. Apparently abandoned, the house bore little resemblance to the grand place Heck remembered so well. The outside walls were unpainted, its cornice rotting and falling off in places. Most of the windowpanes were missing. The swing where he sat with Charlotte was the saddest sight of all. Warped and rotten, it was hanging at a crazy angle by one chain.

Cracker stopped behind a white Lincoln Continental and Norton got out greeting them. Still stunned by the unexpected desolation, Heck stepped out into knee-deep weeds gawking at the place.

Approaching Heck, Norton said, "Figured you'd be early, so I got here in time to put Miss Priscilla's letter in that special place before you showed up."

He looked at the side yards and glanced out back, but saw no other cars. Norton was alone. He looked at the lawyer. "So now, you'll find out if I'm really Heck Tennel, right?"

Norton gave him a nervous smile and turned to look at Cracker. "Who's he?"

"Another innocent man your dear ol' D.A. granddaddy filed false charges on," Heck replied. "But don't worry, he's harmless now."

Norton searched Heck's face. "Well? Are you Heck Tennel or not?"

"Keep your shorts on, lawyer. I'll be right back."

Heck headed for the trees on the east side of the driveway, finding them much taller now. Moving slowly through the dense underbrush, he walked toward the spot where he remembered the old servants' quarters to be. Not finding the ruins, he changed direction and spotted the collapsing chimney.

As he studied the scene, an eerie sensation swept through him. It was overwhelming, much like the feeling he had when Cracker asked if he ever saw Billy again and when he walked to the front of the Panther Holler Baptist Church and took the preacher's hand.

He stepped closer, noting an absence of jonquils at the base of the chimney. Pushing through the pine saplings, vines and weeds that apparently had smothered the flowers, he moved his hand up the chimney wall until he felt the loose brick. He removed it, allowing it to fall to the ground, then reached into the cavity and retrieved a metal box.

Backtracking out of the vines, he examined the shiny black box, obviously new, which didn't appear large enough to hold a significant amount of anything. He lifted the lid with his free hand, shaking with anticipation. There was nothing inside but one small piece of white paper. A wave of indignation and disappointment followed his recognition of Norton's deception.

Placing the box under his arm, he unfolded the paper and read a handwritten message: "The material was too bulky to be left here, Heck Tennel. I have it in my car. Robert Norton."

Feeling better, but a little put upon, he rejoined Norton. "Did I pass the test, teacher?"

"You're a tough nut to crack, aren't you, Tennel?" Reaching through his car window, he picked up a large brown envelope, telling him, "In view of your low regard for lawyers, I'm sure you'll be pleased to know that the orders on the outside of this envelope were not written by me."

Heck examined the bulging envelope with a puzzled expression.

Opening the Continental's door, Norton said, "Don't worry about that reward Miss Josephine put on your head a long time ago. You know how we crooked lawyers are. I found a loophole. I'll be going now, but if you need any legal work done later, you know where to find me. I'll be happy to help."

"Legal work? You mean, like defending me in a court trial? Sounds like you called the sheriff, after all."

"Stop fighting ghosts and read what's in the envelope, Tennel. That's why you came out here, isn't it?" He started his car, then killed the motor. "Do you mind if I ask you a personal question?"

Heck shrugged. "Not if you don't mind if I don't answer it if I don't like the question."

"As I said before, we pulled lots of strings looking for you. The Social Security Administration, the FBI, our congressman. That's after I found out about your assumed name and your military service. It was some notes in your military file that puzzled me. They said you requested to be sent to the Pacific theater after recovering from a wound you received in North Africa. Once you got there, you requested duty after being wounded again, even though you were eligible to be sent home. And when you were sent back into combat, you fought like a man who wanted to be killed. You even volunteered for assignments that you knew were very dangerous."

Heck remained silent, waiting for the ultimate question.

"It may be none of my business, but I'd really like to know. Did the things that happened to you here in thirty-four cause you to, you know, want to stop living?"

Heck sensed Cracker's eyes on him as he pondered the question. It was apparent that his friend was also anxious to hear the answer.

Finally, Heck calmly said, "You're right. It's none of your business."

Taken aback by his response, Norton's frozen smile slowly faded. He shrugged, re-started his car and drove away.

*He could come back shortly with the sheriff,* Heck thought. *Should I stay and take that chance after all these years?*

# Chapter XXXIII

Eager to see the contents of the large envelope, Heck decided he couldn't wait until he drove to a safer place. Ignoring Cracker's questioning look, he put the large container on the trunk of the Ford and studied the writing on the outside. It read, "Heck, the letters within are numbered. Reading them in order will help you understand what has happened during your absence. Priscilla's letter should be read first, therefore, it is numbered one."

There was no signature, but the handwriting looked vaguely familiar. He pulled out his pocketknife and carefully cut open the packet. When he tilted it, three smaller brown envelopes slid out.

Feeling something else in the larger envelope, he ran his hand inside and pulled out a bundle of letters. A notation on the outside of them said, "Read these last."

*Could it be?* The possibilities caused his fingers to tremble, but he decided to abide by the instructions. Placing them on the trunk, he picked up envelope "# 1."

Shaking hands slipped the knife blade beneath the flap and cut it open. Unfolding the white stationery within, he read the date at the top: December 10, 1988.

> *Dearest Heck,*
>
> *I was so happy when I found out, at last, that you are not dead as Josephine reported. I'm so grateful to God that we found out while I still had the strength to resume the search for you that was interrupted a long time ago when she said you had died. I pray you will be found before I die so I might know that you have read this letter. If I do die, I have left instructions with Mr. Norton to deliver it.*
>
> *I want to explain why I was unable to leave Charlotte's letters in that secret place for forwarding. But first, you should know I never told her you got married, which I learned myself by accident. I thought that could best be explained by you, if given the opportunity.*
>
> *As anticipated, Josephine had Charlotte's letters intercepted but for reasons known only to her, not destroyed.*

*I found them after she died earlier this year, and I inherited control of Father's estate. I sent the bundle to Charlotte who will, I'm sure, deliver them too you in the event you are found and agree to return to Two Rivers.*

Heck glanced at the other envelopes. *Is it really true?* His hands were shaking uncontrollably now. He resumed reading.

*I promised Charlotte before she was sent away, and myself, that whenever I had the power to do so, I would try my best to make partial amends for the suffering my family caused you. Having lived a lonely life because I never found no man who loved me as Charlotte loved you, and what I do for others has special significance to me. In keeping with that promise, you will find attached your copy of the dismissal orders on all three indictments so wrongfully returned against you in May, 1934. With Josephine no longer alive, the assault charge was moot, of course. But I wanted it stricken from the record forever, like the others. In doing these things, I prevailed upon our present district attorney to do what no other Hispaniola County official ever dared to do during Father's lifetime.*

*Also find enclosed the deed to the place where you now stand. Charlotte said you loved it so. I don't expect you to forgive Josephine and Father for doing what they did, but please don't think too harshly of me for not doing more sooner. If I am dead when you return, Charlotte will organize these documents and have them presented to you.*

*Sincerely,*
*Priscilla Vandergriff*

With pulse pounding, Heck reread the part about Charlotte's letters and the deed.

Leaning against the car, he looked at Cracker and said, "I don't believe it. Talk about spittin' in the eye of the devil!"

Cracker appeared at his elbow. "Good news?"

Heck nodded, too excited to speak for a moment. "Miss Cilla had those old charges dismissed. How about that?"

"Thank you, Lord." Cracker smiled skyward.

With his face lit up with a big smile, Heck picked up the deed and waved it joyously in the air. "Can you believe it? Miss Cilla gave this farm we're standing on to this ol' washed-out clodhopper."

Cracker stared open-mouthed at him. "So, you finally got that section of land. I'm happy for you, Heck. Praise the Lord."

Heck gave Cracker the deed and picked up the largest envelope, studying the handwriting on it. *No wonder it looked so familiar. Her style hasn't changed since the letter Mr. Meade picked up when I lay hurt in his cabin.*

Gathering all the papers off the trunk, he looked at the old swing. "Cracker, there's more than one special place around here."

Anxious to continue reading, he walked up the rotting porch steps, lifted the swing's remaining chain off the ceiling hook and dragged it to the edge of the porch. Taking care to avoid splinters and the heads of rusty nails, he slowly sat down in it, leaning back with a sigh of relief. He hung his feet off the porch and opened envelope Number Two.

The handwriting bore the same characteristics as that on the larger container. The letter was dated June 11, 1940.

> *Dearest Heck,*
>
> *I have finally admitted to myself that you never received any of my letters. I know because you promised to write after receiving my first one. But I still wanted to write this, and leave it with Aunt Priscilla, just in case some day you'll receive and read it and understand something I have done. I wanted you to read this first because it contains information that might cause you not to want to read my old letters and those I might write you in the future in case you are found and this one is delivered to you.*
>
> *Tomorrow I will marry a man I know you would approve of. I recall you telling me once that lots of Southern girls are hitched by age fifteen, so I believe you would agree I'm now old enough.*
>
> *But age has nothing to do with why I have finally decided to take a husband. My primary concern, you see, is the welfare of our son. He needs a father.*

Shocked that she had a baby out of wedlock, Heck reread the last sentence. "Our son?" he muttered. Turning to Cracker, he said, "Charlotte had a baby by a man before she married him."

He felt the pain that comes when one's idealistic expectations are shattered. He also felt a twinge of jealousy. *Odd at my age,* he thought. *Isn't that kind of nonsense reserved for teenagers?*

He returned to the letter.

> *I said I would never marry as long as there was hope you were alive and would find me. I even waited a year after Aunt Josephine informed me of your death, thinking perhaps she had lied to further her own plans. When finally allowed to correspond with Aunt Priscilla she told me she had only her sister's word about your death until she contacted Josephine's source of information, Willa, who confirmed it.*
>
> *Whether you are living or dead, I will always love you, and have taught your son . . .*

Heck fixed his eyes on the words "your son" with pulse pounding. "My God." he said out loud. "*I'm* the father. I've got a son." He threw his hands up in the air. "Did you hear that, Cracker? I've got a son!"

> *to love you as well. He is a handsome boy, much like his father.*
>
> *His name is Tenny, short for Tennel. You'll find him mentioned in my old letters. I tried very hard to get word to you as soon as I found out I was pregnant, but could not. I'm sorry.*
>
> *If Aunt Josephine did lie, and you some day read this letter, I hope you understand and will not think less of me for doing now what I consider best for Tenny. I hope you have found someone else to love and have been happy.*
>
> *Love,*
> *Charlotte*

"You really are rich now," Cracker said. "All good things come to him who waits."

"Says who?" Heck gave him a skeptical look.

"Just quoting a little scripture. It wouldn't hurt you any to reacquaint yourself with 'em."

Heck seemed not to hear his last remark. Looking at the letter again, he said, "A boy . . . Better late than never, right? I'll bet you never saw a seventy-nine year old man become the father of a bouncing middle-age son right before your very eyes, you ol' clodhopper. I should've charged you admission for such a momentous occasion."

"How old is your son now, Heck?"

"Let's see." Heck did some quick figuring. "Nearly sixty, I guess. Must be the oldest new-born in recorded history."

Cracker shook his head. "You've been kept from seeing your child for more than fifty years."

Bursting with excitement, Heck opened letter Number Three, dated December 24, 1992.

*Dearest Heck,*

*I was so happy when Aunt Priscilla informed me you are, indeed, very much alive, and that she resumed her search for you. How wonderful it would be to see you again. And have you meet your son at last. Since age twelve, he has known about you and longed to see you in person.*

*I was so saddened by Aunt Priscilla's recent death. I could hardly follow Mr. Norton's reading of the will. But I knew if you had been there, you would have told me life must go on, to brace myself. So I did. As always, a part of you gave me the strength I needed.*

*As the sole surviving heir to my grandfather's estate (he refused to recognize our son as an heir), I have abided by Aunt Priscilla's wishes by organizing these letters for presentation to Mr. Norton. I have not read her letter to you, but she advised me some time ago that she would deed grandfather's old place to you, which would, in turn, go to your sisters if it were determined that you were deceased. I'm very happy she did, because you and I had some wonderful times there. It was where you showed me the meaning of real happiness, where I became a woman and where our son was conceived.*

*Aunt Priscilla found all my old letters to you that Aunt Josephine intercepted and had them delivered to me. I have, in turn, forwarded them with these documents in case, after all these years, you want to read them.*

>     *As I said before, I hope you have found love again. A*
> *snapping turtle needs a little love now and then.*
>     *Please try not to be bitter.*
>
>     *Love,*
>     *Charlotte DeHavilland Perradine*
>     *1924 Hugenot Dr.*
>     *Bowdoin, Maine*

Tingling with excitement, Heck read the letter again and laid it in his lap. Without thinking, he pushed his toe against the ground as if expecting the swing to begin moving in cadence with old memories. Embarrassed, he glanced at Cracker.

"If you want to be by yourself a while, I can take a walk," Cracker said.

"No, no. Stick around. If I find any bigger surprises in that bundle of letters, I might need a preacher to say a few words over Blood Money's ghost that's been looking over my shoulder from the parlor window."

A twinkle appeared in Cracker's eye. "You always bounce back, don't you, Heck?"

With a furtive glance at Cracker, Heck touched his eye with his shirt sleeve, nodding toward the yard. "I might not survive these Texas weeds though. The damn things can sure tear up a man's sinuses."

"So I see," Cracker said.

Blinking rapidly, Heck asked, "Do you mind if I take the time now to read all these old letters? Since this is the place where so many good things happened to me, it seems fitting that I do it here, if you have a few minutes to spare."

Cracker sat down at the end of the porch and leaned against the corner post. "The happy expression that's come over your face is ample reward for me. Take your time. I've got nowhere to go but to Heaven, if I'm lucky."

"Thanks. That'll allow me to sit right here in one of my favorite places in this world until I finish. Not even water moccasins crawling up both legs could stop me now."

Heck opened the first letter. Completing it, he carefully re-folded and returned it to the envelope, opening the next. Some he read twice, glancing at Cracker when he couldn't suppress a sniffle, to see if his friend had noticed his continuing allergic reaction to the weeds. When Cracker turned away during one of the watery attacks, Heck sat up erect, thrust out his jaw and turned quickly back to the letter in hand.

After tucking the last one in its envelope, Heck arranged them all in a neat stack and slid out of the swing to the ground. Stretching and doing a few quick steps in place to restore his circulation, he turned to Cracker. "What a day this has been. Almost too much for an old clodhopper's brain to absorb in one sitting."

"Pretty hard on your sinuses too," Cracker observed, with a knowing look. "God has really smiled on you, for sure. And as we used to say in the old days, you're walkin' in tall cotton now."

"Yessir. Shoulder high if an inch. All bottomland stuff that'll yield five bales an acre if it'll turn a pound. And the corn's tall and green as far as the eye can see."

"So when are you leaving?"

"Leaving?" Heck gave him a puzzled look.

"To see Miss Charlotte."

Heck didn't answer him, turning instead to look at the old house, his now. "It's got possibilities. Still square on its piers, and the tin roof hasn't let in much rain."

Feeling Cracker's eyes on him, he stopped evading the question. "I don't know if that would be such a good idea. For starters, it might spoil the beautiful memories which kept me going all these years. We're talking half a century, you know. She wouldn't look anything like that old photo in my billfold. Don't know if I could stand that." He sighed. "But even if she's half as pretty as she was the last time I saw her, she wouldn't still love me. How could she? And she's married. I'm afraid I couldn't stand that either."

Not convinced by the excuses, Cracker said, "You're not afraid of how she'll react to your ol' ugly face, are you?"

"You don't beat around the bush, do you, preacher? That's just like a hard-shell Baptist. Never saw one show a speck of mercy for us sinners."

"Neither one of us has enough time left to beat around the bush about anything."

"You know what? I'd give all my remaining days to feast my eyes on her again. But if I did, I'd have to feel her next to me. And that would get both of us into trouble, if her husband is still living. Her letter didn't say if she's still married, widowed, or what. I sure don't want to cause her any more problems." He gave Cracker a concerned look. "And what if she's sick? I couldn't stand seeing my pretty little lady ill *and* old."

"But I know that ain't gonna keep you from goin' up there, because nothing ever stopped you from doing what you set your mind on. I can see that devilish sparkle jumping around in your eyes like live coals in a north wind. You know what they say about live coals."

"You're really full of it, clodhopper-turned-preacher Maybe I should've left you at home."

"What about your son? You're going to look him up too, aren't you?"

"Ol' Blood Money himself couldn't keep me from doing that, even if he was alive and standing right there in the middle of the porch with a cannon in each hand and passing gas from both ends."

Cracker appraised the house again. "This could be a fit place for a man and his woman to live out their so-called golden years together," he said, closely watching Heck's reaction out of the corner of his eye.

"Cracker, over the decades I've done my best to figure out what life gave me besides a criminal record, lots of kicks to my backside and some bad whiskey. It wasn't until I read Charlotte's letters that I finally realized the answer. I'm grateful to her for that." He paused, turned to gaze out over the trees across the road. "For a short time back there, Charlotte made my life better than it had ever been, better than I ever thought possible up to then. And remembering her has kept me going during dark periods when I was ready to throw in the towel. For that, I'm also thankful."

"I'd say that's pretty levelheaded thinking for an instant rags-to-riches clodhopper. I do believe there's hope for you, after all."

"Seems a man's always having to re-tune his thinking, like he has to with the strings on a cheap guitar. Back when I was a kid, green behind the ears and Ross was still alive, I actually believed life had a purpose. But I was beginning to have doubts before I met Charlotte. When that happened, things started making sense again again. Then I wound up crossways with Josephine Vandergriff and got run out of town. That flip-flop made me wonder if I'd been right in my thinking about life being a bummer." He sighed. "Now, I don't know if I can change back or not."

"The changing might not be as hard to do as the facing up."

"Facing up? What's that supposed to mean?"

Cracker shrugged. "Never believed a man could come up with answers unless he dealt with the problems burning up his insides."

"I thought you were a preacher, not a philosopher. You're beginning to sound like those army shrinks that hounded me with all kinds of dumb questions after the war."

"Like Mr. Norton did when he asked if you were trying to get yourself killed?"

Heck's jaw muscle rippling was his only answer.

"Care to tell me what you wouldn't tell the lawyer? Might help to talk about it."

"You're the philosopher. You tell me."

"You mean to say you really don't know if you were intentionally placing yourself in harm's way over and over?"

"I'm saying I don't think so. But there was a time when I acted mighty reckless and stupid. After things fell apart here, I didn't believe I had much to look forward to. But I don't think I ever jumped into something to get killed in the process. The shrinks babbled about suppressed death wishes, whatever the hell that means, and sub-conscious desires that drive a man to do things for reasons he doesn't understand. Sounded like a bunch of crap to me, and I told them so."

"They must've found out what Josephine Vandergriff and her daddy did to you here in thirty-four."

"As far as I know, they believed I was Roger Wills from Arkansas. All through the war, at least. Don't know what they found out aftwards. But one time I did let it slip out about how my little brother Billy died and how bad I felt about it. Man, they ripped their drawers when I told them that. They concluded I kept offering up my life because I blamed myself for his death."

"That's funny," Cracker said. "I got the same impression down the road there a few minutes ago."

"Smart aleck. Why don't you stick to preachin'?"

"What about that sending in all your medals? What was that all about?"

"That's easy to answer. Why should a man get a medal for killing another man who's out there just doing what he's ordered to do? Wars are nothing but a squabble between the B. M. Vandergriffs of the world. When our Vandergriffs find out another country's Vandergriffs are a threat to their business interests, they pump up their young cannon-fodder with a lot of high-sounding talk about God, the flag and their mothers' apple pie and send them off to wipe out the competition. Well, one day while I was sitting in the V. A. hospital with my back-side showing, I decided against wearing any of my B. M. Vandergriff medals and mailed 'em all back to Washington, D. C., by God."

"If I had a medal right now, I'd hang it on your ugly neck for saying what's needed to be said for a long time."

"Didn't mean to preach, Preacher." He sighed. "Maybe I lost something along the way and ain't smart enough yet to know what. It's been a long haul."

"I think you know what you lost, and I think maybe you found it today. You're just afraid to admit it, because you're scared of losing it again."

Heck continued to be impressed by how insightful a young, carefree fishing buddy had become during his exile from Two Rivers. "You're full of it, you know that."

"Maybe. Maybe I'm just old and sentimental, or sentimental because I'm old. But even a snappin' turtle knows when to turn loose of something so he can swim on up the creek. Quit fighting it. Let what happened here today help you believe in something again. After all, life is supposed to make sense, isn't it?"

"You tell me. You're the preacher."

"It ain't the preacher part of me askin'."

Heck continued thoughtfully surveying the premises. "Does life make sense?" He shook his head. "I might have to travel a few more miles down the road before I'm convinced. But I already know one thing for sure, ol' buddy. At times like these, it's mighty interesting."